THE INEVITABLE COLLISION OF BIRDIE & BASH

CANDACE GANGER

ST. MARTIN'S GRIFFIN NEW YORK

THE INEVITABLE COLLISION OF BIRDIE & BASH. Copyright © 2017 by Candace Ganger. All rights reserved. Printed in the United States of America. For information, address St. Martin's Press, 175 Fifth Avenue, New York, N.Y. 10010.

www.stmartins.com

Illustration on page 305 by Wesley Berg

Designed by Jonathan Bennett

The Library of Congress Cataloging-in-Publication Data is available upon request.

ISBN 978-1-250-11622-2 (hardcover)
ISBN 978-1-250-11623-9 (e-book)

Our books may be purchased in bulk for promotional, educational, or business use. Please contact your local bookseller or the Macmillan Corporate and Premium Sales Department at 1-800-221-7945, extension 5442, or by e-mail at MacmillanSpecialMarkets@macmillan.com.

First Edition: July 2017

10 9 8 7 6 5 4 3 2 1

For Gram, my infinite beacon of light.
And to Joshua, whose brief chapter
on earth has been rewritten.

BASH

The thing about Wild Kyle is, he's never lost a goddamned thing.

So when I tell him about Layla, my recently departed (his word, not mine) ex, I don't even flinch at his response: "Fuck that shit. Hit it and quit it, man."

He offers his monogrammed chrome flask—*KJT*—that's filled with something vile, I refuse, he chugs. "What the fuck is in that?" I ask.

With squinted eyes and a puckered pout, he's trying hard to swallow like it'll really impress all these fine young, partygoers if he can keep the burning liquid down the chute without spewing. He raises a finger while a cloud of sour-smelling gas explodes from his mouth. "Moonshine. Eighty proof."

"Holy shit! *Why* would you do that to yourself?"

A crooked smile crawls up from the corners of his lips. "Why *not?*" He struggles with another sip, nearly blows chunks right on the flimsy card table, and then excuses himself up the stairs to, I assume, his grave. Leaning back in a plastic fold-out chair, I'm in this tiny basement room that's starting to swell. I don't know half these people, and the ones I do, pretend not to know me. The music is blaring, thumping, through the walls of Kyle's cousin's friend's college boyfriend's place just outside of East Clifton. It's close enough for me to crawl home if I need to, far enough that Ma won't hear about it.

"I need a beer pong partner," a sultry voice says from behind. I know those paralyzing, knife-wielding sounds; rasped and smoky as all hell. It's Layla, my kryptonite. I spin around to see a cigarette pressed between her plump, scarlet lips, her lashes batting at me.

"So go ask your dude," I say, turning away from her. She rests a hand on my shoulder, creeps around to my side and crawls onto my lap. She's wearing this black miniskirt that shows off her curves and thigh-high boots, and after that, there's nothing left to see.

"We broke up," she says with a pout. She pinches the cigarette, pulls it from her lips, and gently nudges it into mine. Our eyes are locked, and from the corner of my mouth, I blow a thin stream of smoke into the air. It curls between us, disintegrating into vapor. She likes this, I see, but I know that face. I've seen it a hundred times. It's the same face she dragged into the rink I work at, the same face she made at the dude whose jock she was all up on *at* said rink, and the same fucking face that dumped my sorry ass in front of said dude at said rink just one week ago.

She wants me to break. Part of me *wants* me to break. I mean, *goddamn,* look at her. Dirty blond hair that trails in loose waves below her shoulders, nose pierced, a few tats on her forearm, mostly butterflies and shit, but rock as hell. Her icy eyes sear through me, and a flash of the future pops into my brain, and she's just not in it. Didn't see it last week—I was too close to it. I see it now. With a firm grip on her hips, I lift her from the warmth of my lap and toss her to her cold, unfeeling heart—I mean feet.

Thanks to the height of her heels, she wobbles, nearly falls straight to her ass. "Bash!" she screeches. Her eyes are bulging, and that pouty thing she thinks is working isn't (anymore). "I miss you. I was wrong."

Reminds me of something I saw scribbled on a gym locker. I inhale and blow another cloud of smoke toward her with a wink. "If you're looking for sympathy, you'll find it in the dictionary between *shit* and *syphilis*."

I leave her there to, I don't know, think about how actions have consequences, or whatever, and find myself up on the main level where the awful chest-thumping music streams. No sign of Kyle, so I hang in the corner, where I'm mostly alone. Back against the wall, I enjoy the cigarette still pursed between my lips—her lovely parting gift to me. Thanks, doll. Directly in front of me are about a dozen sweaty bodies, bending and swaying, grinding against each other beneath the dim lights that flicker primary colors. From here, they're just faceless, gestural shapes on a dark canvas—something I could draw if I had my charcoal lump and kneaded eraser.

"Want to dance?" a sweat-drenched girl asks me.

She's grabbing at my hand. I pull back. "I don't dance; just watch."

"That's super creepy," she says. "I like it." She smiles with the jagged teeth of a great white as her hands paw at me to move deeper into the nucleus of the cesspool. I resist still, mostly because, selfishly, I want to smoke this free cancer stick to the nub. I keep my cool because Layla lurks nearby, an amber bottle in one hand, my (metaphoric) balls in the other. She's looking around, probably for her next victim, and this chatty girl, man, she does *not* care I'm *not* listening. She's talking about her phone bill and how she can't figure out where the extra charges come from—"I mean, I talk the same amount every month, so it should be the *exact* same," she says—and I'm still looking at Layla, pretending not to, because I know exactly where that eye contact leads and I don't have enough soul left for her to pulverize a third time. And before you even ask, no, she wasn't worth it.

Behind this girl, who is now spewing a diatribe about the

government spying on us through our phones, I lose sight of Layla for just a moment. The crowd parts in a zigzag fashion and beneath the light machine, where the red, green, and blue hit the hardest, I see *her*—this statuesque beauty—hiding behind a trail of long brown hair and thick-framed glasses. With her hands folded snug in her lap, she's looking around, sinking farther into the couch's wilted threads as if hoping to not be seen, but *I* see her because hiding is typically what I do, too.

"My God," I say. The cigarette hangs from my bottom lip, and this girl, who finally stops talking, is still looking at up me, glitter plummeting from her silver-tinted eye shadow. The flakes dance down to the tops of my boots like little asshole snowflakes. That shit should be banned. She follows my eyes across the floor to the big, plaid couch, letting her smile fade. Losing interest (finally), she drops my hand and disappears into the sea of people from which she first emerged.

With my heart nearly beating out of my chest, I watch Couch Girl. The way she tucks her hair behind her ears with precision, the way she nudges her falling glasses up the bridge of her nose, the way she pretends she's not as earth-shatteringly stunning as she really is. Radiance surrounds her—not a halo, but some kind of ethereal glow—and I can't look away. She looks up at me. Once, twice, three times; tries to avoid my eyes, but can't. For the length of a whole song, my gaze doesn't abandon her, and by the middle of the next song, she's smiling at me. *Score.* Normally, I'd hang back, wait and see if we "accidentally" cross paths, but Layla's determined eyes are on me so I up my game. To finish her.

I push through the haze and find my way to Couch Girl. She looks up at me with these electric green eyes that are more evident through her lenses, and I do something I thought I'd never in a million years do—hold out my hand.

"I don't dance," she says, reluctant.

"Me either. Too many germs." A few seconds pass before she decides to take my humble offering. I pull her to her feet, and our palms smash together and slide across the dampness. This would normally gross me out, but I kind of want to linger in it with her. Gently, I lead her to the center of the floor where *we* are now gestural shapes on this dark canvas, too.

"Help me out here," I say. "See that girl over there?" I point to Layla with my middle finger. A silent dig, if you will.

She nods.

"I need her to see us talking."

She scrunches up her face. "I'm not getting in the middle of whatever *that* is." Her finger is waving around, grabbing Layla's attention. "But thanks."

As she tries to walk away, I tug on her sleeve. Eyebrows arched, and my own full puppy-lipped pout now in full effect. "Please."

She must sense my sadness (read: desperation), because with one sharp sigh and a roll of her beautiful eyes, she digs her feet firmly into the floor. "Okay, fine. Just for a minute though."

We're not dancing, not swaying or grinding, but here we are, in the epicenter of it all. She crosses her arms, I cross mine, too. "So are we going to actually talk or just pretend?" she snaps.

"Who the hell *are* you?" I ask with a smirk.

She looks down. "Who *am* I? You mean *what name was I given at birth,* or *who am I* in a general sense?"

I start to respond, but she interrupts.

"Because, in said general sense, I'm a girl at a party I should've never come to but did and am now trapped in this weird interaction between subjects A and B while I'd much rather be at home teaching my chunky cat how to drink from a running faucet, thank you very much."

With my gaze pressed hard on her porcelain skin, I drop

the last bit of cigarette to the floor and twist the cinder into the grooves until it burns no more. My smile grows, and all of a sudden, I don't care if Layla's watching or not. "Fair enough."

"Who are *you*?" she replies with a touch of snark.

I look down to the holes in my shirtsleeve where the fabric has worn, and I realize I have two choices here. I can tell her the lame, true story of my life and wait for her to walk away, or I can do the opposite and hope that, for one perfect night, I'm allowed to feel this way about a girl who's way out of my league, knowing the second I leave here, this, whatever *this* is, leaves with it.

Plus, it'd totally piss Layla off, and that makes it sweeter.

"Well," I say, "in a general sense, I'm a boy at a party *I* should've never come to but did and am now *gloriously* trapped in this enlightened conversation with, probably, the most captivating girl in the entire house. In an even generaler sense"—she stops me, tells me that's not a word— "I'm nobody. Well, until I saw you." My smile widens. To sell it.

She blushes. Her fingers fumbling through her long, silky strands, she objects. "One, that's so ridiculously cliché, and two, statistically speaking, you're a percentage of this party as a whole house equation. Without the exact number of bodies—I estimate around thirty-seven—you're something like 2.7027 percent somebody without ever seeing me."

My heart drops through this creaky, wooden floor, and this smile that's still pasted—it's about to rip my face in two. The forces of the earth have rumbled beneath my feet and combined, climbing up through the dirt core, into my heart. We stand here, for, I don't know, what feels like an infinity (she abruptly explains infinity is a concept and there's no way to solve for x, so in reality, we can't actually stand here that long), and all these things start flying out of my mouth—how I graduated last year, I'm only in town for tonight—and with every passing lie, I think, *You're no better than Kyle,* which makes me sick—like, physically ill with the sweats and a weird clamminess and all these symptoms that remind me how I felt when I first met Layla.

When the song ends, we hold on to this moment that, in the space between, feels like a million electrodes have begun to rattle and vibrate. I feel it fuse to my bones. It connects us together, grounds us, right here, right now. Layla's gone—*who cares now?*—but just as I start to ask for her number, or the name she was given at birth, a tiny little thing with big, springy curls that dangle over one eye pulls at Couch Girl's arm.

"Ready to go?" the friend asks. She's looking me over in this protective kind of way, and I know what she's thinking because I beat her to it.

While the two of them decide, a hand slaps the back of my shirt hard enough to leave a mark. I turn around to see Kyle's cousin's friend's college boyfriend with a worried look on his face. "Your friend might need to go to the hospital. He's, like, not waking up."

With a heavy sigh, something that follows Kyle's hijinks often, I silently agree to retrieve my sort-of-ill-behaved dog that does as he pleases. Before I can even *think* about what to say to Couch Girl next, I spin around and she, and her tiny friend, are gone.

Just like that, it's over before it even started.

Story of my goddamned life.

Two days have passed since the house party, and I'm still thinking about what an idiot Kyle is. The only chance I had to talk to (probably) the most interesting lady specimen I've ever met, and he totally screwed me. One night to be all the things I'm not, maybe make out a little, and instead, I spent the wee hours of yesterday making sure his ass didn't die of alcohol poisoning—again. And now here we are, hanging out at 8:30 P.M., on a stormy Sunday, in one of his dad's empty developments doing what Wild Kyle does best—drinking.

Kid doesn't use his head because he's never had to. If I had everything he has, I'd be eating three square meals, filling my tank with premium gas, and sleeping on something more than an old spring mattress in a piece of shit trailer—all these things, these simple ideas that most normal people get on a human level—are things Kyle couldn't get if you nailed them to his brain with a stake and hammer.

But I guess if I had those things, or even one, I wouldn't be *me*. I'd be him. And right now, *him* is sitting in a yoga-like position, legs crossed, eyes closed, fingers pinched up at his sides like he's taking a serious shit. He drinks straight from the bottle of his dad's top-shelf vodka, and with one flick of his metal skull lighter, he burns the end of a fresh joint. But me? I've got my legs spread out in front of me, a cheap can of off-brand beer that tastes like asphalt in one hand, a limp cigarette balanced in the other, as I try to sketch with a jagged piece of compressed charcoal on a napkin.

He makes a deep hum and exhales a cloud of smoke through the side of his lips, currently buried under an avalanche of wiry hairs. "You're so whipped! I can tell you're still obsessing over Layla. Didn't know she'd be there, I swear."

I shake my head, surprised he noticed anything more than the toilet rim.

"Forget that heartless bitch. Didn't you see that hottie in the spandex thing? Oohhh! I'm not religious, but goddamn, TAKE. ME. TO. CHURCH!"

I don't dare tell him about Couch Girl. Conversing only encourages the idiocy, and I don't need him fucking up any more of my shit. Besides, I'd rather let him think I'm still hung up on Layla because (1) in a totally whacked-out way, it's kind of endearing that he cares, and (2) it gives him something to focus his negative energy on—that won't fuck up any more of my shit.

"This is good stuff, man. Sure you don't want some?" He pulls the stick from his mouth and offers it up.

"Nah," I say. "My gift for helping with that wretched chem test last week. Besides, Camilla's way past that now, and I sure as hell don't want it."

He nods, knows Camilla—Ma—is the reason we sometimes come drink in this dark, empty neighborhood. It started months ago during her weekly chemo treatments and became this thing I couldn't get out of—I tried. Among the half dozen vacant houses and lots Kyle's dad invested in, this one is my favorite, because even though it's not finished, I can tell it could really be something. Kind of like me.

There's a long silence, a shift in the air between us, as he shuffles around to stretch his lanky limbs. He lifts the joint into the air and unfolds his legs. "So did you pass the test or what?"

I take a swig of the warm beer, my last one, my only one. "No. Goddamn reactions and rates. That whole collision theory got me. How am I supposed to remember what affects the rate of a reaction? If I knew, I wouldn't be in school where you learn things—I'd be Stephen Hawking or some shit. Not trudging through my mandatory four-year sentence like a freakin' dunce."

"*Five* for you."

"Hey—everyone should be a freshman twice. It makes a *real* man outta ya."

Kyle's obnoxious laugh echoes through the wooden slats where walls should be. "Like John Locke says, 'There is only one thing which gathers people into seditious commotion, and that is,'" he pauses for dramatic effect, "'*OPPRESSION!*'"

I focus on the rough charcoal lines and edges I'm sketching,

9

blending with the side of my palm as I go. "I don't think the right to rebel applies at East Clifton High. Unless you have no interest in graduating in the spring. I, on the other hand, have no choice."

He holds his hand in the air and waves his clenched fist, his voice strained. "Then we will take a stand, my brother. We. Will. Start. THE REVOLUTION!"

I shake my head, mostly because I'm used to Kyle's dramatics. "Why don't you get a head start on that and I'll jump on the bandwagon later. *After* I pass my classes."

"Goddamn, man. 'The surest way to corrupt a youth is to instruct him to hold in higher esteem those who think alike than those who think differently.' Why can't we all think like Nietzsche? If you won't help me start the new rebellion, don't sweat it. In five years no one will remember you, me, big-boobed Brittany, or easy Emma or any other East Clifton POS's. Well, *I* might remember those hotties, but that's because I'm a perv. Point is, just get through it, then forget about it."

Even in his drunken philosophical babble, it sounds easy enough, except I have to sweat it. Like flunking out kind of sweat it. If Ma only knew how much I'm really sweating, it would kill her faster than the cancer. Besides, Kyle's got his life figured out. He'll sleep in on graduation day, wake up to a big breakfast the maid will deliver to him in bed, Mr. Taylor will give him the keys to one of their fancy cars, he'll stroll in for the rolled-up diploma (that's just a piece of paper to him), then walk off the stage with a job handed to him on a silver fucking platter. Doesn't matter if he's earned it (because he hasn't), if he's qualified (because he's not), or if he'll even say thank you (because he won't).

A sarcastic chuckle escapes me. I can't help it. "I'm *trying* to get through it, dude. I've got no other options but, what—work at a skating rink my whole life? No effing way."

"Dad could hook you up with a job."

"Buying real estate in shitty places and then selling to a bunch of schmucks? Rather die."

"Then come to New York with me next summer. Use our connections. Work for a bit, save your money, buy your own gallery."

"Thanks, man," I say with a sigh, "but I can't make that much that fast. Besides, I'd rather earn my show, not buy it. Wasn't it one of your half-baked inspirational posters or philosophy man-crushes who said 'Intelligence without ambition is a bird without wings'? I've got wings, and I'll find a way to use 'em."

He looks annoyed, his ramblings backfiring. He presses the butt of the joint into a floor tile with a sizzle. His words are beginning to slur and melt together.

"Psshhtt. Artists don't make squat. They're pretentious hipster assholes who think they're creating something that means something even when it means nothing. Like two circles. There's not a deep, contextual meaning in the round-ness of them. They're fucking circles."

He stares at me, unaware he's dissing the only thing I'm actually good at (other than dodging class and ignoring him). "You don't think there's meaning in something like, say, this?" I hold up the finished portrait of a black grizzly bear with Kyle's scruffy beard. He's sitting on a tricycle in the same yoga-like position as Kyle, joint and all. A swirled cloud of smoke is lifted from the bear's head forming words that read *We. Will. Start. THE REVOLUTION.*

He holds the flimsy napkin between his fingers, eyes expanding, jaw agape. "Bash," he says quietly, "this is," his voice strengthens, "AWESOME! Love that the beard is in full swing."

"Thought your valiant effort should be recognized."

"Given the hairiness of my genetic predecessors, I *thought*

11

it'd be cake." He strokes the few sparse hairs sprouting from his chin. "But look at it—I'm like a hairless cat with a rash."

I laugh, set my charcoal block to the floor beside me. "It's only been three days since you started. Give it a whole month. By then, you might hit sheepdog mode. Never know."

The light from the lantern is flickering, causing our shadows to dance across the wood, and although I'd never tell him in a million years, through all of this, I'm still hung up on Couch Girl. It doesn't even matter. I mean, it's not like I'll ever see her again, so why can't I let it go? I blame Layla. And Global Warming. And Kyle, just because.

I crank up the volume on my phone and select a track—something Johnny Cash, for my ma—and wait for Kyle's inevitable eye roll.

"Ugh," he says. "It's so . . . what's the word?"

"Rustic," I say. "Vintage. Classic."

"More like depressing. Melancholy. Buzzkill."

"Fine," I say, skipping to the next song, "Comfortably Numb."

A smile twists up and out from his squirrely mustache. "Now *that's* the stuff."

"Just another version of depressing. Melancholy. Buzzkill."

"No way, man. HUGE difference. Floyd completely changed the way people get high. It's un-American to have one without the other."

Through the vibrations of the song, the rain beats harder on the roof like it's competing for our attention. Kyle's eyes sink farther, nearly closing completely, his body swaying to keep balance. I shake the last couple drops free from my beer can and crunch it between my fingers, tossing it aside to the pile we've created over the last couple months. Since Mr. Taylor all but gave up on this house and the five others surrounding us.

"You about ready to drop me home?" I ask. His head is now in his hands. The alcohol has officially set in—hard. He shakes his head. Didn't get the title "Wild Kyle" for nothin'. Dude doesn't have an off button, just

1. Go,
2. Go Harder, or
3. Go Until You Pass Out.

"Want me to drive? You can crash at my place." As soon as I say the words, I'm calculating where he would sleep. There are only two options, both equally shitty: the lumpy mattress on the floor or the broken recliner in the front room. I really don't want him on either.

He looks up at me, his eyes glazed over, mouth bone dry. "No to both."

I'm relieved. "Thought your dad was on a business trip," I say. "How's he gonna know if we don't tell him?"

"*No one* drives the Benz but me. If Dad finds out I took his prized gift from Bono or Bon Jovi or whothehellever it was he sold a house to, if there's a scratch or a spot of charcoal, or the scent of whatever cheap-ass Axe cologne you're wearing in the driver's seat, he'll know and I'm dead. Can't let you get dead, too. You've got plans to be the next Van Gogh or Michelangelo or Raphael or Donatello, so dying might, you know, interfere." He laughs at himself, words trailing. "*He* doesn't even drive the thing. You know that. It just sits, locked up like some secret trophy. Someone's gotta appreciate the finer things Dad works for."

My eyes are locked into the ruby metallic sheen. "Imagine all the hungry kids he could feed with the price of this car."

"Rhode Island."

My brows dip. "A lot of starving kids there, huh?"

"A shitload." He stands unsteadily, straightening his

posture and widening his eyes to show me he's okay. "I'm good to drive. Trust me."

Trust him? Can't remember a time I did that. We're barely friends when he's sober, and that's only because we lived with the Taylors after Ma brought her pregnant ass to America so I'd have "a better life and all that shit" (her words, not mine). Apparently she responded to an ad for a chamber maid for some rich, white family, and LOOK AT US NOW! Things were fine until Kyle's witch of a mom kicked us out on the street without warning. I still don't know why all that went down. Needless to say, we look back on those days fondly. Not.

But through all the chaos, Kyle, an only child lost in the shuffle of his parent's fucked-up marriage, clung to me, forced the whole brotherhood thing to happen. After all these years, and as much as I protest, it stuck, unfortunately. I guess he's the closest thing I have to family, other than Ma. The thing is, when Kyle's drinking, a moodier, darker version emerges from his tall, slender frame. I learned a long time ago not to challenge Drunk Kyle, or it's my head on that silver platter I previously mentioned. And right now, I need my head. So when he says to trust him, the only choice I have is to buckle up tight.

He jingles the keys from his pocket, and we make a dash for the car through the pouring rain. As the wind howls, lightning brightens the sky in bold flashes, illuminating an otherwise blackened cul-de-sac. I slip in, wait for the seat warmer to do its thing, and clasp the buckle together. I smell the alcohol on his breath, and when I look at him white knuckling the wheel, I wonder if I should have insisted I drive. Like in a "don't take NO for an answer" kind of way.

He turns the engine, twists the radio's volume all the way up to the heavy metal playlist he has synced. Here we go. The fast drums and furious screams only add to Kyle's state. His eyes lock onto mine for just a second, wide and crazy, as he sticks out his tongue and thrashes his head around to the four-on-the-floor beat like he's caught a second wind. My stomach twists in knots of regret, and it's not from flat beer.

"Slipknot, dude!" he screams. "They wipe their asses with the music you listen to!" He peels out of the driveway, screeching the tires against the pavement, then slams on the brakes.

"Dude," I say, my hands clinging to the seat. "Chill."

"Oh, *I'm* chill," he says. There's a lull, but the crazy is still fermenting in his eyes as he revs the engine. It roars, chases the thunder through the clouds. Ma would kill me if she knew I didn't steal his keys.

"Don't," I say. My face is flat, I'm not kidding, and he knows it. I don't need another ding on my arrest record. I'm nearly eighteen—they'll try me as an adult if we're pulled over for a DUI.

"Okay, okay," he says. "You should probably drive." As I unbuckle my belt, he lays his hand on the shift, pretends to put it in park. The moment I have my fingers on the door handle, he presses hard on the gas, jerking me back to the warmed seat. He laughs like the Joker, his eyes piercing mine.

"What the hell, dude?" I quickly rebuckle and grab ahold of the dash as he swerves around every rounded street. *"Idiota!"* I shout (Ma would be proud I still use my Portuguese). "Slow down!"

His eyes are on everything but the road, one hand off the wheel, then he lets go completely to roll his window down. The rain falls like bullets, coating the windshield with a thick, blurred paste we can barely see through. I throw my hands on the wheel, try to steer from the passenger seat.

"This is FREEDOM!" he yells through the crack in his window. "Total control! Free yourself from the shackles of our screwed-up democracy!"

I'm leaning over him, my ribs collapsing on the middle console as I narrow my eyes and try to see the yellow lines. "Kyle!" I snap. "I'm not kidding—slow down before you kill us!"

He rips my hands off just as we doughnut around the final bend, to the mouth of the neighborhood's entrance. Headlights gleaming in a muddled, choppy ray, something darts out in front of us so fast, I could argue neither of us saw it coming. The object hits the front bumper and the impact flings me into the door, slowing Kyle's lead foot.

"What the hell was that?" he asks. "Did you see it?"

While the car crawls along the road, far past the point of impact, I whip my head back to see a light flicker atop the hill behind us. "Should we check? Might be a dog or baby deer or something. I think we have to call the cops so they can shoot it."

"Shit. Shit. Shit." Kyle's disoriented, sweat forming on his brow. "We can't call the cops! I smell like vodka, and look at me—I'm high as fuck."

Think, Bash. Think. I swallow, look him over, the fear spilling out of him. "Trade places. I'll say I was driving."

"They'll make you take a Breathalyzer, too. No, no way. They'll call my dad, and we'll both get busted."

"I only had one beer. I'm totally sober."

"You're underage—they'll still arrest us, and I can't get another DUI. Dad warned me—he said, 'Kyle, if this happens again, kiss your car, your friends, your life good-bye.' I can't, Bash, I can't."

I bite my fingernail and try to see behind us through the rain, but it's pitch-black. "Then let me drive you home, and I'll come back and check. I'll take the blame or make something up if anyone catches me." Despite his unparalleled ability to fuck my shit up, Kyle's my stupid pseudo brother, and he's gonna leave Clifton and actually be something—run a company or buy a country or something so beyond my

16

comprehension—I can't just stand here and let him throw it all away. Not when he's always been there. Because me? I've got nothing to lose.

Not a dime.

His head wobbles, his eyes nervously darting. He's seriously considering this, because when it comes to Wild Kyle, if it's in his best interest, he usually takes it. "Didn't you promise your mom you'd stay out of trouble?"

"Didn't *you* promise your dad you'd stop drinking and getting high?"

He points his finger at me. "Good point."

"So move. I'll drive."

He pauses, swallows a big burp. "No, wait. They'll wonder how you got the car. Forget it. We're just gonna go. This never happened. It's fine, I'm fine, everything's fine."

"But we hit *something*. Don't you want to make sure it's dead? Like, you know, you have a heart or something?"

He revs the engine again. "Dad gets a ding on one of his other cars, he wears black for a week. If he finds out about this, bye-bye, NYC. Besides, you're an accomplice now. If someone busts me, we're both done."

His tone and eye contact more ominous, I turn my head back once more, ignore the sinking feeling in my gut. My fingers clench the belt buckle tight. "Okay. But drive slow."

With shaking hands, Kyle gently pushes the gas, splashing the damning water up behind us. Now, he's not driving fast, he's driving guilty. In the exact moment I'm begging for my life, I have sudden clarity over the chem test I bonked. The collision theory suggests reactions happen, no matter what, with a few important factors that decide the collision outcome:

1. **Temperature.** Kyle's energy changes when he drinks, making him more likely to collide with something.
2. **Concentration.** If there is more substance in his

system, like copious amounts of liquor and weed, there is a greater chance the rate of the reaction will happen faster.

3. **And pressure.** As it increases, Kyle is more likely to have more collisions.

4. (I'm screwed.)

birdie

What is *love* anyway?

It's not logical, something you can prove. There is no solid data to back up phrases like "soul mate" or "heartbreak." They're not real, just ideas people cling to so they can put names on feelings that are actually chemical reactions in the brain. The dictionary says love is defined as "a profoundly tender, passionate affection for another person." If I rely on that, I've *never* been in love, and if I'm held to the use of *passionate affection,* I never will be. All I know about love is from movies, books, and songs, where everything is wrapped up with some sappy, unbelievable ending. The unhappy truth is, *reality* is, people cheat and lie, keep secrets, and leave. Because it's human nature.

What I *have* are facts. And the primary fact I'm stressing over is, a couple of days ago, I did something incredibly, unexplainably, undeniably, stupid—I snuck out of the house and went to what my best friend, Violet, calls "a rager" in East Clifton. I could say it was only for a few minutes and I didn't have fun and I shouldn't have gone (lies). I could say there wasn't a boy there with beautiful brown skin and dark, silky locks, who absolutely *didn't* intrigue me (more lies). I could blame it on stress from college essays or this random job I'm about to start so I can save for the fall (so true, it hurts), but really, it's much more than that. Plus, my nosy brat of a sister, Brynn, totally caught me sneaking back in, so, there's no way I can pretend it never happened. I know *she* won't.

"What's wrong with *you?*" Brynn asks, with her tongue curling in disgust.

"Nothing," I say. "I'm fine." I shift in my seat to stare out the window but I still feel her staring a hole through the side of my face—something she's done as long as she's been alive.

"You look like you're going to puke. Are you going to puke?"

"No," I snap. "I said I'm fine."

Benny hangs over his car seat to stare at me, too. "I'm fine!" He repeats, his voice rising in excitement at the end.

Brynn shushes him, then whips her head back around to me. Her dingy brown hair is covered in braided beads and feathers from the Americana Festival that happened three effing days ago. It smells like sewer. "You're *not* fine," she whispers, loudly. "It's all over your stupid, perfect face. Ugh. So annoying."

I back away, casually pinching my nose shut so I don't have to breathe the debris embedded in her scalp, or smell her rancid breath. The radio is a low murmur, but even through the rain, I hear the music streaming through the speakers. I draw my attention to the rhythmic droplets that splash the window. There's something about the *pat pat pat,* the smell that lingers long after it has passed. Makes me feel alive.

I roll down my window to feel the cool mist on my cheeks. The pellets, which are about half a centimeter, fall hard and fast (probably exceeding the typical seven to eighteen miles per hour in this kind of weather). But it's hard to calculate. I'm squeezing my brain like a sponge, but it's parched. If I could crawl into the eye of the storm, I would. It'd suck a lot less than telling Mom about the party, and worse than that—about the fact that I went to the party to forget that the major scholarship I had applied for and counted on fell through. So now, with only minor monetary gifts, I'm in financial free fall—no safety net and terrified that everything I've worked toward for twelve years will be for nothing. We can't afford college, so if there are no scholarships or grants, I might as well put feathers in my hair like Brynn.

This time last year, we weren't on our way to our new home. My whole life we'd only lived in tiny apartments. But now, since Dad was promoted to supervisor at the electric company, we're blocks away from the new place we call home. And yet, I have a stomach twisted in so many knots, home is the last place I want to be.

We have to be the only family crammed together on a Sunday night, out buying a Christmas tree before Thanksgiving. Dad says it's because of the deal; Mom argues it's so he has an excuse to play Christmas music earlier than socially acceptable.

"It's a young cypress," Dad rambles, "so we've got to make sure it gets two gallons of water in the next forty-eight hours. If someone sees the water is out, refill it as soon as possible," he continues. "If we don't catch it within two hours, it'll start turning brown, dropping needles. And keep an eye on Chomperz. Don't want a repeat of last year's needle-eating obsession. I lost four pair of shoes in that battle."

"We know, Dad," Brynn says. "We do this every year, so you don't have to give us the same speech each time. And anyway, it's Birdie's job to keep her cat from eating the tree—not mine."

I don't dare comment. It only encourages the little monster.

She continues without taking a breath. "Did you even notice the guy had a sign next to the trees this year that said 'Meat Goats for Sale'?" she giggles to herself. "Meat goats! Disgusting."

Mom sighs loud enough for everyone to hear; Dad stops

talking. A blaring siren interrupts the station, one of those emergency alerts I hear on the television sometimes. Dad turns the dial down, but we can still hear the announcer report the flash flood warning that's been issued for our county. Even though we live only a few miles from the lot, we're still not home because of this violent storm we're caught in.

Dad presses his worn leather boot to the gas pedal, gliding and swerving around the highway's dangerous bend through the torrential downpour that's covering the windshield. The wipers swish and sway, shoving pockets of water off our SUV onto the side of the road. I push my face farther out the window into the air. My fingers cling to the Nikon D3300 camera I got for my seventeenth birthday in January. Mom says I owe her one valedictorian speech at the end of the school year, something I've been working toward since I could speak and still, I feel so unprepared. Brynn sees my fingers fidgeting with the flower-printed strap and sharply cocks her head up at me.

"Maybe after you puke, you can take pictures of it like you do with dead animals," she says. "It's seriously messed up." Now that's she's thirteen, and more of an a-hole than ever, I have to refrain from karate chopping her in the throat on a minute-by-minute basis. It would take me only one shot, and she'd be on the floor, choking for air. I know this because I looked it up (and maybe even practiced on my pillow). Chomperz thinks I have a suppressed rage problem, but I tell him it's just an a-hole-Brynn problem. He usually gets me, but we seem to disagree on all things Brynn.

"*You're* seriously messed up—stop looking through my camera!" I shriek.

"Stop being creepy and morbid like Jeffrey Dahmer. He ate people after he killed them, probably took pictures of them first. Are you a brain-eating zombie like Jeffrey Dahmer—a Dahmbie?"

I shoot her the I'm-going-to-kill-you glance, but she just smirks. "Brynn, I mean it. Shut. Up."

"Brynn, I mean it," she repeats. "Shut. Up."

"*Real* mature."

"*Real* mature." She wags her tongue, dares me to pull it straight out of her throat.

I grunt, forcing Mom to spin around from the front passenger seat to look closely at me. "Are you sick?"

The thoughts are piling up in my head, making me flustered. I see them stacking like files I'm separating into categories: Tell, Don't Tell, Kill Brynn, Schoolwork, Random Song Lyrics, and Cat Videos. Brynn's eyes are still on me with a steely focus, instead of the phone she's usually texting on. I don't know who would ever want to talk to her unless they were threatened with execution, but that's on them.

When I don't answer, Mom turns back to the road.

I meet Brynn's deep-set cocoa eyes that are lightened only by the moon. A half-crooked smile lifts from the corner of her metal mouth in a way that tells me she's totally messing with me. Of course she is, because she's Brynn—queen of her own whacked-out universe where she and I can't possibly coexist like normal sisters. That would be too easy.

"You're going to be in so much trouble," she whispers. "I'm telling them their perfect little princess snuck out of the house without permission. It's going to be awesome."

I lean in, grab a fistful of her plaid shirt—*my* shirt she stole—and lower my voice to something from the depths of hell. "I already paid you off, you little brat. If you say *anything* to Mom and Dad before I do, I'll call Jason Sloan and tell him you're on your period."

She rips my hand off and scoffs. "You better not—I'll die!"

"Try me. Let's see . . . this is day . . . four of your cycle. I know things you don't even realize, little sister."

I watch her deflate and know I've won. She backs away and crosses her arms but in this backseat, there's nowhere she can go that's far enough. Her hair brushes up against me when she turns her head, and now I really want to gag. Thanks to puberty, she completely sucks—a stinky, moody narc who wants to catch me doing anything out of character so she can rat me out and be the hero. Mom and Dad's little Birdie Jay doesn't make mistakes. Ever. That, of course, is according to them, not me. Brynn's determined to prove that theory wrong so she can shove it in my face. They won't even think sneaking out to a party is a big deal, but to me it's everything. I don't want them to see me as one of *those* girls—lying, sneaking around—the kind of girl Brynn will, inevitably, be (and kind of already is). And if I pull at one thread, the whole ball will unravel, and the scholarship thing is a really big ball.

"Vroom!" Benny yells, rolling his toy car's wheels against his leg.

"You like your new car?" Mom asks.

"Yeah," he says—pretty much the extent of his vocabulary.

I look over at him, his unmatched socks pulled high, sparkling cobalt eyes illuminating all of Clifton. He doesn't look as sick as he's been the last couple weeks, and I think *I can't do this*. Things flop in my stomach the closer we get to home.

"I can't believe he's almost two," Dad says laying his hand on Mom's. Her fingers have swollen to twice the size they used to be—before the baby weight from Benny left her permanently heavy—so she wears her wedding ring around her neck instead of her finger.

"Can't believe I'm a forty-three-year-old mother of three with the youngest still in diapers," she says. "Not what I had planned all those years ago in undergrad. I should be a best-selling author, teaching English at a major university, not

24

ghostwriting in my pajamas while balancing a sippy cup and a pack of wipes."

"You've got to let it go, Bess," Dad says. His salt-and-pepper hair—that's more salt than pepper lately—reflects against the moonlight. "You *chose* to stay home, and you're great at it."

"I didn't mean—never mind," she says, mumbling. "Things are just different than I imagined. That's all."

"So goes life," Dad says.

She turns her attention out the window while a long strand of her coarse brown hair unravels from her fingertip. Thunder clashes, scaring Dad just outside of the thick yellow lines, where the water builds and carries along this winding highway—the one we live on. When he tries to regain control, his white knuckles clutching the wheel, he overcorrects and crosses the double center lines around the bend just as an oncoming vehicle is directly in front of us.

The car swerves, howling a *HONK* to show us what idiots we are, but they never slow their speed—something we've realized is the dangerous norm on this stretch of road. Dad eases up on the gas so the rain puddles on the hood. I see his shoulders rise and fall in a sharp, panting motion, and my heart jumps. My breath shortens, my chest is tight, and I can feel my hands clenching shut tight like his. Brynn and I give this look to each other, as if to say, *That was close!* But no one says a word aloud for a solid ten seconds.

"I wish people would slow down on this damn curve," he says, shaking.

As we approach our driveway, I know it's ours by the raised wooden stake with the fresh SOLD sign on the corner that wasn't there last weekend.

Mom places her hand on Dad's shoulder. "I'll drive next time."

He nods with intermittent breaths. Brynn looks to me again. She's a hot branding iron and I'm the animal hide.

Together, we're a violent stampede waiting to happen. All of this combined gives me mixed sensations. I'm cold, with a sweat that drenches my cheeks and I'm hot, with a chill that runs from my toes to my spine in one swift flash. Dad steers up the steep, newly paved driveway that overlooks a string of memorial crosses on the other side of the highway. This part of the road is known as the Devil's Backbone. It's nearly impossible to reverse or check the mail without a car pulling skin off the bone. To be honest, I don't know why anyone would build a house here, but Dad says he got a great deal—just like the cypress—and it's better than the small confines of that apartment where *everyone* could smell Brynn's hair.

I see in the rearview mirror Dad is struggling to find the path of the beastly hill. He punches the garage door opener, but per the new-house kinks we've noted, it stalls. His aggravation is mounting, probably over Mom's underhanded jabs at everything he's doing wrong muttered beneath her breath, but the thing won't budge.

"Piece of shit," he mumbles.

Brynn chuckles. "Dad said *shit*," she whispers.

"Brooks!" Mom says in a huff. "Language." It's the same thing she always says when Dad curses, which happens often.

He pulls the opener from the visor and bangs it on the steering wheel. *Tap tap tap.* One final press, and a light beams onto the lot, making it look like we're at the top of a majestic mountain instead of a puny hill. "Just needed to shake the batteries loose."

He parks the car and looks back at the three of us. "Me and Brynn are on grocery duty, Mom's on Benny patrol, I'll have Sarge help with the tree, and, Birds—you okay?"

I nod, I think. It feels like my head is moving. Everyone is staring at me like it's not, so I decide now would be a good time to actually speak. "I wish everyone would stop asking me that. I'm fine."

He looks to Mom, and they make these faces at each other like I've said something crazy. "Hope you're not catching whatever Benny's been fighting."

We maintain eye contact. "Grab Benny's stroller from the trunk," he orders. He presses the garage door opener again, but the door doesn't close. With a screech, he pounds the plastic opener on the wheel again.

"Birdie—did you hear Dad?" Mom asks.

I nod again. This time it seems like my head is moving, because the doors swing open and everyone goes on with their tasks. Mom is rustling around in her giant purse while Dad and Brynn grab armfuls of grocery bags. Brynn sticks out her tongue before running inside the connecting door that leads to the kitchen and I secretly hope she'll trip and fall. *Now is the time,* I think. *There is no other time.*

Mom slides out of her side, fast. "Mom," I say once out of my seat. I sling the camera over my shoulder and compose myself. She's busy unfastening Benny, the strap strangling her arm as she lifts him, which causes his toy to fall to the ground.

"My car!" he cries.

I inch my way closer to her. "Mom," I repeat with more urgency.

"I'll get it, Benny," she says, setting him down. "Grab the stroller, Birdie." I hear a slight irritation in her tone.

I reluctantly pull the flimsy thing out of the trunk and, without thinking, something I'm *not* known for, unfold the hinges and prop the wheels against the opening of the garage. The rain is blowing inside in gusts as Mom kneels down onto the oil-tattooed garage floor to look under the vehicle.

"Mom," I say, walking up behind her. Through the entranceway, I see Dad and Brynn putting the groceries away while Benny stands here with us. He's rolling the wheels of the stroller between his fingers, ignoring the wetness of rain on his head.

"Go inside, Benny," Mom says. "I'll bring it in when I find it." She's reaching, patting the floor, mumbling something about how lazy Dad is and how she has to do everything around here and though Dad works a lot, she's not completely wrong.

"I need to talk to you," I say. My knees threaten to buckle and leave me with no solid foundation.

"Gotcha!" she says.

"What?" I think my bones have split apart now. One by one, they've unhinged and flung to the outside of me. She already knows what I'm going to say, and she's been waiting, holding it in, until we were alone. A flush of heat tingles across my face.

"His car. Found it."

"Mom, please stop moving," I say, my voice quivering.

"What?" she asks. Her arms are spread wide, daring me to spill every word.

I open my mouth, but the space is void of any truths. The only sounds are of the bellowing winds and rain colliding, blowing streams into us. Through my grunting and stuttering, my grandpa, Sarge, interrupts, his glasses reflecting against the florescent lights.

"Hurry up, Birds," he says, tossing back a popcorn kernel. "*Law and Order: SVU* is on in five. It's the one where Benson is kidnapped." He lingers in the doorway with a grin, then tips his camouflaged veteran hat before he disappears.

"You heard him," she says with her hands pinching at her waist. "Spit it out."

My hands are twisted behind my back while my feet shuffle a nervous number. It doesn't feel like enough time; I can't do this. I have, what—ten seconds to tell her I lost my scholarship *and* snuck out of the house to blow off steam? She won't understand. "I have something to tell you."

"Birdie Jay?" She crosses her arms, and sudden worry drenches her expression. She leans in close enough for me to smell her perfume, the floral one with a hint of peaches, and it makes me remember all the times I confessed things as a kid.

"So," she says. Her silence is deafening, and now I know why Dad feels the need to talk incessantly when he has nothing to say.

Again, I open my mouth, ready to tell her everything, but we're interrupted by a loud banging that originates from the big bay window at the front of the house. And through the entranceway that connects to the kitchen, there are screams. Loud, guttural screams. Mom and I both turn around at the same time to see why the banging, the screams, are echoing louder than the storm itself at a pitch most animals couldn't recognize.

I'll never forget the look on her face.

Her eyes expand to the size of planets, mouth slack in silent horror. She pushes past me and runs like hell after the stroller Benny climbed into, while I distracted her with my stupid, irrelevant news that now seems so unimportant.

The wind and spitting rain pulls at the metal and plastic, forces him down our steep blackened driveway that tips toward Highway 22 like a teetering roller coaster at its peak—the stroller I pulled from the trunk and left propped open. And this series of motions I will never forget, because this is the last time I will ever know myself, my life, in every sense of the word, again.

Brynn continues pounding on the window's glass with her screams, chasing away every last bit of hope that maybe Mom will catch him, it'll be fine, the storm will slow the cars along the bend this time. Dad runs through the entranceway after Mom, and now they're both chasing Benny, in this runaway stroller, down this summit. I look through the door that leads inside our house that still smells like fresh paint, and Sarge is rushing around like he's fighting a battle he can't win. And I'm just here, frozen. My feet are concrete, cemented into the earth that is about to split into uneven halves.

There are moments in life, vivid ones splashed onto blank canvas, that hang in front of you, swing like a pendulum you can't grasp. But you reach, eyes wide open, because if you close them, everything changes. So fast. My fingers are outstretched at Mom and Dad's shadows like if I push them far enough, they'll pluck Benny right off the stroller just in time.

Two headlights appear around the bend at an accelerated speed. The engine's roar is louder than any I've heard around these parts. The way the tires squeal, pushing through heaps of stagnant flood water, I'm reminded of a jet landing on a runway at approximately 870 kilometers per hour—a reverberating sound I can't wrap my senses around, even though I'm right here witnessing it.

The lights don't slow through the storm, they speed up, challenge the thunder and crackling lightning that spills from the clouds. The collision is inevitable, and just as the earth is cut into halves, my heart splinters, too, into an endless chasm, creating the moment those two headlights catch the stroller and fling my baby brother into the air like a ragdoll. The impact crushes the plastic and metal between the wheels, leaving the fabric in shreds and Benny's motionless body next to the SOLD sign at the base of the hill.

The tires don't screech to a stop, and there is no driver checking to see if my brother's heart is still beating. The last thing I hear is Mom's transcendent wail that seeps into the sky and carries through the whole state of Indiana.

And still, my limbs betray me.

"Move!" Brynn cries, pushing past.

Here I am, this solid mass of cancer, infecting the family—like we're not already struggling—and my voice refuses to cry out while my feet don't carry me to the point of impact. Sarge and Brynn run down the slope to where this is happening—it's really happening—and I can't make any part of me stir. My brain tells my feet to take a step, just one step, and all these files I've categorized in my mind have been hurled in all directions. There is no order inside of me right now—only chaos. I can't see past the top of the drive. Is he dead, alive? I hate myself for not knowing, for not checking.

A sour stream of food shoots up my throat like a cannon, spewing all over my camera and strap. I don't hunch over or look for a trash can. I puke, right here, on the cold garage floor where the lighting acts as a sunlamp, heating my scalp. Just as it happens, Chomperz casually strolls through the entranceway with a sort of cat smile, if there is one, and rubs up against my leg because cats are inconsiderate jerks who want to be petted at the absolute worst times. And all this is happening because I wanted to tell Mom something so insignificant, so trivial, before Brynn did.

And just as I think it, the boy at the party flashes through my mind.

And at the absolute worst time, I sort of smile, too.

LESSON OF THE DAY: For a reaction to happen, particles must collide with energies equal to or greater than the activation energy for the reaction. But the thing is, the one thing I can't stop thinking about: Out of all the cars in the world traveling at normal speeds, why, at the exact moment Benny crossed the highway, was this car there? One second faster or slower, one variable changed, and this might not have happened.

Or maybe, no matter what, it would have.

BASH

We haven't spoken since it happened.

I know Kyle's freaked, because his mouth is shut, which almost never happens. He pulls into my trailer park, Grand Estates, and coasts up along the unpaved road. The absent hum of the engine is obvious now that we're just sitting here in the silence. With my hand clenched on my seat belt, I notice he's hovering over the steering wheel, his eyes still darting around in a panic.

I lay my hand on his shoulder, but I'm not sure what to say. "Don't stress until we check the car. I'm sure it's fine."

He nods. "Tomorrow? We *have* to get it done tomorrow."

"Fine."

We step out of the car. The rain has let up on this side of town, just a drizzle trickling over us, clanging on the trailer's rickety roof. He's not worried about his perfectly coifed hair or expensive leather jacket like usual. Hands stuffed in his pockets, he examines the front of the car. I make my way up beside him, afraid to look at the damage.

"Shit," Kyle says. He rubs his hand over a small dent on the hood, trailing down to the hole of a cracked headlight. He sticks his finger inside, pulls it out, then pushes back in, and looks up at me with a grin. "Remind you of anything?"

I punch him in the arm with a balled-up fist while he continues to laugh. "You're sick."

His laugh fades as I squat down for a deeper look. I feel him tower over me, his vodka breath souring the air. "When does your dad get home from his trip?"

Dude can barely keep his balance, wobbling like a tree ready to drop. He burps, holds his stomach. "Next Monday, I think."

"There's a sweet place up the road that will give us a good deal. I'll chip in what I've got saved, and he'll never know." I dip my hands into my pockets, where holes line the edges, the place where money should be.

He's shaking his head. "I know a guy who knows a guy. He'll get it done on the DL. Fast and cheap. Like Layla."

I stand up and meet Kyle's drowsy eyes. If I punched him, he wouldn't remember. I think on this for a few seconds until I remember he's an idiot with no filter. Besides, not that I'm not tough as shit, but my knuckles are too delicate for his GQ chiseled chin. I refocus to his swaying frame and attempt to steady him with my index finger on his chest. "That sounds super sketchy, man. Let's just take it to the place Ma used to go. They know me."

"No, nope, no. This isn't for public consumption. In this small town, word would get out before we could say 'banana hammock.'" He giggles. "Banana hammock. A hammock for your banana."

Now I know he's gone. I roll my eyes, place my hands square on his shoulders and draw his attention to my words of reason. It's a helluva lot harder than it sounds. "Kyle. Look at me." He does, barely. "It was probably just a big-ass dog. We'll get the dings fixed; your dad, and anyone else, will never know. Hear me?"

He takes a long time to respond, rubs his lips together, and pulls his phone from his pocket. I watch as he slowly and haphazardly punches a few numbers. One second later, my phone rings.

I sigh. "Really?"

He nods, his eyes urging me to answer, so I do, though, really, really pissed. "What?"

"Banana hammock," he says. He hunches over, hand pulling at his shirt, barely containing his laughter. Drunk Kyle is officially the worst, which isn't much better than sober Kyle, and coincidentally, they're *both* Wild Kyle, and I'm stuck with him, er . . . them. No one else can handle it, and if they could, wouldn't want to. Hell, if I knew for sure I wouldn't feel like utter shit for bailing on a decade-long shadow, however annoying, I'd stop handling it, too.

"Thanks for wasting my time, douche," I growl, knowing I have exactly twenty-nine minutes left on my pay-as-you-go card, and those are reserved for emergencies only. This doesn't count.

He's still laughing, waking the nosy-ass neighbors now. Their lights switch on, one by one, illuminating the Benz even more. I stomp over and shove my hand over his mouth with force. "Unless you wanna go to jail for being a high-ass drunk who hit something and fled, shut the hell up. I doubt even Daddy's money could get you out of that one."

His eyes are alert now, and with my hand acting as duct tape firm over his mouth, he nods. I let go, shake his germs free, and circle the car to warm the shivers prickling my skin. The rain left a bitterness in the air that bites into my veins. Part of me wants him to get out of here, fast, and the other knows what's waiting for me once I go inside—nothing.

With an out-of-character calmness, Kyle casually walks over to the row of withered bushes that are really just a pile of connected sticks surrounding the rusted tan trailer. It's the place where, every spring, Ma would attempt to plant something, and lo and behold, every spring, nothing would bloom in the weed-covered patch. His finger is waving at me like I'm trying to talk, and he's shushing me, but I've been quiet.

"What are you doing?" I ask.

He hunches over, near the brass numbers, *17,* which are barely hanging on, grabs his stomach, and vomits a thick stream of everything he's eaten today. I turn away, wrap my arms together, and rub, try to ward off the wind while he cleanses. The sounds remind me of Ma, and suddenly I miss her so much I want to drive across town. That's weird, right? Yeah. But with beer and cigarettes on my breath, if she's having a clear night where she isn't higher than Kyle, she'll kick me out before I'm halfway through the doorway. *Why are you killing yourself with those cancer sticks when I don't get to choose how I go?* she'll ask. To which I'll probably respond, *Because even the thought of losing you is its own kind of slow death, and this just eases the pain.* And then she'll lecture me about what it's doing to my body, which will lead to a discussion about life and death and all the things I don't want to hear or say. Not now. So instead, here I am looking at Kyle, realizing *this* is all I can handle right now.

Kyle clears his throat, jolting me from my thoughts. "I feel like a million bucks now!" He wipes the slime from the stray hairs on his chin.

"Get it all out?"

He begins to talk, his mouth half open as if he's going to say something profound. One finger pointed in the air, he runs back to the row of sticks, head hunched over. He always said cleansing is the soul's way of finding balance, so I hope this asshole comes out Even Steven when he's finished decorating our "front yard." This is why I don't drink hard liquor. A beer or two is cool. Beer confirms my beliefs on just about anything, doesn't change the way I act or think. But liquor, it changes people, usually in a very, *very* bad way. Like my ex-stepdad, Joe. I don't want to be anything like that son of a bitch. So I stay away from the stuff.

This time, when Kyle's finished, he doesn't have that smug grin I'm so used to. "Dude," he slurs.

I throw my arm around him and guide him to the passenger seat of his dad's car. "Get in. I'll drive you home."

He doesn't argue about the expensive wheels, and doesn't question how I'm gonna get home after. But that's not just Drunk Kyle. He wouldn't give a shit if he were Sober Kyle (which is a rare form, anyhow). But with only a few miles between us, it's not like I haven't done the walk of shame in days past. Though, it should be known, it was only a few times, when I felt a slight twinge of loneliness at the exact same moments Kyle felt a surge in clinginess. Similar to a weirdly platonic one-night stand, I always disappeared before his witch of a mom ever found out, and *definitely* before Kyle decided I couldn't live without him. Because let's be clear: I CAN.

He falls into the still-warm seat and slouches over to the side, with his head resting on the door panel. I buckle up, twist the keys, and slowly, carefully, drive him home. There comes a point in this small town, that has exactly three schools and a handful of traffic lights, where a definitive line is drawn. There are few good parts in East Clifton, where people drive Mercedes-Benzes and stand on pedestals from which they judge everyone else while waving their gold and arrogance around like flags. Then there are the places I live, which are the exact opposite. West Clifton has more of those cookie-cutter houses, completely lacking in originality, but better than my hood. There isn't much middle ground here. You're either making it or you're not. A town within a town. Those that live like Kyle's family sure as hell don't make their money here. They commute in their fancy suits to their big desks. These places, things, I know nothing about, except in my big pipe dreams. *Maybe someday,* I think to myself. And then I look around at what I have versus what Kyle has and realize, *Not really, though.*

We pull onto the long, winding drive where the front yard boasts a stone bird bath that spits a stream of water from its long beak. Careful not to press on the gas too hard, I coax the car into the open space of the five-car garage. With the engine now off, I look over at Kyle, who is sound asleep, snoring through his clogged nostrils—not a goddamned care in the world. *Must be nice,* I think, *being the one who lives here instead of works here.*

The day we left, the day Kyle's mom, Linda, kicked us out, she said she wouldn't be undermined by "the help." That we should go back to where we came from. She implied we're from Mexico by pointing to a bag of tortilla chips and a container of salsa, like the racist bigot she is, but we're Brazilian, and damn proud of it. My beautiful ma, so dignified and classy, ripped off her uniform and threw it at the salsa with a burly force. It knocked the plastic vessel onto Linda's ivory dress, to which Ma said "We're not Mexican, bitch." She packed our things and moved us into the place I now call home, which isn't home at all. Just a shack with sheets of thin threads to block the wind and light while I sleep. It felt a lot smaller when Joe was here, but he left when his next meal ticket came around. Thank God for that.

But another thing about Kyle is, he never really treated me like "the help." He defended us to his mom, cried when we left, begged for us to stay. Maybe that's why I let him hang around all these years (even though he's the actual worst). I feel like I abandoned him or something. Let him rot in that wretched mansion with all that money and freedom. Maybe I'm the one who's the actual worst.

I nudge Kyle awake with my elbow. His head pops up, eyes bulging in alarm. "Where am I?" he blurts in a huff.

"You're home. Go to bed. Sleep it off."

"Got anymore weed?"

"Get out of here." I shove him out. He stumbles before catching his footing as he mutters something, not a thank-you, and drags himself inside. I linger in the car for a minute, because it's still warm, think about the night, and walk around the front to inspect the dent once more.

I lean down, something between the headlight's jagged teeth catching my eye. My fingers pinch a small, almost invisible piece of fabric. I angle the green, wet patch up against the light. A chill startles me as it sinks deep into the muscle. Animals like deer or stray dogs don't wear clothes. Unless it was a pet tortured by the kind of people who raise their dogs like kids. People like Kyle's family.

I spend a few long minutes rationalizing with myself before deciding the cloth was there before. It's the only thing that makes sense, the only thing I can accept right now. I shove the fabric into the corner of my pocket, close the garage, and exit through the side door like one of Kyle's girlfriends.

The cold thrashes sharpened waves of face-numbing wind at me. I march on, press my feet deeper into the ground as I walk parallel to the highway, through the bare forest and trees. The fallen leaves crunch beneath me, step by step, for a couple miles. Whatever buzz I had is gone, and I'm fresh out of the cigarettes I stole from Vinny at the rink.

I walk up to my door and easily twist the knob because it's never locked, because we have nothing worth stealing. Unless you count dreams and faith. The door won't close, so I slam my body up against it, then flip the light switch. But it's still dark, still cold. Might as well go back outside and sleep in Kyle's warm vomit. I flip again, hoping the house just needed a warm-up flip and this is the one that will cast a light onto all our treasures and gold.

Nothing.

My foot catches on a piece of paper on the sticky floor.

NOTICE: DISCONNECTION OF ELECTRICITY

"Who disconnects on a Sunday—God's day of rest? Sacrilegious a-holes." I think back to the last bill I used as a napkin. Must've been the electric. Ma would lose her shit if she knew I let them "take our light," even though I've explained a million times that's how utilities work. That you have to *pay* for them to *keep* them.

I wad the paper into a ball and see how far I can toss it. Considering the space is only about twelve feet wide, it's not far. With my stomach still churning, I figure a sandwich could calm the storm, so I throw together a slice of stale bread and a slab of bologna that—I hope—hasn't spoiled yet. The jacket stays on in this icebox, and I wander back to my room, where the old spring mattress lies on the floor. My body falls like someone yelled "timber," sandwich still in hand, and I pull my chem homework from the faded backpack I've had since I was twelve. Shuffling through the problems by the light of the moon, I press Play on my phone—more Johnny Cash—and use the extra light to boost my vision.

Staring at summary number three, it's talking about catalysts. How hydrogen and oxygen need a catalyst, like a lit match, to explode. I read a little further.

> When a catalyst is added, a molecule shifts its
> structure or makes two molecules combine, and
> they release more energy. That extra energy might
> create a chain reaction. A catalyst is like a bridge.
> It can redirect the chemical pathway to skip all the
> other steps that require energy.

I lower the paper and think of Kyle, the car, and the cloth.
Maybe I'm overthinking, maybe I'm too sober.
Or maybe I'm onto something kind of huge.

birdie

The red and blue lights bleed into the night sky like melting crayons.

Three police cruisers and one EMT arrive exactly four minutes, thirty-seven seconds after Dad made the call. They drove just a few miles from the local emergency room, but they say it's too bad; Benny needs to get to Children's over in Grove City, and now. Mom crouches beside him, tries to hold him, move him, but they tell her not to, beg her not to. With a face ghostly white, Brynn says there's blood everywhere, and by the way she tells me, she's not processing what has happened. They're just emotionless words, a record on repeat.

As the rain settles, it is clear Mom's in shock. She won't let go of Benny. Dad tries to pull her fingers loose from the threads of Benny's shirt. She cocks a fist back and wallops him in the arm with the strength of ten men. I've seen her do this before, but not like this. She was joking then. This is different. This isn't light. This is pain.

Their mouths move, open and close and close and open, but I can't hear their words. I pull the camera that's covered in bile up to my face, focus carefully with my fingers, and snap a dozen pictures. The smooth black frame knocks my glasses onto the bridge of my nose. I capture the moment so I can go back and remember this, figure out how to fix it.

Without the pictures, the proof, I might not believe this is happening. Because this isn't happening. It *can't* be.

I stand in the garage, camera smashed to my face, until Sarge gently pulls me, and Chomperz, inside. He drags me into the kitchen and plops me down onto a chair before sorting through a drawer. With shaky hands, he runs a cloth under the faucet, silent. I don't move as he wipes the vomit from my chin and sets my camera on the table next to, of all things, Benny's bedtime book. He's slow and deliberate, steadying his hands against my cheeks. I don't make eye contact; I can't. Just look at the floor. It's all I see. The diamond-shaped pattern that weaves through the kitchen and dining room. Connected, like a family should be, not broken.

When he's finished, he pulls back, soft, hands planted down on both my shoulders. There is an obvious shift in the room's energy. He says so much without uttering a single word. He pats. Once, twice, three times, then walks away, leaves me to my thoughts as if to say, *I'm here if you need me.* The red and blue lights now pour into the living room, coloring our new home with feelings, I can't escape. So I don't even try. I just . . . sit.

I don't remember much, like how long the EMTs work to keep my brother alive, or maybe, bring him back to life. I only remember those lights. Like the pulsing rays of a disco ball, alerting the whole town something horrific happened while we wait, another fourteen minutes, nineteen seconds, for the CareFlite helicopter to land near our front yard. We all know that puttering sound of sadness. When it's flying overhead, something bad has happened, something inevitably fatal. At some point, as I sit here, he's airlifted to Grove City PICU and Trauma Center, a half an hour away, with Mom by his side.

Dad and Brynn rush in, and without even speaking to me, Dad grabs his keys. They rush back out, hop in Dad's car to leave. I should go with them. Or maybe I should stay? Or . . .

maybe I would be better off melting into the foundation to never be seen again. I vote for the latter. They don't wait for me to decide anyway. I wander back into the garage to see Dad furiously back down the steep drive, darting into the highway without much care. Sarge quietly follows after me. He tugs on the young cypress that's still attached to Mom's SUV. Moments pass as he struggles with the cords that have the tree wrapped snug. I consider offering help, but don't. I can see on his face, he needs to do this on his own. This is how he must process the events, so I let him.

Through Sarge's grunting, I fall to my knees on the garage floor, just inches from the vomit puddle. An officer, all dressed in blue, as they say, slowly walks up the hill, his head hung just low enough, his eyes are hidden. He approaches with caution.

"Is he dead?" I blurt.

"No."

"I hope he doesn't. Die, I mean." My hands are shaking, out of my control.

"Me, too. Want to talk about it?" he asks. I can't tell if he's asking in an official way or asking because we're sitting near my puke.

"I bet it's a traumatic brain injury," I say. "If he doesn't die, he'll never be the same. Fifty-two thousand deaths occur from traumatic brain injury every year. He's probably going to die." I feel like stone, my heart not just broken but a blank sheet of paper. From the cold, from the slow acceptance that this is *my* fault.

I see his eyebrows knit together with curiosity from the corner of my eye. "You going to be a doctor?"

"Medical examiner." There's a lull in the conversation where part of me wants to talk about the lost scholarship and how I might never actually be a medical examiner, but I decide now is probably the worst time to analyze my path in life.

He pats my shoulder. "I know this is difficult . . . but . . . I have to ask you a few questions."

I nod. My eyes are fixed on the driveway that, now that the bright lights have faded, slithers out into the dark night and fades into nothingness. The moon casts daffodil streaks on the flood that's pooled in the pockets of our yard. I can't look away.

"Seems to be a little confusion on the details of the accident. What do you remember?"

My mind is empty, a black vacuum without a single thought or memory of anything that has ever happened in the history of my life. Except for the file of these random facts that seem to keep forcing their way out of my mouth. "There was a car. It hit Benny."

He clears his throat. "Do you remember what the car looked like?"

"It was fast." He's watching my every move. I'm afraid to do something wrong, say something wrong. I feel my body clenching. Behind us, Sarge thrashes, finally pulling the cypress free from the knotted ropes. He's huffing and mumbling obscenities to himself as if he were fighting the toughest battle of his life. Maybe he is. We watch as he flings the sapling through the doorway with one sharp "HIYAHHH!"

"Okay." The officer is hesitant, pulls my attention back to him as he scribbles a note onto a small pad of paper he lifts from his front pocket. "We'll question neighbors, try to find everyone who drove on the road tonight, talk to body shops in case whoever did this tries to get any damage fixed."

"It was raining, dark, the car hit him," I manage. Now that the garage is quiet again, I feel the words breaking and splitting, but I can't glue them together. He's looking at me, not writing, but watching me fall apart.

"Can you tell me where your parents were when your brother got in the stroller?"

The words drag my weary eyes up to his. "Here."

44

"Were they . . . with him, watching him?"

I nod, furiously, clamp my mouth shut, and revert back to the driveway. How could he think otherwise? OF COURSE Mom was watching him. Well, sort of. Now that I think about it, maybe she wasn't. He stuffs the notepad back inside his pocket and removes a small business card he places in my hand. I'm still staring at the driveway, disoriented, afraid to say another thing. I don't feel the card anyway. My skin isn't a part of me, but this separate entity I see from the outside. This is a dream and I will wake up and everything will be fine.

"You think of anything, anything at all, call me. We'll do everything we can to find who did this."

I nod again. The officer's shiny black shoes pitter-patter down the driveway as Sarge appears behind me, jingling keys in hand. He shakes them the way an owner does to a dog. "Tree's up and watered," he says. "Damn needles started falling and Chomperz already ate some. I knew when Brooks said he was going to that Meat Goat/Tree Farm up the road he'd be ripped off. The guy that runs that shithole is a damn Communist."

"Mmm-hmm," I say.

"You okay to drive?" he asks. I'm so *not* okay to drive. Holes are where my eyes should be; my eyes have fallen into the sockets along with all vision or clarity. But it doesn't matter. I tell him I will drive. With his glaucoma, we're only getting to that hospital if I do. I also can't tell him my legs are numb, my feet won't feel the pedals, so I just slip inside the car—the one he gave me when his depth perception started to go—turn the ignition, and follow the lingering sounds of sirens in the distance without feeling a thing. There are lights I don't remember stopping at, cars I don't remember yielding to, and I think, *Maybe this is what happened to the person who hit Benny. Maybe they were in a daze, couldn't tell what was real or a dream,* and I realize I'm in a bad state if I'm now empathizing with the one who hurt us, instead of my hurt brother.

We drive and we drive. The total only twenty-six miles, almost a marathon's distance, but it feels like an eternity. The car is silent, and we bathe in it, soak, too afraid to say anything at all, and it's fine. He doesn't bring his trusty bubble pops—the blistered plastic wrap meant to cushion packaged items—or I'd have opened my car door, at approximately sixty-two miles per hour (which is almost as fast as a cheetah can run), and let the wheels catch me, churn me into mash. Like Benny. With the wind and rain as variables, taking into account the velocity, I should be street meat about .02 seconds after opening the door.

What's wrong with me? I think. Mom's always nitpicking, asking why I can't be more sympathetic, emotional, think a little *less* sometimes. This—as my baby brother struggles for life—is why Brynn hates me, why they'll all hate me once they know I'm the reason he's here. My brain doesn't work like theirs, never has. I'm not just different; I'm now a danger.

We pull into the emergency parking lot at the Grove City PICU and Trauma Center awhile after the helicopter, and the rain is now just a light dust of cold water. If it had been this calm a couple of hours ago, Benny would be in the house playing with his car. Instead, they've wheeled him into some trauma room to put the pieces of him back together while his car is the safe one.

"I reckon we better get in there," Sarge says, quietly.

I nod, my body paralyzed with fear.

He sighs, lays his hand on my leg, and pats to calm me in the way only he can. "Can't let your head get away. You never have before so let's not start now." He lingers for a second, clears his throat, and steps out of the car. I sit in the quiet for another minute, hope he's right, and reluctantly follow him inside. Even though the rain has stopped, the wind feels colder now, like the car knocked the warmth right from Benny's chest, his soul, and filled the air with bitter frost instead.

Inside the hospital's double doors, a nurse directs us to the Emergency waiting room where Mom, Dad, and Brynn have been put to pace. Their feet have already worn imprints into the tiles. We are the only people here, the only ones who will be on our knees tonight. Sarge offers a hand to Mom. With an empty, teary-eyed stare, she looks up at him, her father, and he blankets her with his embrace. She sobs into his jacket while I quietly, remorsefully, look on.

After a few minutes, Mom plops into an unfeeling chair and buries her head in her hands. Dad sits, rubs her back; she leans into him for comfort. He's hurt, too, but I can see him struggling with staying strong. Brynn is quieter than usual. Her knees are scrunched up to her chest and she's crying into them, staining them with tears.

"They took him to the operating room," Mom sobs. "Please let him be okay. Please, God."

We're all stuffed into this room that's not big but not really small. The walls are closing in, pressing us together in these two rows of chairs that are adjacent. No one says a thing as we wait for an update, and the only sounds are of the book-length pile of papers Mom and Dad have to fill out. Her hands shake as she frantically searches for the insurance card and realizes she didn't bring her purse—she must've dropped it in the garage when all this happened. She's ranting about how she forgot, what a horrible mother it makes her, when Dad calms her, hands over his card instead.

I don't know how much time passes. A minute, an hour, a lifetime. The operating doctor appears in the doorway, his blue scrubs stained with red, much like the police lights, and we all stand, as if standing will make his news seem better. Standing to keep our knees from buckling, pulling us right under into the core of the broken shards of earth. Or maybe standing gives us something concrete to sink into instead of just clinging to a ratty upholstered chair.

"I'm Dr. Cheung." The man with kind eyes says. He removes his paper hat and clutches it to his chest. We're collectively holding our breaths. It's so quiet, only the clock's ticking hands are heard.

"How is he?" Mom asks in a strangled voice. She dries tears on the edge of her palm, smearing them along her jawline. "He's okay, right? Please tell me he's okay."

The doctor sighs. His jaws clench down, hard. "When he was—"

"Benedict," Mom interrupts. "His name is Benedict. Benny. Call him Benny."

He hesitates. "Benny *is* alive, Mrs. Paxton."

Mom gasps, cries into her hand again. "Thank God!"

He continues. "But"—because there's always a *but*—"when he was first assessed and intubated, he was unresponsive and almost died on the ride here. MRI scans show severe head trauma and facial fractures, with extensive swelling around the brain. He lost a lot of blood and needed a transfusion. My team is working to drain some of the fluid through tubes in his scalp. There was also substantial debris embedded in his skin from the road, but we've removed most of it."

"But he's okay—he's going to be *okay*, right?" Mom cries. She emphasizes *okay*, like if she says it with more urgency, he has to agree with her. Dad moves closer; we all follow in rhythmic wave.

"We put him in a medically induced coma so as not to risk shock. I can't tell you how long he'll remain in this state, if he'll ever come out of it, and if he does, that there won't be irreversible brain damage. It's just too early to tell. He's not breathing on his own, but for now is stable and we hope the steroids will help bring the swelling down." He looks

48

away when he says *stable,* and I know it's bad. He's being polite so we don't lose hope, or maybe for his own sake. So *he* can sleep tonight knowing he did all he could.

Mom's eyes are searching like she doesn't completely understand, but I've seen enough medical documentaries to feel confident in my traumatic brain injury diagnosis.

"When can we see him?" Brynn asks, her eyes and nose beet red.

"When he's out of surgery and recovering in his room, someone will let you know. My advice? Get some rest. It'll be touch and go through the night."

Dr. Cheung leaves, and Mom falls into a chair as if standing was a bad omen and sitting will help put things in a more positive light. Plus, sitting gives her something to fall over, to catch her when she's too weak. Sitting means the doctor isn't standing here telling us Benny is dying. Everyone is quiet again, except for the sounds of sniffling noses. The room is swollen with sadness so thick, it's suffocating me. I scratch and claw at my throat to open up the airway.

Mom's face is flat, and she's picking at her nails, one by one. "The police were NO help," she says. "Said they didn't have enough to go on—I know what I saw. And then they questioned me—ME—like *I* did something wrong, like *I* caused this!"

Dad runs his hands through his hair, then over his weary eyes, his wedding ring gleaming against the lights. He sits next to her, but this time doesn't touch her. "What *did* you see, Bess?"

Her eyes narrow into slits as she jerks her head up at him. "Don't talk to me with that tone. You couldn't see. You weren't as close as I was."

"There's no tone," he whispers.

"The car was dark," Brynn speaks up. "And fast. That's all I saw."

Sarge stirs, takes a seat on the other side of Mom. He

fiddles with a patch on his army jacket. "Sometimes . . . our minds, our eyes, play tricks on us, you know? Make us see what we want to see, what makes sense to us at the time. Doesn't always mean it's the right thing."

"Dad," Mom says, "what are you saying?"

"When my friends were killed in combat, I wasn't thinking about the color of the guns our enemies used to shoot at us, because a bullet is a bullet. I wasn't thinking about the size of the grenades they launched, because an explosion is an explosion. And I sure as hell wasn't thinking about the pang in my stomach that burned with fear because I was doing what I had to do. Honestly, I couldn't tell you a god-damned thing about the war except the eyes of those men who died in my arms. And it doesn't matter. I fought, and I lived. Everything else? Things my mind, my eyes, decided for me. Doesn't make them right."

"This isn't about the war," Mom snaps. She always snaps when Sarge talks about the war. She thinks he's senile, doesn't remember as much as he does, doesn't feel as deeply as I *know* he does. Just look into his eyes, you'll see he knows, feels, more than all of us combined. He didn't move in with us because he needed us, but because we needed him—Mom needed him.

"This, Bess, is about *hope.* I'm just sayin', when you're praying for a certain outcome—Benny to live—the details will get foggier, less important. Because all that matters is he makes it another day. As long as we have *hope,* we have life. It's out of our hands." He pats Mom's leg and walks to the door. "I'm getting coffee." His slumped-over shadow fades behind the glass pane, and I feel Brynn's eyes on me.

"You smell like puke," she says. "It's seriously making me gag."

I fold my arms, bury my chin in my chest. "Maybe it's your dirty hair."

She continues staring, and I know she's looking for a fight.

50

"You saw the whole thing, didn't you? You *had* to have seen it. You were in there."

Mom's eyes find me, Dad's, too. Dampness coats my hands, clammy and cool. "I don't know—it happened too fast."

"How did Benny find the stroller anyway? It was in the trunk." She starts crying, her eyes pleading with me. I glance at Mom, who is clenching her jaw, and I know she's angry, confused, maybe as she retraces the events, and I can't speak. Has she forgotten I was there, trying to confess something?

They're waiting. For an answer. The lights above sizzle with a hum that fills the room. "I . . . I . . ."

"Is it because you snuck out to a party the other night?" the little brat asks.

"You *what?*" Dad asks.

"She snuck out of the house Friday. Your perfect little Birdie Jay isn't as perfect as you think. FINALLY! Everyone will see what I've been saying for years. You suck, Birdie!"

"Brynn!" I cry out, prepared to jump from my seat to strangle her. I know exactly how long it would take to revive her if she went without oxygen too long. Plus we're already in a hospital, so it seems like my chance.

"I can't deal with this right now." Mom stands, runs into the hallway to catch a passing nurse, almost saving me from the question. Brynn follows—a chicken that keeps pecking long after the food has run out—but our war is far from over.

Dad walks over to me, pats my shoulder with a light touch that feels different from Sarge's. "Once we know more, I think you should drive Sarge and Brynn home," he sighs. "Everyone's tired. The arguing isn't helping Mom."

I turn to face him, my eyes meeting his. I fall into the sleeve of his crisp shirt and sob. The tears fall, a running faucet with no OFF switch. He stretches his arm around me and rubs the hair from my eyes to wipe the tears dry, but there's something missing in his gaze, and I'm sure it's because he knows I'm the one who unfolded the stroller—because *he* gave me the task of removing it from the trunk.

I agree. He places a finger beneath my chin and tilts my head up. Our eyes meet and linger as if he's searching for some kind of truth. He says nothing before hugging me one last time, then sets me free.

In the hallway, Mom is crying into her hands, Brynn is clinging to Sarge, and the pain in my heart is right here, pulling me under in this massive tidal wave. Flashes of tonight are colliding, creating a new trail of thoughts, and all of my files are splayed out across the vast depths of my brain. They cannot be organized right now. Maybe not ever again.

Before high school, I wanted to be a scientist. Chemistry has always been my favorite subject (aside from physics) because it's interesting why some things shouldn't go together, how fast they react, and what can explode (Brynn) or implode (me). It wasn't until we started learning about decomposition, my freshman year, that I became enamored with bodies and how, in the end, they break apart like all the particles I once loved so much. Thus, I decided to go the medical route.

But now I'm rethinking everything.

LESSON OF THE DAY: I learned a long time ago that activation energy, the minimum energy needed for a reaction, is necessary to make a chain reaction happen. Maybe it was when Dad asked me to get the stroller, maybe it was my own numbing fear of telling Mom about the party, but when I stalled Mom, *I* was the inhibitor, slowing her reaction to a complete stop. *I* am the reason we are here.

Because no inhibitor = faster reaction rate.

And faster reaction rate = possible different outcome.

And no matter what happens with Benny—my family is broken.

And no matter how you calculate it, it's *my* fault.

BASH

It's cold as shit.

I don't sleep much, but when I'm shivering all night, I sleep even less. The sun hasn't yet shown itself through the window above, which is blocked by an old, thin bedsheet hung by tacks. The sky is more dusk than pitch-black so it must be near dawn. I squint my eyes, roll onto my side, where a loose mattress spring jabs my rib, and try to go back to sleep. But I'm distracted by the constant buzz of my phone against the floor. The rattling won't let up, and a sudden wave of fear washes over me. *Is it about Ma?*

I turn over, and the buzzing stops, but there are a dozen missed calls, voice mails, and texts. From Kyle. I grunt, toss the phone down, and roll back over. It can't be time for school because I haven't been home long. The phone dances across the floor again; this time, I answer, thinking mostly about the minutes I'm wasting, how long until I can buy more, and if this isn't the nursing home calling about Ma, what could be so important to wake me from this nightmare.

It's Kyle again, obviously. He asks why I haven't answered, says this is urgent and we need to talk before school, it can't wait. I tell him to come on over, and he says he's already out-side freezing his ass off in his (heated) Corvette. I laugh because he doesn't get it on so many levels, but he's dead serious, so I roll onto the floor and drag my sorry ass out of the comfort of my prison cell.

A minute later, a knock on the door—more like a thunderous banging that doesn't stop until I open the thin metal barrier between us. "What the hell, man?" I ask, wiping the sleep from my eyes. "I literally just left your drunk ass at home. Thought you'd skip school today, sleep it off."

He ignores me, pushes past. He's pacing, wearing an even bigger hole in the middle of my torn-up floor. The sun is brightening now, streaming thin, choppy rays onto the floor, showing how bad the wear really is. Clearly I must've slept at some point, but it doesn't feel like it.

"What's up?" I ask, arms crossed firm across my chest. With a yawn, I think of falling back to the mattress and skipping school myself. What's one more day? It's not like anyone misses me there. I'm not the star football player or the a-hole who knows the answer to every question. I'm just . . . there. Mostly because the state, and Ma, make me.

His pace quickens as he runs his fingers through his freshly washed hair. The ends drip pellets onto my floor. Something has him spooked. Even for a high-strung, privileged, whiny-ass, the way he's filling the entirety of this place with his anxiety is beyond his usual level of whacked-out.

"Why's it so cold in here?" he asks. "It's like a goddamned freezer."

I see the balled-up disconnection notice on the floor. "Saving money on heat."

"It's too cold."

I try to find his eyes, which are bouncing around with his pace. "Is this about the Benz?"

He laughs manically, a questionable look of crazy spinning in his stare. "Oh, yeah. This is about the Benz. It's definitely about the Benz. We're in the deepest shit ever taken. Future is gone, everything we know—gone. I. Can't. Even."

"I told you. I'll help pay to get the thing fixed," I say,

wondering how exactly I'm going to do that when I can't even keep the electricity on. "Might take me a couple weeks to get the money, but I'll help."

He's shaking his head like he's trying to knock loose a clear thought. "I don't want your money, dude. But we've got to get it taken care of today. Has to be today."

"Are you still high?"

"If I were, this would suck a lot less. If the chemo didn't kill your ma, what I have to tell you sure as hell will."

I place my hands firmly on his shoulders, stopping him in his tracks. "Kyle," I say with a firm voice, "you're not making sense, and I'm starting to get freaked out. Just tell me what's wrong."

I guide him to the recliner that won't open. He sinks into the fabric's contoured cushion and takes a deep breath. His eyes are glued to the floor, and mine are on him. "Is your dad coming home early?"

He nods.

"Okay. Is that why you're tweaking?"

"No."

"You're going to have to use actual words and form sentences that make sense if you want my help."

"The news station called Dad. They wanted a quote about how the curve on Highway 22 might affect the value of the development . . . now that this *new* accident happened."

"What . . . *new* . . . accident?" I hold my breath, knowing what's coming, reach into my pocket, and pinch the small piece of fabric I found between my fingers.

"Dad called Mom a couple hours ago, and the phone woke me. When I got up to pee, I heard it on the TV." He pulls out his phone and searches with a few keystrokes. "It wasn't a deer or dog we hit, Bash. It was a person—a little kid."

He holds the phone up to my face, his tired eyes absent of any sort of arrogance or the confidence that usually preceded him. The article says there was a hit and run on 22 late last night, the boy is at Grove City PICU and Trauma Center, and they are searching for suspects with little to no information about the make and model of the car. My heart sinks into the worn floor, absorbs into the rotted wooden slabs, and deteriorates right here as the sun shines brighter through the thin sheet. Now I'm shaking my head like I can't believe this, it *has* to be someone else. We didn't do this—we couldn't have done this.

I drop the phone into Kyle's lap and circle back to lean against the small kitchen counter. "I thought that house was empty," I say, my voice shaking.

"I guess it sold."

I gulp. "We *have* to go to the police."

"We do that," he says, "we're done. They'll slaughter us and use our insides as Christmas decorations."

"No," I say. "There's NO other option. We *have* to do the right thing here—what if this kid dies? I don't want that on my conscience. This is serious shit, Kyle."

He stands from the recliner, shoves his phone and his hands in his pockets. "Just stop for one second and think about how this will play out. You go to the cops, they arrest us. Your ma—who thinks you do no wrong—dies of heartache before the cancer's even finished with her. That will be your fault. Then my dad's agency goes under while we're shoveling shit off the highway with criminals. That will be my fault. When it's all said and done, we'll have nothing left. Nothing."

"You mean, *you'll* have nothing left—is that what you're afraid of? To be like me?" I snap, knowing when Ma goes, however she does, there's nothing left for me anyway.

He walks toward me. "Yeah, Bash," he says. "I am. I like my life. I like having things, and I like my beard. My beard tells people I'm a man. Not just any man, but Jeff Taylor's son. I don't want any of that to change."

The words, the truth, hurt, sting the backs of my eyelids. I slide down the cabinet and fall to the floor, my head buried in my hands. "You should've just let me drive the goddamned car in the first place."

His voice softens; he slides down the cabinet, too. "You're right. But I didn't. Now here we are."

There's a long silence between us before one of Kyle's rants crawls into my thoughts. "If I'm not mistaken, you once told me Confucius said 'A man who has committed a mistake and doesn't correct it is committing another mistake.'"

He nods, with a wagging finger up in the air. "Preach, brother! Guess that's what they call a taste of my own medicine?"

I snicker, but the feeling is more sour than sweet. "How does it taste?"

"Bitter as shit."

I angle my head toward him, hoping for some kind of agreement without a fight. "So we'll turn ourselves in, then."

He pulls himself up and towers over me, his shadow casting darkness over my soul. "You don't get it. We're not telling anyone—ever. This ain't no slap on the wrist like those DUIs or your little spray-painting incident freshman year, Bash. This is hard time, and being closer to legal, we're talking about prison with killers and shit. You know what they do to people who hurt kids. I'm not cut out for that lifestyle— with this baby face? I'd be torn to shreds."

"Prison *with* killers?" I stand to face him. "If that kid dies, *we're* killers, Kyle. Us. You and me."

Tears fill his bloodshot eyes, and I realize I don't think I've ever seen him cry—not really, anyway. I've seen the fake tears fall when he wanted to get in a girl's pants, but not for real. Not because he actually *feels*. In this case, Daddy might strip him of his trust fund, and on some level, knowing how he was raised, I guess I understand. He doesn't know any other way to be—something I say about myself often. So I guess we're at an impasse.

He looks at me with salt-stained cheeks. The tears roll down into his scraggly beard and mustache, and I can see Kyle. Real Kyle. At least I think I do. "I don't want Dad to be disappointed in me," he says. "I've felt it with less important things, like booze or girls. But this . . . this would destroy any relationship he and I might *ever* have. If the cops, media, or any other human on this earth finds out I was involved in this, it would ruin *everything,* and I couldn't live with myself. *No one* can find out. I would actually rather die."

His sobs grow louder until they're rumbling off the walls. With his hands now grinding into my shoulders, his voice strengthens. "Do you understand? If it comes out that I had anything to do with this and it's connected to my father, *his* car, and *his* real estate investments, I *will* kill myself."

I see the intensity in his eyes, the way they shake. A chill goes through me. I've heard Kyle say a lot of dumb shit before, but never this. I peel his hands off my shoulders and hug him. I don't remember the last time anyone hugged me—like, really hugged me—so it wasn't only a comfort to him. His tears soak through my shirt, and I realize how scared he really is. Same way I was when Joe was drunk all those times.

I don't know what to say. My conscience battles with itself, doing right, or doing wrong, and I pull him off to look him straight in the eyes, because until I can figure out how to get us out of this mess, it's all I can do to make this conversation stop.

"Okay," I say.

He wipes the snot from his nose. "Okay?"

I release a long sigh, and all of the regret I know I'm going to have. "Unless the kid dies, I won't say anything."

His tears cease, and a look of surprise covers his expression. "Really?"

I nod, while a sharp pain in my chest tells me what a mistake this is.

"I knew I could count on you!" he exclaims. He says it like it was his plan all along, to ignore anything I said until he got his way. "You really are my best friend—brother from another mother."

"I'm your *only* friend." This is true. "And your brother because, like a lost puppy, you won't leave me the hell alone." This is also true. All versions of Kyle are a combined force I can't escape because he literally has exhausted the shit out of me. That's his thing. To wear people down until they give in. He wins, everyone else in life loses.

His tears cease. "I swear—I'll anonymously send money, flowers—the goddamned moon—but as long as the kid is alive, we can never tell anyone we did it." He holds out his fist, hoping to knock knuckles in a silent form of agreement. "Deal?"

I swallow a lump bigger than I have had since hearing the news about Ma. It's wrong, so wrong, but at this point, there's nothing I can do to stop it.

Except keep my mouth shut.

birdie

Every news station on the planet is telling our story, our *tragedy*, like Benny's already gone. One anchor, whose name I won't mention (okay, it's the local Fox anchor who laughed when telling a story about a man exposing himself in a Walmart; apparently it was *really* cold in there), keeps referring to Mom as Bessie, to which Mom says, "I'm not a damn heifer—it's Bess, *just* Bess. It's not hard." That's usually when Dad replies, "That's what she said," to lighten the mood, but no one laughs because Mom keeps reminding us we shouldn't be laughing at a time like this, and she's right.

Pictures of the tattered stroller and Benny's stray shoe made the front page of the paper. Images, much like I'd take of something dead on the side of the road, have gone viral. The yard has been littered with people, strangers, for days, their feet marking the dried grass around the SOLD sign that's splattered with mud and gunk and a little bit of our hearts.

On this particular morning, I almost forget what life I'm living. Last night's dreams of riding horseback with a crab fisherman named Sig Hansen have me a little dazed. I mean, I'm *pretty* sure the conversation we had about the whole Taylor Swift and Kanye thing was real, but with the way life has been lately, who even knows anymore.

After a garbage-mouth yawn and a sudden realization of my actual life, I toss the covers and jump out of bed. The comforter lands on top of Chomperz, who is, without shame, bathing his embarrassingly shrunken testes that, for whatever reason, he enjoys showing off. "Have some humility, man," I tell him. He pauses a short moment, then continues licking. Squinting, I pry open the ivory plastic blinds that I've just noticed have bite marks in them. "Jeez, Chomperz, we *just* got here," I say. He's sprawled out in the nucleus of my bed, surrounded by the sea of fabric, completely ignoring me—a trait I *really* love about him. "Furry jerk."

When I check my phone, I realize I forgot I'd texted Violet from the hospital but didn't respond to her reply, so, naturally, she's concerned to the point of completely blowing up my phone, as besties do.

> VIOLET: OMG!!! ARE YOU KIDDING? TELL ME YOU'RE KIDDING. BUT IT'S NOT FUNNY.
>
> VIOLET: ARE YOU THERE??? WHAT CAN I DO—DRIVE OVER?
>
> VIOLET: I HOPE YOU'RE OK!!!
>
> VIOLET: HOLY CRAP APPLE, BIRDS—IT'S ALL OVER THE NEWS. WOW . . . ☹
>
> VIOLET: I LIT MY FRANKINCENSE AND ASKED DEITY ALLURA TO WATCH OVER YOUR FAM. ♥ YOU.

I toss the phone and count a slew of faces outside, including one lanky anchor, a bulbous man balancing a camera on his shoulder, and an old geez with the mic and boom whose arm is shaking from the weight of it. Such a production to film these strangers laying colorful flowers and sad-looking teddy bears around the base of the wooden stake. You would never know how many people it takes to shoot a thirty-second clip of news unless you're like me, living this horrible nightmare right now.

I pound at my window, scream, "He's not dead, butt clowns!" For a moment, they stop. For a moment, they see me and offer condolence smiles. You know the kind. A half smile, saggy eyes, with a three-quarter wave. Our eyes linger through this pane of thin glass, but after a few minutes, they decide to pretend I'm not here—the same thing Chomperz does as he moves to other gross areas of his body.

"You disgust me," I tell him. I love this cat so much it hurts.

I shower, dress in my favorite charcoal jeans and navy math tee that reads $\sqrt{-1}\ 2^3\ \sum \pi$ (aka: I Ate Some Pie)—something Violet doesn't think is funny even a little—comb through my long, wavy hair with my fingers, and hide my bloodshot eyes behind my glasses.

"What are you doing?" Sarge asks as I make my way through the house. He tosses back a couple of his heart pills like candy.

"School," I say.

"You're not going to the hospital?"

I shuffle my feet, sling the backpack over my shoulder, and shrug.

Through his glasses that magnify his every blink, he lowers his face into mine, and I can see the clouds of glaucoma swimming around. "You *need* to be with your family, your brother."

I know he's right but can't tell him I don't want to be in that room, listening to Mom and Dad sob over Benny's broken parts and endless bandages. I don't want to see Brynn's dirty hair and bratty smirk. I don't want to smell those hospital scents of urine, sterile needles, death, and all the things I'd rather forget. And I sure as hell don't want to see my baby brother take his last breath because of something *I* did.

I don't deserve to be there. I *deserve* to be strapped to a rolling gurney in an incinerator where I would burn at 1,600° to 1,800°F until my bones fall to ash. According to my height and weight, it would take about an hour and a half;

maybe less. Seems unfairly painless, considering what I've put Benny, and my parents, through.

"You okay?" he asks, his palm on my forehead. "You're clammy."

"I'm fine." I push past him, grab my jacket and keys. "I'll stop by the hospital after school."

"Birds—" He starts toward me, a fierce look in his eyes.

I pause, challenge him with a determined stare of my own. The silence builds until the phone rings. It's Mom checking in on us. "She's fine, I'm fine, don't worry," he says to her through the phone, over and over. I imagine Mom on the other end, tired and panicked she's not here to keep the order. Like the house literally will fall apart without her, shingles and all. Sarge isn't capable of feeding himself, and I'm going to miss my alarm, and Chomperz might starve to death, and—crap, I forgot to feed him. He's got a few extra layers to shed, so he'll be fine.

With Sarge's attention turned away, I rush to the garage. My bitterly cold car heats beneath the fluorescent light that knows all of my secrets, and the garage door opens without stalling. The crowd of people by the base move in one rhythmic line to the side of the grass, aware of my presence. I slowly back down the driveway, my neck craning like a flamingo. At the bottom of this crap hill, the lanky anchor, Julie Sturghill, approaches my window with a light-knuckled tap, and I want to avoid her, but she's kind of unavoidable in that she's blocking my way out.

"Excuse me," she says. I crack the window, let the air slap my face. Her left eye stares harder than her right, so much so that I can't focus on what words are streaming through her lipstick-stained teeth. Something about a candid sit-down, my take on what happened. I don't know, it's all fuzz. This eye won't let go of me. It's like a fishhook is latched onto her eyelid, pulling it down over her pupil. Reminds me of those boys who wear their pants too low. Not that I've never seen anyone with a unique facial thing before. Nan's nose had been broken in a car accident and never healed right. Her nostrils angled up toward each other like a teepee. They were so perfectly triangular, so sharply formed; her nose was perfectly imperfect. But that was my nan. *This* is a reporter who I want to get out of my way.

"Hello? Did you hear me?" she repeats, the microphone gleaming against the morning sun. The crowd of strangers gathers around her, a dark army of curious shadows.

Awkwardly, I shake my head and say the only words I can muster. "Saggy pants."

She looks confused—heck, I'm confused—but taps on the window again, this time with the tip of the mic's metal. There's a real intensity to it. She wants to break the glass, but I'm still looking into that droopy eye. She thrusts her body up against the car, red pencil skirt and the power of all the Spanx beneath, tries to keep me from leaving, and still, her mindless herd watches from behind with sad faces like I'm a tragedy, too.

My foot on the brake, I rev the gas. The engine roars this black cloud of smoke and fumes, because this car is older than me and Brynn combined, and I raise a finger at her, as much as I want to imply my frustration with the strong middle finger. I use the more restrained index finger instead. This should get my point across loud and clear.

Julie backs away. "Is that a *one*? What does that mean? You'll do the interview at *one*?"

I'm furiously shaking my head, wagging my finger as hard as my swollen eyes are pressed into hers, both the normal and lazy one, and as she steps away, I continue to reverse into the highway with screeching tires. The bumper strikes the recyclable-trash can on the opposite corner of the drive, knocking a mound of cans and cereal boxes to the ground, and I'm thinking back to all the times I explained to Brynn you don't recycle them together as I speed away. In my rear-view, a speechless Julie Sturghill and her voiceless fans watch as I clumsily work to find some sort of order both in the car, and in this world.

On my way to school, I pass a peculiar-looking carcass, so I pull my car off the side of the road and lift my camera from the puke-smelling case. I slowly approach and kneel down to see the mass is not one, but three small raccoons, all smashed into an almost unrecognizable sheath of bones and rotting flesh. My nose wrinkles at the stench. But I turn my camera to the black-and-white setting, angle the lens, and snap. Passing cars probably think I'm morbid, as Brynn says, but others just see death where I see collapsible frames that once held life. I wonder, *What were they thinking as they crossed together?* Because the prelude to death is a series of questions, and those questions have answers—answers I want to know. As a gust of wind spins off of a semi's tail end, I decide three pictures for three souls is enough. And I tell them *good luck* and *good-bye* because Sarge promises some kind of everlasting afterlife, or whatever. Amen.

I swerve into the senior parking lot of West Clifton High, the tires squealing to an abrupt stop. My breath dances in front of me through the crisp, stinging autumn air. I keep my head down, buried into my chest, and make my way through the rows of the senior parking lot. *I shouldn't be here.* I wrestle with my conscience. One foot in front of the other, I ignore that voice because twelve years of perfect attendance isn't something I can just scrap. That's a lot of days feeling like hell, struggling through tests with fevers, and still acing my classes. School is more than a place where I learn—it's part of me. But today, of all the days I've walked into those doors, it looks different.

"Hey, Birdie!" Jess Wilson yells. "Saw what happened on

the news." She grabs my arm, keeps me from walking. I feel the need to turn toward her. "How is he?"

Jess and I have never said more than three words to each other, partly because we're not in the same classes, we don't hang with the same people, and mostly because her breath smells like sour apples and Tang. She's a close talker, so it's hard to ignore.

"I don't know," I say, trying to move past. Her ginormous hoop earrings dangle against her shoulder and, in this light, I can see the multitude of turquoise eye shadow layers piled on.

"*Why* are you even here?"

"Why are any of us anywhere?" I quip.

She looks confused. "Okay, well, let me know if I can do anything."

"A breath mint?" I mumble.

"What?"

"Nothing. Thanks." I navigate my way through the doors to find my purple locker in the long row of others just like it. My fingers fumble on the lock's dial. It takes three tries before the bunk latch pops open. The noise squeezes every last bit of concentration out of me, and I start to hate myself for wanting to be here. But the smells—the weathered pages of musty books and old paint lacquer and wooden desks and underclassmen who haven't yet discovered deodorant— comfort me in ways my family can't, won't. I close my eyes and breathe it in as hard as my lungs allow.

On my way to class, a flock of girls I'd rather not talk to, Mace(y), Grace(y), and Stacey (also known as "The Aceys"), move toward me in one giant, swaying herd—much like those strangers at the bottom of our hill. *What is it with everyone today?* Stacey's near the back because, even though she's only a few pounds heavier, the other three refer to her as Fat Stac(k). In their insanely superficial world, they're led by the idiotic pack master, Tracey, and I realize the probability of running into any one of them (let alone as a quad), at this exact moment, out of all 333 kids in the school, is exactly 1 in 333—which is really, *really* sucky. Tracey stops short in front of me as each girl behind plows into the back of her like a set of dominoes; Fat Stac(k), who is about as awkward as me (and thus why she's my favorite), nearly knocks them to the floor, which pretty much makes my day.

"Oh. Em. Gee," she says, grabbing my shoulders. "I am SO, SO sorry about your brother. It's SO terrible. How are you even standing? I'd die. I'd just die. Don't you just want to *die*?" The other Aceys watch this weird interaction, standing there staring at me with these identical great big mascara-tinged eyes. They want me to say something magical and inspirational while all I'm thinking of, really, is how she, and the others, get their teeth so blindingly white. My eyes fall to Fat Stac(k), whose shaky hands unwrap a piece of gum—right here, in the middle of this emergency intervention of grief. It's all I hear—*crinkle, crinkle, crinkle*—and she knows this because she pauses when all eyes fall to her, instead of me—the grieving one.

"I guess," I mutter.

Tracey wraps her sticklike arms around me—I want to scream—and tilts us back and forth like we're dancing. The other girls have their hands placed on their hearts. "Aww," they all say together. I can't breathe, she's squeezing so hard, and my glasses crack between her boney clavicle and my nose. I breathe in a thick waft of her vibrantly scented citrus perfume and have an instant headache. Eyes toward the long hallway, it is only now I'm rethinking this whole zero-absence streak.

"Thanks," I say, pulling back quickly. She holds on, clings to me like a dryer sheet. "I'm fine."

When I finally get free, she smacks her lips together and pretends to shed a tear, but there's no real sentiment behind her stale words; there's not even a real tear. She tilts her head and makes this sad face like I've just given her all the buried treasure in the world. "You are so great. Isn't she great, girls?"

"So great," they say. Fat Stac(k) isn't paying attention. She's already gotten a patch of gum into the ends of her hair and is fighting to pull the gob free. Tracey whips her head around, silky blond hair flying, to punish Fat Stac(k) with a glare. For a second, I forget they're feeling bad for me because, at the look on FS's face, my heart wrenches for *her.* It's a fleeting thought, and when the first tardy bell rings, Tracey flips her hair back behind her shoulder and waves the girls on. "Well, if you need anything."

She walks away, the other Aceys nipping at her heels. Fat Stac(k), with her slight muffin-top spilling out over the band of her skinny jeans, spins back toward me. "Help me," she mouths. Grace(y) grabs her by the arm and yanks her forward, back to the mindless self-esteem booster she's meant to be. For some sick reason, all of this makes coming to school totally worth it because for a short time, I can forget about everything else.

I continue on my way through the corridor, down the hall to where my first-period English class is, and while everyone is dispersed in separate areas of the bustling room, I quietly take my seat without anyone noticing, including Violet.

"BIRDIEEEEE!" she cries when her eyes alight on me. Before I can hug her, tell her everything, the room goes quiet as, one by one, they all move in like this solid wall of comfort I can't escape. I'm surrounded by cold, slimy hands and tight hugs and someone's hair in my mouth and, at the tail end of everyone's sympathy, Mrs. Rigsby's sad eyes. The pack spreads thin. She opens her arms and waves me into her, clutching the back of my head as she whispers, "There, there."

Here I am, nuzzled against my teacher's boobs, with all of these eyes on me—eyes that have barely looked at me all year—and I'm not thinking about Benny. I'm wondering if one boob is an A-cup and the other a C. They feel way off. Like, not normal boobage kind of off. I mean, mine are different sizes, but I wouldn't compare them to an apple and a watermelon. It's a sizable difference that I'd never really noticed just by looking, not that I've ever *looked*. I don't want to grope, but I casually move my head to try and solve the equation before the not knowing bothers me.

The final bell rings, and Mrs. Rigsby lets go with her arms but is still holding my head in her palms. "Poor girl," she says. "Saw the news, and I've been thinking about you, wondering if you'd be here today. How are you and your family?"

"Fine," I say. I try to move my eyes from the heaving right side of her bosom.

She shakes her head. "It's okay not to be."

The others take to their seats. "I know."

She backs away and moves behind her industrial metal desk. "Class, let's just take a moment to dig deep in our hearts and send all the love and support you can gather over to Birdie. For those of you who don't know, Birdie's baby brother was in a horrific accident. When you go home to-night, please continue to keep her and her family in your thoughts. I will do the same."

When she's finished, she just looks at me. *Everyone* is just looking at me. All these eyes, forty-eight to be exact, have decided I am the only thing worth seeing. Violet looks at me with a devious grin like she's got something up her sleeve—I knew I could count on her not to make this worse. She winks, and I don't feel so alone.

Eventually, the morning moves on and we're working independently on personal essays using literary devices. I choose something I learned in chemistry called the collision theory to better explain all the things I can't seem to say, feel. Things that makes sense to me, like coming to school when

I should be at the hospital. I'm thinking hard on different words to string together when Vi taps me.

"I bet everyone's asking why you're even here," she says. Her springy auburn curls are tamed by the medieval head-wrap she's wearing, but loose tendrils bounce as she angles toward me.

"Yup," I say.

She sighs, places a hand on my arm, and with all serious-ness, guides my eyes to hers. "Bitches be trippin'."

I chuckle. "You know me too well."

Her face falls flat, and she squeezes my arm, something Mr. Crouch showed us in psychology to make people feel more comfortable, and tells me how sorry she is this is hap-pening. "He's gonna be fine. I promise."

"You don't know that." I refrain from explaining how all this happened in the first place—how it's my fault—not that she'd judge me, but because I can't say the words out loud yet. Not to her or to anyone.

She releases her grip to unfold a printout and clears her throat. "Today is a fantastic day for new beginnings. Thanks to a play from Uranus"—she pauses to snicker—"Aries to Jupiter, and Leo to the moon in Sagittarius, is about an ex-traordinary flow. This should fill everyone with hope and optimism. And finally, today, focus on any healing, hospi-tals, or spiritual approaches, thanks to Venus in Pisces."

She refolds the paper and sets it on my desk. "See? It's in the stars, babe. Release the negative. Live and let die. Throw caution to the wind. Be the best *you* you can be. Have it your way. Because you're worth it." She falls back into her chair, obviously pleased with herself.

I hold my stare, eyebrows scrunched, because I'm pretty sure she's just shouting slogans. "What?"

At ten till, a freshman student officer struts in and hands a pink paper to Mrs. Rigsby. I remember when I was that freshman, awkwardly tossing papers at the teachers and running out of the room like it was on fire. Everyone wants a pink paper. It means you're being awarded, honored, or saluted. But today, I know what this particular pink is for. Her eyes meet mine, and she signals for me to walk over. I grab my backpack and head over. "You're a wanted woman," she says.

Before I go, she also hands me a business card. "This might be helpful."

HANCOCK FAITH–BASED COUNSELING SERVICES

"Thanks," I say. "But we don't need spiritual intervention. We need a scientific miracle."

"Sometimes the two go hand-in-hand, Birdie."

"If there's any other work, send it with Violet, please." I force a smile and push past her. Vi salutes me from her chair with another wink. I wave, slightly, and make a beeline for the guidance office. When I round the corner, Ms. Schilling waves me in. With shaking hands, I grab on tight to my backpack.

"Birdie," she says, standing. "I am so sorry about your brother."

I nod. She circles around to me, boxes me in between her arms. Ms. Schilling and I go way back to my first day of high school when we thoroughly went over the academic plan Mom and I set in place. She's like an aunt—a stumpy, apple-shaped aunt with short, salt-and-pepper spiked hair and a newsboy cap always resting on her desk. Her voice is deep but calm. She folds her hands and leans in toward me. "I wanted you to know, if there's anything you need, I'm here."

Once she pulls back, the quiet is too much for me. "Is there anything else?"

"Yes." She pushes into my shoulders, grounds me into the floor, but it's in this way like she doesn't know her strength. It kind of hurts, but I don't let on. "I don't want you worrying about the scholarship. We'll find a dozen others to apply for, and with your impeccable test scores and near-perfect grades, something will come through. I just know it. I'm already on the hunt."

I shrug.

"Listen. Be with your family. School, scholarships—all that stuff will still be here to deal with in a couple weeks. And in the meantime, I'll see what I can dig up."

My stomach rumbles, and I think back to breakfast—same as Chomperz—I had none. "But I want to be *here*."

She sighs at me with this long, dramatic breath. "I understand why it might be hard."

"But?" I ask.

"No *but*. I understand, is all. If you feel like being in this place is what you need, then by all means."

I resling my backpack over my shoulder and prepare to leave. "It is."

She stops me. "Just know that *not* being here doesn't take away everything you've accomplished. And *not* being here won't change the scholarship thing. There are no rules when it comes to tragedy, but . . . do what you need to do to feel . . . okay."

There's that word again. *Okay.* My toes curl in my shoes, and I'm eyeing the door.

"Go" she says.

I linger, my face unsure.

"Life is about choices. If this is your proverbial fork, *you* choose which direction to go. Home or class," she clarifies. "Whatever your choice, I hope it heals you. Because I *know* you, Birdie. I can see behind those glasses; behind that huge wall, there's more grief than you realize."

I smile, my lip quivering. "It's fine. I'm fine. We're going to be fine." Lies I tell myself, tell her. School, my safe haven, suddenly feels claustrophobic. The walls are moving, closing in. My feet are stone-heavy, but I hold that smile tight.

Ms. Schilling nods me off, and after the bell rings, Violet comes running down the hall. I know it's her by the sound of her clogs, and I think back to all the times I've said, "Who wears clogs?" and she's said, "Everyone," and then I reply with "who is your everyone?" But it's okay because she grew up what she calls "new age"—which Sarge refers to as "hippie shit"—so it's expected.

"BIRDIEEEEE!!!" She pushes past all the warm bodies in her path, straight down the middle, until she gets to me. It's almost like she can feel my heart breaking with every passing second and knows exactly how to fix it. She nearly knocks me over with her arms wrapped so tight around my rib cage. I want her to squeeze tighter—so tight, I'll stop breathing, at least for a second. At least for the same amount of time Benny stopped. Because, it's only fair, right? His breaths for mine?

Minutes pass, and I try to peel her off, but—God Bless this wacko—she clings tighter. Her stray curls brush against my cheek, and I can feel her crying into my T-shirt. "I just don't know what I can do to make this better for you. I hate it."

"It's okay, Vi," I tell her. "The stars said so." I rub the wetness from my sleeve.

When she finally looks up, red-faced and snotty, she smiles. "I hate that effing shirt."

I smile back. "Bitches be trippin'."

LESSON OF THE DAY: If particles collide with enough energy, they can still react in exactly the same way as if the catalyst wasn't there. Maybe some things are just meant to be and others aren't.

But who decides—Uranus or me?

BASH

"Mr. Alvarez," Mrs. Pearlman says loudly, shaking me from my distracted thoughts. "Can you name one thing that can speed up the reaction rate in an inevitable collision?"

I raise my head, look around at all the eyes on me, including Kyle's. He's mouthing something I can't make out. "Eat," I say, confused.

The room erupts with laughter, and Kyle buries his head in his hand. He's now pulling his shirt away, fanning his face with the other hand. "I meant heat. *Heat* speeds the reaction."

He's relieved I didn't waste his theatrics on another wrong answer, but it's those same theatrics that got the asshole kicked out of private school. Well, theatrics and Ecstasy. And whiskey. And a lady (hooker) named Anna Conda, who, to no surprise of mine, was no lady at all.

Mrs. Pearlman still isn't satisfied—something I think her husband probably says about her. Her eyes are digging into me like she wants more. I look around the room. Some are still laughing, some are trying to mouth other words, but my mind is blank. I try to speak, and all I see, feel, is the impact of the collision, not with a deer, but a human being. It repeats in my head, over and over, making me want to jump up from my seat. "I don't know what you want me to say."

Everyone is giggling, whispering behind my back—

something I'm used to. She moves closer and leans down into my space. "I suggest you study a little more and party a little less. Or you won't pass this class. Got me, *amigo*?"

There's a lot I want to say. I don't party, ever, I don't give a shit if I pass or not, that previous statement is a lie, and for Christ's sake, I'm *not* Mexican. Instead, I smile. "Yes, ma'am."

We're interrupted by a student office helper who hands her a yellow note. No one wants the yellow note. It means you're either suspended, flunking, or someone died. There's no other reason to go to the office. Ever.

She reads the slip, hands it to me. "Take your things." I string the bag over my shoulder and exchange one last glance with Kyle. He's urging me with his eyes, begging me not to rat him out if they're about to interrogate me. I give him a nod, almost to say, *I said I wouldn't, so I won't,* even though the kid should know by now, I'm not the type to rat people out, especially after I give my word.

I feel the eyes of the class on my back. Mrs. Pearlman adjusts her glasses as she flips through a stack of papers and hands me a pile. "Due Friday." She's telling me this because she thinks I'm being suspended, wants to give me advance notice, I guess. I know the drill.

The long, quiet walk down the hallway, I'm stuck on the little boy. He has no face in my mind, like one of those creepy dolls that murder people in the movies, but I imagine his tiny body being flung by the hood of the Benz as we just drive away like cruel, heartless bastards. Every time I remember the feeling, I choke up.

In the main office, there are four doors, the four pillars of East Clifton High. One to the principal, one to the vice principal, one to the guidance counselor, and one to the nurse's station. I choose the guidance counselor because that's where the yellow note tells me to go, and my stomach drops. He sees me before I can knock.

"Mr. Alvarez," Mr. Lawson, aka Big L, says. "Come on in and have a seat." He's scribbling something on paper, his eyes not on me.

I fall into one of the two chairs and hug my backpack. My heart is beating a million times a minute, and I envision police officers rounding the corner with handcuffs and pepper spray. The room is quiet, except for the sound of his pen. I stare at the many pictures on the wall of him posing with all the kids he's helped over the years through his churchy youth program in downtown Indy, Teams 4 Dreams. They trade shooting guns for shooting hoops, which, to me, isn't even close to the same as far as extracurricular activities go, you know, if you're into shooting things, but whatever.

He finally finishes, neatly stacks the papers into a folder, and crosses his heavily tattooed arms together. I like the one of the pinup girl that peeks out from his rolled up sleeves, for obvious reasons.

"How's it going, man?" he asks, reaching out for a shake. It's not the first time we've met; more like we're old friends.

"Same shit, different day," I say. To any other teacher, I couldn't, wouldn't, say this.

He chuckles. "I hear you. That's why I've got some strong liquor waiting for me when I leave this run-down dump." He points to his desk drawer.

It's warm in here. Too warm. He wants me to crack, I know it. I smile, bite my nails to pass the string of silence between his words. He pulls another file from his desk drawer and shoves a piece of paper in front of me. "You see that?" He points to the string of letters and numbers on my most recent grade card. I nod. "You're flunking."

"Yeah," I say. "I'm trying."

"Two years ago it was Algebra I, last year Algebra II, this year, chemistry. I don't know how you're scraping by, but it's time to buckle down, man."

I wriggle around in the chair. The backpack is making me

sweat more, and I'm just wishing he'd get it over with—bring the cops in, lay it on me. "I *am* buckled."

"Look, Bash," he says with concern in his voice, "it's nothing we haven't already talked about. I know school isn't easy, that you're struggling with work and your mom, but in order to graduate, by Indiana law, you have to have pass the Core 40. You're dangling between thirty-eight and forty."

He points to the F again—Mrs. Pearlman's class.

"She hates me."

He leans back in his chair and shakes his head. "That crazy bitch hates everyone. It's not personal. But you still have to do the damn work at a *passing* level. Or all this work, everything we've done to keep you in school, means jack shit."

Now I lean back in my chair, stew on his words. He's right. All the tutoring, extra credit, extra classes—everything he's done to get me that diploma—will be worthless if I can't get past the gatekeeper. "Fine," I say.

"You've got to nail a B next semester to get the full credit."

I think about what that means, having had only a few B's in my entire life. Maybe I should just quit now and save myself the time. We already know the way my story ends, anyway. Typical trash who stays in the gutter, says Kyle's mom. He angles his head at me in an attempt to tap into my thoughts.

"What do you want to do with your life?"

I don't hesitate. "Draw."

He nods with a smile. "I've seen your work. You've got real potential, and I don't say that to everyone. Look at it this way, in order to be the next da Vinci, you've got to know about molecules and reactions and formulas and shit—for now. It sucks, but that's the way it is. But then—*then*—you can flip us all off and go sell some paint scribbles for a hundred grand while you say, *Now who's the idiot?*"

I say nothing, still focused on quitting. Ma would be so disappointed. I couldn't do that to her, could I? He folds his

78

hands again, something I feel like he learned in counselor school, and leans close.

"Look, Bash, I'm sorry for what you're going through. I know things aren't going so great. But you can't cut anymore. Not one day, not one period. We're all sensitive to your situation, but you're almost done here. Get it done, and get out."

His words are eerily like Kyle's, I nod.

"And between you and me, you smell like weed. Get your shit together, man, or you won't have a future to graduate for."

"Tell me something I don't know."

He's serious now, his face is telling me to shut up, so I do. Then I open my big mouth again. "So is that all? You want me to pass chem, but then you pull me out so I can't learn a goddamned thing?"

He wants to smile, but he doesn't. He's fighting it, I think. Four years, *five* for me, with this man, and I know his tells. "Go."

I give him a silent salute, throw my backpack over my shoulder, and walk away. But instead of going back to class, or to my next class when the bell rings in a few, I do the exact opposite of what I promised—I leave.

Through the double doors, I slink out to my car that's near the back. My hands are shaking, I fumble the keys in the lock, but the door sticks. I shove my body up against it several times until it opens. Piece of shit.

Once inside, I toss my backpack to the rear seat. The landing causes my visor to fall, an old picture of Ma and me in full view. My face grows hot, my jaw clenching. The anger boils to a bubble inside of me with every bad thought building, kicking me while I'm down. I can't hold it in. My hands on the wheel, I look into her eyes and think of a time when she didn't hurt, I didn't hurt. But it was so long ago, no matter how hard I stare, I can't remember the feeling.

My jaw presses harder, and tears burn my eyes, blurring my vision. I bang my hands on the steering wheel so violently, it leaves my palms red, while releasing a scream so loud my ear drums muffle. All of my energy permeates into this stupid car, this space where I am all alone in the world (Kyle does NOT count), and suddenly my heart feels like it's sitting right here in front of me, barely pumping.

"I won't let you down," I say to the picture as I catch my breath. "But until then, I *have* to let you down," I say, referring to my shit job I decide to drive to so I can take my mind off things.

When I get to the skating rink, I park in my usual spot near the back of the empty lot and head inside, using my super special employee key. It sticks, like always, and I freeze my ass off out here in this wind that lashes out against my bare hands. The awning screeches and dangles above, threatens to give out, fall on my head, which might be the best thing to happen to me, really. The rink isn't actually open until five on weekdays, but there's always gum to peel off a table or skates that need disinfecting. I toss my stuff to the small office counter just as Vinny pops his head in.

"Thought I heard ya," he says. "You're early."

"Don't ask."

"Wasn't gonna." He's holding a steaming cup of coffee in one hand and a holiday hat that would barely fit his short, fat head in the other. He tosses it to me.

"What's this?" I ask.

"You're gonna wear it every shift through Christmas. It's festive." He smiles the kind of smile that says he's taking too much pleasure in my misery.

"Thanks," I say, putting it aside.

He stares at the hat. "Wear it now."

I'm reluctant, but his eyes don't move, so I slowly put the stupid thing on my head. The little, white ball falls over my eye and he laughs.

"Ho ho ho!"

I blow the ball out of my vision and start to walk out of the office, but he stops me. "I'm actually glad you came in when you did. I've got an important job I need done stat, and no hands to help me with it."

He points to a stack of papers and the envelopes beside them. "Stuff and seal. I want those mailed to all the schools and businesses within a fifty-mile radius."

I pick up one of the pages splattered with red and green ink. SKATE 4 THE HOLIDAYS. I grunt beneath my breath. Coupons are at the bottom of each page. Vinny makes his way toward me to point to the bold print as if it's not staring right at me. "They *cannot* double the coupons, so make sure when you're working the window they know they can't get in for free, or it'll come out of your check." He's nodding with his eyes like I won't understand. "Got it?" he asks, sipping from his cup. The dribble sticks to his bushy mustache and drips onto his shirt. "God damn it! First the cable goes out and now this!"

"Cable's out?" I don't care.

"Since yesterday morning. Evie's losing her shit not getting her stories or her *Housewives of Whatever*. I'm like, 'There's news—actual news and important things—happening in the world'—and she thinks *I'm* the asshole."

"I haven't had TV in years," I say.

"No cable in years? She'd die."

"No. Like no TV, at all, in years."

He's quiet. "Sorry for your loss."

I laugh, because he's a moron. He's almost out the door when he spins around. That coffee drizzle left a pretty huge splotch in the shape of pretzel on his precious sweater. "By the way, I've got all the new girl's stuff in that file by the computer. Told her to stop in and fill out the forms before Wednesday, so in case she comes by when you're here, there they are." He says it as if he has a full staff when really, there are only three of us.

"There they are," I repeat. It's like swatting a fly.

He disappears somewhere into the rink, probably to change his festive sweater and put on another that looks exactly like it, because I've seen them all, and dear God, they're the same.

I fall into the swivel chair and spin around to my workstation. My fingers fumble through the papers that I really want to push through the shredder. I pull out my phone to see if Ma called; she hasn't, but there are six texts from Kyle.

KYLE: WHAT HAPPENED W/ BIG L?
KYLE: BASH?
KYLE: WHERE THE HELL R U?
KYLE: WE GETTING CAR FIXED?
KYLE: R U IN JAIL?
KYLE: SAY SOMETHING!!!

I ignore them. They just remind me of the mystery boy and the choice we've made. Or more like the choice *I've* made. It's a feeling like quicksand, and I'm going under fast.

I slide my chair over to the computer on the other side of the counter to search for any kind of news update. Link after link, they all say the same things with different words. No change in his condition, family asks for help finding the hit-and-run driver. One thing that's clear is the community is grieving and hopeful they *will* find whoever is responsible for such a horrible act of cowardice. My first thought? I damn sure hope they do.

I try to swallow, but the lump sticks in my throat. *Enough wallowing.* I click out of the window and start my project. Fold, stuff, lick, stamp. Fold, stuff, lick, stamp. When I glance at the clock above me, I realize hours have passed by the time I've finished. My phone vibrates, indicating a missed call and new voice mail, but my phone never rang because the rink is in the cell tower's black hole. The message says to call the nursing home right away, so I do.

Nurse Kim puts me on hold. I'm so nervous my hand slides sweaty against the plastic phone's case. The Christmas music Vinny is playing through the speakers doesn't make me feel cheery; it makes me angry, reminds me of the hat I'm wearing. I rip it off, check the minutes balance on my phone. Sometimes it takes bigger chunks than a minute at a time. I don't know how it decides, but I'm almost always getting screwed out of the minutes I pay for. It's down to twenty-two. My heart pounds. I'm just waiting, wasting away the metaphorical time I have left.

"Bash?" Nurse Kim says. She's been taking care of Ma since day one. From the first time we realized this is it—this was where she'd go to die. Kim's seen Ma's wrinkles deepen, her eyes sink, and what's left of her hair fall out. Her voice is soft, calm, like she's trying to keep me soft, calm, too.

"What's wrong?" I ask, panicked.

She hesitates, which is never a good thing. "You might want to get over here as soon as possible."

A burning lump lodges in my throat, making it hard to swallow. "Did something happen—is she okay?"

"It'd be better to talk about this in person."

"Tell me something. Please. I can't go there until I get off work unless it's an emergency."

She hesitates again, and my heart thrashes. "The preactive phase is nearing an end. We had some things happen today and . . . she wants to see you."

I know exactly what she's talking about—death. She explained when Ma was admitted there are two stages of dying, preactive and active. She was the former when admitted—an amount of time left could not be estimated because everyone's different. Except, they don't know Ma. Single mother, tough as shit, sixty-hour workweek, take-no-bull-from-anyone kind of woman. She's a goddamned fighter. They said it could be a few weeks once we stopped all treatment. No more chemo or radiation, no more weed for the pain. Ma wanted to go out on *her* terms. Free and alert.

That was three months ago.

But in these three months, I've watched this brilliant, insanely vivacious woman with a knack for genius one-liners, my hero, disintegrate into a frail pile of bones and broken smiles.

"Sebastian?" Kim asks. "Do you understand what I'm telling you?"

I shake the tears free and clear my throat. "Yeah. Be there as soon as I can."

With the phone clutched between my fingers, I hang up and squeeze so hard, I hear the plastic creak. She seemed okay yesterday, but I've learned that *okay* doesn't mean much at this point in her disease. My frustration is interrupted by a knock on the metal door. The clock says it's nowhere near time to open, but I unlock anyway to see who's there. Kyle pushes through, shoves me into the wall in what he thinks is a playful way. His touch sends an electric voltage through my fingertips, firing up all the rage that's been buried, and I shove him back, hard, without a second thought. He trips, falls backward over the red velvet rope that divides the Enter and Exit lines. Now I'm looking down on him, panting. I could argue I didn't mean to, but I won't, because in this moment, maybe I did.

"Dude—what the hell?" he shouts, smoothing his shirt.

I pull the doors closed and help him up. "Sorry," I say.

His eyes are bugging out of his head as he paces across the tiled floor the same way he did before when he told me about the boy.

"Why are you here?" I ask.

"You didn't text me back. Why'd you ditch school—did you talk to the cops?" He's an inch from my face, close enough for me to see, smell; he's on something more than adrenaline. I'm not talking to Drunk Kyle or even Wild Kyle right now. It's full-on Tweaked Kyle. Anxious, sweaty, with an almost irrational string of rambles. I poke a finger at his plaid button-up shirt and nudge him away. "Cool it, dude. I haven't said *anything* to *anyone*."

He runs his fingers through his oil-slicked hair, but it keeps falling in his eyes. "Okay, okay, okay." He chews on the words, his eyes racing. "Just making sure. I didn't hear from you, and I thought—"

"Chill out, man," I urge. "Vinny's here, so you need to split before he sees you. I can't lose this job, and you know that. I didn't say shit, so let it go." He stares at me, through me. I wave my hand in front of him, but he's suddenly turned to stone. "Kyle!" I shout, shaking him out of his daze. "Get lost. I'll text you later."

"Like what time later? I have shit to do, but if you tell me when, I'll be ready for it."

I stare at him, Kyle in all his annoying glory. My teeth grind against each other. Vinny appears in the office behind me. He stops to look at us through the glass window and signals to me with one damning finger. I shoot Kyle a look and head back to Vinny before he notices the level of weirdness that's filled the interior entrance.

He leans in real close, the coffee still lingering on his lips. "We're not open yet."

"I know," I say. "He's leaving."

"You know my number one rule here. No drama."

I nod, my eyes on Kyle. He's chewing his thumbnail, spitting the pieces onto the floor.

Vinny wraps his hand around the back of my neck and squeezes, pulls me into him like a godfather ready to off me. "Good. Because drama drives away business, and if business goes, so do you. Keep personal shit outside of those doors. Capeesh?" I nod again. He pats my neck, takes one last look at Kyle, and disappears to a place I can't see. But I know Vin, and he's always watching.

I rub my brows, pinch the skin between my eyes as if causing enough friction will erase what's happening, and walk back to Kyle. "You gotta go."

He walks backward into the door. My chest is puffed out, my arms swollen from the aggravation. He must see this transformation because this tall, cocky asshole is cowering suddenly. "Text me later, then," he mumbles, tripping over his feet. I shove him into the cold outside air and lock the doors behind him before he finds one more way to slink into another part of my life and fuck that shit up without permission.

Hours later, after the rink rush of germy kids and couples trying to "keep the magic alive" comes and goes, I have only one thing on my mind. I can't get to my car fast enough, and even as Vinny is shouting something at me through the doors, I peel out of the lot and don't look back. That's what gets most people—the looking back. I don't believe in it. The tires grab the pavement and squeeze, screaming into the air. A black cloud spills from my tailpipe and follows me all the way to the side of town that holds both the dark (the thieves, the poor, the Bashes of the world) and the light (Ma).

She likes tiger lilies for their "courageous" stripes.

"I'll never bring you those," I always tell her, "because those *courageous* stripes mean wealth and pride—two things we ain't never gonna have, ain't never gonna be, and that's a good thing." She'll usually grunt, make a comment about my posture, and we're all good.

I stop in the floral department of the market, like I do when I have a couple bucks, and buy a single calla lily because it means splendid beauty—one thing she's always had. Sometimes, when I'm real broke (always), I linger in other hospice rooms where flowers and plants are overflowing, make fake conversation, and if there's somethin' pretty, I'll pull off a crisp stem or two and sneak it in. The recipients are usually on their last leg and don't notice anyway. But I *never* show up empty-handed, or she'll know something's up.

I poke my head around the corner of her room, 318, with my hand behind my back. My knees buckle at the sight of her, but I hold myself together the best I can. For her, not me. She's lying still, her arms crossed over her stomach, her eyes focused in front of her, and I wonder what she's thinking.

"My little Picasso," she says. "Get in here."

She doesn't use her hand to wave me over. They're swollen, like her legs and feet. The edema has given her elephant trunks that are hard to lift. From here, I see she's not even wearing any of her usual baubles and bangles around her small wrists. She loves things that sparkle and shine, the kind that make people stop and ask, awestruck, "Where did you get those?"

I walk over to the thin, frail ghost of my ma. She's got a silk scarf knotted around her head where her hair used to be. Now, all that's left are a few strands that were spared. Her long, beaded earrings dangle across the bare part of her shoulder where her shirt hangs loose, and her electric hazel eyes are dimmed by the discoloration in her skin. But behind those eyes, she's still here, fighting the good fight others would have already succumbed to. It's hard to believe it's been only a year since the official diagnosis—Stage IV ovarian cancer—and in that year, Ma stopped working and had surgery that didn't remove everything we'd hoped. So now here we are.

"*Sentar-se*," she says, which is *sit down* in Portuguese. She flicks her eyes to the bedside chair. I show her the lily, place it beside the other things I'd brought in the last few weeks—a few drawings, a picture of us like the one hanging from my visor, and an old teddy bear I used to sleep with, to remind her I'm here, even when I'm not.

Before I sit beside her, I load up on the hand sanitizer that's sitting next to her bed so as not to risk giving her an infection of any kind, slathering it through every crevice and ridge of my hands. Hers are ice cubes, colored in blue and purple swirls. Even though I see her every day, her gaunt face looks embarrassed at her appearance. Gently, I teepee my hands over hers to warm her. She smiles her trademark ruby-lipstick smile, her teeth looking more yellow than white, but that's from years of smoking, not the cancer—a lesson I *should* recognize every time I light up, but purposefully choose not to.

"You smell like smoke," she says. "Tell me my nose is wrong."

I sniff my jacket, pretend to be shocked. "Vinny smokes, Ma. I told you."

She looks me over with one big eye, the other squinted. I know that look, because nothing gets by her, never has. "You'll ruin your perfectly pink lungs."

I laugh, nervously. "I know, I know." She holds her stare as if to scare me out of doing it again. It kind of works. I clear my throat and compose myself. *Don't give it away, Bash.*

"So," she says, "how was school? Tell me everything."

I hesitate. *Everything?* As in hit-a-kid-who's-now-in-critical-condition *everything*? I stutter, try to form a whole sentence without saying too much.

Little lines web out from the corners of her eyes like cobwebs. "Don't slouch. Makes you look angry."

I pull my back straight, roll my shoulders, and shake a loose hair from my eyes. "I, um . . . had a meeting with the guidance counselor today."

Her smile sours, and my heart cracks. "Said I'm top of the class. Might be a candidate for valedictorian." I say the words, and all I can think of are the times she'd say, *Don't lie to me, Sebastian,* her eyes lasers that cut to the core of every fib I'd ever told. I challenge her stare and swallow. Her smile lengthens, and I know what I have to do.

"Yeah," I continue, "said I should think about running for prom king, too. Might do that after I pick which college I want to go to in the fall. Scholarships are lined up. Now I just need to make some decisions."

She nods, pleased with my lies. "How'd you manage to go from flunking out to valedictorian without me there to crack the whip?"

I shrug.

"Maybe I should've gotten sick sooner," she jokes.

It's a Band-Aid. It fixes things for now, but I know eventually I'll have to rip it off. I'm hoping it won't come to this, accepting the truth, until she's passed.

"That's wonderful," she manages. Her voice is raspy. "Glad to know you don't need me."

"I'll *always* need you." My voice is rough.

She squeezes my hand just enough to let me know how much it hurts to let me go. I swallow a wave of tears that want to erupt. "How's the rink? You work today?" she asks.

"Mmm-hmm. It's great," I lie. "Vinny promoted me to assistant manager, today actually, so I'll be making more money. I'm pretty stoked about that."

Her smile disappears, and I feel the air leave the room. "You didn't mention Layla a couple of days ago. Was afraid to ask."

I swallow again. Thought she'd have forgotten about the demon who wanted all my attention, every second of every day, followed me here to see what I'd been hiding, and when she finally saw my mother lying in this bed, sleeping with an apnea mask on so she wouldn't suffocate and die in her dreams, told me the relationship was too heavy and bailed. The next night, she started dating that new dude. And, well, the rest is history.

I feel the tears building, change the subject. "She's not you."

Her lip quivers. "You'll have girls lined up for miles. Forget her. How are Kyle, Jeff, and the grand wench of Clifton?"

I know who she means, but because of the bad blood, she won't mention her by name. It's conjuring bad juju, Ma used to say. I shuffle in my seat. "Fine."

"I wonder what kind of man Kyle's gonna grow into, *if* he ever grows up. With all that money and no responsibility, I feel like he's probably looking for any trouble he can get into. For attention, because he can. Do you remember when he was little and used to steal money from my wallet? The little shit didn't need it—*we* did—but he knew there wouldn't be consequences, and there weren't. I don't miss watching him one bit. I hope he doesn't cause you any trouble, because God knows you don't need any more of that."

I'm quiet. I move my eyes away from her and try to avoid the topic, but she continues. "Does *he* ever drop by? To see how you're doing?"

"Who—Kyle? We're together all the time. Too much."

"No. Jeff. Does *he* know I'm sick?"

"Uh, I don't know. *Should* he?" Her question is weird. For years she's cursed his name for letting Linda kick us out onto the street. I wonder, *Why now?*

"Well then, as long as Kyle's a good friend and doesn't drag you into becoming a mess with him, I can die in peace." Her glare slices me in half. We sit in this uncomfortable silence until her eyes grow weary. They told me she might be in and out of conversation, might fall asleep and wake, forgetting everything we'd talked about, or that I was even here at all. I already told her about the Layla breakup. She forgot. I've already lied about school and my job—last week—she doesn't remember. Her mind is going, fading faster than

I'm ready for. They said this could happen toward the end; they told me to be prepared.

I'm not.

I force another smile, but I know she can see behind it. At least before she got sick, before the cancer spread to her lungs, she could have. Now, I don't know.

Nurse Kim breezes in, closing the thin curtain behind her. "Hey, Bash," she says.

Mom interrupts. "He's top of his class, Kimmy." She's beaming a light so beautiful, it brightens the whole room. "No money, no nothing, but somehow I managed to raise a good boy."

Kim looks to me, one deliberate eyebrow raised because she knows better. "He *is* one of the good ones, isn't he? Must've done something right, Ms. Camilla."

I look at Ma and nod.

Kim raises Ma's bed, fluffs her pillow, and administers more pain medicine through the IV drip. The liquid slithers through the long plastic tube that's connected to her hand. She told me before that sometimes it burns when it hits the entrance, so I can't help but flinch as it inches closer to the open wound that's blistered and swollen from the needle attached.

Moments later, Ma's eyes relax. Kim looks at me with a curious smile, half-cocked. "I've got to drain some of that fluid from your hands and feet, Ms. Camilla," she says. She opens a sterile syringe and needle and stuffs her hands into a pair of latex gloves.

"I'll wait in the hall," I say. This process, the needle, things leaving her body so it can deflate to a normal size . . . I can't watch. Watching means it's happening, so if I turn my head or linger in the hallway, maybe Ma will reemerge into the woman she once was.

As I stand, Ma grabs my wrist, tighter than she has in a

long time, and pleads with her big eyes. "Don't go. Please. I don't want to be alone."

I see a fear I haven't noticed before, or maybe I have and didn't want to, so with a nod, I sit back down and look away as Kim removes Ma's socks and pushes the needles into the thick skin on her feet. "You're ice cold," she says. "I'll be quick so we can get those fuzzy socks back on. Want me to turn the heat up?"

Ma's trying to nod, but her movements are slow. "Bash"— her lips are weighted now—"can you lay your head on mine? I want to feel you close."

I look to Kim. Her eyes well, and she silently agrees. Our heads touch and Ma is quiet now, the medicine fully immersed in her veins, filling her body with a freedom she desperately needs. Kim is sitting on a chair on the other side of the bed, and as Ma's eyes drift to a close, she looks up at me, wipes a tear from her eye, and focuses hard on the needle in Ma's foot.

"She's proud of you," she says with a quiet voice. "Talks about you all the time when you're not here."

"Wish I could be more for her. You know, like all the things I *tell* her I am."

She pauses. "Bash, you can be anything—a valedictorian, the president, a bum under the highway bridge—she wouldn't give a damn. She's proud of the *person* you are, not the things you accomplish."

I'm quiet, maybe because I don't believe her. "Doesn't matter. She won't live to see if I make it or not."

"In her eyes," she says, "you've *already* made it. Let her die with that."

We lock eyes as she sticks another hole in Ma's foot. Now my eyes well as I linger on the words.

"I'm surprised she was coherent that long. It's been coming and going."

"How long do they—" I stop myself.

She pauses, looks up at me. "It's hard to say, but she probably won't be here come Christmas. I'm so sorry."

I hold back the flood of tears prickling the backs of my eyelids and gently drop Ma's hand to pull out my spare drawing pad and a block of charcoal from the drawer. My fingers move freely, faster than my brain can keep up.

"Whatcha drawing?" she asks.

I don't look up or tell her I'm sketching a frail, motionless bear. His body lies on a pile of crisp, dead leaves in the center of a barren field that once occupied a lush forest. I don't say his lips are pale as ice, eyes nothing but slits, and there's a dark, gaping hole to symbolize the place where healthy organs should be. I don't mention, through all of this sorrow, there's another bear—one full of life, with soft, plump lips; big, hopeful eyes; and a whole, complete body etched lightly—who hovers above the corpse like a wild spirit set free. I don't say a word about any of this, and maybe she knows I won't, because she doesn't ask again. When I'm finished, I sign my name in the lower right-hand corner and set the drawing upright on the bedside table. I stare at it. Seeing it for the first time.

I'm letting her go. Or at least I'm trying to.

birdie

Instead of braking up the slope of our driveway with caution, I tap the gas in short bursts.

Eyes focused, fists clenching the steering wheel, I plow right over that wooden SOLD sign, and all the vibrant flowers and depressing teddy bears around it. Amidst my destruction, the pile of flattened trinkets are no longer a reminder of all that's happened. Now, they're roadside litter for the garbage truck to claim.

Maybe I should be sorry, but I'm not.

When I finish surveying the wreckage, I navigate the car up the hill, into the garage, and walk inside the house. Sarge is on the couch popping a roll of bubble wrap—something he does a lot when he watches old war movies. You'd think the sound would make him cower, scare him into remembering the bloodier times in his life, but it seems to comfort him instead, like some weird Pavlovian experiment gone horribly right. It's a sound that took us a long time to tune out after Nan passed and he moved in with us, but now it comforts me, too.

Dad and Brynn are in the kitchen, slinging their coats around their shoulders. "You guys leaving again?" I ask.

He nods. "Last night was rough on Mom."

"Then the news segment today," I say.

He pauses. "Yeah, that too."

"Mom looked so bloated," Brynn says.

"Shut up, Brynn," I say.

She looks offended. "What? That's what Mom said—I didn't say it first."

Dad's eyes move to Brynn. "Go to the car."

She sighs or grunts or something Brynn-like and stomps off into the living room to sit with Sarge instead of to the car. Her underwear pokes through the top of her jeans where her shirt rises. I can't help but laugh to myself. What a tool. I can only hope that at thirteen I was, at most, half the tool she currently is. Then I glance down to my math tee, which isn't much better. I'll settle for three-fourths the tool. Brynn helps pop the bubbles a few at a time. She likes to do it in clusters; this annoys Sarge. He calls it *wasting*. I look to Dad, wait for him to say anything about anything but he's hyper-focused on folding Mom's clothes perfectly. It's all I can do to get a glance from him.

"Dad?" I urge.

"He made it through surgery and they've got him in the PICU for observation, but he's still not breathing on his own." And with a shiver in his tone, he pauses again, but this time it makes my chest hurt. "I don't think he's gonna make it, Birdie. It's bad."

I feel a sour kind of pain rise from my stomach, up into my throat, that I can't swallow down. Dad sees this, intervenes as he wipes his own eyes. "Why did you go to school?" he asks. "We needed you."

I begin to sort the file in my mind of all the ways they *don't* need me. "Twelve years, not an absent day. I can't just throw that away."

"Mom tried to make arrangements."

"I don't *want* arrangements."

He leans close enough to whisper. "We all know Brynn won't be valedictorian. She still has those damn feathers in her hair from last week. But, and I mean this with all the love and support in the world, there's a bigger battle to be won right now, Birdie. School can wait."

My gaze drifts to the space behind him, where the wallpaper strip is full of ninety-degree angles, much like the diamonds on the floor. Hundreds of them. And we're just ignoring them, flat-footed, unappreciative of all the perpendicular glory amongst us on the walls.

My hearing grows fuzzy while Dad says words like *irreversible brain damage* and *10 percent chance of recovery*. All things I previously concluded on my own, before he ever went to the hospital. Only now it's real. Then he throws in this word *IF*. That is, *if* he wakes. *If* is such a sucky word. It implies a reaction can only happen *after* variables collide. Maybe I don't want to wait for *if*. Maybe I want *when*. Like, *when* he wakes.

"Get Brynn, go to the car." He disappears into the bedroom, his voice fading.

I walk into the living room; it's dark, just the way Sarge likes it, and I stand between the TV and the couch.

"Move!" Brynn yells. She's stroking Chomperz like the evil genius she *thinks* she is.

"Dad said get in the car."

She sighs, flops her arms around like a wild octopus. "I'm tired. Do I have to go again?"

I squint angrily toward the little beast. "Are you kidding me?"

"I was there all day. Benny didn't move once. He doesn't even know I'm there, and all Mom does is cry over him. It's boring."

Sarge mutes the TV and rips the bubble pop from her hands. "Young lady, get in the goddamned car, or I'll drag you out by your cold, dead body. It's not a request, it's an order."

With a huff, she stomps to the garage and slams the connecting door—something I wish I'd done last night, making

sure Benny was inside first. Sarge's narrow, deep-set eyes—
that always seem to look sad even when he's smiling—are on
me now.

I hold my posture tall. "How are you not freaking out?"

He sighs. "Right now, you all need something concrete
to ground you, not more chaos. I have to be that. Doesn't
mean I'm not scared shitless, because believe me, I am. I
don't have any magic words. There's no way around it—this
sucks."

I nod in agreement.

"I know you don't want to walk in that hospital and pretend you're not broken, too. Like you don't deserve to feel
pain or sadness, but you listen here—you do. You feel however you feel, damn it."

I pick at my fingernails now, not sure of what to say. My
lip quivers, so I bite it. "I want to fall through the center of
the earth and never be seen again."

"That's okay," he says. "If that's how you feel."

My stomach gurgles.

"Can't hide from feelings. Believe me, I've tried."

"I miss Nan," I say. "She'd know how to deal with this."

He smiles to hide the tears. "Yeah, me too. She'd tell you
to think in terms of two. There's before, and there's after.
Like life has been split down the middle right along with
your heart. You can't be who you were before. It's not possible. Nan's gone. Now there's only the me, or you, that
comes after. I think right now, you're somewhere in the
middle, trying to find your place."

"What if the person I become after sucks?"

The corners of his mouth turn up, and I see that twinkle
in his eyes. "If no one else can stand you, come to me—no
one can stand me either."

He pulls me into him, wrapping his arms around me so
tight, I can't breathe. Because Sarge never hugs, ever, it's
okay, I don't flinch. I don't need air. I breathe in the scent of

him instead. Dad walks in and clears his throat, forcing me and Sarge out of our embrace. He pulls back, his eyes still full of pain and regret, and salutes me with two fingers. It's his way of saying good-bye without being too sappy. I salute back, my way of being sappy without saying good-bye.

"Let's go." Dad carries a large bag filled to the brim and stuffs it in the trunk. Inside, Brynn has one half of her earphones in, while the other hangs free. She's blasting music through an old iPod Mom gave her, and I know she won't put the other half in because that would be too easy. She stares out the window, blissfully soaking in my annoyance. I grab my camera from my car and settle into the front seat. As Dad turns the ignition, he looks at me.

"You and Brynn need to knock it off with the arguing. We've got to rally behind Mom. She's not taking this well."

Brynn holds the hanging iPod between her fingers. She and I look at each other through the side mirror. Our eyes lock, and we silently agree to do as Dad says, but it doesn't feel right. This is pretend, a lie. We aren't the kind of sisters who share makeup and gossip about boys; never will be. Fighting with Brynn has to be the only thing that feels normal right now, and we're both clinging to it with all of our might. Without it, life feels wrong.

The longer we hold our stare, the more I realize she feels the same way. With Dad's eyes now glued to the road, she flicks the back of my shoulder, and smiles. I smile back. And everything feels okay again.

The drive feels especially long. I pass the time snapping shots of roadkill along the way, secretly hoping it will spark an argument from Brynn, but she doesn't bite. When we arrive at the old, brick hospital that towers twenty stories high, Dad checks in at the head nurse's station near the elevator because we have to get name tags with Benny's room number on them to go inside the PICU room. The hallways are already decorated for Christmas, and I think back to our bare tree and decide, since it was this time last year Nan died and Sarge moved in, I *officially* hate Christmas and I will not partake in any festivities. You can put that on the record.

"Two visitors at a time," the nurse tells us. "Everyone else can sit in the waiting area." She's stern, her face made of cavernous wrinkles, so we don't argue. We agree Dad will go in first, though; Brynn and I follow him to poke our heads into the room. Mom is slumped over a tiny chair next to Benny's bed. The beeping sounds from his breathing machine are loud, competing with the other monitors and tubes spilling out of his little body. He looks like a science experiment.

Dad sets the bag on the floor, pulls out a teddy bear and a box of milk chocolate turtles—her favorite—and places them on the small table next to her chair. Delicately waking her, he brushes the hair out of her eyes with one careful swoop. The room is loaded with stuffed animals, balloons, and trinkets like the memorial at the base of the hill. I'm afraid to look closer. From far away, Benny doesn't look like Benny. Things are bandaged and covered, and he's so frail and lifeless—nothing in the way of my lively little brother who wakes us all up at four o'clock every morning.

Dad's touch startles Mom awake. "What the hell are you doing?" she snaps.

"Sorry," he says. "Why don't you go home for a little bit? Shower, sleep, eat."

"I'm not leaving," she says, pushing the chocolates and teddy away. "You know a news crew was here earlier? Wanted a shot of Benny. Said someone has asked to set up a fund—quote—*in his honor*—like he's already dead! I told them to fuck off."

He rubs her back, trying to calm her. "You're exhausted."

"I'm broken." She turns to see us lingering in the hall, but says nothing and turns back to Benny. "They come in every hour, check the same things, rearrange him, tell me nothing's changed."

"He looks so small," Brynn says, creeping closer. "Like a doll."

"Let's go get some coffee," Dad says. Mom looks up at him with these pleading eyes, then to Benny. She can't let go, not for a second. Letting go means he could die without her right there, beside him. But it's obvious she's in need of something. Dad nods his head toward the door where we are standing, hopeful, and pulls her up by the hand.

"Okay, fine. We'll be right back," Mom says to us. She touches my back lightly, kisses my cheek, then Brynn's, and leaves with her purse in hand.

"It's like he's gone," Brynn says, stepping to the side of his bed. "It's only his body here, and his soul is, like, somewhere else."

I walk up behind her to look at him from a short distance. His mostly bandaged face is black and blue, broken like the rest of us. His body is cast in different casings, holes grab onto the tubes that ventilate, feed, and soothe him. I want to tell her she's wrong, that he's right here listening to us, but I'm not so sure. It feels empty in here.

"Say something to him," I say. "He can hear you."

"How do you know? You're not in a coma."

"Studies say coma patients show improvement when people talk to them."

She looks at me like I'm lying, then turns back to him. "Benny, wake up. I miss you." Then, she waits. "He's not doing anything."

I roll my eyes. "He's not just going to wake up the second you talk, but he's probably talking to you inside his head. You just can't hear him."

"I wish none of this ever happened," she says with a quivering lip. "It's not fair. You know if that car were driving just a little bit slower, it probably wouldn't have hit him."

I lay my hand on her shoulder, impressed, something that feels unnatural, and pat. "I know."

"Where do you think we go when we, you know, die?" she asks, her eyes wide. "I mean, do we go *somewhere,* or are we just . . . not here anymore?"

I stop and think, try to clear the scientific answers from my vocab, because Brynn never was at the top of her class. "I hope we're not just gone. Otherwise, what's the point of life?"

I can see I've got her thinking, stewing, and I wait for some profound response.

"To fight the aliens when they invade."

I open my mouth, then close it. Because, aliens.

We sit in total tolerance of one another, listening to the harmonious sounds of beeping machines, and reminisce about the day he was born. His thick, dark hair looked like Sarge's old toupee, but his dimples, those were mine. All the way. Dimples so deep, Dad used to say he could fall in and swim around.

A while later, Mom and Dad come back, coffees in hand, while Brynn and I are laughing about things Mom yelled at Dad when she was in labor. Things we'd never heard of before—things I so wish I could go back to and hear again. Because that would mean Benny was here, awake. We're joking about all of the happier times and then suddenly our laughter peters out. It's not often Brynn and I are on the same page, but once the silence settles in, we realize together this is no time to laugh, to feel *any* kind of joy. Our faces fall flat simultaneously.

"I need a break," I say.

"Don't be too long," Dad says.

"Okay." I stroll down the hallway where some of the doors are open. Urine smells and murmured cries drift into the open space. In this wing, every one of these rooms holds a small person who might die. The reality hits me, and I want to fall to my knees.

I take the elevator to the second floor to explore the sanctuary. It's a dimly lit room filled with candles, crosses, and prayer cards. The pews are empty so I grab a seat and bow my head as my insides churn and tear. I grab ahold of my stomach and close my eyes hard as tears stream down my face.

"*Please* let Benny wake up," I whisper. "I'll give you *anything*."

I cling to the row in front of me and cry, unaware of anyone else in the room. A hand touches my shoulder, makes me flinch. "You okay, miss?"

I can't stop the tears. This room almost pulls them from my soul.

"Tell me about your troubles," the man says. Tattoos shade every visible inch of his arms. He's clasping a Bible between his hands as he takes the empty seat next to me.

"My brother might die," I cry.

"Are you seeking forgiveness?" The light hits the top of his bald head and black, thick glasses that are similar to mine.

"More like mercy."

He nods, flips to a marked page in the Book of Psalms, but instead of reading, pulls the note card out that holds the page and places it in my hand. I look at the man, confused. I offer the paper back to him. He closes my fist and urges me to take it, so I do.

FORGIVENESS BEGINS IN THE MIRROR.

"In other words," he says, "the only person you need mercy from is *you*."

I open the paper and read the words again, my eyes soaking into every letter. When I look up, the man is gone as quickly as he appeared. In that short time, I forgot about the pain, about Benny, about everything I've screwed up. Holding the words close, I close my eyes and pray to the lighted chapel where the candles flicker. Maybe someone is listening, or maybe (and probably this) no one is.

When we get home, all I hear is Sarge's bubble wrap—the *pop pop pop*—and it's making me crazy. There's not even an ebb or flow to the rhythm. I imagine ripping them from his arthritis-stricken hands and tossing them into the garbage. But with his reflexes, he'd probably drop-kick me in a nanosecond, grab the bubble wrap, and flee.

"Has anyone watered the tree?" I call, noticing the needles scattered all over the brand-new ivory carpet. A box of ornaments is nestled up against the wall, the cardboard weathered and frayed. Sarge can't hear me through the bubbles, and as I get closer to Brynn's room, where she's already shut herself away, I hear the swells of bass and treble pour from the cracks. It's the kind of music that makes me want to bash my head into the wall until my ears don't work, but I guess it's her way of blowing off steam, so I deal.

I check my phone to find that Violet sent a few quotes from her Book of Silver Linings (that isn't the actual playbook but an old notebook she writes affirmations in).

VIOLET: YOU ARE STRONGER THAN YOU THINK.
VIOLET: TOMORROW IS ANOTHER DAY.
ME: THINK LIKE A PROTON AND STAY POSITIVE.
VIOLET: I DON'T GET IT.

When I've finished every possible piece of homework and extra credit, I find Dad at the kitchen table. He's surrounded by piles of paper and bills, and he's on the phone talking real loud. In between words, he's grunting, mumbling to himself. From here, it's clear how much this has affected him. From his tousled hair to the creased frown lines. I don't think he's even changed his shirt.

"Yes, I understand that but—" he pleads. He doesn't look up to see me, so I grab a can of Coke from the fridge and pull up a chair beside him. "No, thanks for nothing," he adds. He hangs up and throws his phone across the room, waking Sarge who had drifted off, gripping his bubble wrap. He tosses away the pops that are stuck to his fingers, mutters something about the colonel giving a direct order, and drifts back to sleep.

Dad's face is pale, not an actual color of white, but like all the color has faded, washed out, from the heavy kitchen lights. I snap open the Coke and take a sip while he stares at the pile of papers that cover the table.

"What happened?" I ask, afraid of the answer.

He shuffles around and grabs a beer from the fridge, twisting the cap with his bare hands before chugging half the bottle. His eyes avoid mine, so I know it's bad. He falls back into the chair, his hands still locked onto the frosted amber glass, and tells me about our insurance and how they basically want to pull the plug. Benny costs too much.

I hold my stare, try to understand what he's saying. "He's not brain-dead. They would've told us that. There's still hope he'll wake up, right?"

He's silent, takes another sip of his beer.

"Right? Dad?"

He looks up at me, a ring of redness around his tired eyes, and forces some kind of crooked smile from the corner of his mouth. "There's *always* hope, Birdie."

I ask if we have enough money, and just like a star combusting, he starts throwing numbers around like $3,953 and $101, $9,235 and $8,050, and I get lost in the infinite space of them and all the things those numbers add up to—all the money in the world we don't have.

"I don't know how people survive, even when they walk out of the hospital alive," he says.

"I could start hooking," I say.

He wants to laugh, but doesn't. "Still not enough."

"Ouch."

Now he laughs. I chug more Coke to chase down that stinging feeling in my throat. The one that's burning the surface of my eyes. I blink faster, try to ward off any tears. The silence is long. He chugs, too. My eyes find a picture on the fridge of the five of us. We're smiling, all of us but Mom. I can still taste the hot cocoa from that pumpkin trip, still smell the hay bales, still feel Benny's hand in mine as I help him walk across the gravel lot.

"So what do we do?" I ask, my voice cracking.

He shakes his head. "Whatever we have to."

He flips through the papers, hoping to find something he's missed. I reach my hand over and lower the paper from his face so mine is in his clear view.

"I start at the rink Wednesday. My paychecks are all yours."

His eyes soften. "How'd you get so unbelievably awesome?"

I shrug. "Born this way."

"Thank you, Birds. But, you need to save that money for college. We'll get by."

He holds my stare, and the words erupt from me like a volcano. "Maybe I don't even want to go to college."

His brows furrow as he leans in closer. "Of *course* you do—it's all you've talked about since you were six."

With the secret loss of my scholarship, I stop to think about how much money I need to go through with my dreams, but most of all, what I'd be leaving. "People change. It's called spontaneous evolution."

He grabs my hand and pats it gently. "It's called growing up. But you're going to college."

We sit in this discomfort, our pain a thick wall between us, until eventually I go lock myself behind the bathroom door, where I can't hold it in another second. I try to think of Violet's quotes, of anything else, but my heart bangs against my chest with these sharp, aching pains. I sit here for a while, until my tears stop, then I run a warm shower, let the beads pour over me until I'm clean, inside and out. Before I hibernate in my room, I turn off the television Sarge is snoring to and sneak into Brynn's room. She's sound asleep, nestled in one of Benny's old blankets. I pull her comforter over her and shut the music off—something Mom would normally do.

Chomperz is still in the exact position he was when I left this morning. He looks up at me and yawns like he's had such a hard day. "You lazy bastard," I say. As if he understands, he drags his chunky body from the covers and strolls out of my room, not a care in the world as to how my day has gone. "You're inconsiderate!" I call after him. He does not look back, and I love him even more.

I have my own blanket waiting for me in bed—Benny's absolute favorite, the one with the blue stripes. It should probably be at the hospital with him, next to him, but right now, I need it more. His smell is buried in the fibers so deep, my every breath is filled with Benny. I don't know what time it is, I lose count of the seconds. I'm lost in his scent. But some time later, after the moon arches over the trees, I shoot up out of bed with an aching kind of feeling. It's not Benny. I roll over, and toss, and turn, but it's a funny thing I can't explain:

I see the face of the boy from the party again, and it stings a little.

Because, maybe like Benny, I'll never see him again.

And maybe he's exactly the kind of distraction I need right now.

LESSON OF THE DAY: Reactions usually slow down as time goes on because of the depletion of the reactants. But maybe the reactants aren't really gone, maybe they're hiding, lurking, waiting for the exact right moment to speed back up.

Or maybe this growing-up thing sucks, no matter what happens.

BASH

Dave sinks farther into the chair and kicks up his feet.

"I'm telling you, man," I say, "women are trouble. Straight. Up. Trouble. Only good one is Ma, and God didn't make two of her."

I'm busy switching the skates around so most pairs have different sizes. Makes people feel like something's wrong with their feet and entertains me. "I mean, *sometimes* you fall for the wrong girl and she breaks you into a bazillion pieces, but *sometimes* you meet someone different and you think, *This could work.* But it doesn't matter; none of it matters . . . I'm just rambling."

Dave nods with a grin.

I sigh. "Maybe *I'm* the one who's trouble."

He's still nodding, still grinning.

"Good, man. That's why I like you. You cut the bull. The truth will set us free and all that shit—that's you."

He points at me, his smile lengthening wider, and suddenly I think of how ironic those words are. Swallow, breathe, lose eye contact. Vinny busts through the door. He tells me about our new hire—a senior from West Clifton High, our rival school—who never made it in to fill out those papers when he last mentioned it. He tells me today's the day and to "be nice and un-Bash-like," to which I say "to do so is to deny my right to live" and he tosses a box on the side counter and ignores me. It slides into a stack of print-outs, knocking them to the floor.

"I'll need to send these out now because there was a typo on the last batch," he says. "Sorry. Looks like all that time stuffing envelopes yesterday was just practice." An evil smirk rises from his mouth, and just after he leaves, I flip him off so hard, I swear I can feel my finger jab him in the back of his fat little head.

Between Vin and Kyle, I can't decide who's a bigger pain in my ass. My phone vibrates.

KYLE: GETTING SHIT FIXED 2NITE. COME WITH.

Well, that answers that.

I'm reluctant to reply. I don't want to waste my minutes on a back-and-forth text war he'll probably win, so I make it short and sweet.

ME: CAN'T. VINNY NEEDS ME LATE.

Three little dots form on the screen; he's responding, and it's taking a long time. I nervously toss the phone between my hands, hoping it'll come through before Vinny sneaks back in.

KYLE: YOU PROMISED.

I pause for a moment, my finger lingering over the Delete button, and I know I have two choices here: Cave so he'll shut up now, or ignore and risk him stalking me until I do what he wants. I've played this game so many times I shouldn't even have to think about it.

ME: FINE. MY HOUSE AT 9.

The words sting to type, as if I'm signing some kind of formal contract, and in a way, since we're going to cover up something so terrible, I guess I am. I'm no better than my father, no better than the murderers we should be locked away with.

KYLE: YESSSSS!

I pass the next few hours restuffing envelopes and charging holiday prices to the weeknight crowd, which really only consists of a handful of middle-aged couples, one family, and a sixtysomething widow who comes in to hit on me every week. I can't lie; she's kind of hot.

At 8:45 P.M., I tell Vinny I have to jet early. Something about Ma. Most of the skaters have left, so he gives me a nod, says he'll see me tomorrow. I grab my leather jacket that's bunched up in the corner and run to my car. The air is frigid, causing my door to stick again. I slam my body up against the cold metal, thrashing the already rusted dent in the side until it unsticks. Once inside, I take a deep, nagging breath and drive home, where Kyle is already parked outside in the Benz, his heavy metal blasting through the speakers.

I don't bother going inside the trailer. The lights are still dark, empty as though there's no life left between the mobile walls and in a way, that's true. Kyle swings the passenger side door open, and I fall into the warmed seat.

" 'Sup?" he asks with a devious smile.

"If you're trying to *not* get caught, turn the music down," I say in a stern tone. His smile dulls as the realization of what we're doing kicks in.

"This isn't a game," I tell him. "Since you won't let me go to the cops, let's get this taken care of so we can move the hell on." Just saying this makes my stomach churn. There's no moving on from something like this, not really.

111

He spins the volume dial down and nods, shifting the gear gently. The car is quiet, and the only sounds are from the whir of the engine. He drives along the back roads, away from light, careful not to accelerate, to draw attention. He's obviously nervous but steady—two things I never thought I'd witness from Kyle Taylor at the same time.

"Where we going?" I ask.

"Skeevy Steve's."

My head jerks toward him. "What?! No way, dude—turn the car around. After what happened last time? What in the actual hell?"

He's silent, eyes focused on the road. "It's cool," he says. "I haven't bought any bad shit since then, and it was only probation. I got off easy."

"We can*not* be seen over there, Kyle. Think. He went to jail for selling—BECAUSE OF YOU—and he's just gonna help you out, no strings?"

He looks at me, dead serious. "Yeah."

"Bullshit."

"I've got something he doesn't."

"Hell, *I've* got something he doesn't and I ain't got much, but I'm not makin' a deal with the devil. Let me fix this—turn *myself* in, take the blame so we can all sleep tonight. It'll all be done before you can say Skeevy Steve three times fast."

He chuckles, the smile only halfway formed. "I'm a gamblin' man. You're not making the deal, Bash. I am. If anyone goes down for letting it all ride on Skeevy Steve, I promise—it won't be you."

I won't win this fight either, so instead, I think of all the ways this will go wrong as I stare out the window. Eventually, we pull into a back alley in the next town over—a deceptively safe town, New Castle, where streets are eerily vacant. In the daylight, all is well, but after dark, no one should wander through without caution.

Kyle slowly approaches the deteriorating garage door and puts the car in park. "Wait here," he says, stepping out. His voice shudders. My legs do, too, but I pin them to the floor to prevent the fear from crawling up into other limbs. He walks up to the big door and knocks three times. The big, rusted mouth of the cave opens, revealing Steve on the other side. His shadow drags far behind his compact frame, and his beady eyes rival that of any rat I've ever seen crawling through the trailer park.

At Steve's signal, Kyle drives the car into the empty garage space. When the car is in Park, the giant door closes behind us, trapping us where we stand, maybe forever.

"Long time no talk, man," he says, shaking Kyle's hand. He holds a long time, an uncomfortable amount of time, staining Kyle's clean skin with oil. Kyle pulls back, but Steve still grips him tight. When he lets go, it flings Kyle backward, into me. He wipes the slime on his pocket and I can see his eyes nervously beginning to twitch. The lighting is bright enough to see Steve in his full douche-bagginess which is pretty stellar.

He inspects the car, circling it three or four times, his eyes flittering up to us every few steps. "What'd you hit?" he asks.

Kyle and I don't even make eye contact, but our mouths open at the same time. "A deer."

Steve smiles, his gold tooth twinkling under the lights. "Pretty small deer. Did you call the cops? Make sure the thing was dead?"

Kyle stutters. "No cops. Saw the thing, and he was dead. Really dead. As dead as a deer can be." I elbow him to shut him up.

Steve is watching us intently, his smugness never fading. "Good. Don't want a repeat of last time. You're lucky I'm a forgiving guy." He laughs, steps inches from my face. He's close enough that I can see the tar stuck between his teeth, smell the rank tobacco on his breath. "Because this time, if there's cops, they won't be after me."

We collectively shake our heads while I plunge my hands into my pockets. Kyle does the same, too. "How long will this take?" he asks.

Steve angles his head. "What's the rush? You didn't kill nobody, did you? I can't go to jail for that."

We laugh nervously. Beads of sweat ball around my hairline. The lights are bright, hot, too hot.

"Are you serious?" Kyle laughs. "It was a stupid deer, and I just don't want my dad to find out I drove his car while he was gone. That's all."

The words sound believable enough but I can tell by the way he's shifting, Kyle's about to lose his shit, and if Tweaked Kyle takes over, we're done. On so many levels beyond cops. Steve's known for a lot of things; forgiveness isn't one of them. He won't let Kyle off again. And me? A civilian casualty caught in the cross fire that he won't hesitate to take down, too. I know all about this guy and what he's capable of. Kyle does, too. So why are we here?

Steve walks back to the car and lays his hand flat on the hood, running it across the smooth, shiny finish. "I can take care of this for you in about an hour."

Kyle breathes a sigh of relief. "Thanks, man. You're saving me—"

"But," Steve interrupts, "it'll cost ya."

"How much?"

Another smile drapes his face. "A grand."

A laugh escapes me. "Come on, man," I blurt. "It's just a couple dents and some glass."

"Take it or leave it."

I can tell by the way his eyes narrow into little, evil slits, he's not joking. Kyle is now quiet. The only sounds are a wafting of bills he's counting. The thick stack of greenery blows a gentle breeze in my direction. Kyle flops the money into Steve's blackened hand. We watch as he re-counts each crisp bill. He licks his thumb and forefinger between passes, makes an *mmm* sound through the split between his two front teeth.

"Good to go." He waves us over to the plastic lawn chairs near the back wall and offers me a smoke from his half-used pack that's covered in black oil. I don't flinch. My eyes on Steve's, I push the pack out of my space.

"Don't want to be charged for this, too," I say.

He presses one between his lips and burns the end with a lighter. It sizzles and smokes when he inhales. "This one's included in the price of the car."

Kyle takes one because he doesn't think, doesn't realize we pay the price for anything that happens here. He ignores my glare and lights up. My mouth kind of twitches like it wants a taste, but I'm not doing it. Steve is slow to get to work, like we've got nothing better to do than sit here. After a minute or seven, he pulls out a metal box of tools and various parts from the shelves built into the wall.

"This is bull," I whisper to Kyle. "He's totally scamming you."

"A journey of a thousand miles begins with a single step," he says.

I turn my head toward him, annoyed. "Now's not the time for your philosophy shit."

"Maybe *he's* the one getting scammed." He smiles like he's been preparing for this all damn day.

"What are you talking about?"

"Don't let these good looks fool you, my man. I've got a plan."

I shake my head because the last plan he had was the equivalent of lighting a spark in a room filled with hydrogen and oxygen—explosive. "I won't even ask."

"Good idea. More of a surprise when you see the wheels in motion."

I lean in, my eyes locked onto Steve. "Have you read any-thing about . . . the kid?" I whisper.

Kyle's head jumps. Ashes drift to the floor in a loose pile. "No—did he die?"

"I don't know. I keep checking the papers, the Internet, but it says the same stuff. Seems like something should've changed by now. Like he should either be better or dead."

"It's only been a couple days. Maybe they don't know yet. Doctors are so full of it—you know that better than anyone."

I nod, run my fingers through my hair, and lean in closer. "I was thinking of"—I kick my feet around—"going to see him."

"WHAT?" Kyle practically shouts.

"Shhh!" I shove my hand over his mouth, casually smile at Steve like nothing's going on. "Unless you want Steve in on this, shut up."

He nods, slowly. I lower my hand enough to see the panic cover his face. He's three shades whiter than when he told me about the boy in the first place. "Are you *trying* to get us busted?"

I prop my hand on my knee where the hole in my jeans has grown. Kyle's looking at me, waiting for some kind of answer or epiphany or shit—I don't know *what* else he wants from me. Steve's lying on the garage floor with his hands in the headlight, hopefully unable to hear any of this. "Dude," I say, "I need to see for myself. I don't even know what he looks like. It's bugging me."

Kyle's still examining me, but I hold my gaze to the oil-spattered floor. Looking at him means we did this—we really did this—and there's nothing I can do about it. He sucks in a long hit and exhales the smoke, plunging the butt of his cigarette into the floor beside us.

"Look," he says, "I hate that this happened, but it did. It sucks, and I really hope the kid pulls through, but, Bash, like I said before, think about the rest of our lives. From the day your ma got sick, you've become everything she's ever wanted you to be, and more. Doesn't matter if you're lying through your teeth, because it makes her feel better, and you two are seriously twisted like that. Don't throw it all away. You could be a seriously famous artist in New York or something if you just hang on long enough for this to pass. Because it will. You don't want your mom's last memory of you to be this gigantic a-hole mistake. Don't be a fuckin' idiot."

"Says the idiot," I snap.

He laughs in this way that makes me want to choke the shit out of him.

I sit on his words, letting them sink in, and the more they do, the angrier I feel. "To be the person Ma thinks I am, I *have* to do the right thing. I told you I'd tell them it was me so you won't have to sweat it. Whether the kid lives or dies, I can't just hang out and let that family wonder. They deserve to know it was an *accident*. That we didn't mean it and we're not bad people. We just made a bad choice. But the longer we say nothing? The worse it's going to look when we're caught."

He's shaking his head at me, a look of disappointment in his eyes. He's firm now. "You can't go to the hospital. Ever. You can't turn yourself in. Ever. It's done. Let it go."

I hope he can tell by the look on my face I'm struggling with this friendship, brotherhood, or whatever mistake of a relationship this is. "You're a selfish son of a bitch; always have been. This isn't about *you*. Think about those parents, what they're going through—think of anyone other than your goddamned self for once. Hell, if you have to, think about me. *I* need to tell someone. To feel okay with *me*. Because I sure as hell am *not* okay right now. I'm not okay with you, either."

He stands from his chair, towers over me with a balled-up fist like he wants to punch me. Because the truth hurts.

I don't cower, don't flinch. Even beneath these hot, blinding lights, I'm resolute.

"You guys are talking about that kid over in West Clifton, aren't you?" Steve interrupts. He's up from the floor and walking toward us as he bats a thick wrench in the palm of his hand. It's big enough to knock us both out with one swift smash and I have no doubt he's capable of hiding our bodies where no one will find us.

Kyle lowers his hand, looks to me, then Steve. "Yeah," he says. "So?"

"Sounds like you know more about that accident than the police do."

Kyle looks to me again. His legs tremble. I stand from the chair and cross my arms firm against my chest, use them as a shield.

"Don't know what you're talking about, man," Kyle says. He shoves his hands into his pockets, probably to dry his clammy, truth-telling palms.

Steve chuckles. Up close, the wrench is even bigger. The places where the metal has worn, near the head, have stains of rusted red. It could be tarnish or it could be dried blood. I know not to ask questions so I move my eyes up to Steve's and pretend I'm confident in our denial.

"No worries, I won't say nothin'," he says.

Kyle relaxes his body and shakes it loose, and I'm thinking, *You jackass.* "Thanks, man," he says. I punch his arm, and he realizes what he just said. "I mean . . . nothing. Wait . . . what?"

Steve raises his wrench and points it in Kyle's face. "Come to think of it, a female deer can weigh up to a hundred twenty-five pounds, while a buck, well, a buck can weigh as much as three hundred."

"What the fuck does that have to do with anything?" Kyle blurts out. I elbow him. Hard.

Steve pauses. "That car ain't been hit by no deer. No dog, either. It was that kid, wasn't it?"

I try to stay chill, but my heart races. Kyle looks like he's choking, can't seem to spit out a word, and I kind of wish he would *actually* choke on something right about now to keep him from fucking up more of my shit.

Steve shakes his wrench at us, then walks to the other side of the garage to dig in a large, plastic bin. "Don't worry. I won't say anything. Unless . . ."

"Unless what?" Kyle asks in a panic. It's clear he now realizes we're in trouble here.

Steve pulls out a small disposable camera and circles to the front of the car. Kyle is anxious, fidgeting with whatever he can get his hands on. He whips his head toward me. "What the hell is he doing?"

Steve snaps a few photos of the damage, then walks back to us. "Unless this finds its way to the station. I've got a few legal binds I need to get myself out of. This might be my golden ticket."

I don't move, try to hold it together, to look like I'm not fazed, but I completely and totally want to bolt. Kyle doesn't even hesitate. He pulls his Gucci wallet from his back pocket and counts what's left. Steve's eyes expand as the bills fly, fanning the three of us standing in this tiny circle of lies and deceit.

"Twenty, forty, sixty, eighty," Kyle counts. "This is all I've got on me," he says, laying the bills in Steve's palm. Steve has wedged the wrench between his armpit and miniscule biceps while he gawks at the green in his hand. The look on his face shifts into something more sinister as Kyle backs away.

"This ain't enough," he says.

"What do you want?" Kyle asks, fear in his voice.

"What do you think your freedom is worth?"

Kyle looks to me, per the usual. I raise my eyes from the grimy floor and shake my head, silently beg him not to do this, not to dig this hole even deeper. He ignores my plea, also per the usual.

"I'll withdraw my savings if you keep your mouth shut."

"How much?"

"Five grand."

Steve pulls the wrench from his arm and smiles. "Ain't your dad like the real estate king of Clifton?"

Kyle swallows. I pinch the skin between my eyes, close them tight. I can't watch this train wreck another second. Or in this case, two-car pileup. "We're not struggling, if that's what you mean," he says.

When I open my eyes, Steve is looking at me, rubbing the front of his teeth with the tip of his slimy tongue. It only accentuates the gold and I'm suddenly thinking about the jewelry Ma sold to pay her doctor bills. He looks back to Kyle, whose knees are about to buckle completely. He holds the wall to keep steady. I'm planning my exit before we're both dead. Only one door in, one door out. No one would hear us scream, no one would know to find us here. He pokes the wrench's tip at Kyle's chest. Kyle inhales sharply, closing his eyes as if he's waiting for the blow.

Steve sighs. "If I remember right, when the cops busted me on that coke, you got nothin' but some trash pickup. Bet Daddy and his fancy lawyers helped with that. I still smell the chipped paint from the inside of my prison cell. Five grand is . . . a start."

"I have restrictions on my other accounts until I'm eighteen," Kyle stutters. "I have a limit on withdrawals without permission."

And for the first time since we've been here, the black in Steve's eyes expands, and I know now we're making a deal with the damn devil himself. "Find a way."

I open my mouth to speak, but I'm empty. Most things in

life don't scare me, and any other time, I'd pop that wrench from his boney fingers and make a run for it, but there's something about his intensity that's made me frozen. Kyle's not looking to me for approval this round, either.

"Fine."

Steve holds his hand out for a shake, but Kyle falls back to the chair, probably so he doesn't faint. "Finish the car. I'll get you whatever you want."

Sighing, I sit on the edge of my chair, too, and think of the boy. If Kyle had been driving a little slower, a little faster, if the kid had rolled a little slower, a little faster, we wouldn't be here.

Kyle leans over and whispers in my ear. "I'm not giving him shit. Just play along."

I angle my head up at this stupid idiot and decide right here, right now, this is over. I'm done.

No more Steve.

No more Kyle.

No more lies.

No matter what.

birdie

The doctors give up.

They say Benny's a vegetable. Broccoli or a carrot or something in the ground. He'll never make it, just take him off the machine, let him go, let him "be free." The insurance company, greedy bastards, tells Dad we're maxed out. They won't pay if there's no improvement, no hope. I toss between my unforgiving sheets all night. When I awaken, all those little broken hairs along my hairline are creased and bent into tiny curls from tears I must've cried through the night.

I rise up, stretching my arms high overhead. The grim realization—my life will never be the same—sets in like a punch to the gut. Legs hanging off the edge of my bed, I rub my hand over the comforter's creases, smooth them so they're not bunched up and ruining the beautiful flower-sewn lines threaded throughout. Chomperz is sprawled out on the floor where one thick streak of sun shines through. "Hey," I call out. He doesn't even flick an ear, so I put on my glasses and check my phone to see a mass of texts.

VIOLET: YOUR HOROSCOPE SAYS TODAY IS A GOOD DAY
    FOR LETTING GO.
VIOLET: BUT I THINK IT MEANS LET GO OF THE NEGATIV-
    ITY, NOT BENNY.

VIOLET: BASICALLY HOLD ON TO BENNY AND LET GO OF
   EVERYTHING ELSE.
VIOLET: AND MAYBE THAT NERD TEE THAT DOESN'T
   MAKE SENSE.
VIOLET: HOPE THE NEW JOB IS INSPIRATIONAL!!!

I hear clanging in the kitchen, so I put my phone away. As I throw on black leggings and a long, comfy sweater, a glimpse of my reflection catches me—a bag lady—in the dresser mirror. "Violet's gonna have a field day with this outfit," I say. "But I don't care." Chomperz looks up briefly then drifts back to sleep as if I'm not even here. Typical.

In the kitchen, Brynn pours herself a cup of freshly made coffee, black.

"What?!" she snaps when she sees me looking.

Sarge is asleep on the couch, snoring louder than the TV, which is set at 25 when the rest of the world listens at 12. It's no wonder he has (selective) hearing loss.

"Nothing," I say, choking down the thousand things I really want to say. "Need a ride to school?"

She takes a sip from the mug of steaming hot java, the mug that says #1 MOM, and grumbles as if she actually knows what a bad morning feels like. "No." She stomps off to her room, slamming the door behind her. The sound startles Sarge awake. Hands fly through the air, legs swinging. He is now upright in the most patriotic of ways, seemingly trying to figure out where he is, what year we're in, and more than likely, which platoon he's in charge of.

"Mornin'," he says with a gravelly voice. It's the sound of no sleep. He lifts his glasses from the coffee table and plants them over his nose.

I force a slight grin, however much it hurts, and take a seat next to him. I lay my head on his shoulder to feel the warmth radiating from his boxy frame. He pats my arm in his usual way, *pat pat pat,* unsure of how tight to hold, how close to pull, how much to say. "There, there," he says, not knowing which well my stray tears have sprung from. To be honest, I don't either.

He sighs again. This time the words churn beneath his breath. "Things will work themselves out. I have faith."

I look up at him, the sleep still lingering in my eyes, my lips still quivering the way they did all night. "Maybe they won't."

He pushes me back with a gentle nudge and tosses the old army blanket to the floor. "You know what Nan would tell you?"

I shake my head.

He swipes a tear from the corner of my eye. "It's kismet. If things stayed the same, we'd never grow into the people we're meant to be. There's a plan bigger than we can understand, Birdie. Everything will fall into place as it should, however He"—Sarge points to the ceiling—"wants it to."

I think on his words. "But it's not about religion. It's science. Like how single reactions happen as part of a larger series of reactions."

I've confused him, but he smiles anyway. "Okay . . . if you want to think of us as atoms and molecules, then yeah. Change will come, somehow, some way. It's human nature. If you ain't changing, you ain't human."

I want to frown, but the gleam in his eyes won't let me. "You're smarter than people give you credit for," I tell him.

"So are you." He smirks. We sit in silence for another moment before he nudges me off the couch with his elbow. "Go on, now. Don't want to be late."

"Fine." I grab an apple, my camera, backpack, and keys. On my way out, I brush past the bare baby cypress that's nestled in front of the big bay window where the collection of stray needles has mounted to an actual pile. The morning sun catches Brynn's fingerprints that haven't yet been wiped clean on the window pane. This tree looks lonelier than ever, each branch still naked and vulnerable. Hoping someone will notice. Hoping someone will be kind. The image grips me, forces me to my camera. I snap a few shots, sling my black lifeline over one shoulder and make my way to the car, where Brynn is quietly sitting in the backseat. No earbuds, no phone, just her. And I notice something I hadn't before—she and I are kind of the same, naked and vulnerable, like the cypress. We are each hoping someone will notice, hoping someone will be kind. And maybe someone—maybe each of us—will offer the other the comfort we so desperately need right now.

She doesn't meet my eyes in the rearview mirror when I slip inside, so I let her be. Instead I sneak peeks at her once we're on the road. She's unusually sullen. I want to ask if she's okay, but the words won't form behind my tongue. I don't want to ruin the absolutely perfect silence where we're not drowning in sorrow or bickering like children. We're just . . . here.

I drop her off *near* the middle school because she's never allowed any of us to pull up in the drop-off spaces that are actually meant for dropping off. *It's, like, so embarrassing,* she'd say every time, slumping farther into the seat. But today, as I put the car in Park about a half block away, she finally looks up at me in the mirror with her big, droopy eyes that are just like Dad's, and I feel like she wants to say something. She hesitates, though, as our eyes lock. In the stillness of this silence, we *are* speaking, we *are* civil. And it's just too weird. I'd much rather fight right now so as not to break down completely. It seems she feels the same.

After a few moments, I spin around in an attempt to nit-pick something stupid, but as I do, she flings the back door wide open, jumps to the curb, and walks away from me, from this. She looks over her shoulder once, something else she's never done, and I wonder what's going through her weird little head. I linger in her shadow until it fades beyond the large middle school doors, melting into all the other weird little heads that will gather to be weird together.

As I drive to my school, only a few blocks away, my thoughts drift back to the night Benny was hit. Over and over, I see myself unhinging the stroller, propping it up against the garage door. If the grand plan Sarge talks about really exists, the series of steps I was inevitably going to take were written before I was born and this choice was out of my hands. But it's something I can't wrap my brain around. I believe in free will, not prewritten. This is on me. Maybe if I hadn't kept the stupid scholarship thing to myself and snuck out, I could have changed the grand plan—changed the reaction—and there would have been no collision in the first place.

The thoughts consume me so deeply that I don't see the green light change to red.

My foot is on the gas, my eyes on the road, but I'm not here, in this car, in this world. I don't see the red SUV coming at me until it swerves out of my way with a screech and a loud honk. I slam on the brakes, heart beating out of my rib cage, and suddenly, I'm here—back in this car, in this world. I feel the gas pedal and see the road and the others around me who've just witnessed a near accident, and I'm gasping for air like there isn't enough left in the entire universe, and now I see—this must be how the person felt when they hit Benny. Paralyzed with fear, confused as the out-of-body haze melts away and life becomes crystal clear. Just now, *I* could've hit that car, caused another domino to fall. *I* could've been the one to put some kid in the hospital. *I* could've ruined someone else's life. When I think of it like that, it's hard to reconcile being angry with the person responsible for Benny. It could literally happen to anyone—including me.

When I finally get to school, Violet is waiting at my locker clutching her books. She catches me before I'm halfway down the hallway, wrapping her arms snug around me. A few of her soft tendrils make their way into my mouth, and I gag.

"Did you get my texts?" she asks.

"Yeah. I'm letting go," I say. "Well, *trying.*"

This makes her happy. She releases me from her grip, locks her arm in mine, and pulls me to my locker. "So, last night, at eleven eleven, I lit a candle and wished for a miracle. There was an INTENSE Scorpio moon that was basically purging all the sadness out of me, so I know it's going to purge from you, too. You just have to believe."

Her big, brown eyes sparkle at me through a thick stroke of purple eyeliner as she pumps her fist in the air.

I smile. "You are the BEST friend I could ever ask for."

"I know," she says just as the Aceys pass. Fat Stac(k) is MIA, and a new Acey is in her place near the back—Lacey—who seems confused as to why she's part of the group. In fact, I'm pretty sure her name is Laney Hodge and they've just renamed her Lacey to keep their group consistently shallow. Laney tells them she has to get to class, and that her name is not Lacey, but they shush her, pulling her along with complete disregard to our actual reality.

Violet snickers. "What are the odds of another Acey in the group?"

"About as good as that miracle you wished for. Poor Fat Stac(k). The intense Scorpio moon must've purged her."

When I pull into the rink's parking lot after school, I apply a thin layer of the strawberry lip gloss I never use in an attempt to appear more put together, then I comb my fingers through my hair and *try* to look happy. Vinny, the owner, said he wouldn't be here today but that everything I need to get started is inside. Through the rusted metal doors, I nervously fumble inside to a small counter that hangs lopsided off the wall.

"Hello?" I say, ringing the little bell. *Ding ding ding.*

A boy backs into the room, midconversation with someone else. "Make sure you're pushing the Lysol all the way into the skate, Dave," he says. "Or everyone's foot fungus will get together and procreate. Let's preach germ abstinence. Get that shit in there—deep. Yeah, I know—that's what she said. Beat you to it." He spins around to face me. His beautiful brown skin pales as he makes eye contact. "Hey."

A draft crawls up my spine. "I *know* you."

He squints, looks me over, but it's obvious my presence has him startled. "Nah, I don't think so."

I inch my head beneath the small window to pinch the sleeve of his shirt where the holes are. "You were wearing this when we met, actually."

He swallows, kicks his feet around. With a blush and trickle of sweat, he loses eye contact. "Oh, right. The, um, party last weekend."

There's an uncomfortably long silence as I stand under the vent's draft.

"What are you doing *here*?" he mumbles.

"Vinny hired me."

He coughs or grunts or something I can't make out. "Why would *you* apply *here*? It's literally the worst option in the mid-Indiana region."

"*You're* here."

"Only because Bill Gates wasn't hiring."

"Yeah, well, same."

His eyes find mine. "You can put your shit back here, I guess."

"Awesome." I push through another set of metal doors and walk around to the office.

He keeps his back to me as he speaks. His silky dark locks shine under the sizzling lights. "Throw it anywhere. Doesn't matter. It's all one giant Dumpster fire."

I lay my purse between piles of papers and cross my hands

in front of me. The room is silent except for the vague sounds of Christmas music streaming from the computer's speakers. I clear my throat and study the disheveled layout. Files are unevenly stacked across every inch of counter space while coffee mug stains saturate the sparse, open laminate. The old carpet is worn and frayed, dirty footprints soaked through. It sort of resembles my brain this past week which makes me feel eerily at home here.

He's quiet, too quiet, not like at the party. He falls into one of two chairs and drags his glare up to mine. It's intense. He's not looking away. Not to check the door or behind me, or down the front of my shirt like some boys do. He's, like, inside my brain. Big, honey-glazed stare, coming right at me like an arrow. "Tell me, Couch Girl," he says.

"Couch Girl?" I interrupt.

"Yeah, that's what I named you at the party."

"Kind of demeaning, but whatever. Continue." I like it almost immediately.

"What are the odds of us running into each other again?"

I run the numbers. "Based on the assumption you are, in fact, in town longer than *one* night, unlike what you said at the party," I sneer, "take the odds of us meeting once, multiply by the odds of meeting again, and," I grab a pencil, shove him out of the way and scribble on a blank Post-it.

7.47467%. "Boom."

His jaw falls open, but the corner of his mouth is slightly turned up. "Hot damn! Wasn't expecting a real answer there. I was thinking you'd say something about fate or destiny or some shit."

"You don't know me."

His half smile fills out. "Yeah, I see that."

At a small knock on the door, the boy spins around in his chair, his eyes still on the paper between his hands. "Dave, this is New Girl. New Girl, Dave." The man is older. Like Dad's-age older. His eyes are kind—something I notice about people because I think you can tell a lot about a person through their eyes. The boy's eyes are kind, too, but I wouldn't dare tell him so. The man steps forward and holds out a hand for me to shake while balancing a pair of skates in the other.

"Birdie," I correct. "Or, Couch Girl, apparently."

Dave's smiling, brimming almost, but doesn't say a word. He looks to me, then to the boy, then back to me.

"Now would be a good time to stop staring," the boy says. "If I were her, and I saw your face right now, I'd haul ass out of here. You scare people, man. Ease up."

His honesty makes me laugh. Not because it's really that funny, but because I wish I could say things like that without analyzing. Dave dips his head and waves slightly before turning away.

"Bye, Dave," I say. "Is he shy?"

"Um, no. He has aphasia. It's a speech impairment. The most outgoing fuckin' quiet guy I've ever met, too. Dude won't shut up—I mean, in his own way."

I laugh harder, while simultaneously trying to conceal how funny I think he is so he doesn't get a big head about it.

"So . . . ," I say. "Your name is?"

"Most people just refer to me as 'that asshole.'"

"I see why."

He hesitates. "Bash. Or if you want to chew me out, Sebastian."

"Okay, Bash. Did you *really* graduate, or was that a lie, too?"

He ducks his head away, and I've got my answer.

"And that's why I don't do parties. Lying. Boys. Like. You."

He grabs his chest, appears hurt. "Burn. You don't know me, either, kid. And my guess is that's not the only reason you don't do parties."

"Right." I sigh. "You're SO different. Anyway, since we

have to work together, let's pretend we never met, start over. Are you training me, or what?"

He smiles, grabs a stack of papers, and tosses me a pen. "Fill all these out and give me your ID."

"What? No way!"

"For Vinny. He needs it on file for taxes. Jesus. Have you never had a job before? What would *I* do with your ID?"

I grab the chair next to him and scribble my info on the sheet, my hands sweating, thanks to the plug-in heater that's nestled between paper piles. "Maybe you're obsessed with me. You could be a total creeper. I don't know."

"Yep," he says, "you got me. This was all part of my grand plan. To get you, a complete stranger—"

"Who you met once," I interject.

He chokes. "A complete stranger I *didn't* meet once because we're starting over—to apply for, and get, this shitty job so I can steal your"—I hand him my ID—"*really* terrible ID to hang up on my wall of Couch Girls. That really gets me off. Like, more than you know."

I scowl. "I don't know you. Maybe that's your thing." He copies the ID on the scanner and tosses it back.

"Girls, women"—he points at me—"are soul-sucking, time-wasting hangovers waiting to happen. Remember the girl at the party I was trying to piss off? Point made."

"I see where I stand." I'm joking, sort of. Because while right now may not be the best way to reunite, I felt *something* at the party, and I thought he did, too.

"I'm not interested in being analyzed."

I shift in my seat, away from him. Doesn't faze him, though. "Good—neither am I."

The silence stings.

"So . . . how long have you worked here?" I ask.

"Too damn long."

"If you hate it, why don't you do something else?"

"Yeah, good luck with that. Everyone says they're hiring, but no one is really. Some of us need whatever we can get."

"I know the feeling." My thoughts drift to Benny, and the room feels like it's shrinking.

He's looking at me. I'm staring at these piles of random papers, but I feel his eyes hard-pressed on the side of my face. It's warm, a little like when you open the door to a sauna and it hits you—*BAM*—right there on your cold, vulnerable skin. I've started to ask another question when Vinny bursts through the double doors. A tiny lady nips at his heels only a step behind. He's balancing a big cardboard box while she's covered in the fur of something exotic. Her jingle bell earrings dangle and ding, something that seems to match her very, *very* scarlet metallic lips. Gold jewelry hangs off her, and even the tips of her heels have little gold bows on them. She's like a miniature Christmas tree about to topple over.

The woman makes eye contact with me and rushes around the back, into the office door like she's being chased. Her arms wrap around me, knocking the papers and pen to the other papers and pens lying in stacks on the floor. And suddenly, there go the files in my mind, too.

"My God," she says, pulling back, "I cannot imagine what your family is going through. How is your brother? Is he okay? I can't stop watching the news. Well, once the cable got all fixed up. That was a long couple days without. Every single morning, I think of you all, and now here you are— right in front of me. This *has* to be a sign. Our paths were meant to cross." She pulls my head back into her, the fur fully inside my mouth, and I'm thinking about Sarge and if she says the word "kismet," I'm going to—

"It's kismet. It *must* be."

(Insert silent scream.)

"Your chinchilla is in her mouth, Evie," Vinny says, handing the oversized box to Bash. "Step back and let her breathe.

So glad ya could finally make it in. Welcome—this is my wife, Evie, by the way. She's a hugger, if you can't tell." They're all standing here, waiting for me to say something. She pulls back again, her hands tilting my head up at her crystal blue eyes that have streaked with mascara.

For a second, I forgot about the pain. And I liked it that way. "They don't think he's going to make it . . ."

She rubs the hair on my head in a way resembling motherly and offers a sympathetic pout.

"There's nothin' they can do?" Vinny asks.

I shake my head. "I don't know."

Bash's eyes are glued to the floor, and I can't tell if it's because he feels sorry for me, too, or if he's not interested in my sob story.

Vinny pats my shoulder. "Well, we're glad to have ya, and if there's anything else we can do, let me or Evie know."

They hold their stares for a solid minute while I keep nodding. It won't stop, and I feel it going, going, going. "Thanks."

"Well, you look great," Vinny says to lighten the mood. "I hope Dave didn't say anything inappropriate." He laughs, turns to Evie, and she laughs, too. "Kidding, kidding."

I force a pseudo-laugh and glance at Bash, who is not even trying to smile. He looks like he wants to disappear.

"Bash, can I talk to you for a second?" Vinny asks. "Evie, go wait in the car. I'll be right out."

"So nice to meet you, honey," she says. "I'll drop off a casserole and keep you on my prayer list." She squeezes me again, but this time, I don't squeeze back. Bash meets Vinny at the doorway, a few footsteps away. I go back to my spot near the clutter, next to the other clutter, and awkwardly pretend I'm not listening while gathering, then filling out the endless pages of paperwork.

"I don't care what shit you have going on—stealing my cigarettes and a twenty from the drawer is strike two," Vinny whispers in a loud voice. He's pointing his finger in Bash's face.

"I didn't steal—I borrowed," Bash jokes. "I put the money back."

"Two weeks later."

I try not to listen, not to stare, but I can't help it.

"Sorry."

"One more strike, Bash, you're out. I'm sorry. This is a business. And replace my cigarettes."

Bash's head is low, his jaw clenched. "You *know* why I need this job."

"Then don't fuck up again." He places his hand on Bash's shoulder but catches me watching. He turns to me. "I'll have a schedule for you in a couple days, but until then, just come and go as you please while you learn the ropes. I know you've got a lot going on, but we're glad to have you onboard. If you have any problems, my cell is on that list by the computer." He points to a faded sheet with barely visible numbers.

"Thanks," I say.

"Bash will teach you everything you need to know." He leaves, and Bash flops back into his seat. The mood of the room has shifted. Feels like the ceiling is falling down on top of us.

"What should I do?" I ask.

He grabs a bottle of hand sanitizer and spreads a thick streak in his palm, rubbing until it's dissolved.

I scoot my chair up next to his, pretend not to have heard what Vinny told him. Our knees touch in this way that kind of grazes, kind of shoots a jolt through me. I pretend not to feel it, and I can tell he does, too. "Teach me, Yoda," I say.

His eyes find mine, and we're close enough that I can really see into them. My reflection and everything.

"So there's nothing the doctors can do . . . for your . . . brother?" he asks.

135

The question catches me off guard. I shift in my seat. "Uh, they want to take him off the ventilator. See if he can breathe on his own. But our insurance doesn't want to pay much more and . . ."

He leans in to me. I smell him. Can't say it smells good, but for whatever reason, I like it. "And what?"

"It's like a *Dateline* mystery. We don't know who did it, probably never will."

He turns away. "That sucks."

"I just want him to open his eyes," I say. I wipe away a tear with the tip of my pinky finger before he can see. He shuffles the stack of papers, pretending we weren't having a super-serious conversation, just as someone comes through the door.

"Well, hey, hey, hey," a boy says, making a kissy face toward me. "Who's the new fox? Ho-ly guac-o-mol-e." Bash jumps up from his chair and runs around to the boy, who towers over him, trying to usher him out before I get a good glimpse. The boy resists, pushes his way up to the counter, where I now see him clearly. He's a total cliché. Tall, dressed like he's got money, diamonds in his ears, and slicked-back hair. It's like he knows what he is, where he comes from, and doesn't even try to fight it. He opens his mouth, and the smell of alcohol wafts out—hard liquor.

My nose crinkles.

"Doesn't matter," Bash says, pulling on the boy's arm. "We're not open yet. Out."

The boy pushes Bash away, knocking him into the concrete wall near the exit. "Stop, dude!" He turns back toward me and ducks his head inside the small window while Bash is reaching for him. I scoot my chair farther back from the opening, just out of this boy's reach. "I'm Kyle. Are you single? I'm single. Wanna mingle?"

I say nothing, instead look to Bash, who is now rubbing his arm. "You've got to go," he says.

Kyle, or whatever his name is, grins with a smugness that screams insecurity. "Silence is a true friend who *never* betrays," he says, pointing to me, then to Bash, then to me again. "Hmm? You got that? Confucius—my script magician of life." He's stuttering, slurring his words.

Bash gets ahold of Kyle's shiny leather coat and shoves him out the door. Hard. "STOP DRIVING AND CALL A CAB, YA DRUNK DOUCHE!"

He pulls the door shut quickly and twists the lock behind him.

"You *know* him?"

"Unfortunately."

"Sucks for you." I look at the clock. "Also, it's like four in the afternoon. Why is he wasted?"

He rubs the skin between his eyes, his hair falling into his face. "Because that's Wild Kyle. He does whatever the hell he wants."

"I remember seeing him wasted at that party and, no offense, but he seems pretty terrible."

He glares at me, but his face softens the longer he looks at me. "My mom used to babysit him. He's been following me around ever since. Like a bedbug. He's really not *that* bad once you get to know him." There's a short pause. "Yeah, he is. I don't know why I said that. He's the worst human being I've ever known. But I guess I kind of care about what happens to him or something. I've got a death wish."

"I get it. Sounds like my little sister." I scoot my chair closer to the window where my feet disappear beneath the desk. He looks up at me, through this thin sheet of pain, and in his eyes, I feel that warmth again. He smiles, then quickly retracts it.

"There's a binder in the filing cabinet. Read it. If you have questions, ask Dave."

"But Dave can't talk."

"Sorry, gotta make sure my idiot friend doesn't kill

137

anyone. Later," he says, rushing out. He disappears, only the scent of him, something terrible, lingering behind.

I don't see Bash again for a few days. He bails, leaving Dave and me to figure things out with no verbal communication whatsoever, which if you've never tried, is *really* hard. When my time is up this shift, I make my way home. I debate texting Vi to tell her I now work with the mysterious boy from "the rager," but I know she'll lecture me about "dudes like him," just as she did when she pulled me away from him. It's not like us to keep secrets but these days, I'm doing a lot of things out of context. What's one more?

Dad's car is gone. Judging by the temperature of the space, the coldness of the leaked oil I swipe across my finger, he's been gone a while. Like maybe he never came home from work, if he went at all. I walk inside and toss my things on the muddled kitchen table. A loud blaring boom spills from Brynn's room, where the door is wide open. Her back is to me as she glides a jet-black pencil around her eyes.

"Where's Sarge?" I scream.

"Hospital with Mom," she screams back.

I walk over to the laptop on her bed and punch the volume down. "Dad, too?"

"Dad's working. Again." She spins around to face me so I can see her more clearly, the pencil lodged between her freshly painted black nails like a cigarette. She's dressed in a black miniskirt that looks more like underwear and a white V-neck that's been cut at the midriff.

"Uh, where are you going?" I ask.

"Out."

"Like that?" I hear Mom's voice, not mine.

"Yeah, so?"

"Mom and Dad said it's okay?"

She huffs. "Before, it was all about you, and now, it's all about Benny. They don't give a shit *what* I do."

My brows knit together as I study this girl who's transformed overnight. Or maybe it's been happening, and I didn't notice until now. She isn't a kid anymore—it's obvious by her curves—but she's not a woman yet, either, obvious from her words. She's in between, trying to navigate her place, her body, her boundaries—things I get more than she knows.

"They care," I say. "You want Benny to wake up, too. Imagine what Mom and Dad feel right now."

She laughs, tosses the pencil into a case on her dresser. "If Benny doesn't wake up, this is just the beginning."

She sounds different, more cynical. A jealous hatred leaks out of her, and I'm wondering how she could be so cold. I think of Violet's horoscope that promised new beginnings. Goose bumps coat my skin.

"Did something happen?" I ask, afraid to know the answer.

She shakes her head. "Nope. Just realized life is too short to sit around and watch everyone frozen in this weird parallel universe where good things *don't* happen—where we all die a little every day *without* good things happening—*without* MIRACLES!"

Her words sink all the way in as I watch this almost-fourteen-year-old twist her hair up into a high knot where a few loose wisps fall free. Maybe this little brat has it figured out more than any of us.

"Just so you know, boys, the good ones, will like you even if you don't dress like that."

She glares at me, at another one of my big sweaters fluffed up around me. "This coming from . . . the town bag lady. Might as well be a nun in those gross clothes."

"I'm just saying . . . there are some boys who see what you're wearing and think it's an invitation or something. Like you're—"

"Like I'm what—asking for it?" Her hand is on her hip, and she walks toward me.

"Yeah."

"Maybe I am."

Her eyes challenge me. I back down, move toward the door so she can't see my own mistakes scribbled across my forehead. Truthfully, I envy her confidence. Instead, I prefer to hide behind my clothes, my glasses, and my scientific facts because it's safer that way. I open my mouth, but the moment I do, a horn blares from the driveway. I poke my head around the corner to see two headlights gleaming through the window right into our bare cypress.

"Welp, good talk," she says. "Later, loser." Her lips upturned, she throws a skinny jacket over her shoulder and slams the door behind her. I watch from the window as she piles into the backseat of this car, with these friends—who are apparently old enough to drive—I didn't know she had, and I think *maybe she's right* about everything.

I watch the headlights reverse down the driveway, careful at the base where everything changed so quickly, and my heartbeat accelerates. I feel those moments all over again. Like even though we've never been super close, I've lost Brynn, too. Maybe I'm destined to walk the earth alone, inside my head, always.

Short of breath, I open the front door, and the wind hits my face. Plunging my hands into my pockets, I walk down the hill to where a new pile of stuffed animals and trinkets encircles the crash site. I squat and pick up each item, one by one, to say hello. Even for a highway, it's quiet now. No one wants to drive here anymore. I count how many cars pass as I sit here—two—and relive the night in my head, retracing every step, every choice. If only I'd talked to Mom about the party, the scholarship, this boy now known as *Bash* sooner, if only I hadn't let these completely normal things fester and grow into monsters inside my mind, we wouldn't be here. I don't know much about a grand plan or fate, but I know it's my action, or inaction, that is undeniably part of the equation.

While I'm lost in thought, the full moon breaks free from the clouds. The illumination casts shadows that stretch far and wide and a strand of glowing light shines down on the prayer sheath I'm sitting beside. Out of the corner of my eye, I see something reflect off my glasses. I poke my finger into the dried-up grass and brush away the dirt to pinch a hollowed silver metal circle with a triangular-pointed trinity molded inside. I angle it up toward the moon, one eye shut to study the object and think, *Surely the police didn't miss this; it couldn't be related to Benny's accident.* Cars pass through here all the time. Or did. I look up, clutch the metal in my palm, and decide to do the only thing I can think of in my dreary state: Hide it. I don't know why this feels okay, but right now, what does?

Through the night, Chomperz sits on me and locks me into one position. When I turn, he paws at me with his clawless little nubs to remind me who's in charge. I dream Benny is gasping for air, blood vessels bursting through his eyes, and I'm reaching for him, but I'm restrained just like this—by something sitting on my chest. And I'm screaming at the top of my lungs the same way Mom and Brynn did when he was hit, but not a sound escapes me. When morning breaks, my eyes feel puffy and raw as I crawl out of bed. Chomperz thinks it's an invitation to spread out between the sheets as I get dressed for the day. It's not, but he doesn't care what I think.

"Something you want to talk about?" Sarge asks on my way out the door. His bushy brows perch on top of his thick glasses.

"I can't take Brynn today. She'll have to ride the bus." I'm lying. I just don't want to be near her. His eyes study me, making me fidget. I look away, try to pull myself free from his grip.

He pats the couch—*pat pat pat.* "Come here."

I glance at the clock and resist. "I'm going to be late for

school." The words, the lies, are hard to form, especially to him.

He smiles, urges me onto the fluffy couch cushion where the shape of his body has imprinted. "Birdie Jay—SIT."

My face flushes as he mutes the TV and sort of angles away from me. Eye contact isn't his thing; emotions, feelings aren't either. Except, for some reason, when it comes to *me*.

"I've been thinking a lot about this. About you. And here's what I've come up with."

"Okay?"

"The heart breaks harder than bones," he says.

My eyes are locked onto those little nose hairs that flare in and out as he breathes. With all his war stories, you never know what the point will be, so I hold my tongue. The light of the muted screen shines across his face and the few gray hairs left on his head. "I'm just saying the pain . . . the pain is what will kill you, not the act itself."

I look up to his aging square face and find my reflection in his magnifying-glass lenses. Our bare Christmas tree stands, overlooking us, mocking. "It doesn't matter what happens. I've ruined us."

"Hmm. Grief is a black hole. You've got to find a way to walk around it without falling in."

I let his words sink in as my eyes follow the way his lip trembles. He's trying to hide it by cupping his hand around them, but I see—he's thinking about Nan. We all are, would be even if this hadn't happened. Sarge would rather have broken bones, too. I lay my hand on his, and he looks at me with a smirk.

He sucks it up. "Go on now. Get to school." He leans in with a whisper. "Or wherever you were really going."

He falls back to the couch in a slump, remote in hand. This is it, my opportunity to slink away, disappear into the bitter Indiana wind. I get in my car, the hill of terror in my rearview, and carefully reverse into the highway. Straightening my front wheels, I leave the corner memorial, not the SOLD sign I flattened, but all the other wooden stakes that have lined this section of road, behind.

With a heavy sigh, I drive to the far side of town to the Gardens of Memory Cemetery. On the winding back of the paved spine, through the old weeping willows whose branches have dried up for the impending winter forecasters say will be "the worst in a long time," I make my way to the farthest western corner, near the ivory mausoleum I used to pretend was a princess castle.

The sun pokes its flame-colored rays through the cotton clouds, spilling onto the headstones. The light almost makes them look alive. One foot in front of the other, I find it: Nan's final spot, bound by earth and granite. The grass is cold when I kneel down; it pierces through my pants like tiny, icy swords. I lay my hand on the words LOVING MOTHER, WIFE & GRANDMOTHER and bow my head in prayer.

"It's been a long time," I say quietly. "You probably thought I'd never come. But here I am." The wind picks up, whistles past my ears. "I have a favor to ask, and I'm sorry if it seems rude to just show up and ask for something, but . . ." I stop myself because my heart is pinching, bleeding through my nerves into a giant pool of grief. "I don't care what happens to me. It's Benny. Help him open his eyes. If God wants something in return, tell him to take me instead. Please."

I slowly raise my head, tears drenching my face just as the sun brightens, shines a warmth to dry them. Maybe she hears me, maybe she doesn't, but at least I can say I tried. I spin around, resting my back on the stone, and pull my knees up to my chest. As the sun rises into a full scene of majestic beauty, I can't look away. The oranges and yellows pour over me like a bath, heat me inside and out. I close my eyes and I drift along with the clouds and maybe, with Nan.

Later, about the time Mrs. Rigsby might grab at my arm,

force me in front of the class for everyone to cock their heads at and pity, I pull myself up from the dried grass and dirt, giving Nan one last look. "Thanks for listening," I tell her.

She doesn't respond, which I've heard is a good thing.

LESSON OF THE DAY: There will always be one step in a reaction that happens at the slowest speed. That step is called the rate-limiting step, and it determines how fast the overall reaction can happen. I didn't see it before, but maybe the only thing preventing me from evolving, moving forward, isn't the accident.

It's *me*.

BASH

Of all the places in this shithole town (okay, there aren't many), she walks into mine. My stomach feels like someone's punched me with a two-ton brick right here—right in my center of gravity. This must be part of that chain reaction shit Mrs. Pearlman always talks about—the actions Kyle put in motion. Wait. What am I saying? *I* was there. *I* was in the car, too. This is *my* chain reaction, *my* cross, because I know Kyle won't bear shit.

I couldn't sleep, tossed and turned all over those damn mattress springs until one finally poked straight through. Now the sun is up, almost shaming me, and I'm in my car driving fast, too fast, but I can't force my legs to stop shaking. They're lead, all the weight down on that rusted pedal. It's as if those two-ton bricks sank into my toes. Just feeling Birdie—what kind of name is that anyway?—there so close, behind me, beside me, around me like the atmosphere incarnate, made my vision dark, my hands tremble. What if I said something wrong? Maybe I did. Shit, I don't even remember. Maybe I confessed, told her everything. My shirt is soaked through with sweat, so I wouldn't doubt it. I'll probably have cops at my door any minute now, ready to bust down the flimsy piece of sheet metal, kick in the blanket that hangs over the frame where a door should be, handcuffs bright and shiny with my name all over them.

WHAT THE HELL—I ALMOST MADE OUT WITH HER!

Shit. What was I thinking? To be fair, I was thinking, *She's hot,* but had I known I was going to sit in a car that would run over her brother, I might've steered clear. This is all Layla's fault. Had she not been at that party to fuck with me, I wouldn't have met Couch Girl, and Couch Girl wouldn't be completely sucking the logic and reason from my brain. I'm a mess.

I wonder why Vin didn't tell me beforehand to "be nice to her; she's from that news story." Or maybe he did, and I blacked out. Hell, I don't remember. Isn't that what happens when you black out? I can't catch my breath; I might be having some kind of panic attack. I drive faster, before anyone can tell Ma any of it. Try to save her so she can go peacefully and not be held back by this unfinished business or some shit like I read about with dying people. Doesn't matter, I guess. If shit's gonna happen, it's gonna happen. Nothin' I can do about it now but hope that if I am busted, she's too far gone to understand.

I get to the nursing home and fling the door open to dodge the cold. I forgot the lily, but I can't think about that now.

"Hey, Bash," Nurse Kim calls from the front desk. "She might be sleeping."

I ignore her, round the corner, and run down the hall to her room near the end. The slot on the door where her name usually hangs is prematurely empty like they're just waiting for her last breath so they can toss her out, give someone else the chance to die here.

Fear courses through my veins as if I've just killed someone, because maybe I have. I poke my head inside to see Ma hooked up to all her usual machines, medicines flowing, thick tubes pushing air in, pulling it out of her lungs. She's sound asleep, snoring so loud it bounces off the paper-thin walls. In between labored breaths, there's a gurgling sound. This is new. She hasn't gurgled before.

I smooth my clothes and slowly walk to her fragile frame. She doesn't flinch, so I squirt a puddle of hand sanitizer in my palm, pull up a chair, and sit along the edge to grab her swollen hand. I gently bury her frozen fingers between my thighs, hoping they'll warm, but she still doesn't wake. On her bedside table is a small faux Christmas tree with teeny-tiny bulbs of light that flash in a rhythmic motion. My latest bear drawing is nestled up against the bristles like a present.

Nurse Kim pokes her head in. "Been sleeping most of the day."

I gulp. "How is she?"

She lowers her head, her frown deepening. "You want the easy answer or the truth?"

I angle my head and purse my lips. "Come on, Kim. Give me the real stuff."

"We called hospice."

"She doesn't want more meds."

"She changed her mind, Bash. The pain was too much. They came this morning, and . . . they don't think she'll make it much longer. Few days, maybe."

I can't swallow now. Once I do, the tears will fall, and I won't be able to stop them.

"I'm sorry, kiddo," she says. "If she needs anything, buzz me, but just know, she might not wake while you're here . . . if at all. The rest periods are getting longer." Ma gurgles again, startling me. The sounds are loud, as if she's in pain. Her chest is clotted with saliva she can't swallow, and, *God*, it's never felt like the end before, until now.

"That's normal, too," she whispers.

My eyes fall to Ma. Her face is thinned and pale. But her lips and cheeks are still as rosy as ever. "She put on makeup, so she can't be too far gone," I say, with hope.

"I did that, sweetie," Kim says.

My head, and heart, drop again.

"Treasure the time you've got left with her."

I nod. My throat is tight.

"I know she doesn't have much family, no friends—none that visited. You may want to call whoever you need to—like that brother she has in Utah—let him know it's almost time."

"He died a couple months back."

"Oh, she didn't mention it," she says. "I'm so sorry."

I dip my head away from Ma, lower my voice. "She doesn't know. Didn't want to stress her out."

Nurse Kim's eyes soften with a hint of pain. "You're a good boy, Bash." She stares for a moment, then pulls the door shut.

If she really knew me, what I'd done, she wouldn't say that. She'd be on the phone with the cops to collect her reward. Who wouldn't? I sure as hell would. Some punk-ass kid, hanging over his comatose mother, hiding, lying about the things he's done, the person he *really* is. Ma would be so ashamed. And *that* is the worst punishment of all.

The more I overthink, the tighter I grip Ma's hand. The purple and blue colors deepen so I release her, lay it on top of her sheet, and take a long, deep breath while I relive the conversations Birdie and I had at the rink. Now that I'm calm, the words are clearer. Maybe she didn't figure me out just yet. Besides, there are no cops, no signs of my arrest here, so why am I freaking out? I try to relax as much as I can while I watch Ma struggle to breathe—something so simple, so natural, and yet, it's the hardest thing for her to do. Every third breath, she gasps for air like there's nothing left in her, and I know the feeling, because every third breath, I gasp, too.

I fall asleep in the chair, my neck cockeyed. I'm awakened by Ma's gentle tap on my knee some hours later. The hallway lights have dimmed, and the shuffling feet have slowed.

"Go home," she says. She pulls the CPAP mask—an unsettling breathing contraption that looks like a villain's disguise—off her mouth and nose. She settles a hand on my leg. "Go lie in your bed, crank up the heat, and dream about everything you'll be." A smile stems from her hollow face. It glows brighter than ever. But her eyes are empty, gray.

I pick up her hand and plant a soft kiss on the top. "I'd rather be here with the most beautiful woman in the world."

"Oh, Sebastian." Her voice is strained. "You've always been the only man for me. . . . You'll make some girl . . . very lucky . . . someday. . . . I wish . . . I wish I could be here to see." Her glow fades as her tired lungs struggle for air between words. Even now she's fighting to breathe. She coughs, violently, the jostling nearly knocking her unconscious. Her lashes fall heavy, fluttering closed. I place the CPAP mask over her mouth and nose once more, but she pushes it away. I brush the sparse curls off her face and think of all the times she's done the same for me.

"You need something? For the pain?" I ask.

She shakes her head, opening her eyes once more. "No more. I'm ready. Tell *him*."

"Who?"

"Fate."

Now I'm beaming. "How do you know fate is a *man*?"

Her eyes make brief contact as her breathing worsens. "Only a man would be cocky enough to decide the huge responsibility of destiny. Probably some . . . middle-aged piece of shit . . . in his parents' basement . . . after *Call of Duty: Clan Wars* weekend. He's . . . jacked up on . . . taking people out, and he grabs his . . . iPhone his mommy bought him (like Kyle) . . . because a pen and paper is . . . beneath him . . . and he makes a note of how everyone . . . will die. This one—death by . . . rat poison. That one—death by . . . military execution. And me—death by . . ."

"What, Ma? What would fate do to you?" I ask.

"Heartbreak. For leaving . . . the . . . greatest son ever made."

My expression sours, but I can't let her see. Even though they're trying to spill out of me, I hold back the words about everything I've done, lied about, and focus on her eyes. They dart around like she's half here, half not. I clear my throat.

"Fate *can't* be a man," I say to break the pain. "It's impossible."

She's looking at me intently. "Why's that?"

"If a man were in charge of everyone's destiny, he'd fuck it up. That's what we do—fuck shit up. We need a good woman to set us straight, make the fucked-up shit right."

She chuckles, a sound so beautiful, it makes my heart swell. I forget about everything else for just this moment.

"I'd tell you to watch your mouth, but I know who gave it to you," she says. Our snickers melt into each other and fade away completely because it's true. She's looking at me in a way she never has before, and somewhere deep inside, I see that twinkle I'd been missing. In my gut I know her disappointment in me is better than lying to her. How can she die in peace if I've betrayed all she's taught me?

"Ma," I say, my head hung low, "there's something I need to—"

"Tell me about work," she interrupts. Her chest expands as she gasps for another breath.

I look up. "Work?"

"I want to hear it all."

My jaw is open, I know. "There's a new girl. That's actually what I wanted to—"

"Oooh," she says. "Tell me all about this girl." She pulls her CPAP mask up to her face and presses the little black button on her handheld controller that releases pain medicine. The liquid feeds into her veins; her body relaxes now.

"I might close my eyes, but I can hear you. Just keep talking so I know you're here." She pats my leg again, and it sends a tremor up my body. She wiggles around between the sheet and blanket, tucking her arms into the sides. I stand and gently tuck the sheets under her. The machine is loud, but I talk through it.

"Her name is Birdie," I start, with a heavy sigh. It's like letting go of some pain I've been holding on to, a weight lifting. Almost. "She asks too many questions. Seems to be some kind of genius or something."

Ma lifts the machine off long enough to speak. "Boyfriend?"

I shake my head with a smirk. "I don't know."

"What does she . . . look like?" She rests the mask over her mouth and nose and folds her hands back under the sheet.

I latch my fingers together and stitch a coherent string of thoughts. "Uh, I don't know," I say. "Kind of tall, long brown hair, thick white glasses. Pretty, I guess. Not like Layla kind of pretty. More like awkward kind of pretty. I mean, she's really kind of gloriously beautiful, but in this weird way," I say. My face softens, and then I remind myself who she is—off limits.

Ma's movements are slowing, words slurring, but she lifts the mask one last time. "He came to see me, to say good-bye."

I crouch toward her. "Who did?"

She mumbles something I don't understand. "I wanted him to take me back to Brazil where we met. So I can give him the letter."

"What are you talking about? What letter?"

Ma's eyes grow heavier and heavier until her lashes shut completely. I fall back in the chair and try to figure out what she was trying to tell me. Nurse Kim tiptoes in to check her vitals, fluff her pillow. She catches me in deep thought and waves her hand in front of me.

"You okay?" she asks.

"She said something about a man and a letter."

Nurse Kim nods. "She's been rambling quite a bit about this man. Says he's tall with eyes like crystal. The other day she told me he wanted to pay her, but she refused it. The closer her mind and body get to the end, the more hallucinations she'll have. I know it's confusing, doesn't make this process any easier."

I bite my lip and nod.

"Go home, get some rest. She needs hers, too."

"Few more minutes?"

She grins, nods.

I give a thumbs-up as she leaves us and turn back to Ma, her mask filling her body with oxygen. I wonder how many more times I'll be able to sit here with her, look at her, feel her next to me. For as afraid as she is to leave me, I'm afraid to be left. Despite all the shit I've given her, she's the only person on the planet to never give up on me—to see I *am* worth something (although, I'm not even close).

I lean over her and close my eyes, inhaling her scent. "I'm going to turn myself in," I whisper. "Take responsibility, be the man you raised me to be. When you go, I'll have nothing left anyway." As I lean on her, my phone vibrates. I pull it from my pocket and see Kyle sent a few texts I didn't get until now because it's a cheap-ass phone and we're in the dead zone everywhere.

KYLE: DAD'S CREW IS GOING TO THE HOUSE NEXT WEEK.

KYLE: HE'S MOVING FORWARD WITH THE PLANS TO KEEP BUILDING.

KYLE: WE HAVE EVIDENCE THERE.

KYLE: CALL ME ASAP!!!

I shove the phone back into my pocket so I can just look at Ma for one more minute. The lights from the small Christmas tree flicker against her pale face. I brush her stray hairs back and kiss her forehead. "Love ya, Ma. Always."

As I walk away, she pulls the mask off her face one last time. "Whatever you did, just fix it, Sebastian."

I stop dead in my tracks, my eyes bulging.

Busted.

birdie

Dr. Morrow's pulling the plug. Dr. Schwartz agrees.

Two people, completely different Ivy-league schooling, completely different families and beliefs (probably), and they're in agreement about one thing—unhook him, see what happens, see if he can make it without the tubes and needles. Insurance is done, we're broke, and Mom and Dad have begged, borrowed, and scrambled to come up with enough money, barely, to fly a specialist in for another opinion.

Time seeps into one runny mess, like the yolk of an egg filling the sides of a cool pan. After some discussion, they make the decision to do the exclusive interview Julie Sturghill's station has been asking for. Dad's worried about how desperate it makes them look, while Mom is still stuck on the whole Bessie thing from that brief clip last week. Right now, we need all the press and donations we can get, and everyone agrees. It's for Benny.

I watch from Benny's bedside chair, his hand in mine. On air, Mom, whose voice cracks when she speaks, pleads for three things: (1) to find the driver of the car that hit Benny, (2) donations to cover the cost of Benny's specialist and hospital stay, "but most of all," she says, (3) "whether you believe in God or not, pray for us." Old Bessie is composed, hands crossed, good posture, big, bright eyes like she hasn't been hunched over a hospital bed all this time. You wouldn't know by watching this that on the inside, she's completely, irreparably broken. But in those cracks of her voice, I hear it.

Dad fidgets with the cuff of his shirtsleeve, his worry not so easily masked. He keeps swallowing, blinking, and wiping the beads of sweat from his brow. But even through his pain, he does most of the talking so Mom doesn't have to stay so strong. Every time her voice even threatens to hitch, he jumps in to her rescue, without so much as a stutter or stumble. They've always been like this. Where one falls, the other catches. Even when all else seems lost.

I squeeze Benny's hand. It twitches every now and then. They say this is normal, doesn't mean anything. I don't believe them. I *know* he hears me. He has to. I look at the clock. It's nearing the end of the school day, so I decide I should go. Just as I do, every little finger on his hand wraps tighter around mine. He's squeezing back. I gasp. This is *not* a reflex, a normal part of a coma; this is real. He wants me to stay, so I do.

"Hey, rascal," I whisper into his ear, "if you can hear me, you have to open your eyes." I wait for some sort of divine response, for minutes, an hour, but he doesn't squeeze again. It's enough, though. Enough for me to believe he'll make it, and *that* is everything.

A nurse, Shelly, glides through the door. She's petite with golden ringlets that spiral down to her waist, held back from her face by a flower barrette. She's the most delicate with Benny of everyone I've seen, smiling with sympathy at us, but not in the pitiful way. More like a hopeful kind of way.

"I've heard of people being in a coma for years and then one day, they just wake up," she says, adjusting Benny's levels on his monitors. The cords are intertwined between her fingers. She grabs Benny's hand, the one I let go of, and holds it for a moment. I watch how gently she wraps her fingers around his. For sixty seconds, her eyes are firm, steady on her watch as she counts his pulse. I watch the tube pushing air into his lungs, breathing for him. His lashes flutter the way they do when he's sleeping.

A few years back, I saw a segment on the morning show Dad watches about a woman who'd been in a coma for weeks. The day they pulled the plug, her body became restless—something known as the last rally. It's what happens when your body approaches death. But her movements didn't stop, and her words became louder. She was *not* dying, but instead, screaming to live, and from what I remember, asking for Mexican food.

I will not let Benny endure the last rally.

Shelly pats my shoulder on her way out. "Miracles happen every day."

I linger over him, inhale his scent that's lost in the starched hospital sheets. Brynn's right—he's a tiny doll, so fragile, he could break right here beneath these tubes and cords and casts. "If you don't wake up, I'm keeping your blankie."

The 22 SKATE CLUB sign splashes a sultry glow across the highway. Its deceptive beam makes me forget everything else, and that's okay with me. Bash, who sees me struggle to get through the door between gusts of snow-blowing wind, is sitting in the swivel chair, hunched over a thick textbook. I make a point not to acknowledge him when I eventually make my way in—on my own—and flop into the other vacant chair. Minutes pass before he cranes his neck in my direction. "Hey."

"What are you reading?" I ask.

He grunts. "Chemistry. It's *killing* me." His face suddenly deepens seven shades of red before turning back toward the book. "I'm sorry—that wasn't cool. I mean with your brother and everything."

"It's okay," I say. I glide the chair close and pat his arm

without thinking. Maybe because from the second I met this strange boy (who I thought I'd never, ever see again) at that horrific party, I've wanted to touch him. He looks at my hand on his shirt—the same plaid shirt I've seen him wear nearly every day here—and I quickly remove it. The room is quiet again.

"Chemistry is kind of my thing," I say. "If you need any help, you know."

"Obviously."

"What does *that* mean?"

"Some of us carry our hearts on our sleeves. You carry your brain."

I scoot away. "It's not a *bad* thing to be smart. I have a plan, a future."

He laughs. "Well good for *you*."

I bite my tongue, unsure as to why he's being so rude. "I just meant, if you need help, I've tutored before. That's all."

He's staring at the book, his hands now gripping the edges. They shake, nearly ripping the page straight out. I keep my distance, pull out my phone to pass the time, and scroll through the various feeds of nonsense that only distract me from life. The Christmas music streaming from the computer speakers breaks into a commercial, blaring louder than the music. Bash turns the knob to low and flings the hair out of his eyes like you'd see in one of those dumb hair commercials. And I can't look away. But I don't want him to notice me noticing him. Now his legs are jittery, his heel bouncing off the ground in rapid succession.

"What are you stuck on?" I ask, reluctant.

"Reactions and shit. I mean, not *shit,* but, you know."

"Let me see." I scoot my chair close enough for our elbows to touch—*zap* goes my heart—and lean over the thick book where all the words look so comfortably familiar. I inhale the smell of Bash and old ink as my eyes scan the page, and I feel him looking at me the same way I just looked at him, the same way he did the night of the party. I felt it then; I feel it now. The intensity grows—an electric spark that could ignite in the space between our hearts—but when I look up, he turns away. We play this game a few times, but I'm not sure who is the cat and who is the mouse in this scenario. I suppose we are both the mouse, afraid to make the first real move that doesn't include small talk or sarcasm. Especially because, no matter what becomes of us, of whatever this is, we still have to work in this tiny space together. So maybe it's best not to make any move.

Staring into the spine of the book, I make two columns in my head. I list the qualities he has going for him and against him. Here's what I've concluded: Judging by the way I can't actually focus on those two lists or on the numbers between these two pages (because he's touching me, and when his eyes catch mine, I feel like I could fall into him and melt away forever), I'd say that the list is null and void and I have no answer.

"You need to balance the equation," I tell him, finally looking up. Facts. I have those. And while the numbers don't exactly settle into my brain, seems like the most logical response in most situations.

He stares at me blankly.

I angle the book. "Here," I say, grabbing a pencil, "I was taught by an awesome teacher a few years ago and learned this method. Draw boxes around the chemical formulas and do an inventory of how many atoms you have of each, in a table format, both before the reaction and after. Makes it easier to see the work you need to do."

I ramble for a bit, get lost in chemistry's glorious rules, sketching all over his once-blank page. His eyes briefly watch what I'm writing but soon find their way back up to me. "Cool," he says with a sharp tone. "Thanks."

"Now you try." I hand him the pencil and hover as he slowly learns the process, erasing, and backpeddling the first few times. When he's finished, he holds the paper out in front of him, but he's not smiling. His brows are arched like he's looking for some sort of approval.

$$2H_2(g) + O_2(g) \rightarrow 2H_2O(l)$$

Impressed, I lean back and prop my hands behind my head. "You know how to do it; you just need someone to push you."

The excitement fades as he puts the paper in the book and claps it shut. "Yeah, well, my teacher might not agree. Or the principal. Or my guidance counselor. Or really anyone."

"You'll get it."

"I don't have any other choice."

Vinny pops his head in from beyond the office door. "Hey," he says, knocking the little white Santa hat ball to the side of his face.

"Hi," I say, waving.

"We saw your parents on the news today, and Evie wanted me to be sure and tell you she's sending a check to the hospital. We want to help with the cost of that specialist. It's not much, but—"

I stand from the chair and throw my arms around him, holding back tears. "Oh, my gosh! Thank you so much! My parents are going to be so happy!"

He pats my head the way a father might, then peels me off. "Glad I can help a bit." He looks to Bash. "We're about to open. Put your homework away and look festive. We've got a shitload of kids coming from some youth group in Indy."

"It's not Teams 4 Dreams, is it?" Bash asks, a wash of fright coloring him.

"How would I know?" Vinny points to the two Santa hats on the desk and motions for us to wear them. Bash is reluctant, but slides it over his dark hair with a look of annoyance.

I do the same, but with an enthusiastic smile. Vinny pats me on the back. "Thatta girl."

Bash slides his book into a ratty backpack that's buried beneath the desk and, as soon as Vinny leaves, pulls off the hat.

"He wants us to wear them," I say.

"You want to kiss ass, be my guest. I'm not sticking that hot, germ-infested sock on my head. It's gross, and with all the people who've worn it, unsanitary."

He tosses it aside, and I can't help but giggle. "What's with you and germs?"

"What do you mean?"

I slink back into the chair. "You wear the same dirty shirt every day, and I've seen your hand stuffed into those dirty skates. You don't make sense."

"*You* don't make sense."

I'm shaking my head at him, speechless. He wins.

A while later, a swarm of fifth graders from a basketball youth group, Teams 4 Dreams, busts through the door with their coach. Bash is friendly with the guy, explaining "Big L" is his guidance counselor at East Clifton and I immediately want to know more about this other side of him. After shushing my stream of questions about classes and why his guidance counselor swears so much, Bash grabs a roll of tickets, and together we work to get everyone in the right size skate and into the rink. I watch him from afar as he interacts with these kids not much younger than Brynn; he's gentle in guiding their feet inside the skates, helping them to the railing along the wall, and even cracks a joke or two that has the kids falling over with laughter. He's this whole other person I haven't seen since that party, a switch that just flipped on again, and I find myself looking at him a little harder, wondering the same thing I did when we met, *Who is this boy?*

With kids inundating the rink and arcade areas, Bash takes to the microphone to introduce the Hokey Pokey. I watch from the carpet because skates and I don't mix. Not since puberty made my body an uncoordinated, awkward mess and even before, my ability was mediocre, at best. He, on the other hand, glides across the shining floor, crouches low, one leg pushed out, and seamlessly stands tall to skate backward. It's like he's being transported to another place and time. As I look at the holes in that dirty shirt, I think maybe he is.

When it's time for the chicken dance, the lights dim and the disco flashes across the wide-open space. The sight of pulsing colors, red and blue mostly, catches me off guard and forces the breath out of me. Police sirens, the ambulance, the night Benny was hit, and every thought and feeling of that night rush to the surface before I can understand what is happening.

My stomach gurgles, chases a stream of food up into my throat. I barely make it to the tiny bathroom stall, where the door won't latch. I throw up everything I've eaten today. Toast with grape jelly. Noodles. That weird hamburger that really isn't hamburger at school. The sounds echo around me. There is no main door to this bathroom. Only a short hallway. I can hear everything beyond the toilet rim, so I know everyone can hear me. I hold my long hair back with one hand until I catch my breath and hang here, my knees on the cold, tiled floor, until everything settles.

"Birdie?" a voice says. "You okay?"

It's Bash. "I'm fine."

His skates roll up behind me. "You're not, though."

I look up at him, my eyes still watering. "You're in the *girls'* bathroom."

He scoffs. "Does it look like I care?"

I try to stand, but the moment I do, my legs buckle beneath me and my stomach pumps the very last bit of food out of me. Bash pushes forward to grab my hair so I can grip the toilet freely. "Did you eat something rank?"

"No."

"Pregnant?"

I flinch. "Ugh. Not even possible."

"Not possible, like you're not getting any, or not possible because you're getting some but know for sure you're not?"

"Not possible, like I might punch you in the throat."

He laughs, a sound that carries.

"The lights. They remind me of the accident." I move from the stall, turn on the faucet, and splash a handful of water into my mouth, using my shirt sleeve as a towel. He helps me find balance when I'm a little unsteady.

"You okay to walk back to the office where you can sit?" He's propping me up and, even on his skates that threaten to give way, is strong. A pillar. I let him help me into the office, to the chair I'd abandoned. He fills a cup of water from the cooler in the corner of the room and offers it to me.

"Drink," he says. "You're probably dehydrated now."

I look up at him and drink the water, fast. He stops me. "Sip, don't chug, or you'll puke again." His eyes on mine, connected by an invisible string, I drink slower. He plunges a hand into his pocket and tosses me a stick of gum. "This is more for my benefit than yours."

"Thanks," I say, embarrassed.

"Work the door. I'll do the rest. Go home if you need to."

"I'm okay, really."

"Well, do whatever then."

As he disappears behind the door, I realize he's not so tough, after all. He's just hiding, pretending. Maybe we all just hide, pretend to be things we're not, because it's too scary to let people see the real person, the bruises and scars, the broken heart, the gaping, restless soul that's too afraid to let anyone in. Because it might sting. And suddenly, without really knowing why he's flunking, what his mom does, or even his last name, I feel like I *know* him.

I sit here, alone, until the end of the night. Vinny splits early, so Bash does all the gum peeling and skate disinfecting. When he counts the drawer, he makes a point of counting out loud, holding up the bills high when he's finished, so I know he's not stealing. I pretend not to pay attention, my eyes pressed on next week's schedule.

"Done," he says grabbing his backpack from underneath my feet. He slings it over his shoulder, and we head outside, where he twists the door's lock before we separate to our cars. He doesn't ask how I'm feeling, if I'm okay again. It's like it never happened.

"Later," I say.

"Yep." He thrusts his body against his car door. It takes a few whops before the thing swings open. A bright light coats the interior of his car—*beater,* really—from the phone he's holding in his hand. The look of concern on his face pulls at me—not that I'm *trying* to stare—and as I watch him peel out, without thinking (something that is getting me in more and more trouble lately), I follow him, ignoring the little orange engine light that pops up on my dashboard.

Down Highway 22, past my house, Bash pulls into a small parking lot on the side of town where the police blotter stays busy, the trailers are lined like an army, and you'd think twice about leaving your car unlocked. He couldn't have seen me because I calculated the distance between us— distance (d) equals rate (r) times time (t) or $d = rt$, $r = d/t$, and $t = d/r$. So simple, it's ridiculous.

The wind knocks the branches of a nearby tree, casting deep shadows. I have this unsettled feeling in the pit of my stomach and decide if there's ever a good time to have a backup plan, now would be it. I pull out my phone, shield the light, and text Vi.

ME: CAN'T EXPLAIN, BUT IF U DON'T HEAR FROM ME, I'M NEAR 22 AND MULBERRY. BY THE DUMPSTER.

I don't stop and think about how badly worded the text is. When Bash moves, so do I. A generous space between us, I read the sign on the approaching overhang:

CLIFTON NURSING AND REHAB CENTER

He slides by the front desk where two nurses are deep in piles of paperwork, their eyes buried, ignoring those who enter—including me.

"She asked for you about an hour ago," one nurse says to him, without looking up. "Thinks it's your birthday."

He pauses, rubs his brows. "It will be. On the twenty-eighth."

"Happy early birthday, then. Whatcha wishin' for?"

"You already know."

I melt into the passing people, where the smells remind me of Benny's room, and follow Bash as he disappears into a patient's room that he quickly comes back out of, a long-stemmed flower now in hand, the little thief. I keep my head down, try not to let anyone see my face, and follow him to a room on the left where the hall is quiet. He pushes through a wooden door and walks inside. I stay back, my body clinging to the wall where I can see and hear, just barely. I don't know what I'm doing or why. I just feel like I *need* to.

Bash pumps what appears to be hand sanitizer into his palms and rubs. He then sits at this person's bedside. I can't really see who. He, or she, is buried between tubes and blankets and all the things I've seen on Benny. He bends down and kisses his or her forehead. I shift my position for a closer look. The person is still. A man passes behind me, so instead of alerting everyone to my creepiness, I pretend to text something on my phone, as if I'm *supposed* to be here. I glance in again, and Bash is pushing a spoon into the person's mouth. He's careful, gentle, just as he was with the kids. I'm lost in this sweet sight when a nurse—the same from the desk—walks up to me. Her name tag reads KIM MCDONNELL.

"Can I help you?" she asks, her voice booming.

I shake my head, my cheeks flushed. Bash jumps up from his chair. His angry face, the same as Mom's, moves toward me faster than I can think of an excuse as to *why* I'm here.

"What the hell are you doing here?" he growls, tugging at my arm.

"Is there a problem, Bash?" Nurse Kim asks.

I look at him with pleading eyes.

"Who's there?" the person, a woman, asks from the bed. "If it's Gloria, tell her I can't make it to work tomorrow."

"Bash?" the nurse asks again.

"Come in here," the woman calls, her voice raspy. "Ray? Did you drive all the way from Utah for Bash's birthday?"

Bash sighs. "It's not Ray or Gloria," Bash responds. He looks to the nurse. "No problem," he says. "Unfortunately, I know her."

The nurse looks me over with a condescending eye and tightens her lips. "Okay. Let me know when Ms. Camilla's done with her soup." The look on her face is telling me to go; the look on Bash's face is telling me to run. When the nurse leaves, it's just Bash and me standing under the glow of overhead lights.

"Sebastian?" the woman says. "Who's here?"

He looks like he wants to kill me, but instead walks me over to the woman in the bed where a small, nearby Christmas tree is lit. He leaves me at a distance, as though he doesn't want me too close to the ailing woman. She's frail, moving slowly. Her jaw is hollowed out like a skeleton, eyes sunken in and gray. Little wisps of hair poke through the colorful scarf wrapped around her head, but even in this state, her lips are adorned with magenta lipstick that rivals a blossoming poppy on a clear spring day.

"This is Birdie," he says. "From work."

Her eyes light up. *"Pássaro?"*

"Huh?"

"Portuguese for *bird*," Bash says. "Close enough, Ma," he tells her. "We're Brazilian—we speak Portuguese. You know, the language?"

The woman reaches for my hand, grabbing my sleeve instead. Bash panics, pumps hand sanitizer into my palm and quickly rubs it inside my lifeline's cradle in a frenzy before the woman's hand slides into mine, and now I see—he wants to keep the germs from *her*.

I stare into the woman's eyes, unsure of what to say. My stomach growls, filling the silence with more things to make me uncomfortable. "Is this your mom?" I ask him.

"Camilla," she interjects.

He nods.

"I . . . I didn't mean to interrupt," I say.

She pats my hand. "You're even more beautiful than Bash said."

My eyes expand toward him. He glares at his mom, then to me. "I didn't say *beautiful*, Ma. I said kind of tall with brown hair and glasses. And awkward and weird. That's it."

I bite my lip. *He's talking about me to people? What does this mean?*

The woman glares at Bash. "You said 'gloriously beautiful,' actually. And even if you didn't, I saw it on your face, heard it in your words. *She* makes you happy."

He's shaking his head, his face bright red. I want to look deeper, but as I sit here next to his mother, I can't seem to do it.

"You go to . . . school together?" she asks me, already forgetting that Bash said we work together.

"We work together," I repeat.

"Work, yes, I remember now. Forgive my memory. It's . . . not as strong as it used to be."

"It's okay." I smile, holding her glassy-eyed stare, grateful she doesn't recognize me from the news like everyone else.

"You're here for his birthday?"

"No. I didn't know it was his—"

Bash pulls me back toward the hall urgently. "It's not. Birdie has to go now, Ma."

"Nice to meet you," I say.

His boots nip at the backs of my heels. We round the corner, and he's so close, and my back is now smashed flat against the ivory wall and for a split second, it feels like he's about to kiss me—right here in this open hallway. "What the hell are you doing here?"

I stutter, look to the passing people—basically everywhere but in his eyes—as I try to find an actual reason, because the truth is, I don't have one. This is what Violet would call "my intuition." My eyes focus in on his lips, his really, *really* nice lips.

"Stay out of my shit."

I look away again.

"I'm sorry. But now that I've seen her, I know what you're going through, and—"

His eyes narrow into slits, and his voice is low and grumbled. "I don't want your apology or understanding. I don't want you anywhere near my ma, or my life. Just leave."

"For what it's worth," I say, my voice breaking, "she's lucky to have you." I push past him and hurry down the long hall, my head ducked low to my chest. The hopeful part of me wants him to chase me down and beg me to stay. The other part, the logical part, knows it won't happen—people don't really do that. Not in real life.

I find my car in the cold, dark night. The stars twinkle high above me. When I get closer, I realize my door is wide open, still twitching like a body that's not quite dead yet. Footsteps fade into the night, and even farther in the distance, sirens. My heart thuds loudly in my ears as I approach.

The spare change, $1.47, and Dad's outdated GPS are gone.

The outside feels scarier than the inside right now, so I quickly jump in, shut the door, and lock it. My eyes dart across the lot, but my hands are shaking too hard to do anything that matters. I could scream, maybe. Or go inside for help. But screaming might bring the thief back, and going inside, where Bash doesn't want me, isn't an option. I try to turn the ignition but that light—the orange one Sarge says is a lying, Commie-made POS—is still on, and this time the car won't start. I twist three more times, but the engine just rolls and coughs.

I pick up my phone to call Dad, to make sure Vi isn't gathering a search party in my honor, but the battery is dead, too. I'm frozen, paralyzed, just as I was in the garage the night of Benny's accident. I don't know what to do so I slink down into my seat and . . . wait.

I'm bundled up with my knees tucked up into me. Chilled and terrified, I guess I'm waiting for Mom and Dad to check the locator app that tells them where my phone is (and me), but it could be hours before they even begin to worry. I bury my head in my knees, close my eyes, and wait for something. A logical sign or a religious miracle, maybe. I don't even know anymore.

No more than a few minutes pass before a tap on the window scares me out of my seat. I scream, and pee a little. It's Bash. He's making this face like *what the hell?* so I roll the window down with the old-school manual handle that's missing a knob, and it feels like it's taking forever to get to the bottom.

"Stalking is a felony," he says. He's not smiling.

I try to make my teeth stop chattering. "Car won't start."

"Fuck. Why didn't you call someone?"

"Phone's dead."

"You have an answer for everything. Almost like you planned this."

I'd be offended if it didn't look so well thought out. "My car was broken into. I'm freaked out. I just want to go home—can you help me or not?"

He sighs, expelling a plume of cold air from his mouth and nostrils like smoke. "I want to say no but I don't really have a choice here, do I?"

"Unless you want to be a sucky person." My body is still convulsing from the cold.

"Still will be, even if I fix it." He sighs again, this time louder, more dramatic. "Hold on," he says. He walks to his car and pulls it as close to mine as possible, nearly scraping the paint. "Roll up your window," he says, opening the passenger door of my car, "and come here." He doesn't hold out a hand but instead nods with his head for me to get out of my car, so I do, my hands hidden in my sweater's sleeves. I bunch them up to my mouth and blow warm air, but it's just too cold. *Frigid* would describe it better. Or maybe even *arctic*.

He takes off his jacket and throws it at me. I don't get my hands out in time, so it falls to the ground and he just looks at me again with that *what the hell?* face, which is becoming his trademark, like I'm supposed to just *know* when he's about to toss things toward me. I lean down and pick it up, draping the warmth of leather over my shoulders. "Thanks. Should I call the police about my missing change and GPS?"

"No. Let's just get your car started and get you out of here." Now he's shivering but pretending not to. "You want your jacket back?" I ask, hoping he'll refuse.

"Nope." He lifts my car's hood and hooks up the jumper cables he pulled from his trunk. I don't mean to, but I'm hanging over him. To collect the warmth or just to be close to someone, maybe. "Get in my car," he orders. "Heat's on."

"Sure you don't want your jacket back? You look cold."

"Get in the damn car."

I roll my eyes, try to lift the handle, but it's stuck. Thrusting my body up against the cold metal like I watched him do, I finally get it to fling open. He doesn't look up, but a slight grin forms from the side of his mouth. The vent is blowing a hot, dry air that smells like bologna. The cracked cassette radio is broken, and random trash and empty cups are scattered throughout. Bear and fox sketches litter the space by my feet. I lean over and pick one up. This bear is lying on its back, gazing into the clouds; one billow is in the shape of another bear, a paler version, peering down. The closer I study, the more I see the bear in the grass is crying.

The drawing is heartbreakingly beautiful. I fold it up and stuff it inside my pocket because I don't know if I'll ever find something that describes exactly how I'm feeling more than this. Bash moves from the rusted hood to the inside of my car. I lean back and attempt to look like I've not taken a thing from this mess. A few minutes later, the engine revs and he flashes me a thumbs-up. He's quick to unhook the cables, slamming the hood shut. He motions for me to get out of his car.

I kick the door open and, as I start to take off his jacket, he stops me. "It's cold. Keep it."

"My car is on; I have heat now."

He shakes his head, arms crossed tight over his chest. "Bring it to work tomorrow."

I shuffle awkwardly. "Thanks. And . . . about me following you here—"

"Forget it."

"She's dying," I blurt out. The words escape before I can catch them.

He nods. "Fucking cancer."

"I can tell she's a fighter. I see where you get it from." I see a slight twinkle in his eyes I've never seen before. I've made him happy. Not in a joking way but for real this time. My cheeks warm against the cold night.

"I don't know what I'll do when she's gone," he says. "She's all I have."

The air is quiet between us; a string of hair blows into my mouth. "Bash . . . I . . . I hurt for you."

He kicks some loose gravel, in obvious discomfort at sharing this news, in hearing my compassion. "Hmm. Now you know something about me pretty much no one else does, so, whatever." He slams his body into his door until it swings open, and I hold my stare as I slide into the seat of my car. He's not looking at me, but he doesn't have to. He backs out of the spot, but before he goes, rolls down his window just enough for me to see his warm breath curl into the cool air.

"She likes you," he says. "Doesn't say that about anyone."

Before I can speak, he pulls away. I sit in this spot a few more minutes, unsure what to make of all of this. *Does he like me or doesn't he?* And I realize this is why I like science. Because factual answers are inevitable. But with love, feelings, sometimes they aren't.

The drive home feels carefree, my body relaxed, my mind somewhere in the stars. As I pull up the steep driveway, my stomach starts to twist itself back into knots. The feeling intensifies as I pass the SOLD sign. The uphill acceleration forces my mind back to the accident. Through the window, I see all the lights are on, all cars present. I don't want to get out of this garage, out of Bash's jacket. I walk into the corridor that leads into the kitchen where everyone is sitting with a pile of papers and a box of used tissues.

"What's going on?" I ask.

Dad walks toward me and grabs my arm. His eyes are wide and misty. "Benny crashed. They had to bring him back."

I throw my things on the table. "Why didn't anyone call

me? Come get me at work—anything? He squeezed my hand earlier—he was getting better!"

Mom's shielding her face from me, shaking her head, and Brynn is blowing a pile of snot into her own personal mound of Kleenex.

"We *tried* calling. It went right to voice mail. They're telling us he's brain-dead," Dad says.

"He's not!" Brynn cries. "He's gonna wake up, they just need to give him more time!" She tosses her tissue and runs to her room, where the door slams, and honestly, I wish I could do it, too.

My mouth hangs open, speechless, as the tears build and well in my eyes, splashing across my cheeks.

"*They're* killing him," Mom mumbles. "We need to move him."

"What about the specialist?" I say.

Mom moves to the sink, away from us. Dad's eyes follow her. Sarge takes a big sip of his coffee, then clears his throat. "He only takes a couple of cases a year and doesn't think Benny's is anything significant for his portfolio. In other words, he's a black-hearted jackass. Probably fought for Nazis."

"Then we'll find someone else—tonight," I say, tears welling. "We don't just give up! We FIGHT!"

Dad bows his head as Sarge stands to empty his cup at the sink by Mom. The lighting in here only exaggerates the emptiness of the Christmas tree, this horrible symbol of our lives without Benny here. "We're not giving up, Birdie," Dad says. "We just don't know what else to do. There isn't enough money to pay for Benny to stay on life support."

"My boss and his wife are sending money—he told me. And I bet after seeing us on the news, others will, too. We just need to buy time until we can find another specialist— someone who doesn't care about his *portfolio*." My eyes are swollen with fear and hope all at once.

Mom looks over to Dad, and he shrugs. Sarge walks over and squeezes me into his side. "Bess, order another CT scan." His voice is firm.

Mom laughs in a condescending way. "Dad," she says, "we can't just give an order with no reason. Insurance is already up our asses about all the charges. They're questioning the need for his catheter, for Christ's sake."

Sarge glances at me, then back to Mom, who looks about a hundred years older than she did a few weeks ago. "They want a reason? Make one up. He was sick before the accident. Use that. Exaggerate."

She tilts her head to the side. "What?"

"Tell them you forgot about a previous head injury or fever or something else believable and you want to make sure they didn't miss anything. If they do it and find nothing, it buys you another day or two to get a specialist. If they don't do it, threaten to sue their asses for causing his death. You might not win, but they'll want to avoid the suit."

Mom and Dad make eye contact as if Sarge might be onto something. I watch them, hope in my eyes, and there's that word again—*hope*. Can't seem to avoid it, and maybe that's a good thing. Mom nods, Dad does, too.

"I'll go now," Mom says, grabbing her keys. "Brooks, do an Internet search for the best neurosurgeons and doctors who specialize in head trauma. Look at clinical trials, alternative medicines—everything."

Dad nods, and as Mom tries to brush past, he pulls her into him and clings to her. At first, Mom doesn't hug back. Her arms hang free and limp. A few seconds in, her hands climb up Dad's burly arms. She buries her head deep in the collar of his shirt, and as Sarge and I watch, we hear her sniffles escape into the air. It's this feeling of watching a broken heart be put back together, stitch by stitch. Dad looks like he's never going to let her go and I'm almost hoping he won't. I don't know how we got here, how they became so broken and fragile the last couple years. But seeing them now, I feel there's a chance we can save Benny.

When Mom peels herself off, Dad wipes a smattering of tears from his face and moves down the hall to their bedroom. Sarge pats my shoulder with a firm grip. "See that?" he says. "They're just bent, not broken. We'll get it figured out. That's what family does."

Seeing them like this makes me think of new beginnings. Before all of this, they argued. A lot. Didn't know if they'd make it work or not. But now, things feel different; another shift in the formula. I pull the cardboard box of Christmas ornaments from the corner to unstring the tangled lights. My fingers carefully intertwine with the strands, pulling apart each layer. The big, yellow moon glares through the bay window where Brynn's handprints are forever etched. I can see down the driveway, onto the highway, and the irony hits me. But I refuse to be stuck. I unwrap the ceramic and glass bulbs from the old newspaper and twirl the lights from top to bottom, pushing them partway into the branches to hide the cord. I then step backward, about ten feet, noting any light or dark spots.

"You're such a nerd," Brynn says, spying from the hall. I ignore her and hang the ornaments. I start at the top and calculate how much space is needed between each one for a uniform appearance. She grabs a couple of old bulbs from when we were babies, her eyes looking mostly sad, but kind of happy. She remembers the good, too. And as she reaches to hang those memories, she looks at me and grins.

The world transitions into a new light. Not like the past hasn't happened, but more like it happened and we're still here, fighting. Not long after, Sarge shuts the TV off and helps, too. None of us talk, but I feel like we don't need words. We're almost finished when Dad walks out of the bedroom, laptop in hand. His eyes expand as he sees what we've done, and behind his eyes, there's gratitude.

"I was wondering who would cave first," he says.

Brynn points to me. "She couldn't help herself, Dad."

I shrug as Sarge puts an arm around my shoulder and squeezes. Dad's eyes light up as he presses the switch to illuminate the dying baby cypress in the most glorious of ways. "Thank you for this."

We stand in the glow of the tree—Nan's tree—for a while, soaking in its beauty. When we finally part ways, I fidget in the dark corner of my room for my phone charger that's stuck in an outlet. When the screen lights up, there are a few new texts.

VIOLET: I HOPE YOU'RE JOKING.

VIOLET: ARE YOU JOKING??

VIOLET: IF I DON'T HEAR FROM YOU IN FIVE MINUTES, I'M GETTING A SEARCH PARTY.

VIOLET: SPOKE TO YOUR DAD. SAID YOU'RE AT WORK, YA WEIRDO.

UNKNOWN: HOPE YOU'RE STAYING WARM. -BASH

I ignore Violet, biting my lip as I wrestle with a reply. My stomach drops. Five minutes pass. Type, delete, rewrite. Type, delete, rewrite. And finally, Send. Gulp.

ME: HOW'D YOU GET MY NUMBER?

BASH: STALKING.

I smile, touch my lips with the tip of my finger.

ME: YOU SAID THAT'S A FELONY ☺ BUT . . . THANKS AGAIN FOR THE HELP WITH MY CAR.

I pull out the bear drawing, unfold and smooth the edges, laying it on my bedside table propped up against the lamp so I can see it clearly. He doesn't write back; I don't expect him to, but I stare at his words for a long time, until I fall asleep sometime in the night. When I wake up, I'm still wearing his jacket, a smile beaming across my face.

And Chomperz pawing at my hair.

LESSON OF THE DAY: Some reactions take hundreds, maybe even thousands, of years, while others can happen in less than one second.

Like this infuriating variable I can't quite figure out.

Named Bash.

BASH

My guilty reflection in her glasses.

That's the only image in my mind; the way my eyes stare back at me, the way hers plead to know me. I couldn't sleep thinking about her. This isn't just dangerous, it's lethal. A chemical combination that shouldn't mix, ever. A parallel to Kyle's and my relationship.

Explosive, possibly deadly.

She left my jacket, scented with something floral and girly, at the rink. It was carefully nesting a chemistry printout with practice equations and answers, along with a note saying Vinny gave her a few days to be with her family. The scent overcomes me like a freakin' schoolgirl with a crush, and I know I've got to quit her in a bad, bad way. This *can't* be happening, I won't let it.

I heard what they're asking for, what they need to happen for the kid to live another day. So last night, when I'm closing the rink by myself, and the lights are off and everyone's gone, I sneak another twenty from the drawer and put it in an envelope. Vinny will survive, minus twenty, and if he doesn't, well, tough shit. I sniffed the damn jacket all night, until my nose nearly bled, and now know exactly what I have to do.

This morning my thoughts are tornados spinning up in

the air, spitting debris all over everyone, and pretty soon, they're going to crash down so hard, the impact alone will kill us both. So why do I have to feel these . . . things for her? She's not like Layla. She's different, good. When Ma goes, I'll have nothing, but Birdie still has her family. It should be whole, not broken. So if I can salvage one of our lives, it might as well be hers.

"Mr. Alvarez," Mrs. Pearlman says, snapping me from my daze, "care to join us here on earth?"

The class laughs. Sebastian A., class fuckup, never fails to impress. I've been doodling lovestruck bears, some ending in death with wooden stakes through the heart. So, as the beast of chemistry approaches, her tight curls frolicking across her cheeks, her squinty eyes narrowing down at me, I quickly hide my etchings with a cupped hand. "Sorry."

She reaches beneath my hand, pulls the sketch into view with a smirk, and leans down into my personal space so close I can see the coffee stains on her teeth. "If you could learn as well as you draw, you'd have graduated by now."

I back into my seat as far as I can, but her breath is a long string of air that bites into me. "Thanks?"

One hand on each side of the paper, she rips right down the center, breaking the two biggest bears apart, and the whole class erupts with a collective "ooohhh." She struts back to the front of the class like she really got me. I'll just draw another, no biggie. Everyone's eyes are on me like they can't look away—the freak who draws, flunks chem—what will he do next? Entertain us.

"Back to what I was saying," she continues. With my hand shielding my eyes, I ignore Kyle's deadpan stare and whatever he's trying to telepathically tell me, and manage to get through class without another incident.

"Next time, detention," Mrs. Pearlman says, grabbing my backpack strap as I'm pushing past. Nearly breaks the damn thing. I say nothing, grunt so she knows I heard, and find my locker. I'm two numbers in when Kyle pulls on the back of my collar as if I'm some little runt on the playground.

"I've been texting you," he says. "Why haven't you answered?"

I think back to the inbox full of messages I haven't read because, as I told him a million times, it uses up all my data, and I'm running low on minutes (and patience). These are just minor details to him.

"Sorry," I say, grabbing the next period's books. "What'd ya want?"

He leans in closer, too close, and whispers loudly in my ear. "I was snooping around Dad's office and saw an old picture of the Benz with one of those car ornaments on the front hood, and I can't remember if it was there on the night I drove it or not."

I want to throw my book at him, but I don't. "What does that have to do with anything?"

He gulps. "It's gone. Realized it when Steve sent me those pictures he took."

I sigh at him angrily, because he's more of an idiot than he or I realized, which I didn't think was possible. "So you're saying . . . we lost it."

His fingers comb through the slimy strands of his hair that keep falling out of place. "Yeah."

"Well that's it now, isn't it?"

He falls back against the metal and rubs his hands over his face. "I know," he sobs in a totally fake way. "I should've listened to you. I don't know what to do."

"I do." I slam my locker closed and think of the tiny bit of cloth I hid beneath my mattress. It's the only place I could think of. "I'm going to the station today. I can't hide this anymore—it's eating me up."

He shoves his arm against the metal to block me from moving. "No way, dude. I hear the boy is getting better. No point in going to jail if he's better, right? That was the deal."

I make a face like *what the hell?* Something Ma perfected and passed on to me, and duck under his cologne-drenched arm that's lacking any muscle at all, despite his constant weight-lifting. "They find that hood ornament, they'll connect it to your dad, then you. We're toast either way for not coming forward on our own. And the kid isn't better, FYI. They're about to pull the plug."

"How do you know?"

"I just . . . know."

His eyes are examining me too closely. Straight, no emotion.

"You're better than this, Kyle. It could all be over if you'd just trust me. You know I don't bullshit."

His expression flattens. "No."

"No?"

"Yeah," he says, "just . . . no."

Now I lean in, challenge him. "I'm not asking for permission."

He corners me in the space between where the lockers end and the wall begins. "Why do you care so much?"

I don't cower. "Why *don't* you care? It's a kid, man. How are you so effed in the head that his life means nothing to you?"

He holds his glare, twists his patchy mustache ends with the tips of his fingers. A thick, gold ring gleams against the bright hall lights. Eyebrows arched, he's breathing all over me. "What do you want?"

I scoff. "What?"

He reaches into his jean pocket, brings out a stack of fresh bills. "Five hundred? Seven fifty? If it's a grand, I'll have to go back to the bank."

I shove his hand as far away from me as possible. "Get out. I don't want your damn money."

He's chasing me like a farmer after his herd, but I ain't no naïve cow. I feel him over my shoulder, hot on my heels.

"You live in a shit trailer, no electricity, you're flunking out, not gonna graduate, and your mom's about to take her last breath." He waves the money in my face again, tempting me to take it. "Without my money, you have nothing but that old shirt and a pipe dream."

My eyes water with rage that begins in my toes and erupts, surging out through my fingers. I ball my fist but refrain from punching him (like he deserves). Face frozen in an angry grimace, I stand on the tips of my toes, chest puffed, look him directly in his nervous eyes.

"At least this old shirt and my pipe dream are *mine*. Take your stripper money and get out of my goddamned space before I do something that'll get us both kicked out."

After a tense moment, he releases a slight smile. He's nodding as if he's impressed with me. "Balls. That's what I've always liked about you, Bash. You're a *real* friend, willing to sacrifice in the name of righteousness. I respect that."

I release the breath I've been holding, pretend it's cigarette smoke and blow it right up his nostrils.

"But," he continues, "those balls and that sacrifice are gonna get us into trouble. You turn yourself in, and all roads lead back to me, to *my* family. I can't have that." He shakes his head, ticking between his two front teeth. I didn't hear the first bell, but now the final bell has rung and we're late for class.

"It won't," I promise. "All those beer cans, my drawings in the house, just leave 'em—they're not gonna look at you if they find those. Tell Skeevy Steve to back off. I'm going to the station. Call his bluff. Come on, Kyle. You've known me forever. You *have* to trust me."

He doesn't want to. I see it on his face. But he releases his body block anyway. "I'll think about it."

"Okay," I say. "We'll talk later."

"When?" he asks.

I sigh. "I don't know. Later."

181

He stuffs his sweaty hands into his pockets with a twitch and we part ways. Because of our block scheduling, I don't see him again the rest of the day, and when school gets out, I race to my car with only one thing on my mind: turn myself in before Kyle loses his shit. I figure if I get there, I can explain, and because I'm a man of my word, if I say I won't let Kyle take the fall, then I won't.

On a near empty tank of gas, I coax my puttering car into the trauma center lot. I'm on a stealth mission to blend into the crowd as I sneak onto the kid's floor without notice. I know it's the stupidest thing I could ever do (well, not *the* stupidest, but it's up there). I've got to see him in person, so I know for sure. I wonder if this is what Birdie felt like when she followed me to see Ma. A strange mix of nerves and butterflies—it sucks.

It's the holidays, so more people than normal seem to saturate the halls. Up the elevator, past the nurse's desk, I approach the kid's room just as a couple lingers nearby. There's a line drawn between them. His hand on her waist, she pulls away. I notice these things, contexts and hidden meanings you won't see unless you're looking. This I learned by studying some of the great artists before my time: Picasso, Monet, da Vinci—everyone who shook the norm, broke the rules, lived with a ferocious passion most can only dream of. I'll never be the next Jackson Pollock or Andy Warhol, but looking at these two and all their restrained heartbreak that is bleeding into these halls, I could grab my charcoal block, fall to the floor, and sketch what I *really* see, what they're hiding from everyone else—trust—and debut as the one and only me.

In this real-life drawing etched in black, I don't just see pain. Too obvious. Look deeper. Something more subtle. My eyes are magnets, stuck on them. Reminds me of all the times Ma tried to hang on to me before she was sick and I pulled away. I couldn't let her love me, couldn't let her hold me close. Because that meant letting her see how completely fucked-up I really am. It was easier to stand back, keep her at a safe distance so when I messed up as I often did, and still do, if she loved me less, it wouldn't hurt so bad—lessons I learned by watching her with my stepdad, I think.

I quickly move to the kid's door and walk quietly up to his bed. I sit on the edge of the chair that's nestled up against the bed's cool rail, pulling the wadded envelope from my pocket. His stillness startles me. He's so small, it's hard to believe *this* is what we hit—*this* is what we did to him.

"Hey, little buddy," I say, "got a favor to ask." I reach for a pen that's lying on the bedside table and quickly sketch a bear on the envelope's face. In the drawing, the bear is lying amidst a bed of lush forest greens that grow tall and wild like sunflowers. Tubes spill out of his thick fur from all directions while four foxes encircle, bleeding hearts seeping out of them. This isn't just any bear; he's special. Even though he's helpless, lifeless, in the middle of the wilderness where death looms over like a dark cloud, his eyes are wide open.

I tuck the envelope in between the kid's free fingers. They're cold like Ma's. "Time to wake up."

"Can I help you?" a voice asks, startling me upright. I wipe a tear from my eye, shove the pen in my back pocket.

"No."

She studies me as I fumble to get out the door. "Only family allowed in here."

The lights are bright, hot, on me. Putting my head down, I push past the woman in animal-print scrubs. "Saw the story on the news. Sad. I hope he pulls through."

"Excuse me," she says, tugging at my jacket. Her grip is tight. "You don't have a name tag. You shouldn't be up here at all."

We make brief eye contact, a silent contract, and I take a huge gulp. "Stay right here." She rushes in the other direction, toward the stairs, toward the couple—his parents, probably—

and I make a break for it. I sprint down the hall, through a slew of distracted doctors and nurses, nearly tripping on a crash cart that's sitting right here in the middle of the hallway (trying to tell me something, fate?). My finger punches the elevator button repeatedly, and the doors come together just as the nurse approaches the desk nearby. With only a slit of space between us, our eyes meet again, and this time, my face draws itself in her head—a mug shot. My heart is racing; I'm sweating, soaking through my shirt.

Outside I don't even notice the cold, the flurries sticking to my skin and hair. Three thrashes against the car door, and it swings open. I pull out of the lot too fast, the wheels spinning beneath me on the paved lot. I could argue this is a sign that I'm not ready to turn myself in like I thought. Truth is, maybe I'm not as good as I want to be. Maybe Ma failed. Maybe I'm everything the old stepdad said I would be, everything I say Kyle is.

Everything Birdie should stay away from.

birdie

Time, an unfeeling measure of our pain, is something I've lost track of.

Dad's phone has been permanently stitched to his ear, making conversation *not* about Benny impossible. He makes call after call, pleads with this new neurosurgeon in Chicago, Dr. Stein. Dad wants him to take on Benny's case, but again, there's been resistance. No one believes Benny can be saved except for us. Mom spends endless hours at Benny's side. She's become a ghost, a memory of the woman I once knew. To say I miss her would be an understatement. But this isn't about me.

Despite giving them fake reasons, Mom says Doctors Morrow and Schwartz won't do another CT scan until, or unless, we have something called "just cause," which is a fancy way of saying they want more proof than her word. They're short with us, fed up. *We're* wasting *their* time. Benny's wasting a perfectly good room that could be used for another. Dad's tried to reason with them, too. But time is not our side. Time is our enemy, waging a war we can't win.

The hospital and doctors were patient in the beginning when they appeared to understand, to care, about our circumstances. But now, with insurance pounding on their backs and news crews and random people in and out of

Benny's (now infamous) room, they want us out. We're "a distraction to all other patients on this floor."

They repeat the same things. "Does he have a history of head injuries or not? We want to help Benedict the best we can, but we can't do that if you're not telling us the whole story."

Mom starts to sob as the lie unravels. "I just want you to fix him. You can't take him off the ventilator yet. Give him more time to show you he'll wake up. He *WILL* wake up."

"Believe me, Mrs. Paxton," Dr. Morrow says, "I hear you. I've got kids of my own, and if I were in your shoes, I'd be making the same plea. But we have to diagnose and treat based on facts. Your son is in a persistent vegetative state. He is not aware of his surroundings. He is legally brain-dead."

"NO! He squeezed my hand!" I pipe up angrily. "I felt it!"

Dr. Morrow looks to Dr. Schwartz with a sigh of aggravation as he wipes the deepening creases in his forehead. "We've said it before. He's incapable of voluntary movement. On the off chance he progresses to wakefulness, it is our opinion, and the opinion of the doctors who have examined him here, he will *never* have a higher brain function—*IF* he wakes at all. There was too much damage and swelling, even with the steroids and drainage. It's irreversible. Based on what we've seen, we don't think he will be able to wake up or even breathe on his own if he did. It's in his, and your, best interest, to start thinking about organ donation and funeral arrangements." He folds the chart beneath his arm. "I'm sorry. Really, I am."

Mom cups her hand over her mouth to stop the cries that fight through. She's shaking her head, flinging the tears from her lashes while Dad rubs his hand on her shoulder, and we all sit in this room where the walls smother us until we threaten to stop breathing altogether. I dig through the files in my brain for something factual, something we can hold on to, shove in their condescending faces. But I'm empty—they're all . . . empty.

"Go ahead and take him out of the coma," a rasped voice says from the doorway. A short, thin man with smooth dark skin, and a thick, graying beard pokes his head inside. He's dressed in a navy suit donned with a silken reindeer tie. "See if he survives. I've seen it happen."

"Excuse me?" Dr. Morrow says. "Who are you?"

The man saunters up to Benny's bed and pulls a stick-shaped light from his top pocket. "Dr. Frederick Stein, director of the Pituitary Tumor and Neuroendocrine Program at the University of Illinois and chief neurosurgeon at the University of Chicago Medical Center." He emphasizes his titles in a way that says, *Shut up and listen.*

Doctors Morrow and Schwartz trade glances, then to Dr. Stein. "Okay. What are you doing here?"

He turns to us, ignoring the two doctors, and holds his hand out toward Dad. "You must be Mr. Paxton." Mom sobs louder into her hand.

"I can't believe it. You're here. You're really here," Dad says, tears in his eyes.

My eyes meet Brynn's. Our expressions mirror images of hope and wonderment and all the things this very room has lacked for days. I wish Sarge were here, instead of at a doctor's appointment of his own, so his face could do the same.

Dr. Morrow reaches for a shake, but Dr. Stein turns away again. He shines the stick light into Benny's eyes and quickly pulls back with a confident kind of smirk. "Ah-ha! A flicker!"

"Excuse me?" Dr. Schwartz says. He fidgets, holding Benny's file close to his body as if the walls are suffocating *him* now.

Dr. Stein continues checking Benny's vitals while the two doctors move in closer to watch his unorthodox approach—lifting Benny's arm and letting it fall, tapping the skin on his forehead, and tugging on his ears.

"You can't see it unless you're trained to," Dr. Stein says, softly, "but there's a flicker of light in the very back of his cornea. He's *not* gone, he's right here, aren't you, Benedict?" He tucks the sheets into Benny's sides and reaches for the chart that's now buried under Dr. Morrow's arm. "May I?" He doesn't wait for an answer before sorting through the chart's notables.

Dr. Morrow is silent for the first time since we've been here. Dr. Stein flips page after page as if he's looking for something specific. A diagnosis or verbiage, maybe. We aren't really sure what to make of him, or anything else that's happening, so we just hold our collective breaths and watch. His finger traces the paragraphs with urgency, and he stops suddenly. "There's your proof. Schedule another CT scan and a full blood workup. NOW."

The two doctors appear confused as they move in to see what Dr. Stein sees inside the file, but he quickly flips it shut.

"We've already done the testing," Dr. Schwartz argues. "There's been no change, and in our opinion, no reason to continue."

Dr. Stein looks at us again, satisfaction drenching his face. "In 1998, a boy, similar in size, weight, and age, was struck by a pickup that was driving eighty miles per hour on a county road. Doctors pronounced him brain-dead and called for euthanasia, but instead of giving up, the parents called me. The boy is top of his class now."

Dr. Schwartz chimes in, his bushy mustache clinging to his lips. "With all due respect, that's a unique incident. Not likely to happen again."

"In 2007," Dr. Stein continues, "a three-year-old girl's skull was nearly crushed by a piece of farm machinery. Doctors gave up on her. I didn't. She asked Santa for a skateboard this year."

Mom looks to Dad, and I can feel the room swelling with a kind of hope we hadn't felt before. The cracks of my heart pulse, try to knit themselves back together.

"I'm not saying miracles *don't* happen," Dr. Schwartz says, "I just mean—"

"In 1948," Dr. Stein says, his voice more serious as he grabs ahold of Benny's hand, "a two-year-old boy stood behind his father's car and, without the driver's knowledge, was run over, nearly flattened, and just like Benny, it was said he would never open his eyes again. We didn't have specialists as we do today. My baby brother didn't make it because they gave up on him. That's when I decided to devote my life to saving as many people as you're willing to throw away."

The room falls silent. Dr. Morrow clears his throat awkwardly. "Uh, I'll order the scan and, uh, blood work. One more try couldn't hurt, I suppose. But insurance won't—"

"Don't you worry about that part," Dr. Stein interrupts. "It will be taken care of."

Dr. Morrow nods, bows his head as he and a speechless Dr. Schwartz leave. They avoid eye contact with any of us, because they know—they have to know—they haven't done everything they could or we wouldn't be hearing this conversation about a "flicker."

Dr. Stein pats Benny's hand once more, then trails toward the doorway.

"I can't thank you enough," Mom says, wiping her nose with a crumbled up tissue. "This is everything to us."

"Don't thank me yet," he says. "I don't make promises, but I *do* make sure no metaphorical stone is left unturned, by the grace of my brother, may he rest in peace. Take comfort in that. I'll get back to you in a bit."

Dad wraps his arm around Mom and lets her cry into him as Dr. Stein's shadow fades around the corner. "There's still hope, Bess," Dad says into her ear. "There's still hope." I hang back in the chair against the wall and watch their two hearts collide. Mom isn't fighting it for once. She's letting it happen—the way it *should* be. By the way Mom and Dad never seemed to fall into each other in this particular way before, I always thought love was square. Perpendicular angles meeting at just the right points, so no matter which way you turn the shape, it's the exact same. They've been stuck inside these angles for as long as I can remember. Not in motion, more like running in place. But what I'm learning is, maybe I'm wrong. Maybe love—*their* love—isn't a perfectly angled mass, and maybe love isn't meant to be. Maybe it's flexible, wavering with ebbs and flows, more like a circle or oval or even a heart, and they've got to find a way to navigate through it without losing sight of the beginning point or the end. Watching them, my mind drifts to Bash.

I haven't heard from him in days.

"Where'd that come from?" I ask, noticing an envelope with a bear drawn on the front. It's nestled in between a plush teddy bear and a fruit basket on Benny's bedside table.

Mom sniffles. "I found it clutched in Benny's hand when we got back from the cafeteria. The nurse said a young boy left it, but he ran out when she asked who he was. Weird, right?"

I reach for the envelope, trace the drawing with my fingertip. "What . . . was in it?"

"Twenty dollars," she says. "Donations are trickling in, but every little bit counts. I wish I knew who left it so I can thank him."

I shouldn't be smiling, blushing so many shades of crimson. Heat prickles my cheeks. I hold the envelope tight, close to my heart. *So he does like me,* I think. Maybe my heart isn't so square after all.

A while later, Dr. Stein enters the room slowly, with a heavy, almost weighted frown on his face. His head drags. After a long, breathy sigh, he folds the chart down to his waist. We hang on to the air as if it were a dangling cord that could float us to safety. Five seconds pass. Ten. Nearly fifteen before he looks up with a stifled smile.

"So?" Mom says, standing from her chair. Dad stands, too. And for the hell of it, I stand with them.

He tells us about all the fluid that's gone down, the blood pressure that's in a normal range, but most of all, more important than anything else I hear, that brain activity has been detected, "however vague."

"Benny is a near perfect candidate for me," he adds.

"So what's the next course of action?" Dad asks, gripping Mom's hand and puffing out his chest. In this light, he looks kind of like a superhero, and the way he's remained strong and steadfast even when we've all crumbled around him, I suppose he is.

Mom stops crying long enough to look up from the floor tiles. It's obvious she had been awaiting more bad news, because it's all we've heard for weeks now. That thing, hope, is hard to keep when everyone says our situation is hope*less*. My heart clangs loud in the quiet room, competing with the noisy beeps that pour from Benny's machine entourage.

"The next part isn't going to be easy. We have to bring him out of the coma to see if he can survive without the machines," he says.

The words kind of fade in and out as I think back to the moment everything changed. My hands still remember the movements of unhinging the stroller. I watch through a fuzzy cloud of semifocused lenses while Dr. Stein explains lowering the pain medicines' dosage little by little, until he either wakes or he doesn't.

When all is said and done, Dr. Stein pauses in the doorway, beside me. I can smell his cologne wafting under the vents. It's sweet like coconuts and reminds me of the vacation we took to Florida many years ago.

"If you're religious at all, pray," he says. "If you're not, drink. Hard liquor is best."

Thanksgiving, a holiday usually spent stuffing our faces with all of Nan's butter-laden recipes, is spent at Benny's bedside this year. No fine china passed down from Nan's Gran

Gran. Instead, we eat off foam trays that section our preportioned hospital turkey and gravy, which tastes more like rubber and literal nothingness than, say, food. It comes with a side of starchy mashed potatoes with liquids not fully incorporated into the flakes, and the crème de la crème—cranberries floating in some sort of strawberry Jell-O. Less than a stellar way to give thanks, but as Dad puts it, "We give thanks for every day of Benny's life. And especially the lives of everyone involved in the making of this chocolate pecan pie I bought from the bakery."

A few days later, after the "feast" has settled, I tiptoe into the rink, crouching low under the front window, like a stealth animal on the hunt, and sneak up behind Bash. Deeply invested in a textbook, he doesn't flinch.

"Even when you're *trying* to be quiet, you're loud as shit," he says. "Plus, I have eyes. I saw the door open."

I say nothing and push the textbook away to make room for the yellow cupcake I place in front of him. It's covered in pink frosting and rainbow sprinkles—things I know will bug him. A single candle stands tall in the middle, unlit.

"What's this?" he drops his pencil.

"Happy birthday!"

He pushes the cupcake away without so much as a "you remembered!" or "that was SO nice of you!" and draws his textbook near. "What's so happy about it?"

I scrape a dollop of frosting from the icing's peak with my finger and smear it on the tip of his nose.

He slowly cranes his neck up to meet my eyes. I smile a big, cheesy smile. He wants to look glum, upset I thought of him, but after a few seconds, he smiles back.

"Light it," I tell him, pointing to the candle.

"Nah, I'm good."

I swipe another lump of frosting and paint it in one flat line across his forehead. "LIGHT IT!"

With an aggravated sigh, he digs deep into his pocket,

revealing a blue Bic lighter in one palm. He lights the candle then wipes the frosting from his face with one finger. "You're really not very nice, you know."

"Thanks! No one ever says that about me!" I hold my grin while the flame dances between us, flickering shadows across his face.

He devours the sight of the burning stick, seemingly indifferent. "Please don't sing."

"Fine. Make a wish."

He closes his eyes, his long, dark lashes at rest, and blows the flame until it disappears into the air. I feel his breath, warm, across my face.

"I won't ask what you wished for, but I had my friend Violet look up your horoscope, and she says today is a good day for surprises so—SURPRISE! See? Horoscopes are real if you read them first, then *make* them happen."

He chuckles, turns back to his work. "I'd rather forget I'm legal now, though."

With frosting still on my fingertips, I fall into the chair next to him and lick them clean. "Why? You get to vote and serve our country and get into R-rated movies without a guardian and . . . that's it. I'm out of good news."

Silent, he moves his swivel chair close to me, pats my leg the way Sarge might—*pat pat pat*—except Sarge doesn't send shockwaves through my spine the way Bash does. He's reluctant to touch me, though. His nails barely scrape the top of my jeans, which only makes me want him to press a little harder. He's delicate about it. I bury my hands in my lap, anticipating. Our eyes meet again. His hand rests there now, unmoving. But now that the flame is gone, I see the pain swimming around in his stare. I know what he wished for, for his mom to get better. I wished for it, for him, too.

Christmas lights have been strung around the small room. The ones still working beam an angelic glow across the front

193

desk. Garlands and candy canes line the room, and somehow, a scent of pine permeates through the candle's burnt wick.

I sigh. "You know . . . I thought when my nan died, Christmas couldn't get any worse," I break the silence. "She was the glue that held us all together. Held *me* together. We sort of broke apart when she died last year. We hadn't even put ourselves back together yet . . . Then this thing happened—this *monumental* thing."

"You mean the accident?"

"I mean *you*." I smile. That butterfly feeling flutters around in my stomach, and I wonder if he feels it, too. I don't know what makes me say it. Maybe I just want something real, something I can understand.

He clears his throat, removing his hand. "You think *I'm* some monumental thing in your life?"

"More like . . . a nice distraction."

He clears his throat. "You and your nan must've been close."

"We were." I smile sadly. "I've been thinking about her a lot lately because of—well, because. She tried to teach me how to use my heart more and my brain less, but I always fought her on it. I hope I haven't let her down too much . . ." My words fade and I blot a stray tear, smearing the mascara smudge across my fingers. Bash chews on his lip, biting the skin; his face is sullen and flat, but I feel him look at me, then away again, that same old game we continue to play with one another without skipping a beat. I sink into the chair and melt into the smoky fabric just as he jumps from his. He tugs on my wrist and pulls me up, too.

"Come with me," he says. And I do.

He leads me around the vacant rink that echoes our every movement. With no one here, it feels like an abandoned playground we have all to ourselves, which is both exhilarating and totally creepy at the same time. Around the corner, he ducks into the room where all the skates are lined in rows along slats bolted to the wall. We weave through them, this maze of wheels and wonder, to the very back door I've never opened before. He swings it open and urges me to go down a set of steep stairs to a nearly black basement.

"No way. I'm the brains, man," I smile. "The pretty one always dies first." I lower my voice to a whisper and dig my fingers into his jacket. "I mean you; you go."

"Yeah, I get it." He jogs down the stairwell that feels never ending into what feels like a pit of darkness. I slowly follow, gripping the railing as if my life depends on it (maybe it does). When he flicks the light, it's a dim, yellow shade, calming like a nightlight. I can see where I'm going now and move fast behind him. We walk through stacks of broken-down cardboard boxes, old skates—some with wheels, some without—and various other (what I would call) trash, to a metal exit door he props open with a large, gray stone pulled from just outside.

"What are we doing?" I ask. "It's almost time to open."

He pulls something the thickness of a pencil, the length of a lollipop stick, from his pocket, purses it between his lips, and lights the end with that blue Bic lighter. He inhales, long and slow, releases a puff of smoke in my face before placing it between my fingers. "Here's to fighting the good fight."

Somehow, the small, hand-twisted cigarette thing is now in *my* hand. His eyes squint to avoid the smoke cloud that's moving between us, and I'm not sure what I'm supposed to do. Unlike everyone at school, I only know it's marijuana from the D.A.R.E. program; never been the girl invited to the parties where it was everywhere or the girl who *knows* a guy who *knows* a girl who has it. I wouldn't have even known what it looks like, smells like, if it weren't for this moment right now. And to be honest, it's nothing like I imagined. I hold the paper stick like a pencil and sniff it. His eyes stare through the open door's slit, into the open lot that's directly behind us.

"I don't want to get in trouble," I say, my eyes wide.

"If it makes you feel any better, I *never* get high anymore. I'm doing this for you."

The cold air floats in from the cracked door. "Thanks? Um, but no thanks."

He plucks the stick from my fingers, inhales again, holds the drug in his lungs while he opens his mouth to speak. This time, he blows the smoke out the side of his mouth. "Just want you to keep that, you know, happy feeling, or whatever."

There's a long silence between us. We're both shifting, shuffling our bodies together to keep warm, but in a way that's not so obviously obvious. His eyes find me, anchor me into the floor. My heart kind of drops. I don't want it to—I hate it, actually—but it falls straight to my feet. He inches closer, the specks of gold in his eyes clearer to me now. My hand is tucked in his arm to hold my balance, really just to hold him at all. I smell his dirty shirt beneath the smoke. It comforts me.

"Why?" I ask.

"Why?"

"Yeah. Why do you want me to 'keep that happy feeling or whatever'?"

"Because it's nice."

"Me being happy is nice?" I joke. "Okay."

"Maybe it's not. Shit. I don't know." He shifts his stare to the outside.

The sound of the gusty wind is all I hear. It whistles and bends and sways, a song written just for us. I decide he's right. Maybe I need to let go for once in my perfect life— more than just sneaking out to some lame party—more than anything even I can rationalize. So I lean my head in toward his. My lips are soft and open, and with all his attention focused on my next move, I pinch the cigarette and pull it from his mouth with mine—something I saw his ex do to him at that "rager." He probably didn't know I saw him sitting with her before he approached me, but I did. Couldn't take my eyes off of him, actually. But when he stood, I quickly retreated to the couch.

My mouth wraps around the paper. Our eyes sync and I inhale, slow, like I've done this a million times before. The corners of his mouth are upturned. It pleases him to see me break character, and it's the same face he first made at me when we spoke at the party. I couldn't say it, but it got me then, it gets me now.

Secretly, breaking character pleases me, too. The only problem? The breath I take is too big, not that I know the right way to do this, and I instantly choke, losing all sexy credentials fast.

"That was ambitious." He laughs.

I try to stifle the cough, gurgling and clearing my throat. When everything settles, he offers me another puff. "Nope. I'm good, thanks."

"My ex used to do that."

"What—get high?"

"Pull it from my lips."

"Oh," I say, knowing this already. "Then I take it back."

"No." He's still smiling, those lips turned all the way up as far as they can go. "I like it."

I already know this, too.

He drops the stick to the floor and puts the lit end out with the tip of his boot, then crosses his arms as he leans his back against the door's frame to watch the clouds. My fingers fall from the crook of his elbow and hang free. I can't pretend we didn't have a moment just now. My blood is warm, and I'm overly aware of it flowing through every inch of me. I wish he would kiss me. *Please, kiss me. Pull me by the waist and press your lips to mine.* It's everything he probably wanted to do at the party and everything I didn't realize I wanted him to do. Until now.

"So how often do you do that?" I ask, awkwardly filling the quiet.

"Do what?"

"The weed."

He laughs. "I don't think I've done"—he uses his fingers to make air quotes—"*the weed* in, like, a year."

"You just happen to have it today, of all days?"

He bows his head, plunging his hands into his pockets. "Cleaned out Ma's dresser drawer. She used to smoke for the pain."

I scoot closer, enough to make him nervous. My fingers climb up between his elbow and chest and gently grab ahold of his arm. He scrunches his body up against the door frame but his eyes, and every bit of gold, are locked into mine.

"Thanks for the money you left at the hospital . . . ," I say.

He swallows and loses focus. "Don't know what you're talking about."

I nod. "Must've been someone else who draws bears."

He shrugs, keeps his head away from me now.

"Seriously," I say, "thank you."

"It was like, literally, nothing. A fraction of nothing."

"I *do* like fractions." I slide my hand down his arm, slow, where it lands in the center of his hand. Our fingers interlock. The contact pulses a jolt through my whole body, and by the way he's looking at me, his, too.

No more thinking, Birdie. I lean in with my lips puckered. My voice softens to a wisp of air into his ear. "It was *everything*."

He's biting his lip, hard. The closer I get, I notice, the more he backs away. I suddenly feel my cheeks flush. I back away, too. *What am I doing?*

"You hungry?" He kicks the rock out of place and lets the door slam shut, breaking the space between us as fast as he possibly can. A thunderous boom echoes, and while I'm watching the vibrations settle, he's already on his way back up the stairs without me. I follow him to the food court, which is really just another tiny booth stuffed with random snack foods and the liquid cheese they use for pretzels and chips, and linger while he hops behind the counter. He tosses me a bag of chips and a candy bar while opening a bottle of pop.

"Is this okay?" I ask. "I mean, does Vinny care if we do this?"

His mouth is stuffed full of junk as he sits on top of the fractured vinyl table top, his legs dangling. "Who cares? Stop thinking. Good things are happening, Birdie. Revel in the now and get out of that beautiful head."

I'm blushing again, every rosy color of the spectrum. "So you *do* think I'm pretty."

"No," he says, stern. "Not pretty—beautiful. There's a difference."

I toss back a handful of chips and try not to overthink how intriguingly complicated this boy is, because if I do, all those files will combust. "Oh, yeah? Do tell."

"Pretty is this sort of mediocre idea people hold on to because they can't decide if something's amazing or not. When you're pretty, it's like saying you're a flower or a doll or a fluffy-ass cat. There's no real feeling behind it. But when you're beautiful—*my God,* and you are, and don't even know it—it's like seeing a sunrise for the first time. The way the colors streak the sky with a kind of hope you won't feel any other part of the day. You, Birdie, *are* that hope."

I'm midchew and. I. Just. Stop. *Whhaaaat?*

He's not moving. I finally crunch down on the final bits trapped between my teeth when he jumps up and pulls me by the arm into the skate room. "Skates—what size?"

"Seven, but I don't skate."

He looks me over. "Your feet look bigger than that."

I purse my lips and begin to counter that argument, but

once he tosses a pair at me, he disappears into the DJ room. The lights pop on and paint the rink in bold colors, only this time, there is no disco ball to remind me of the red and blue lights I so desperately want to forget. With a loud stream of feedback over the speaker, his voice bounces from wall to wall. "Now, we skate."

He glides onto the floor, urging me on with a nod of his head. I tie up the last lace and wobble my way out as if I've just been given legs. My arms are spread out in front of me, my knees are shaking, and I feel so completely out of control. I hate it, but I also like it. He smirks as he continues speeding in circles past me to show off his talent.

"Could you help me?" I yell.

"No!" he yells back, laughing to himself. "Life is about learning to help *yourself*."

I mumble something under my breath like *I hate you* but manage to grab ahold of the side rail and pull myself along. Just as I get my footing, Bash pushes past me, knocking me flat on my back. Humiliated, I pull myself up, inch to the seated area, and toss my skates to the floor. My eyes sting with tears, and that nagging, sour pain that bites the back of my throat, returns.

"What are you doing?" he asks, skidding to a stop in front of me.

"You're an ass. There are times I think maybe you're not, but no—you really are."

"Took you long enough to figure it out. But really, are you okay?"

"No." Sore and humbled, I toss the skates over the counter, not paying attention to where they land. My mood is definitely not still "happy or whatever."

"But it's time to unlock the doors," I grunt.

He looks at the clock—"Shit"—and does the same with his skates, letting them land somewhere in skate oblivion for Dave to handle when he arrives. Near the front, he unlocks the door where people are waiting beneath the awning in a line that wraps around the back bend.

"Weird crowd for a Friday afternoon," I whisper.

"Discounted rate," he says. "Price goes up after five, remember?"

"They're cheap*skates*," I say with a smirk. I can tell he's trying not to laugh, but the corners of his lips lift anyway.

He pulls a ticket stub off the roll and hands it to an older lady who's exploded through the door. By the way she's aged, I estimate her to be in her sixties. "How's it going, Gina?" he asks.

She lays her hand on the counter and sighs. "I woke up today and realized it's been seven years since I lost Hugh. SEVEN. Where does the time go? I think I've been in a daze."

She digs around in her purse and hands him a couple dollars, but he pushes them back to her. She looks surprised. "Is it more than that? Because I only brought—"

He shakes his head. "No, no. On the house today. In honor of Hugh."

She looks to me, then to Bash with a grin. "Thanks, doll. Who's the new girl?"

"No one," he says. I shoot lasers through the side of his face with my eyes.

"What's your name, honey?" she asks me.

My eyes are still on Bash. "Birdie."

"Don't sweat it. Hugh never introduced me, either. Must be love." She winks, moving into the main room to lace up the skates she brought with her. All the regulars bring their own.

"What's with you?" I ask him. "Everything was fine and then, I don't know." He's fidgeting with the ticket roll.

The doors burst open again, sending a polar wind through the office. A couple comes through, hand in hand. They've got their own skates, too, slung over each shoulder; hers pink, his brown. The man, bald in all the weird places, slides his hand beneath the glass window to shake Bash's.

"Hey, man!" Bash says. "Haven't seen you in a couple."

"Sebastian," the man says, his smile turning the corners of his mustache up. "We were in the Bahamas for our anniversary." Bash purses his lips, makes an *oooh* sound. "Don't know why we ever came back to this shit weather."

The woman lets go of his hand, slaps him on the arm. "Skip."

"What?" He winks at me. And then there's a long silence like they're waiting on Bash to say something about me. He doesn't.

"Let me guess," Bash says. "Janie *likes* the shit weather."

The three of them laugh like they're sharing some inside joke. The woman is nodding and the man is, too. "You know us too well. So who's this?" They're pointing at me like I can't answer for myself.

Before Bash can talk, I do. "No one." *Beat him at his own game,* I think. He's not smiling, though.

There's an awkward silence before the man speaks again. "So . . . you doing okay?"

"Still working in this dump, so . . . what does that tell ya?"

The man pulls his wallet from his back pocket and fumbles through the bills. He hands Bash enough money to cover another hundred skaters. Bash pushes it away. "It's way too much."

The man insists, handing it back, "No," he says, "I counted. It's *exactly* right. Merry Christmas."

Bash's face is red as he folds the change into his pocket. "Merry Christmas."

With a quick swivel of the chair, he jumps up and moves to the other side of the room to thumb through a thick stack of papers. I can tell he doesn't want me to say anything, so I don't.

"Be right back," he says.

"You said that the other night. Then you ditched me."

I can't see his face, but I think I hear him laugh to himself. "Things are different now, Couch Girl. Just going to the bathroom. Relax."

When he leaves, I move to the chemistry book lying face up on the desk next to the uneaten cupcake. Being the curious nib-nose I am, I flip through it. Standard chemistry—something I took my *freshman* year. I get lost in the text, unaware of the faces staring at me through the window.

Tap tap tap.

I move my eyes up to the glass, where I see something I'm not expecting—Brynn. My baby sister, with raccoon eyes and bloodred lipstick, stares back at me. Her hair is in spiral curls, and judging by the three cup sizes added, she has on Mom's push-up bra, or three. I shove the chair back and stomp out toward her. "What are you doing?"

She clings to this boy she's with—this *man's*—biceps. Her face sours. "We're on a date."

I'm laughing, like, hysterically, manically laughing. "You're kidding, right?"

She looks confused. The glitter pressed over her eye makeup flakes onto her cheek. "This is real, Birdie. Jeremy and I are in love. Not that you know anything about that."

"Neither do you." I shove my finger into his chest. "She's thirteen. How are old are you, Jeremy—like twenty?"

He shrugs. "Almost."

"Ugh." Just the sight of him. The way his long sports tee hangs over a faded pair of saggy jeans, baseball hat cocked to the side that reveals the hint of bleach on his yellow strands. Brynn clings tighter to him. It's gross and illegal. But mostly gross.

"Get away from him," I tell her. I drag her away, shoving the perv toward the door just as Bash skids across the floor to where we're standing.

"What the hell's going on?" he asks. He's moving toward this man, stops at eye level. His fists are balled up tight. "This asshole bothering you, Birdie?"

"Yeah—that's my little sister." I point to Brynn, who is slumped in the corner, biting the tips of her nails clean off.

"It's none of your business!" Brynn snaps.

Bash grabs a fistful of the guy's shirt and forces him back into the wall. His body slams, hard, and soon he's vibrating anger, ready to unleash it on Bash.

"Leave him alone!" Brynn shouts. She runs into the middle of the two alphas and pushes back at Bash, but he repels her. There's a fire in his glare, something I've not seen before.

"Easy, Bash!" I yell. "And Brynn—go sit down!"

"You're not my goddamned mother!"

The way she turns her head, a stray feather catches my eye, and all the rage I've buried rises to the surface. I reach my hand into that dirty nest of hair, pinch the soft grooves of fur, and pull. The feather nearly disintegrates in my hands.

"Ouch!" she screeches.

"She was good, Bash," the man says with an evil smile. It's as if they already know each other so I step aside.

Bash pulls him forward, then slams him back into the concrete wall again, this time, harder. "Shut up!"

"If I close my eyes, I can still taste her."

Before I can think, like really *think*, about these events, Bash cocks back one of those tightly clenched fists and whops the man square across the side of his jaw at the exact moment Vinny pops through the door. I see this happening, like Benny's stroller gliding down the hill, a symphonic melody streaming to void the noise, but I don't, can't, move. Brynn screams to break them apart but they're locked in some weird dance to prove who's the toughest.

Vinny drops the box he's got lodged between his arms, tries to break up the fight, but gets caught in the cross fire with one of Bash's fists striking him right in the eye. His head wallops back, then flings forward. Everyone freezes as Vinny writhes in pain.

"What. The. Hell?" Vinny cries out. He kicks the box on the floor three times to get his point across.

I look to Brynn, who looks to Jeremy, who looks to Bash.

"If I have to ask again, it's going on a police report." A redness forms around the punched eye, a bruise sure to follow. "You"—he points to Bash—"tell me what happened."

Bash says nothing, just focuses on the floor.

"Strike three. Get your things and get out."

I paw at Vinny's arm. "No—it's not his fault—please!"

"Don't bother," Bash says to me. "I hate this fucking place."

He crams his chem book into his backpack while I try to explain. Vinny asks me to drive Brynn home, tells the man not to come back, but Bash, he says nothing else to me or anyone.

In the parking lot, Brynn pulls away from me, runs after gross Jeremy, and jumps into the front seat of his car. Before I can reach her, the wheels claw at the pavement, howling as they peel onto the highway. I throw my hands in the air. *I give up.* Bash throws his body up against his car door that, apparently, won't open. He does it two, three, four times before kicking the metal with his boot. The top piece of rubber flies off the tip, exposing the very tip of his sock-covered big toe, and for a second, he's calm—for a second, he's okay.

"GOD DAMN ITTTTT!" he screams. With his back pressed to the door, he slides down to the ground as if he's saying *I give up, too.* I walk over, slide down next to him. His eyes are closed, hands folded on top of his knees. I scoot closer for warmth. When he doesn't back away, I scoot more.

"We used to be kind of close," I say. "I mean, don't get me wrong, she's a jerk wad, but we used to laugh about things. Now . . . we're strangers."

He's still quiet. I count the stars above, find Orion's Belt, then the Big Dipper.

"I fucking hate that d-bag," he says after a while. "Such a piece of shit."

"You *know* that guy she was with?"

He turns his head away so I can't read his eyes. "He's just using her."

"Who, Brynn?"

He sighs. "Layla."

"Layla?"

He makes eye contact, seemingly annoyed. "Yeah—*Layla.*"

I shuffle my feet, not knowing what to say. "Did you . . . love her?"

His eyes search the sky as if he'll find an answer between the spiraling balls of gas. The silence grows, until finally, "Couldn't have been love. She cheated on me. With him. If that's love, I'd rather be alone forever."

I want to give him an anecdote, a formula for healing a broken heart, but like solving for infinity, I don't have those answers. "Well, I've only had one *real* kiss—not like the peck you get at a middle school dance, and actually, I didn't even get that much. And it was like the *worst* thing ever. His tongue felt like a soggy fish poking around in my mouth. Nearly choked on all the spit. When we were done, he was all 'that was awesome' and I was like 'did we just have the same experience?' "

He laughs, and the tension releases.

"Now you know something about me pretty much no one else does, so, whatever," I say, bumping my elbow against his arm.

A few minutes pass, and he still hasn't said anything.

"I better go home to check on Brynn," I say, brushing the dirt from my pants. "You okay?"

He doesn't move, just nods. He's rubbing his eyes, an obvious struggle inside his head.

"Well, text me," I say. "If you want."

He looks up, watered eyes that bounce the light of the moon back into mine, and nods. And we leave it there, whatever it is we have, which feels a lot like a broken heart. Maybe because it's unfinished or because we're too different or maybe—and I'm guessing—because neither of us knows how to navigate these feelings through our already broken lives.

When I get home, Brynn is standing in the bathroom with a washcloth pressed over her face. I hang on the door frame and tilt my head. Under these lights, her clean skin looks the way it did when she was little, with her pink bunny slippers staring up at me like they have for years, and I remember a time I didn't think she was a complete tool.

"I keep forgetting you're not a kid anymore," I say. "Forget what happened tonight. I hope someday . . . we can be friends."

She kind of smiles, but doesn't want me to see it, so I make my way into the kitchen, where three casseroles are sitting on the counter like a food memorial.

"Why so many?" I ask Sarge.

He stops popping his bubbles long enough to see me and mutes the TV. "People have been dropping things off. They think pans of noodles and creamed vegetables will heal us. There's more in the fridge, freezer, trash can, and homeless shelter on Madison."

As I'm headed back to my room, Sarge unmutes the TV, and a car commercial catches my eye. I stop to watch. The frame zooms in on something silver, rounded with a trinity in the center.

A hood ornament.

LESSON OF THE DAY: A French chemist named Henry Le Châtelier said if things are in equilibrium, you have a happy life. But, if you do something to mess it up, rip it into ruins—that system called "your life" will do whatever it takes to get that equilibrium back.

So basically, I should brace myself.

BASH

The trailer's cold, dark. Not where I want to be.

I pace around to keep warm, light the few candles I found in Ma's room, and pile on everything I have, which is only a few layers. Nurse Kim hasn't called, and right now, I couldn't handle it anyway. The wind blows against the frail, aluminum frame. Reminds me of a paper tower about to fall straight over. The forecast calls for snow soon, which means I'd better pay the electric bill somehow, or I might actually freeze to death. I know that's a thing. People can die from being too cold, I think. I know I've definitely come close here.

I pull out my chem homework and do the extra credit Mrs. Pearlman gave me to up my grade with the words "LAST CHANCE" written in red ink. I'm distracted, though. The money Skip gave me is burning a hole in my pocket. Sure, I could pay the electric bill, feel warm until the next bill comes and goes.

Or I could give it to Birdie's family.

The crisp greens feel good smashed between my palms. Even the smell, like a dirty piece of card stock, gets me. Someday I'll have enough of this to have heat *and* help Birdie's family. I'll sell my art from a shack outside of the city where rent is less than a small fortune, be a reclusive art genius no one's ever seen. "Dream on, Bash," I say, reading the next problem.

To produce water and calcium chloride, calcium hydroxide is treated with hydrochloric acid. Write a balanced chemical reaction that describes this process.

I stare at the formula for five goddamned minutes all while imagining Birdie's sea green eyes shooting right into mine. With my phone already in my palm, I wrestle with my thoughts. *Do I? Nah.* I toss the phone aside and refocus. I'm looking at the letters, but they're not registering, and eventually, my eyes slowly wander to my phone again. Fingers on the buttons, I go for it. Before I can edit, reread, or delete altogether, I press Send and exhale, mostly because I'm stressing about how many minutes this will eat up.

ME: STUCK ON SOMETHING. HELP!

Entire lifetimes—minutes—pass before she responds.

BIRDIE: WHAT ARE YOU STUCK ON?

I hesitate.

ME: YOU. *SHIT! WHY DID I HAVE TO TYPE THAT?!*

I'm clutching the phone as if it's air for my lungs.

BIRDIE: YOU'RE TROUBLE.
ME: I KNOW . . .

Pencil in one hand, phone in the other, and I'm sitting in the worst recliner ever made, in this dark, cold-as-shit metal ice box, with a huge grin on my face. Not because I don't feel bad for what I've done, or for not telling her, but because, for the first time in forever, I feel something more than numb. There's a long pause, the bright screen lighting the room. The phone vibrates again, and I lose my smile. It's Kyle.

KYLE: DAD'S HOME. I'M FREAKING OUT.

My finger lingers over the letters; my stomach in knots.

ME: DID HE SAY ANYTHING?
KYLE: NOPE. GOT HOUSE CLEANED OUT BEFORE CREW GOT THERE, SO WE'RE GOOD.

It really would've been the easiest way. Just let them find my shit, piece it together, and come after me. So I don't have to do it. So they leave me with no choice. I know it isn't rational, isn't like the man Ma raised, but now that I know Birdie, I'm torn. The thought of hurting her now . . . but, it doesn't matter.

By not telling her, I know I already have.

I don't respond to Kyle again. I keep my eyes on the light of the phone until it fades. Birdie doesn't write back, and in a way, it's best, I know, but I want her to. I finish my homework, most answers blank or sketches of tiny bears. My eyes begin to close as the pencil falls to the side of the bed. My phone vibrates again, forcing me awake.

BIRDIE: FIST OKAY?
ME: BETTER THAN DUDE'S FACE. TOOK A CHUNK OUT OF MY KNUCKLE.
BIRDIE: UGH. GROSS. I HATE THAT WORD!
BASH: CALL ME. TIRED OF TEXTING.

A few minutes pass, and although I know I don't have enough minutes, her voice is all I want to hear right now. The phone rings.

"What's to hate about *chunk*?" I ask. Her voice sounds sexy through the receiver. More than in person. The phone people do this on purpose, to make me want something I shouldn't have.

"It's on my Worst Word List," she says.

"What else is on that list? Let me guess—*moist, juicy, gelatinous*?"

She's laughing and screaming at the same time—a beautiful sound. "AHH!!! And don't forget *panties*. If you ever call women's underwear"—she pauses to gag—"*panties,* I'll probably drop-kick you."

"Is that a challenge?"

She's silent.

"Panties." Can't help myself.

"AHHHH!!!!" she screams again, I laugh. "I'm hanging up now."

I'm clutching the phone tighter as if it'll make her stay. It's too quiet here; her voice fills the space. And then it happens—this sentence I can't stop, a freight train barreling out of my stupid mouth before I can rein it in. "Go out with me."

There is no hesitation, no long pause, just a slight crack in her voice. "Okay."

Now I know for sure, it's no longer a theory or a guess. It's fact (something Birdie will approve of):

I'm (completely, utterly, and happily) screwed.

birdie

Violet calls to tell me today's horoscope:

"I hope you're sitting down," she says. "Are you sitting? Go sit. It's a rough one."

I'm already sitting, but I pretend to do it again. "Okay, go."

She sighs, her voice aggravated. I can almost hear the worry stone she's probably vigorously rubbing in her free hand. "Today is about working through transformations that are intently reshaping our lives, thanks to the Capricorn moon pushing at the Uranus/Pluto square. Free yourself from anything in your path, though to do so, there may be dark passages to conquer first. Today is not for sissies."

I'm nodding, saying, "Mmm-hmm," like it makes sense to me.

"But don't worry," she adds. "I talked to Althea last night," referring to the 7-Eleven gas station attendant who is also an iridologist—she believes the iris tells a person's whole story better than a palm or, you know, better than asking said person. "And after looking into my eyes, she concluded there's an issue with a major organ, so I tell her I'm fine, everything's fine, but maybe because you and I are so close it's one of *your* organs, and she nodded and flashed the light a little deeper and—"

"Vi," I interrupt, "did you have an energy drink?"

There's a pause.

"I thought your mom said you can't have those because of your insomnia?"

Another slight pause. She speaks slower this time. "I only had half a can."

"No judgment."

"Fine. I had three."

"So *my* organs, huh?"

She smacks her lips into the receiver loud enough for me to hear. "Your heart."

After listening to another long-winded explanation of how to handle my organs and irises and dark passages, I stop by the children's hospital, where they've moved Benny to a different room—a downgrade from the PICU, which should be celebrated to the nth degree. I'll take it as a sign from Nan that she heard me. Or, scientifically speaking, his vitals are improving, despite the odds. Maybe this was the heart Althea droned on about, or maybe Vi believes what she needs to, and maybe I should, too.

Mom is slumped over the hospital bed in the same pair of pajamas she's worn for days while Dad reads a crisp newspaper from the corner of a couch that's held probably thousands of other worried bodies before him. They barely acknowledge me, the fatigue evident on their faces.

"How is he?" I ask.

With a vague hint of a smile, Mom looks at me. "He's alive, Birdie. He's alive."

Dad tosses the paper aside and rubs the creases on his forehead; the lines are deeper than before. He stretches his limbs and kisses the top of Mom's frizzed hair that looks more like Violet's patch of curls right now than any of my waved strands. "I've got to get some sleep. You coming, Bess?"

She gazes at Benny. "Not yet. I'll call." Mom turns to me, looks me up and down. "You look nice. Plans?"

I dip my head, smooth the wrinkles from my shirt. "Meeting a friend."

"Sounds fun." She turns back to Benny. "Brynn should take notes." She looks at me again. "Dad told me about her latest stunt at the rink—the clothes, the makeup. I don't know what's gotten into her."

"She's thirteen. Doesn't think."

"And you think *too* much."

"Wish I didn't. It's exhausting."

She smiles. "But I don't have to worry about you. Your head's on straight. No boyfriends or shady friends. You know what you're doing with your life. But Brynn? I'll always have to worry about her. She's too free, and too much freedom is dangerous."

My nail finds its way into my mouth, and I start nervously biting the tip. "You don't worry about me?"

She turns her body toward me and rests an elbow on the chair's rest. One hand is used as a prop for her chin while the other holds Benny's hand. "We're similar, Birdie, you and I. I worry about you in a completely different way."

I'm nodding, agreeing, though I'm not sure I understand. Maybe now is finally the time to tell her that all those things she's so sure of for me might not happen. My mouth opens.

"I—"

"*Oh my God!*" she squeals. "He squeezed my hand— Nurse! Nurse! Come here!" With an energy I haven't seen in weeks, she jumps from the chair and runs into the hallway, her shoes squeaking against the tiles, and I'm so glad I didn't just ruin this moment with news about money or boys or reminders of the past. Moments later, she pulls an attending nurse to Benny's side. "He squeezed my hand! I felt it— not just a twitch—a real squeeze!"

The nurse checks all the usual vitals, a smile percolating. Her hand tugs at the long, thin paper that has piled onto the floor in a lavalike mound. The readings are scattered—not one linear line like before. "I'll get the doctor!"

After a thorough check, they tell us it's working—his

lungs are adjusting to the lower doses. Mom and I celebrate by singing "You Are My Sunshine" into his ears. I don't know if it helps him or us, but the point is, he isn't just a vegetable anymore. Dr. Stein gave us that thing we needed—hope—and made it something tangible.

A while later, I leave. The sun now peeks out from the gray skies we just sang about and I feel a little more free, lighter even. The air is still cold, though. Little specks of snow flurries are falling through the pillowy clouds. I can't help but stop and feel the flakes as they land on my cheekbones and the sun melts them away. And I think about the next time Benny will be able to do this, because *that* moment will be the moment we will have come full circle.

On my gloriously happy drive, vague thoughts of Vi's horoscope downer still echoing, I stop at the only drugstore in a ten-mile radius. There is this aisle I always loved walking through as a kid that I just have to find. Most people would say it's the "junk aisle," but I like to think there are hidden gems buried, like treasures. This time of year, the "junk aisle" is filled with Christmas items that are only a couple dollars, and sometimes what I find is worth a hundred times that in smiles alone.

I scan each bin, thinking back to all the times Dad would let us pick out gifts for each other with the five-dollar bill he'd give us. Usually, we'd all end up with crap, but this one year, one of my favorite Christmases ever, Nan joined in on this tradition and bought me one of those ceramic rectangular ornaments with a faceless woman, her hair all gray, holding the hand of a small child whose hair, arguably, was just like mine. On the back, the words *Love that transcends the years* was inscribed. The ornament was lost in the move, but those words are still with me, almost like Nan is.

I dig through the pink bin, the one with the discounted ornaments, and although I know it's a long shot to find something as perfect as Nan's gift from all those years ago, I search anyway. My fingers scrape the side of a hard object near the bottom. It's round, sandy in color, with the image of a mother holding her infant son—almost like the picture on mine—but the words are even more powerful:

If I could give you anything, it wouldn't only be the world, but the hope to fill it with.

With the ornament firmly cupped in my hand, I rush to the register to pay before anyone else claims this treasure. It is mine, and I know just the person to give it to. Outside, the snow thickens, clinging to my glasses and the hair I've delicately pulled up out of my face. Little wisps fall against my skin as I move.

I slide by the front desk of Clifton Nursing and Rehab Center, and when I get to Camilla's room, I tap on the side of the door, even though it's wide open. Her eyes are open, fixed on the wall—this blank, desolate kind of stare I'll never forget. Her CPAP mask blows angry bursts of air into her dying lungs, and I imagine being seven, blowing into a favor at a birthday party.

She doesn't hear my knock, so I hesitantly step inside, afraid to disturb whatever daydream she might be having. Her left leg is sticking out of the blanket, swollen and puffy from the edema—the same kind of swelling in Benny's brain. She turns her head, and through the mask, I see that same smile, not so ruby anymore, but plum. She motions for me to sit next to her, removes her mask, and lays her hand on mine. Hand sanitizer is resting on the bedside table, but as I reach for it, she tells me not to.

"No need," she says, her words are labored. "Germs can't . . . hurt me now, honey."

I set the bottle back down, let her frail hand fall into mine. "Been thinking about you," I say, nervous.

"Bash was here earlier."

"I'm on my way to see him," I tell her.

"I know." She holds her stare. "Wouldn't stop . . . talking

217

about . . . you." She pauses in between words, struggles to get them out. The life is draining from her body. I can't fully explain the feeling even as I sit with her, but I feel it—the room is more empty than full. When I sit with Benny, I don't feel it, death, the way I thought I would when they said he was too far gone. But with her, it's everywhere. In the air, in her words, her eyes, and suddenly I feel so grateful and guilty for feeling grateful at the same time.

"When it's . . . all over"—she places the mask on for just a moment to breathe, then removes it to finish speaking—"take care of him. My worst fear is him being alone."

Unsure of what to say, I bite my lip, my heart squeezing too tight in my chest.

"Promise me . . . he won't be alone. And make sure he gets . . . the letter. Promise." She presses on my hand with whatever strength is left.

"What letter?" I ask surveying the room.

"He'll understand when it's time. Please. I need to hear the words before I go."

"Everything will be . . . okay. I promise." My stomach's all bunched up, twisted. She presses a little red button with her free hand. Medicine slithers down from a giant robotic machine and into her bloodstream. Within minutes, she smiles again from the place the ruby lipstick has faded, places the mask over her face, and closes her eyes.

I pull the ornament from my pocket where it's warmed, and wrap the flimsy yarn around a tiny tree branch near Bash's drawing. The tree almost topples but doesn't. It hangs on for dear life, kind of like Benny, kind of like Camilla.

Kind of like me.

I gently place her hand beneath the sheet, and with one final look, almost a good-bye, I leave.

Driving is effortless now, my mind not so gloriously happy as before, but in this strangely empty space. I'm not running equations or stopping to take pictures of the last three pieces of roadkill I passed. Instead, I'm thinking about fate. If things *are* destined to be the way Sarge says, a grand plan we're not in control of—something kismet, out of our hands—do my choices even matter? If I hadn't snuck out to a party, if I hadn't unhinged the stroller, propped it up against the garage, maybe:

a) I'd have never met Bash (at least not that night), had no reason to confess, to distract Mom.
b) Something else would've distracted her anyway.
c) I'd have gotten out of my head long enough to get Benny's car so Mom could take him inside, where he'd be safe.
d) None of the above. Maybe it was *literally* just an accident—something that should've never happened, but did.

I contemplate going to the gas station to see Althea, have her give my irises a look, but quickly remember that's Violet's thing. And I can't anyway. Bash agreed to meet me at the ice skating rink, which is really Hyde Park's frozen pond where the center is always a questionable experiment with said fate. When I arrive, he's sitting in his car blowing warm air into his hands. We make brief eye contact and meet around my driver's side door. He's obviously annoyed.

"I'm not late," I say, challenging the look on his face that seems more angry than happy to see me.

"I know."

"What's your deal?"

He scans the lot, points to a car that's struggling to fit into a skinny spot. The tan clunker reverses then drives, reverses, drives again, and finally lands cockeyed with its tail end spilling into the open aisle.

"If you're not going to use a turn signal or learn how to park between two yellow lines, your fucking tires should just blow off."

I'm laughing, but confused. "What?"

"A warning to everyone who doesn't use it—like, if you see someone's tires explode on the highway, you know that idiot didn't use the little stick connected to your whole driving console and he didn't make it, so you should probably use yours. The blinky thing and those two lines actually have a goddamned purpose . . ." His words trail off under his breath, but I'm still laughing, which makes him stop and smile. "Never mind." He briskly rubs his hands together again so violently it's like he's trying to erase the previous conversation from his skin.

"Don't you have gloves?" I ask.

"Nah."

I look around at the snow. It's becoming more of a blanket that's coating us.

"Sure you want to do this? We could just go to the—"

He sears a look into me that stops me cold. "Come on. Let's go."

I walk to the window, where a long line of anxious skaters has formed. He pulls me to the side of the building where the trash reeks.

"What are you doing?" I ask.

He's picking the lock to the gate. I offer to pay for both our skates, but even though my voice carries, he pretends he doesn't hear. "Too easy. Live a little, Couch Girl."

The lock pops and we slide inside, closing the iron gate behind us with a loud *CLANK*. Filled with people from this county and the surrounding area, the giant, uneven circle of ice looks as if it's daring us to come fall straight through the center to where we'd never be heard from again. The crowd—from the wobbly to the strong, the confident to the unsure, and my favorite, the falling to the completely eating it—are crying, laughing. All these emotions jam-packed into one family-fun (or first-date) outing.

"We don't have skates," I say. Bash looks around, a deliberate something in his eye, something devious, and walks over to a young couple in the midst of removing their shoes. It's so crowded they don't notice Bash as he casually lifts their skates when he passes by. He bumps into me, pushes me along to the other side of the rink, before the couple notices. "Are you kidding me? I have money."

"Money is boring," he says. "This is an invaluable life skill. Can't buy that."

"Stealing is a life skill?"

"Not stealing—surviving." He flashes a crooked smile, and despite all the negative thoughts stacking up in my brain, file by file, I don't fight it. We lace up these skates that barely fit and hide our shoes near the gate we snuck in through. Heavy and awkward, I wobble like all the others eating it out on the ice. This must be what being a baby giraffe feels like. This is even worse than regular skating. *Much* worse.

"Ever done this?" he asks, unnaturally graceful on the two thin blades.

"When I was little." Dad held my hand so I wouldn't fall. He always caught me, made sure I knew he was there.

Bash holds out his cold, red hand. I hesitate, remembering when he let me fall at work. He grabs ahold of me before I overthink it and pulls me across the ice to the ominous center. We weave through the crowd of laughing children and smiling faces, and every time my arms flail, my legs buckling, he catches me, never lets me fall.

The plummeting snowflakes melt in my hair, dampening the stray pieces around my face. A thrill shoots through me as we glide along. I feel alive. With Bash's hand against the small of my back, I fling my arms into the air, close my eyes, and feel the wind brush against me. He pulls me closer, and with all my trust in him, my hand in his, he guides us along the turns. When I blink open my frost-laced lashes, he's looking at me in this whole new way, like he's seeing me, the *real* me, for the very first time. Our eyes linger, until everything around me fades. All I see, and feel, is Bash.

He pulls me off to the side where others are awkwardly falling onto and off of the ice, to the concession window of a tiny brick building. He digs deep in his pocket, produces a fistful of change; the bigger, more valuable coins jump from his hand onto the ground and roll away. I offer to pay, but he refuses, says he'll take someone else's hot chocolate before he'll let me pay, then likens it to another invaluable life skill—sacrifice.

Fifty cents, mostly pennies, later, we're sharing a lukewarm cup of powdery hot chocolate. We hide out near the shelter where wooden benches line the government center building across from the rink/park. We're laughing at how stupid we look in these skates that don't fit right, our reflections mirroring our every movement in the center's glass doors.

"I'm sorry if I was ever a jerk to you," he says.

"*Was*?" I joke. "You still are!"

He rolls his eyes, changes the subject. "How's your brother?"

"Better, I guess."

He looks as relieved as I do. "Good . . . good."

I sigh as my fingers unlace the skates to let my feet breathe. "I mean, he's not awake yet, but other than that."

He nudges my arm with a playful punch. "He's not missing much. Have you seen that new"—he uses his fingers to make air quotes—"'meat goat farm' over by the Christmas tree lot?"

My jaw falls open at the familiar reference. "What kind of signage is that—meat goats? When I think of eating a hamburger or bacon, I don't say they came from meat cows or meat pigs. Should be implied. The words just sound unappetizing. Better feed the meat goat before the meat goat starves. I need to buy a meat goat for my meat farm. Gross."

He laughs kind of hard, the skin between his eyes pinching in a cute way. "You and your words."

There's a shift in the conversation now, a quiet that lingers. I listen to the sounds of the ice skaters from afar. "You know, I tell everyone I've got this hope—*hope* Benny wakes up, *hope* this, *hope* that—but the truth is, I don't even know what that means. *Hope* couldn't, didn't, save my nan. It's just a word."

He stops me. "You don't need to intellectualize everything, you know. Hope isn't just a word—it's a feeling. Like Love. Hate. Sorrow. Regret. It's all the same. If you feel it, that's all the scientific proof you need. And sometimes it means something else. Like believing what is happening is the best thing. Like in Ma's case, she's had the shittiest year ever, so I *have* to believe her leaving me is the best thing. Not for me, but *her.* If she's okay, I'm okay. That kind of hope, the stinging kind that's mixed with love and fear and, well, complete shit, it's not a word—it's my lifeline. Without it, I disappear."

He looks away, then back to me with a forced smile. He swipes a stray tear that starts to run down. "Anyway . . . what are your plans after graduation?"

"I have a morbid fetish with dead things, so thought I'd make something useful out of it and go to UC Denver, study to be a medical examiner. If we can come up with the money in time. My scholarship fell through."

"You want to play with corpses?"

"Who doesn't?"

"That explains . . . so . . . much." He laughs, but there's something nervous in his eyes, his whole face, something I can't place. The silence sits between us for a whole minute, and I suddenly think of Brønsted–Lowry. According to the theory, acids are divided into groups by how powerful or how feeble, and right now, by the look on Bash's face, I can't tell which I fall into.

"Sucks about the money. I know from experience if you have it, life's a damn ball; if you don't, it ruins everything." He fumbles with his hands, and I notice he's still wearing the only shirt I've ever seen him in. The collar pokes out of his jacket.

"What about you?" I ask him with a smirk. "Since I now know you didn't actually graduate and *weren't* only in town for that one party night."

"*Funny*, Couch Girl. I can't think that far ahead. Life has a twisted way of fucking me."

"Like Newton's Third Law."

"Like what?"

"You know, that whole 'for every action there is an equal and opposite reaction' thing? Forces come in pairs." I smile bigger, he smiles back with one eyebrow arched. Suddenly embarrassed, I cower and adjust the glasses hanging on the bridge of my nose. "Never mind. That was stupid."

"Don't do that."

"Do what?"

"Pretend you're not smart. Your brains are the hottest thing about you."

I look down at the ground. "Gee, thanks."

His hand grips my arm. "No, I mean, you're beautiful, not pretty," he smiles, "but that brain is what separates the two. Don't hide it."

My face warms to what I'm sure is the color of beets or tomatoes or something completely metaphoric and perfect for how much blushing I have going on.

His phone buzzes. He hides the screen, reads the message, then shoves it back in his pocket. "So . . . any news on who hit your brother? I mean, have they found any leads?"

I chew on the words, so abrupt, the blushing fades. "No. In some ways, it feels like everything is stuck in the exact position as when the accident happened, and in other ways, everything is being propelled forward faster than any of us are ready for."

"Yeah, I know what you mean."

There's this weirdly long silence. He's looking at the ground. I am, too. We're both kicking our feet in the air, moving to stay warm.

"I kind of wish we'd stayed in the apartment," I say to break the quiet. "Then maybe none of this would've happened."

"Yeah," he says.

Our conversation fades. Words dissolve almost as fast as they're said and it's clear neither of us know what to do, or say, next. I let a minute or two pass before I cut through this moment.

"Well . . . I better get going," I say.

He's quick to unlace his skates, and we toss both pairs near the bench for some other couple learning "invaluable life lessons" to find. We're barefoot, nearly hopping across the snow-covered ground, to the spot we left our shoes. I feel like he's not ready to go, part of me isn't ready, either. He walks me to my car door. My back is leaning against the cold metal. He steps closer, a lot closer, with his face close to mine, his eyes drinking mine in. He reaches behind me and pulls on the handle of my car. I feel his warm breath on my skin again. It forces those little hairs on the back of my neck to rise.

"You really should start locking your door," he says.

A grin forms. I see it, lingering an inch from my mouth. My lips twitch, daring him to do something—anything. He brushes a piece of hair away and tucks it behind my ear and moves to my cheek, where his lips gently press down. I close my eyes and feel every part of his mouth on my skin until he leans back again. The skin pulses and tingles until it's numb.

"Be careful in this weather," he says, his voice soft. "Roads might be slick now."

I'm nodding, wondering why he won't kiss my mouth as I get inside my car. *Was it the fish story? Or maybe my breath is wretched. WHAT IS IT?* Maybe it's because I told him I've only had that one kiss so I couldn't possibly be any good at it. Or maybe it's because I'm just a game to him—the mouse. My thoughts are racing. I need an answer. *Why?* I watch through my window as he throws his body up against his door. This time, it's five slams. He waves, I wave back, and make sure to use my turn signal as I heave up the rounded drive so my tires don't blow off. Once I'm far enough away, this feeling overcomes me—something sickly and pukey and kind of tingly and awesome at the same time.

I'm a mess.

I'm in love.

LESSON OF THE DAY: In chemistry, there are two kinds of heat. One is caused by chemicals, and the other, physical activity. Extra activity (i.e., kissing, wanting to kiss, dreaming about kissing) makes more molecular collisions that create heat. Some of those collisions, like *love,* or whatever that means, are inevitable, no matter what you do to stop it.

I can only hope it won't hurt too bad.

BASH

I knew I couldn't go for it.

Her eyes, lips, wanted me to. Hell, *I* wanted to. But aside from the fact that I cannot be just another fish wading around in her mouth, I shouldn't be anywhere near her heart. I know I've crossed a big line already. I just don't know what to do about it. I will *never* be one of those guys who believe women are things we use—we being this collective group of completely clueless boys—to make myself feel better, less alone. Ma always said a real man doesn't have a lot of women hanging on his arm when he doesn't give a shit about them. He has *one*. And a real man knows when to walk away from something before it breaks that special *one*.

If there's anything I need Ma to know before she leaves this earth, it's not just that I'll be okay, but that she did her job as a mother. All those times she made me hold a door open, helped me with all my, you know, feelings and crap, made me stop and think about what it must be like to be a woman and how hard it is when there are so many d-bags out there ready to pounce. Well, Ma, please know, it paid off. You taught me about respect. To treat women as the treasures they are, just like *you*.

Except, I can't seem to walk away from the treasure I want the most, even if she is everything I should avoid.

As I'm driving home from the ice rink, I trace my lips with

the tip of my fingers and think about how her face felt against them. Warm and soft, even in the frigid winter air. And she tasted like powdered sugar and cherries and that feeling she keeps going on about—hope.

The snow is still falling in waves, so I'm careful along the winding highway. The large flakes melt into the windshield just as quickly as they fall. My wipers work to clear the glass, but they suck, and the window is just one smudged, blurry mess I can barely see out of. My phone vibrates as I'm pushing my neck as far forward as it will go to see through the sludge. I quickly glance at the screen.

It's not Kyle, not Birdie. It's the nursing home.

"Hello?" I ask.

"Bash," Nurse Kim says, softly. "I'm sorry . . ."

I choke on the silence. "No . . . no . . . she was fine earlier. I just saw her."

My heart is pounding so hard, it's going to explode, I know it. I can't speak. My tongue is glued down, pinned to the gum line. She continues talking, rambling, but it's a fog. I swerve to the side of the road and flip on my blinker. After all these months of fighting this goddamned poison eating away at her organs, Nurse Kim tells me that's not even what killed her—an aneurism did. A swift, uncontrollable force that sped through her brain and stopped her heart, almost instantly.

"Wait, wait, wait" is all I manage.

"Get here as soon as you can. We won't move her," she says.

"Wait," I say again. She's silent, waiting for me to add something. "I don't understand."

"Just get here."

I clutch the phone to my chest. The sound of the blinkers—*bleep bleep bleep*—is all I hear. I want to swallow. *Why can't I swallow?* It hurts deep down in my throat, all the way to the back of my eyelids. I feel the tears stir, but I don't cry.

Instead, I twist the wheel and press on the gas, violently steering back onto the road without even looking to see if anyone is coming or going. The car veers into the other lane, crossing the yellow lines that are snow-covered and hidden. An oncoming car slows, nearly drives off the side to avoid me. I slam on the brakes, spin the car around with a loud, screeching howl, and drive in the opposite direction toward the nursing home. My foot is heavy on the pedal, but I don't feel it; I don't feel a damned thing.

In about half the time is normally takes, I pull into the nursing home lot, askew, and fling my door wide open. I don't think it shuts, and I don't care. My feet have never moved so quickly before. At the entranceway, the slow automatic doors only fuel my fire, so I use my hands to pull them apart faster. There is no time to waste. (There is all the time to waste now.)

In the doors. Past the front desk. Down the hall. There are voices and faces I'm sure I saw, spoke to, but if you asked me to recount them, I couldn't. I am one solid motion, while everything else, especially time, has paused.

Ma's door is half cracked. I slow my pace and tip my head inside first. The room is quiet. I'm slow to approach. It feels as if she's just napping, and I don't want to wake her, so my steps are light. Her body is unmoving beneath the crisp linens I saw her alive in only hours ago. I breathe in the last scent of her I will ever have, the last sight of her I will ever have, but mostly, the last feeling of her next to me. No breathing machine, no tubes, no nothing. These are all the things Nurse Kim prepped me on months ago. To prepare me for this moment. But I'm not prepared. I could never be prepared for this.

A small, rolled-up towel is stuffed under Ma's chin to help keep her jaw closed while the muscles stiffen. Two thin strips of tape hold her eye lids shut, because Kim said when someone dies, their eyes may be open which is, I guess, not something I should see. She said this magical tape won't pull off her lashes; it's *gentle,* and I remember thinking, *She'll be dead—she won't feel her lashes,* but I'm glad to know they won't come off when the tape does, now that I'm sitting here looking at them.

The air is thin, feels like Ma's not here anymore, even though I'm looking right at her. I pull the upholstered chair up next to the bed, squirt sanitizer between my palms, and rub briskly until dissolved. Careful with my movements, I grab ahold of her hand. It's ice cold . . . lifeless. I hold her palm to the front of my mouth and blow warm air. Every part of me pretending just a little longer.

"Bash," Nurse Kim interrupts. She walks over and offers a hug. There are tears in her big, brown eyes. "I'm so, so sorry."

"I wanted to be here," I say. "Why didn't anyone call me sooner? It was just a couple of hours ago. She was talking, awake. I don't understand. I don't . . . understand." I hear the words repeating, but can't make them stop.

"It just happened so fast, and she's DNR so we couldn't resuscitate." I'm shaking my head. She says something about a blood clot, but it all sounds like TV static, and so I keep saying "I don't understand" to connect the empty space in my heart to what they're telling me.

"I know it doesn't make this any easier, but you knew this was going to happen soon anyway," she says, patting my shoulder.

But I'm not ready, I want to tell her. "I thought I'd get to hold her hand when she took her last breath, that's all." I'm crying now; a dam burst out of nowhere. I hide my face in my palms. I'm the same lost little boy I was all those years ago when we left the Taylors. I didn't know how we'd survive but she held me, told me we'd be okay as long as we had each other and now, I'm just as lost, only, without her.

She wraps her arms around me and I hear her crying, too.

"I know, honey. It's never easy to let someone go. Especially someone like her. Take as long as you need. There's no rush."

When she disappears, I slink back into the chair and grab Ma's hand again, kissing her cold, thin skin, now wet with my tears. The glow of her tiny tree coats her face in a subtle glow. Her scarf is tilted, not covering the entire space of her mostly bare head, but in true Camilla style, she's wearing her trademark red lipstick, probably thanks to Kim for my arrival. If I squint hard enough, it really does look like she's sleeping. She used to look like this when I was little. All those times when it was too early for me to be awake, I'd tiptoe into her room, sneak under the covers, and pretend to sleep. Except I would just watch her. She'd play my game, pretend not to feel me next to her, and then wrap a warm arm around me, anchoring me into her space.

I wish she would do that now.

My drawing has come to life. Those early days after the diagnosis, when they said the chemo and radiation should get it all, we believed. Our hope faded, though, when we saw our belief wasn't enough, that maybe it didn't matter how much we *hoped* for the cancer to go away. All these things: Watching her hair slowly fall out, her appetite disappear until she was wafer thin, hearing her puke in the middle of the night, seeing the blood, the pain, feeling her agony, and there was nothing I could ever do to fix any damn thing. Part of me wants to bolt, forget chemistry, graduation, Kyle, even Birdie. Just run. Get out of this shit town and disappear until there's nothing left of me to hide. The other part of me, the part Ma would want me to listen to, says stay here and be a man, the one she raised me to be.

I stay for an hour, squeezing her hand, never feeling like she can still hear me from wherever she is now. Maybe that's just something people say to make themselves feel better about death. But maybe not. I guess it gives me some comfort to think she's looking down, telling me to sit up straight.

So I do. Shoulders squared, I sit until I can stand without crying. On my way out, a new ornament catches my eye. Reminds me of Ma and me, chokes me up even more. I hold it in my palm for a moment, then let it drop.

"Good-bye," I say, with one last look. I don't turn around again.

I walk past the desk, where Kim has a box of Ma's things gathered. She says, "Hold on," runs down the hall, and when she returns, tosses the rest of her things—my stray drawings, the tree, and ornament, into the box. "She loved this stuff. So I left them there as long as I could."

After a moment of silence, she hands me a thick envelope. "I'm sorry to do this now. It's the death certificate so you can register her death." She cups her hand to the side of her mouth to keep her words between the two of us. "I paid the fee, Bash, so no worries. You'll just have to go to the Registrar of Births, Deaths, and Marriages and—"

My stare is blank. She pauses, lays her hand on mine. "I'm sorry. Forget it. I'll call you in a few days, and we'll deal with it then."

I shake my head, I think.

"The funeral director says he can have the service ready a week from Monday. Ms. Camilla already had everything set up, paid for, so all you have to do is show up."

"I can't." I swallow another wave of tears, turning my head away so she can't see the pain about to erupt.

"I'll help any way I can." She steps closer, finds my eyes. "Just tell me when you're ready. An obituary she'd prewritten will be in Sunday's paper, so if you're not up to calling people, they'll see it then."

"Tuesday—the service *has* to be Tuesday. She loved that song, 'Tuesday's Gone.' It needs to be on Tuesday." She nods with a sympathetic smile, pretends I'm not unraveling right here in front of her, and hands me that damn box. It holds what few things Ma owned: her gaudy jewelry and old makeup, some papers, my other drawings, and her colorful bandanna collection.

With an aching heart, I plod to my car, where the door is, in fact, wide open. The cold air and snow have floated into the driver's seat, soaking into the fibers. I brush the wet pile into the lot, sit on the soaked cushion, and slam the door. Then, I just . . . stare.

I don't know how long I sit. Could be a minute, could be a day. It's until my windows are coated with a thick avalanche of white. I'm shivering, but I don't let myself turn on the engine. I *want* to be uncomfortable, to feel some kind of pain. Pain is better than this numb straitjacket. My tears have dried and frozen to my lashes, and though my heart hurts, I feel nothing else.

When I counted change at the ice rink for hot chocolate, I'd forgotten all about the money I'd been gifted from the regulars at the skate club. It's still burning a hole in my pocket, and I've got nowhere to be, so I drive to my usual place in a haze, the one where this oddball cashier who likes to look into my eyes and tell me the weirdest shit, Althea, doesn't ID. I grab a few bottles of whiskey and a pack of cigarettes and then I drive. I'm not sure where I'm going at first, but the car kind of takes me where I need to be. As I approach Birdie's house, I slow the car. Headlights off, I pull along the side of the road, almost in the ditch, where the wooden crosses are gathered.

I unscrew the first bottle of whiskey and chug, coughing when the liquor hits my throat. From here, I can see that spot, the one where the Benz hit the kid, where people have been praying and leaving things. I light a cigarette, too. Everything burns. I ignore Ma's voice in my head telling me to stop, because she's not here anymore. That is the *only* thing I know right now.

The lights are on in Birdie's house, their Christmas tree gleaming in that big bay window that overlooks the whole yard and highway. It's so perfect, makes me feel like the sludge I really am. I take another swig. A car whizzes by as it rounds the bend. "Slow down," I whisper. I drink again, put the bottle down, and with a scorching fire in my throat, I step out of the car. My boots sink into the snow, leaving tracks, proof. My vision blurs, and I cross the road without looking, because *who cares now?*

But I don't stop at the crash site to pray, or whatever.

I walk up to the front door, my balance off, and with my finger on the doorbell, I think, *it's now or never, you coward. Come clean. Like a man.* My finger shakes. I can only imagine the look on Birdie's face when I tell her the truth—that I was in that car with Kyle. That the moment she walked into the rink to start her job, I felt torn. Because even though I've been lying all along, I was too afraid to tell her I didn't just feel guilty for the hit and run. I felt guilty for wanting to be with her.

My eyes narrow in on the button with laser-like focus. But when it comes down to it, I can't press the bell. I drop my hand. A few steps backward, I realize what I'm doing. Voices murmur from beyond the door, and I panic, tripping in the bush behind my feet. I crawl down the hill and run to my car before I'm seen. With the engine revved, I peel out onto the highway and get the hell out of there before anyone sees me.

I don't remember the drive home or the snow or the way any part of my body feels or just how slow my heart beats. I don't remember Ma's last words or the way Birdie looks at me or any damn thing. My eyes barely open, I haphazardly park over the sidewalk by my place, nearly grazing the car in my spot.

"What the hell?" a voice says as I fall out of my car. I'm on the cement, in the snow, my hands holding me up on all fours, and Kyle walks over to help me to my feet. "Where have you been?" he asks. "I've been trying to get ahold of you for hours."

I say nothing, wave him off, and grab the bag of bottles from the seat. I feel my eyes closing. He holds me up, helps my flimsy body to the door. I kick in the weak-ass door and toss my bag of whiskey into the room by my bed and fall into the recliner. My arm covers my eyes. I can't look at him, at anything.

"Are you wasted?" he asks, breathing in my face. I ignore him. "Bash—I need to talk to you about Steve. It's bad. We're in deep shit now."

"What shit?" I ask, barely feeling the words leave my mouth. Everything is numb.

"Skeevy Steve called Dad; the police arrested him but let him go—it's worse than bad. It's . . . what's a word *worse* than bad?"

"Gravvvve." I let the word drag on the end, laughing to myself.

His eyes are bugging out. "Yeah—grave—like the graves we're gonna be living in."

"It's okay," I slur. "I'm gonna tell her everything."

"Tell who—are you listening to me?"

"Kid's sister. She'll have to know. Because we talked about meat goats."

"Dude, you're not making any sense. Why would you tell his—" He hesitates. "You son of a bitch. You know her? We made a deal."

I drunkenly point my finger in his face, try to shove him away from me so I can move to my mattress. "*You* made a deal. *I* wanted to turn myself in because I don't have shit left to lose. Now, here we are, *amigo*. Just you and me and all my whiskey. Hey! That rhymes." I slink down and sing in a low, piratey tone. "You and meee and alllll my whiskeeeyyyyy!"

With fear in his eyes, he steps back, studying me, realization sparking as he twists a weirdly long beard hair between his thumb and forefinger. "Bash . . . is your mom okay? Is that where you were?"

"Stop with all that. It's not an imposition." I mean *inquisition,* but my mouth isn't connected to me right now.

Wild Kyle looks like he wants to cry. "Did she . . . die?"

I stop twitching, eyes closed, and I feel that sharp pang all over again. "Yeah."

He pauses. "That sucks, dude . . . you know," he says, "Confucius would say, you'll learn wisdom by three methods, and I feel like, and stop me if I'm wrong, this applies here."

I don't stop him. Because I'm drunk.

"First, by reflection, which is noblest. Second, by imitation, which is easiest. And third, by experience, which is bitterest." He continues rambling for, I don't know, seventeen hundred hours, but his words fade into the darkness, until I hear nothing, see nothing, feel the kind of nothing I need to.

And it's damn all right with me.

birdie

It's been a few days since I've heard from Bash.

Vi says my horoscope promises "a romantic encounter," so naturally, I look to Chomperz, the only man currently in my life, for advice. The verdict's in: He has no opinion on the subject and just wants a *full* bowl of Meow Mix, as opposed to the half bowl Mom's been feeding him to "shed some pounds."

I catch Brynn with the door to her room open. She's sitting cross-legged on her bed with the laptop's glare reflecting off her eyes. With everything in this weird middle-ground where things aren't better or worse, I decide it's now or never. I knock on her door frame.

"What?" she asks in a snotty tone.

"Can I come in?" Head down, no eye contact.

"Do whatever you want."

I walk to the edge of her bed, sit right on the ruffle's seam. "What are you doing?"

She doesn't look up from the screen, continues typing. "Homework."

I'm silent, stewing. All I hear are her fingers against the keys—*tap tap*—fast, then slow. She finally looks up.

"Brynn," I start, "I just want to tell you . . . I want to say . . . well—"

"It's okay," she interrupts. "I'm sorry, too."

She shuts the laptop, tosses it aside. Her hands are clamped together tightly, shaking and white-knuckled. She's wrestling with something—something dark that's rising to the surface. "Anyway, it was dumb. I didn't love that jerk. I just wanted . . ."

I grab ahold of her hands to make them stop moving.

Her eyes meet mine, they're filled with tears. "I just want someone to see me."

"I know how you feel."

"No way," she says, wiping snot across her arm. "People *see* you, Birdie. I mean, why *wouldn't* they? Look at you. Even with glasses, you're sooo pretty, and when you talk and use words like, I don't know, *dead bodies,* people listen. They wouldn't listen if *I* said that. Mom would just make an appointment with Dr. Judy to ask me why I'm talking about dead bodies again."

"That's because you're really weird."

She purses her lips, shrugs, and eventually agrees.

"Brynn, you see these things in me, but *I* feel like I fade into the background. The only thing anyone wants to talk to me about, ever, is school and graduation and grades. Like I'm only this one note and never the melody. Does that make sense?"

"No. You're more than the melody—you're the whole song that plays on the radio over and over until people get sick of it. You're, like, *everything.* Even that Bash guy at the rink noticed. I could tell by how he looked at you. I wish Jeremy—or anyone—would see me that way. With all of this crappy stuff happening, I needed you, and you haven't been there. And . . . and I'm scared." And the way she says it, the way her voice cracks, I realize that all these things I never thought I was, I am to her, and maybe Bash, too. Only, I didn't see it in my *before*—just the after. I smile at the little brat.

She looks up at me and smiles, too. Because through all the pain and arguing and fighting, we're always going to be sisters. She'll always be a constant in my life's equation.

"We don't have to, like, hug," she says, breaking through the silence.

"Nope. Just know I, you know, feel things for you."

"Gross."

She pulls her laptop back to her lap, but not before stopping me once more. "Birdie?"

"Yeah?" I ask, rising from her bed.

"If you tell anyone how much I *actually* want to be like you, I'll murder you in your sleep." She moves a finger slow across her throat. "No one will hear you scream."

A grin forms, stretching toward my ears, because now things are totally normal (for us) again. "Mom—time to call Dr. Judy!" I yell.

I'm half awake, sleep still crusted in the corner of my eye, when Mom dangles the Benz hood ornament in front of me.

"Where'd this come from?" she asks.

I yawn, shrug. "Found it outside."

She clutches it in her palm. "You didn't think it was important to tell me or Dad?"

"I didn't know what it was."

"Birdie," she says with tight lips, "you found it out where? In our yard?"

I nod. Slowly. "By the SOLD sign."

"This came off a car, a Benz—maybe the car that hit Benny."

Cold washes over me. "I . . . I didn't think it was anything to worry about."

She sighs. "What's going on with you lately? It's not like you to *not* think about something. The old Birdie would've given this to me or Dad right away, analyzed the type of metal used to make it, and drawn a lengthy conclusion as to the make and model of the car it was sitting on top of."

My voice wavers. "I'm sorry."

"Listen, I know it's been a lot, with Benny, and school, and work, and I haven't been here, and Dad's working, and Brynn's being, well, Brynn, but you've never been the girl who stops using her head. This could solve Benny's case. Or someone else's. You've seen all those crosses out there."

I'm silent, afraid to speak. She can see my reluctance. "I called the investigator from the accident and told him about it. They're going to track down all Benz owners in a hundred-mile radius to see what comes up. If there's anything else you want to tell me, now's the time."

Her eyes almost hurt, the way they're stabbing into me. I shake my head. "Nothing else."

She lingers in my stare long enough to make me uncomfortable. "Okay, then. Get ready for school."

I jump from bed and zip over to my camera where I've taken about a dozen pictures of the ornament from different angles. I press Delete.

Click click click click.

What am I doing? What reason do I have to not tell the police I found it? Honestly, I'd kind of forgotten I had the thing until just now. It's probably nothing. *Probably.* As in, my chances of it being nothing and being something are split fifty-fifty. Not great odds to bank on.

I flip my laptop open and do a quick search of different styles of Mercedes-Benzes, unsure as to what I'm looking for. My eyes scan the pages, scrolling with each picture. News flash—there are a lot, and I can't really tell the difference between them. Until I see something familiar; something I think I saw before:

S65 AMG IN RUBY/BLACK METALLIC

"This *could* be it," I tell Chomperz. Doesn't even open his eyes. Now I *know* I'm onto something, I'm just not *exactly* sure what that is.

A while later, I pull into the school parking lot sort of dazed. I'm going over the night of the accident, bit by bit, trying to see the car in my head. I remember the rain, the smell of my puke, and the sound of Mom's screams. But the car, even from my view up on the hill, is absent from my memory completely. So if I don't remember, why am I stuck on that image and hood ornament?

On my way to class, I hear the sound of Violet's clogs quickly approaching, akin to a fighter pilot's helicopter picking up speed. I spin around before she can tackle me. She does, anyway.

"Ohmygoshohmygoshohmygosh!" She's frantic.

"What's wrong?" I ask, extracting myself from her.

She drops her backpack. Pain etches across her face.

"Vi—what happened?"

"It's Zoe," she says, referring to her acupuncturist. "She said my energy channels are all blocked and then, after a few of the needles wouldn't go in, she looks at me and says, 'Maybe it's not your channels that need the help,' and it hit me, like, here I am looking for all these ways to find answers for you when really maybe all you need is me to be there."

I cock my head to the side and make a pouty face. "Aww—you *are* here for me. No one else makes a wish at eleven eleven every night on my behalf."

She sighs, giving a half smile. "But is there something else I can do? I feel like I'm not doing enough, and I just want to help make things better. Because you're, like, the best person I know, and none of this should be happening, and—"

I wrap my arms around her and squeeze. "You're a nut, and I love you."

She's crying a little. It's this tiny, mouselike *squeak-sniffle-squeak*. "I love you so hard."

I grab her backpack and shove it into her arms. "No. More. Energy. Drinks."

She nods. "You know me too well."

Mrs. Rigsby stops me as I enter the room; Vi moves ahead to her seat. "How's your family holding up?" she asks.

For a split second, I wonder if something's happened in the time since I left home. Things do that. They don't give any warning. They just . . . go. From the way she's looking at me, I'm not sure. "Better, thanks."

"Mmm-hmm. I'm sure it's been hard."

She's never asked like this. Not yesterday or the day before or the day before that, and I'm starting to panic. "Did my parents call the school? Is something wrong?"

"Oh, no. I caught the news this morning. Just wanted to check in."

I lean into her. "What do you mean?"

"Police have a suspect in custody."

My eyes widen. "They *what*?"

"It's great news, right?" She pats my shoulder and moves behind her desk as the bell rings. Vi sees my face. Her hand finds its way to my arm, and she keeps it there for the rest of class.

After school, I weave through the crowds to my car and peel out of the lot. I drive to the hospital, where Mom and Dad are sitting at Benny's side. When I reach the room, I'm out of breath.

"The police arrested someone?" I ask, out of breath.

Mom doesn't turn toward me. "Oh, yeah. But they let him go."

"Why?"

"We don't know. They're not telling us anything."

Dad pats my leg, looks to Benny, and smiles. "He's doing good, though. That's all that matters. Dr. Stein says it's the fastest he's seen anyone come out of a coma. Especially in Benny's state."

I smile, too, but my stomach is still in knots. Something feels off. With Mom's back still to me, I walk toward her. "I found out what kind of car the hood ornament belongs to. If I found it so easily, the police will, too."

"There's the Birdie I know," she says.

I sit with my parents in the room for a while to watch Benny's twitching hands and eyes. He's moving more than he has this whole stay. Christmas music streams in from the hallway.

"I'm not ready for Christmas," Mom says, sighing. "Not without Benny."

"No one would blame you if you wanted to skip it," Dad says. "Thanksgiving was weird enough."

"Brynn's wish list is a mile long," she says, rubbing her temples. "She doesn't get that we're going broke just to keep Benny alive." She looks up at me again. "But you, Birdie, you never ask for anything."

My mind starts pinging in all different directions. "Mom, Dad," I hesitate, "what if something happened to you guys? I don't even know your wishes, what you'd want to happen."

Dad grins, looks to Mom. "What would we care at that point? Just make sure you feed Chomperz. And Sarge."

After a while, I tell them I'm going to work. But instead, I drive to the nursing home to see if there's been any sign of Bash. Checking my phone hasn't magically made his texts appear, and if no one else can tell me where he's at, maybe Camilla can. Life is in this strange transitional state. Unsure of which direction to move, I just go forward as fast as I can, hoping it will unstick the rest of life with me.

I'm empty-handed, no flower or gift, when I stroll around the front desk and down the long hallway. Her door is open, her room is clear. My stomach lurches.

"She died Saturday," Nurse Kim says from behind.

"What? No."

"Thought Bash would've told you by now."

I can't take my eyes off the uninhabited bed, the place where his mother had lain just a few days ago, talking to me, and I can't help but think about Benny and how quickly everything can change. Close your eyes and everything you know is gone. Just like that.

"He won't return my calls, texts. I haven't heard from him since . . . Saturday. Oh my God." It hits me. I know now, selfishly, it *isn't* me. It's her.

"He's devastated, probably doesn't know how to reach out. Not his style. I stopped by yesterday, and even though I saw him through the window, he wouldn't answer the door. He's hurtin' bad. She was his world."

I grab ahold of her arm, plead with big eyes. "Where does he live?"

She backs away. "I can't give that information out. It's against HIPAA laws."

My lip quivers beyond all control. "I know what it feels like, what he's going through. I just want to be there for him. Please."

With a quick glance down the hallway, she grits her teeth as if she's trying to fight the urge to spill something she shouldn't. "Like I said. I can't tell you he lives in the trailer park off Ridge Avenue. It's against HIPAA laws to suggest he might be at number seventeen, near the end. I'd lose my job if I gave that out." She smirks and pats my back. "Take care of that boy, sugar. Lord knows he needs it."

I nod, backing away. My heart pounds with a heavy thud as I walk back to my car, where I'd left the door unlocked—a lesson still not learned. But this time the only thing missing is that little piece Bash took from me.

My heart.

LESSON OF THE DAY: There are reasons—*many* reasons—some particles shouldn't combine, no matter how curious you are about the outcome. Sometimes things explode; sometimes they dissipate, evaporate, disintegrate. And sometimes they collide and become something so much more than you ever thought they could.

Consider this my little experiment.

BASH

I crack open my eyes.

Sunlight streams through the sheets hanging over the windows. I smack my lips together, pinch the skin between my brows, and roll onto my side with a deep groan. It feels like I've been sleeping for a year, a bear waking from hibernation. I glance at the time on my phone—4:01 P.M.—and see four new texts from Kyle.

KYLE: TEXT ME BACK.

KYLE: COPS QUESTIONED ME. DID WHAT U SAID. TOLD THEM IT WAS U WHO STOLE THE CAR.

KYLE: TIMING SUX BUT DON'T HATE ME BRO.

KYLE: I'M SURE THEY'LL LET U GO ONCE YOU EXPLAIN ABOUT YOUR MOM.

There's nothing left in me to feel any kind of rage. The feelings just settle and dissipate in my guts. Feels like a dream, a nightmare. One I won't wake up from. I miss Ma. Her eyes are all I see when I close mine. She's looking at me with that face, the one that sees past all my wrongs, all my mistakes. I'm not easy to love, but damn it, even after all the trouble I caused before she got sick, she never gave up on me.

And now I'm alone.

I reach over and grab a near-empty bottle of whiskey from beside my bed, next to the untouched box of Ma's things. They still smell like her, and I get a huge waft as I lean over. That goddamned Christmas tree stares me in the eye. No blinking lights, but that ornament is latched around the top where a tiny angel should be. I wrap my fingers around the circle and read it again. *If I could give you anything, it wouldn't only be the world, but the hope to fill it with.* I swallow. *Ma, I don't want the world if you're not in it.*

I chug what's left of the whiskey and launch the bottle at the wall. The glass explodes into a thousand pieces, like my heart. I slam my head back into my pillow and sink into the spinning room. My head throbs, but nothing hurts worse than missing Ma. Nothing. Doesn't matter how long she groomed me for her death, the world is frozen, tipped on its axis. There's a complete emptiness in the trailer, the city—the whole damn world. Her spirit is somewhere I can't see or feel, and with it, she took mine, too.

I close my eyes again and drift to a place that comforts me. Ma smiles as I'm about to blow out thirteen candles on the small cake she made from scratch. I remember how long she stood in the kitchen. With flour on her apron, she brought that cake out and sang to me. I still hear the way her voice cracked as she hit the high note at the end. I laughed, and she poked her finger in the icing and pressed it onto the tip of my nose. Kind of the way Birdie did. That's all that's left now. Memories. But the worst part is, wherever she is, if she's looking down on me, she'll know what I've done.

And that kills me.

I grab my phone and drag myself out of the twisted sheet to take a pee, my balance off kilter, and when I'm finished, I see something sticking through the door. It's a bereavement card from Nurse Kim. She wants me to know she's here for me, I'm not alone. I laugh out loud, because they're just words. Words that don't mean shit. I *am* alone. And when

I'm not, it'll be because I'm in jail. So basically, everywhere I look, it sucks.

I grab another bottle of whiskey and slink back over to the recliner. Flipping through my phone's playlist, I find something dark—a Johnny Cash remake of that Nine Inch Nails song, "Hurt"—and let my eyes close. The pain washes over me, cleanses me. My eyes burn and crackle. The vessels feel red, swollen. The more I think, the more I drink. Ma's face, drink. Ma's last words to me, drink. Kyle's stupid face, drink. *Damn.* I can't remember the last time I was hungover *and* drunk at the same time. Probably before Ma got sick, when I fucked up on the regular.

I join in, waving my arms in the air, bottle in hand, singing. As I'm deep in the middle of the first chorus, a knock on the door grabs my attention.

"Go away!" I yell, continuing to wave my fingers to the beat.

"It's me, Bash," Birdie shouts.

I ignore her, lost in the song.

"Let me in," she says. "I see you. I know you hear me."

Still, I ignore her, take another swig.

She pounds on the door's pane, harder this time.

I pretend she's not there. Pretend I'm not here.

She pushes through the door and, in a matter of seconds, is standing in front of me grabbing for my bottle. "Get your own," I say, pulling back. "This one's mine."

"I'm worried about you."

"Go home," I say, bitterness on my tongue. The whiskey swishes like a cyclone.

She kneels in front of me, her big, teary eyes looking up at me through those dopey thick-framed glasses. She grabs my hand. "I'm so, so sorry. There is nothing else I can say. I'm just sorry."

I rip my hand away, take another drink.

"Talk to me," she says. "Let me help."

My eyes still avoid her. "You can't help me. You don't even know me."

"I *do* know you. You're just hurting."

"If you knew me, you wouldn't be here."

Her eyes wander, scanning the place. "I'm not leaving unless you get out of that chair and physically throw me out." Her feet are planted on the floor, so I get up from the chair and yank on the fabric of her jacket.

"What are you doing?" she squeals.

"Throwing you out."

She resists, cocks her arm, and shoves me back into the recliner, where it's still warm. "Let me rephrase—I'm *not* leaving."

I look up at her, my vision wobbling side to side. Her face is stern. "Do whatever you want. I don't care," I say.

She kneels at the side of the recliner again, her chin resting on the arm. The sun streaks her brown hair, highlighting the golden strands.

I hold her stare, challenge her. "Stop. Go be with your family."

"Stop what?"

"Pretending to care about me. Leave. Act like we never met. Trust me. It's for the best."

My intended arrow finds its mark; her face falls. "Haven't you heard of the Butterfly Effect—if I change one thing, it changes *everything.*"

"Isn't that what you want? Everything to change?"

Her hurt turns to confusion. "Not if it means never knowing you."

I swallow that recurring lump that crawls to the top of my throat, choking me. It's prickly and hurts like hell as it goes down. "When you know me, *really* know me, you'll wish you'd never met me. That is a fact. You like facts."

"And maybe I won't. You don't know. It's not a fact, it's a

possibility. They're different concepts—what *will* happen versus what *could*."

We hold our gaze, I think I smile, but I can't feel my mouth. I throw back another swig of whiskey. "She was six months pregnant with me when she left Brazil."

"Why'd she leave?"

My stare goes blank. I feel my muscles tighten, the anger still very much right where I left it. "To get away from my dad."

I start to take another drink, but she pulls the bottle from my hands, wraps her hand around mine. "Did something happen?"

"I asked about a hundred times, she never said," I say, "but the way Ma always tensed up at the question, her body visibly shaken, I didn't need to hear the answer. He wasn't the nicest, and into some bad stuff, if you know what I mean."

There's a long pause, but I see more questions brewing. Her brain never stops.

Stupid fucking beautiful brain.

"Then you moved in with your crappy friend?"

"Ma's first job here in the States was cleaning their house, picking up their shit, basically wiping their asses. But after Kyle's mom threw us out, she met Joe, and I did everything possible to piss her off, make her see he was worse than anything she left in Brazil. Took years, but when he finally left, it wasn't long before she was sick."

She's quiet, tears streaming down her rosy cheeks. "Sorry."

I bite my lip, nod a little. She stands and walks over to the cabinets, flinging them open until she finds a cup. She brings me water and orders me to drink it. I hesitate, shoot her an annoyed look, but I drink it anyway. Because I'm thirsty, not because she gave it to me.

"She mentioned a letter," she says. "Did you get it?"

251

I think back as far as five minutes ago but my brain is mush. "No idea what the hell you're talking about."

"I'm sure you will. She made it sound important."

"I bet."

"When's the funeral?" she asks.

"Week from Tuesday."

She nods. "You know . . . sometimes good-bye is like . . . a second chance, or whatever."

I slowly roll my eyes over to her. "I'm pretty sure you're just quoting Shinedown lyrics now."

She smiles, her face lighting the dark, stale room. "I just mean . . . good-bye is the only way to move on. There's a before and an after that defines you when something big happens. There's before your mom died, and now, after. *You* decide who you're going to be. My grandpa, Sarge, told me that."

I let her words sink in, think what Ma would want me to do, who she'd want me to be. Then I remember I don't have a choice anymore. I gave up my choice to decide when I let Kyle drive that night and then let this mess go on and on and on until Kyle's mouth flew open before mine could.

She fusses with her nails. They're all bitten off. "I went to see your mom again. I mean, before she . . . you know . . ."

I don't flinch. "I know."

"You know?"

"The ornament. Just seemed like something you would do."

Her cheeks flush.

The longer I sit, the more the room moves in waves. I move toward her with my clunky limbs, my face now in hers. She takes her glasses off, cleans them with the hem of her shirt, and I see her, like, *really* see her now.

"You should get contacts," I blurt.

"I have them, just never wear them. It's easier to hide."

"You should never hide. You have really . . . beautiful

eyes." I linger in them, swim around the colors of her ocean for a minute. She smiles at me with only one corner of her mouth upturned. I close my eyes, listen to the sound of her voice.

"So, tell me something. You can draw anything—why bears?"

Her voice echoes now, far away but right in front of me, like tunnel vision in my ears. "They're one of the most solitary carnivores alive, don't need any damn one for any damn thing. I like that."

She pushes her face into mine. I feel her breath on my face. I pry my eyes open and find the center of her light. "You're like Jack in *Titanic*."

"Who?"

"The movie, *Titanic*," she says. "You know—poor, hot boy on a ship, snags the rich guy's girl but dies in the end when the ship hits an iceberg? He saves her. Everyone's seen it—haven't you?"

I shake my head. "Icebergs don't exist anymore. Global warming."

"I hope you're kidding."

I smile.

"Will you draw one for me?" she asks, her voice rising at the end.

"An iceberg?"

"A bear."

"Why? You already stole one from my car." I grin.

She playfully punches my arm. And maybe it's the smell of her perfume or the look in her pleading eyes, or maybe it's just because I'm empty inside and desperately want to feel something—*anything*—but I press my lips onto hers and nestle her face into my palms. She doesn't pull away but sinks into it, wrapping her arms around the back of my neck. Her fingers comb through the strands of my hair with soft, downward strokes, trailing along my skin, all the way down my back. An electric force climbs across my limbs to reignite everything that's been lost. She's breathing life into me. It takes a full thirty seconds, but when it happens, I realize how completely screwed up this is. I pull back. She's out of breath, her big eyes still looking up at me.

"You should go," I tell her. I'm breathless, too.

She's quiet, her head shaking back and forth with a slight smile. She pushes me to the side of the recliner and squeezes in beside me. "Like it or not, you're not a bear. I'm not going anywhere. I'll be the sodium to your chlorine."

"What are you talking about?"

"Together, we're NaCl—you know—salt?"

"Oh my God, you're such a nerd."

"Thanks." She forces her head beneath my arm and snuggles up against me, her hand holding mine. I'm sure I smell like dog shit, but she doesn't seem to care. She's leaning against my chest, her ear to where my heart is beating fast. I let her curl up into me because maybe she needs this as much as I do. I close my eyes again. Ma's face guides me into a deep, dark, slumber. Only this time, I am at peace.

It's around midnight when she elbows me in the rib. "Oh no, oh no, no, no," she's mumbling, trying to pull herself out of the chair.

I rub my eyes. It's still dark, but she's panicked. "What's wrong?" I ask.

"Didn't you hear it?"

"Hear what?"

I follow her finger to the door she's pointing at. "It's the police! Oh, no, no, no. My parents are probably freaking out that I didn't come home!"

I'm half asleep when I hear her words. But with a jolt, I realize what's happening. I grab her arm with urgency to pull her back. "I need to tell you something."

She pulls away, and I drunkenly stumble backward. "Not now, Bash." She's fumbling for a light switch, flicking it on and off, but no lights shine. "What's happening—where's the light?"

"Stop," I tell her. I'm trying to grab ahold of her, but I have no control over my hands. She won't stop moving, rustling farther and farther away from me.

"Don't answer it! Let me talk to you first!" I yell. She turns to look at me one last time, those green eyes catching me through her lenses, as the door swings open. Two officers let themselves inside, and Birdie's face turns ghostly white.

"I'm so sorry," she rambles. "I lost track of time. I . . . Wait . . . how'd you know I was here?"

"Sebastian Alvarez?" one officer says, inching toward me. My face feels hot. "Yes."

He pulls my arms tight around my back and rings the hard metal cuffs around my wrists, binding me to him. "You're under arrest for the hit and run of Benedict Paxton, fleeing the scene of an accident, and theft of Jeffrey Taylor's Mercedes-Benz the night of November seventeenth."

I don't want to look at Birdie's face; I feel her gaze on me already. "Bash?" she asks in a panic. "What . . . what are they saying?"

I'm quiet. My lip bleeds into my mouth I'm biting it so hard.

"BASH!" she repeats. "You *didn't* do this! It's not him—he *didn't* do it! What's happening? Tell me, please! I don't understand!"

The officer gently nudges Birdie away from me. "You have the right to remain silent. Anything you say can be used against you in a court of law."

Birdie pushes through to find my eyes. I try to turn away as the tears fall, soaking into my shirt. She's violently trembling. This is the moment I wanted to avoid. I hear her heart shattering into glass pieces right in front of me, and all I can do is try not to make it worse. So in turn, I say nothing.

"No, no, no," she's mumbling to herself. "He didn't do this. You're wrong. He wouldn't."

I don't know what the cops are saying. My ears are muffled by a high-pitched squeal, the kind you might hear during dead radio air. The officer drags me outside and shoves me by the head into the back of one of the two police cars. So *this* is what eighteen looks like. Not a fan.

I hear her, Birdie, screaming from the front stoop of the trailer where the goddamned 17 is still drooping. The second cop is consoling her, patting her back to calm her even as she runs to the car window. With her fists pounding against the glass, her words stream through, loud and clear. I think she says "I love you," so I turn my head away because I've caused enough damage already.

"BASH! Tell them you didn't do this! Please! Plleeeaasssee!!!" The officer pulls her back again.

The last thing I see before we drive to the station is Birdie crumpling down into the sidewalk. Her head is in her hands—she's probably cursing the day I was born—something most people probably do anyway. The blue and red lights flicker shadows along the dirt road, much like they probably had after we struck her little brother. Guilty, I'm so guilty. I close my eyes and lean my head back on the leather seat. But this time, it's not Ma I'm seeing in my mind. It's Birdie. If she wasn't broken before, she's *officially* broken now.

And I'm the one who broke her.

birdie

I can't breathe. Why can't I breathe?
  Breathe, Birdie. Breathe.
  Inhale, hold. Exhale.
  But . . . Bash . . .
My lungs are deflated like a balloon that's been pricked by a stray twig. I'm slowly falling back to the earth, to reality, and it hurts. So bad. There are layers and layers of ventricles and valves in my heart that seem to break apart with every new ache. And it won't stop.

Officer Hall wants to drive me to the children's hospital. He won't let me behind a wheel in "my condition." He says I'm in shock and shouldn't drive. I think I swat at him a few times as I try to find my keys, so he handcuffs me to "calm me down," which only makes me scream louder. I'm not calm. I don't want to be. My wrists struggle between the clanging metal that's rubbing my skin raw and bloody as I gasp for air, for a clear thought, and I wonder what this all means. I can't seem to piece things together so they make sense. Because to me, *none* of this makes sense. All I know is, there is *no* way Bash had *any* part in what they're saying. The odds of that happening are . . . are . . . and now my brain is broken, along with my heart.

"How long have you known Mr. Alvarez?" the officer asks as I collapse onto the sidewalk.

I try to find a sentence in all the muck. "Work—we met at work. Actually . . . a party first. Then work."

He sits next to me, the moon peering down over us like a big, yellow shadow. "Small world."

"It's actually not *that* small. The circumference of Earth is a mere 24,900 miles, but in comparison to the sun's 2,715,400 miles, I guess . . . yeah. It is." I sniffle, feel my breaths grow longer as I convince myself this is a dream and everything will go back to normal soon. Whatever that means.

He smirks, pulls a tissue from his back pocket, and rests it beneath my nose. I am calmer now, my lungs still palpitating, my breaths growing stronger. "I'll take the cuffs off if you promise not to swing."

I nod. He twists the key in the little hole, and I'm free. He doesn't seem to know exactly what to do or say.

"Sir, why did you arrest him? He didn't do anything. I don't . . . understand. . . . Please."

He sighs. "I'll drive you to your parents first. Then, we can talk."

"What about my car?"

"Don't worry about that right now." He stands, holds out a hand to help me to my feet. I grab hold and wearily dust myself off. He opens the back door of his police car where I reluctantly slide in and try to imagine what Bash is thinking as he sits in another just like it.

"Don't worry," he says. "I won't turn on the siren. Unless you want me to." He spins around to smile, but I turn my focus out the window.

There's a four-mile-long silence before he tries again. "I remember my first love. Couldn't live without her, I thought. Looking back, as real as the feelings were, I see them now for what they were—practice. My heart got broken about a dozen times after that, each one harder than the last. But what I learned was, sometimes no matter how much you love someone, it doesn't mean you should be together. Some chemicals don't mix."

I hear him, but pretend not to, and he's silent the rest of the ride. My thoughts are busy sorting all these new files: Bash, More Bash, Bash Again. This *has* to be some kind of mistake because he couldn't have done what they think he has. Could he? He'd have told me, wouldn't he? I'm not so sure anymore. I *want* to understand—*need* to understand. But I just . . . don't. This is new for me. I text Violet to comfort me, knowing she won't be asleep yet.

ME: GIVE ME TODAY'S QUOTABLE SILVER LINING, STAT!

Not a minute passes before she responds. She sends me an image of a grumpy looking cat with the caption *Every silver lining has a cloud.*

Ugh.

Along the drive, we pass two different pieces of disheveled roadkill I'd normally take pictures of. Instead, I feel like I'm lying right beside them. Smashed. When we get to the hospital, Officer Hall walks me to Benny's room. I'm slow to follow. He seems to know where he's going. A couple steps before we're there, he turns his cherry nose and cheeks to face me. "I saw your story on the news. The whole department has been on the case nonstop. That something like this could happen here . . . horrible. So I've checked in on your little brother a time or two, because, well, I've got a little boy. I've been praying for you all."

He turns before I can respond, rapping his knuckles on the door's frame. Mom and Dad are inside, nearly asleep. I trail behind the officer, a little ashamed, but I'm not exactly sure why. I've not done anything wrong. *Or have I?*

"What is it?" Mom asks, rising from Benny's bedside.

She's wearing slouched sweat pants and an oversized tee with the picture of the three of us from before I began eighth grade.

Officer Hall beckons me. Uneasily, I step into the spotlight. The buzz sizzles overhead as I take a deep breath.

Officer Hall looks at me, then back to them. "We've arrested the person responsible for your son's hit and run."

Mom clamps her hand over her mouth and immediately starts crying what I assume to be happy tears. Dad is smiling but holds back. He's restrained. Arms crossed tightly over his chest, eyebrows knitted together, he knows there's more. "When? How?"

"Well, you already knew we busted that dealer in New Castle but let him go. What you don't know is we let him go in exchange for information. He had proof—pictures of the car he fixed the day after the accident—but didn't realize was the car in question until afterward. The car was stolen by a Sebastian Alvarez. We took him into custody an hour ago."

Mom walks closer, as if being closer makes the words clearer. "Wait, why is my daughter with you, then? It's after midnight."

"He—" My voice cracks. "Bash, he . . ."

"Birdie—you okay? I'm confused. Did that boy hurt you, too?" she asks.

I'm vigorously shaking my head, fighting their words. "No. No. He *didn't* do this. He couldn't have."

"I don't understand," Mom says. She's hugging me, then pulls back. My eyes can't find hers. I'm swimming through all the things I've ever said to Bash, all the things he ever said to me. And in all of that, I feel a deep, sinking stone floating down the length of my body like an anchor.

Gently, Officer Hall places his hand on my shoulder. "She's in shock. We found her *with* Mr. Alvarez when we arrested him. I don't think she knew of his connection."

"What?" The word rings sharply in my ears. "Birdie, is all this true?"

I finally move my eyes up to hers, and it stings. "I . . . I don't know what's happening."

"I need to understand this, Birdie. How do you know this boy? Where did you meet him?"

The officer interjects. "She said they met at a party *and* they work together."

"You've known this boy ALL THIS TIME?" Mom shouts at me, grabbing my shoulders and shaking them. "And you SAID NOTHING?"

I flinch as Dad pulls her away.

"She didn't know, Bess," Dad says, to my rescue. "If she had, she wouldn't have been with him. Right, Birdie?" The way he says it, though, it's like he really doesn't believe it and honestly, I don't blame him.

"There must be a reason," I mutter. "He wouldn't lie to me. Not about this. He wouldn't." I think I'm crying now, because everything blurs. The room shrinks in size. Everyone is in my face asking things, pointing at me, yelling at me, and I have no answers—for once in my life—and all I can think is, Brynn would love this.

Dad's nodding, pinching his lips. "Okay, okay," he says, brushing the hair from my face. "She didn't know. This *isn't* her fault. Let's take a breath and figure it out. Okay, Birds? It's okay. We'll figure it out together." He pulls me into him, and I bury my face in his sweater, hiding.

"What will happen to this young man?" he asks the officer. He's rubbing my back in circles, trying to make sure I know he's on my side, maybe. And I wonder, *Who is on Bash's side?*

"Indiana hit-and-run laws are pretty straightforward," Officer Hall says with a firm voice. "Mr. Alvarez stole a car, hit and nearly killed a boy, and fled the scene. We also have reason to believe he was impaired at the time of the collision. *If* your son pulls through, he could be looking at three to five years in prison, plus fines upwards of five thousand dollars, or more."

"And if he doesn't . . . pull through?" Mom speaks up.

"Let's just hope it doesn't come to that."

My eyes sting as I look up. "Please don't press charges. I'm sure you have the wrong person or maybe it was an accident or . . . I don't know. Please. You don't know him like I do. I'll never ask for anything ever again. I won't even see him. I just want him to be okay. Please. I . . . I promised his mom before she died."

I'm pleading for his life, knowing I shouldn't. Maybe he isn't worth my pleas. I should feel the way Mom does right now, appalled and disgusted. But for some reason, he *is* worth it. Mom and Dad are silent.

"It doesn't work like that," Officer Hall interrupts. "He broke too many laws, so it's out of your parents' hands. If it makes you feel any better, the owner of the car isn't pressing charges for theft. He *is* grateful to have his hood ornament back, though, so thank you for turning that in, Mrs. Paxton."

"Who owns such an expensive car in this area, anyway?" Dad asks. "They told us it cost something like two hundred grand. I can't imagine someone lives near us with that kind of money."

"Indy's not that far, Dad," I blurt out. "Probably commutes the hour like everyone else in the area."

Officer Hall clears his throat. "The car is registered to Jeffrey Taylor. He was out of town when this happened, so he didn't know about any of it."

"Jeffrey Taylor, as in Taylor Real Estate Investments?"

Officer Hall nods, rests his fingers on his belt buckle.

Dad's focused on the wrong things, scratching his head like he's solving a mystery. "Thought he lived in Indy."

Mom's hand drops to her side. "Oh my *God*. He called me! It didn't make sense before, but now—"

"What? When was this?" Dad interrupts, the concern in his voice growing.

"A few hours ago, when you went for coffee. He said if we needed anything, he'd take care of it. I didn't understand why. I thought, because he owns the housing complex, it was about our house, but then he said something about a Kyle? I couldn't remember anyone with that name helping us with the sale. I don't know. The nurses were trying to check Benny's vitals, and I was half asleep, so I just hung up."

"Wait," I say slowly, my heart skipping into my throat. The pieces suddenly string together like magnets. "Bash's friend is Kyle—*he* did this—he *has* to be Mr. Taylor's son. The money, the car . . . It makes sense now—Bash is innocent! He *didn't* do this! I knew it!" I turn to Officer Hall, plead with him to hear me. "Please let him go. Talk to Kyle!"

Officer Hall seems perplexed, but reluctantly jots down my notes. "We already had Kyle Taylor in for questioning but couldn't keep him. I can't make any promises, but I'll look into it," he says. "So if you don't have any other questions, I'll get back to you when there's news."

"Thank you for dropping her off," Mom says. "We'll take it from here."

He nods, reaches for a handshake from Dad before turning to me. "Remember what I said in the car? No matter how much you love someone, doesn't mean you should be together. Some chemicals don't mix." He tips his hat and disappears. Maybe the words should echo or I should feel like they mean something. They don't.

The moment he leaves, Mom's eyes zero in on me, but she says nothing; she doesn't have to. In exactly four weeks, two days, thirteen hours, I've somehow gone from knowing exactly where my life would take me to becoming our family's inhibitor. *I* am preventing us from moving forward because maybe—and I didn't see this before—*I'm* not ready to. To move forward, to go away to a college we can't afford, to let Nan go, to leave Sarge and Brynn and everyone else, to accept all the damage I've caused with Benny (and Bash), all because *I* lost traction in my *own* life, would mean I'm flawed in more ways than I can process. I am *not* perfect. I *will* mess up. I *will* fail.

And Bash? He's a bear—doesn't need "any damn one for any damn thing." And yet here I am. Maybe I should hate him for being part of our tragedy, keeping the truth from me, whatever the truth is. *How could I even consider forgiving him?* I wonder.

But more so, *How could I not?*

In the middle of this long, drawn-out silence, a series of beeps grows louder. My ears pop as if I'm hearing for the first time. I follow Mom's wide eyes, Dad's too, to Benny's twitching limbs, all the way up to his half-bandaged face, where, finally, his lashes flutter.

And his eyes, they open.

LESSON OF THE DAY: This variable in any reaction is unexpected because that is, literally, what it's supposed to be—a surprise element. Like a twist in the plot. Or wind velocity that suddenly picks up during a rainy night. There are so many variables in everyday life, things I don't always notice at first that can change the outcome dramatically.

That's the beauty/pitfall of science/love.

BASH

"Name?" the officer asks, barely looking up from the glaring computer screen.

"Sebastian Matéus Alvarez," I state.

"Ahh, yes," he says smugly. "Repeat offender, Mr. Alvarez. Looks like we didn't leave a lasting impression."

"Don't remember."

He laughs. "Hopefully this time does the trick, then. You're eighteen now. This ain't juvy. This is a serious felony, with a multi-year sentence up for grabs. That's a lot of time to remember."

He continues with the obvious questions. I can almost say the words before he does. Date of birth, social security number, address. Blah blah blah.

"Could you please recall the incident, in your own words?"

I lean into him, my cuffed hands propped on the desk. "You know, I'm missing my mother's funeral planning for this. How about you let me go, arrest me tomorrow, and we'll start over." I smile, something plastic.

"Sorry, compadré. Arrest warrants don't care who died. But off the record, I'm sorry for your loss."

I lean back, take a deep breath. "Thanks, I guess. So if I tell you what you want to know, can we get on with act three already?"

"Absolutely."

I tell him how it went down, how Kyle had *no* idea I snuck into his house to get the keys to his dad's Benz, how I drove, drunk and high (things I could've probably left out, but at this point, what the hell?), on a dangerous highway bend, struck this kid, and left the scene almost immediately. I tell him I thought it was a deer, because I (we) did. I say the impact scared me (us) shitless, so I drove the car back to the house and snuck out the garage door. And finally, when he digs deeper into the file and asks if recently released Kyle knew about, or helped, with any part of this, I look him straight in the eyes. "No."

My answers don't satisfy the curious cop. "Perjury is punishable by up to five years in the slammer, so if you had help, don't cover."

I don't flinch. "You wanted my story. You got it."

He taps his pen against the desk. "How'd you get in the garage?"

I don't even hesitate. "We used to live there. I remembered the code." *This* satisfies him—*this* helps his case more than anything else I've said. Because now I have credibility. Now I have access. Now they might believe every lie I tell them.

He notes my dark hair and hazel eyes, the clothes I'm wearing (the same I'm always wearing), and pushes my fingers onto a pad of black ink, then onto the document. He doesn't make small talk, not that I expect him to, but through the noise of the precinct, it's still stifling and uncomfortable. I look away, bite my tongue, so not to make it worse. Whiskey hangover intact, my head's thrashing a thunderous bass line through my skull. He eventually guides me to my mug shot photo session.

I blink. "Can I do that one over?" I ask.

He ignores me, taking me over to a small area where he tells me to put my hands up. His hands pat every inch of my body, digging into my back pocket where my phone is nes-

266

tled. He takes it, throws it into a bin. "You'll get your phone call from our phone."

I keep my mouth shut, let him push me into a holding cell where four others are waiting for me. Their eyes are transfixed by the fresh meat walking in. I'm obviously a decade, or more, younger; a shade, or twelve, darker; and a little less sure of my place. The one on the bench slides over. He's built like a Tonka truck, large and in charge, but his eyes are soft, and he nods at me like we're old friends.

"What are you in for, little homey?" he asks. The others turn away from us to sink back into their own thoughts.

I dig my head into my chest and keep my voice low. "Car accident, my fault."

He nods and points to himself. "Robbery, strike three. Good thing we're not in Cali, or I'd be shit outta luck."

We make eye contact, but just for a second. He looks me up and down. "You can't be older than fifteen, sixteen. Why you in here?"

"Eighteen. The kid I hit might not wake up."

He makes a whistling noise through his teeth. "You hit a kid? That's cold."

Another man pulls his sights from the bars and spins to face me. He's pencil thin with eyes the color of coal. "I thought your face looked familiar. It's all over the news. We got ourselves a celebrity in here."

There's that lump again. "It was an accident."

"Some accident," the thin man says. "Police have been lookin' for you for weeks." Tonka Truck Man slaps his legs. "He's just a little girly man." He pulls my shirt back, flings it against my skin, then musses my hair. He pretends to search for a bug in the air—"Probably wouldn't swat a fly if it landed on him"—and smacks his hands together as if he's smashed it.

I don't say anything. My arms crossed tight, I back away, bury my head deep, and keep looking down. *Just get through it,* I tell myself. And finally, they leave me be. I sit in this exact position for five hours, watching, waiting. In this five-hour period, each of the other four people go on to their own fates. When the officer opens the door, I'm the only one left in the quiet, urine-scented cell.

"It's your lucky day," he says. "Someone posted bail."

I look up. A wretched crick in my neck momentarily paralyzes me. "Who would save *me*?"

"Your guardian angel." He points to a tall man in a navy suit, with silver hair and golden skin from the California sun he's been basking in recently.

"Mr. Taylor," I say, confused. "What are you—"

"Get your things," he orders, briefcase at his side. "We need to talk." His shadow fades beyond the door, and I'm still frozen to this goddamned spot. My heart beats faster. I sign everything I need to sign, plead whatever Mr. Taylor tells me to plead, and with my phone back in my pocket, drag my sorry self out into the morning sun, where my breath nearly freezes in the air in front of me. His new car, a navy BMW, is parked in the front row, the engine warming with a cloud of smoke that clings and separates as it moves.

I hesitate, but he opens the door. "Get in."

I stare at the floor, try to find a way out of this. He beats me to it. "Sebastian," he says, angling his body toward me, "*why* would you do this?"

My hands are shaking. Partly from the cold, partly because of this man I looked up to for so long. "I thought it was a deer, or dog. Not a kid. I'm sorry for—"

He's shaking his head. "No, I mean, *why* would you protect Kyle?"

I raise my eyes to his, unsure of what to say. "Why would you think I—"

"Stop," he interrupts. "I know my son. He's manipulative like his mother, charming like his old man, and when our backs are turned, reckless."

"Sir," I say, "Kyle didn't—"

"I knew it when they set him free. He did this, not you. My lawyer is working on getting the major charges cleared. Hell, I'd have had you out of here sooner if I'd known they arrested you through the night."

"I'm *not* innocent. We were both drinking and smoking and—"

"You were scared of losing your mom," he says, with a firm hand on my leg. "I'd have wanted to fall into a black hole, too. Who wouldn't?"

My eyes drop. And it's now, right now, I see her face again.

"I know you were *there,* but I also know you weren't behind the wheel. Kyle thinks he's invincible. That's my fault. Let him get away with too much, too long, and now look where we are."

"Mr. Taylor," I say.

The sunlight catches on his wedding band, sending a direct gleam onto the dash. It's a reminder of the line drawn between us.

"After that New Castle dealer called me, said Kyle had been paying him to keep his mouth shut and he wouldn't do it anymore unless *I* gave him money, I confronted Kyle, and of course, he denied it, said it was you. He tried to tell me that you and Camilla were still pissed over Linda kicking you out. He actually said you had it in for me, after all these years, and probably went on a joyride to hurt someone the way I'd hurt you. Like payback."

The words singe my insides. "Kyle said that?"

He's nodding slowly. "Finally, after cops questioned and released him, he was so damn cocky around the house, I got it out of him that he anonymously called the cops on you. He said it was to protect me and the agency, but I knew it was to protect him from paying for what he'd done. I guess he told them he had proof you'd been breaking into one of my empty houses in the development by the boy's house. But I knew better."

I look up at him, afraid of what he'll say.

"It's not just that the keys to that Benz are in a locked drawer in my study or that the station was turned to something heavy metal, Kyle's favorite, but it was something else, something bigger that told me *you* didn't do this. You."

Confused, I'm careful with my words. "I . . . I don't understand, sir. I *was* there. I deserve to be punished for not coming forward. I'm an accomplice."

A slight smile forms. "Sebastian, I don't disagree with you. You're guilty, too. Keeping quiet was wrong. But protecting Kyle was worse. I'm of the mind, like most might be if they actually knew you, that maybe you've already suffered more than a kid should. Maybe you've already paid for this mistake long before it ever happened."

I swallow. It hurts.

"I remember when you were little. Kyle blamed you for everything, whether you were there or not. He thought I liked you more. At times, I did. You were grateful, never talked back, and liked hearing about all the 'boring' details of my job. You and I have always been more alike than Kyle and I, and it bugs the shit out of him *and* Linda."

I open my mouth, but snap it shut quickly, not sure what he's trying to tell me.

"I went to see your mother last week," he blurts.

"What?"

"At the time, she was clear and coherent. Honestly, I was surprised she even knew me when I walked through the door, but the nurse said she hadn't seen her like that in a month, and it wouldn't last. I had no idea she'd go so soon after, and I'm very sorry. Truly."

He gives a heavy sigh. "There's something you should know, Sebastian. I feel I owe it to you."

He pauses. *Please don't pause.*

"I *never* wanted you to move out. That was all Linda. We fought over it for months."

"You don't have to explain."

"No," he says, firmly, "I do."

"I tried to make it right and give Camilla things—a place to stay, money, whatever you needed to grow into whatever person you wanted to become." He pauses again. "She wouldn't accept it. Refused it all. Didn't want the trust fund I tried to establish to secure your future, wanted to teach you to work for things. I tried to keep in touch, but she didn't want to cause more problems in my marriage. She'd probably have kept you away from Kyle if you didn't go to the same school."

"She tried."

"Let me guess—Kyle's dedicated persistence is the reason it didn't stick."

I try not to nod, but it slips.

He clears his throat. "She always put you first, the man in her life. She wanted to teach you right from wrong. And she has, because look at you. I can see how sorry you are over this. Others will, too. I don't want you to worry about a thing. I'll make sure you have what you need, make sure you graduate, get into whatever college you want. I owe that much to Camilla. This isn't your cross to bear, Sebastian. It's Kyle's."

We sit for a while. Until the sun is glaring its blinding golden rays onto the dash. I'm acutely aware of how valuable his time is and grateful he carved some of it out just for me. Even more so to hear answers to all the things I never had answers to.

Before we leave, he tells me his attorneys will help clear my name so the accident won't haunt me wherever I go. I won't get off entirely; I'm an accessory, however unwilling.

But he assures me he—and his lawyers—will not rest until things are set right and Kyle has real consequences to his careless choices. I breathe a long sigh of relief, letting the guilt float away into the wind and hoping that somehow Birdie breathes it in, too.

In the end, he begs me not to worry, instead to take this time to grieve for Ma. And he thanks me for being Kyle's only friend. I don't know what to say, so I just nod. Eventually, he shifts his car into gear, and we ride in silence.

A few minutes later, we're parked in front of my trailer, the same spot where Kyle parks his car. I look up at my crappy shack with regret and hesitation in a way I've done so many times before, and yet, not. I now see what Birdie was talking about:

This is my after. And it royally blows.

Mr. Taylor watches intently as I open the door. I look at him one last time, knowing after this I have nothing to go home to. "Thank you," I tell him. My voice cracks.

He nods, reaches into his pocket, pulls out a crisp white envelope with my name on the front, and offers it to me. "Take care of yourself, Sebastian. I hope this helps you find some peace." He lingers for just a moment, his smile fading with the sun. "We'll be in touch."

I slam the door shut and watch as he pulls away, leaving me here, in literal ruins. My fingers poke inside the envelope to pull out a crumbled piece of paper.

My eyes spring wide. *The tall man with eyes like crystal.* There really is a letter, just as Birdie said. I smile because Ma wasn't crazy in the end, and that comforts me.

I choke on the sloppy writing because it feels like her hand was just here; her pen dragging these words out of her fingers not long ago. The paper smells like her perfume. It's small, folded in half, with the header CLIFTON NURSING AND REHAB CENTER at the top. I close my eyes and see her, hear her, speaking to me.

My dearest Bash,

You don't yet know how special you are, but I always have. From the moment I first held you, I saw it in your eyes. That spark, that flicker; most people don't have it. I won't be there to tell you how proud I am (a ton) or how much I love you (more than a ton), but know I am here, cheering you on from the bluebird sky. My first, only, and one true love, you are so beautiful to me (having a little Joe Cocker never hurt anyone). I have one request and you'll probably think I'm a buzzkill (or lame or rank, or whatever word you kids use these days): Finish school. Just because you're grown and I'm not here to force you doesn't mean you can quit. We may come from drunks and addicts, but we're hardworking, loyal sons of bitches, and we're sure as hell not quitters. Never have been, never will be. And when you want to let chemistry, or whatever subject you're failing, get the best of you, think of me—I fought until the very end (mostly because they wouldn't give me enough morphine to end it sooner) (kidding) (sort of).

I'm sorry there's no will. No point. We ain't got shit to give away. In fact, take that trailer, every-thing in it, and burn that mother down. But tell the neighbors first. We're not quitters, but we're also not inconsiderate arsonists. Start over. Somewhere big and beautiful, somewhere deserving of you. But more than this, my little Picasso, be everything I know you can be. Believe in yourself. I always have.

Love, Ma

My tears drip onto the paper as I crumble it to a ball in-side my fist. Pain surges through me. My veins are electrical lines, lit with the kind of power that could either come alive or burst into flames. I fall to my knees and sob into my hands, right here on the cold, hard sidewalk where I watched Birdie do the same for me. I want the pavement to crack apart, open a hole I can fall straight through. *I miss you so much, Ma, it physically hurts.* Like someone pulled all of my bones apart, one by one, and tossed them into a fire. I don't care if anyone hears me, sees me. I just want to sink into the earth and disappear, forever.

Without her, there's nothing.

The wind picks up, nearly blows the envelope out of my hand. I slap my hand down on the flap and notice another piece of paper tucked inside, the tip barely visible. My shaking fingers grab it.

It's a check. Written to me.

The memo: Via Sebastian's Trust Fund.

The amount: $100,000.

And signed: Jeffrey Taylor.

birdie

Dr. Stein says, "Pigs *do* fly."

I get the reference but don't laugh. He's waiting, standing here for the rumpus to erupt, but there is none. We are not that kind of family anymore. You could say we've become a bit jaded, or maybe he's just not funny. Benny's eyes have been open a few days now, his fingers twitching more, and that flicker of light Dr. Stein swore he saw, well, we see it now, too. Everyone does, which means Mom spends a lot of time prancing around with a smug look on her face as if to say *told you so*. Doctors Morrow and Schwartz have been in more frequently, examining Benny, commenting how "astounding" his progress has been. They've even asked if they could document his case in one of their studies that would be shown to hospitals around the world.

As far as money goes, thanks to an angel donor's check and donations from people around the community, Benny's bill has a huge dent in it, and Mom and Dad can finally breathe, *I* can breathe, while we figure out the rest. Ms. Schilling even found another scholarship for me. It's a little less than the last, but it's something. And right now, though I've yet to tell my parents about the lack of college money, it's enough. It's like the stars have started to align or something—not that I completely believe in all that. But something definitely shifted in our favor. Part of me wonders

275

if Nan had a hand in this, while the other part knows there has to be a logical explanation instead.

I've been working less hours at the rink, not that I ever worked much in the first place, but it feels strange. It has nothing to do with needing the money, or Benny's condition, or because I dislike scraping gum off the bottoms of tables, but because there's no Bash. I've asked Vinny to reconsider, but he says Bash is a lost cause. Hearing his name or seeing the chair he used to sit in makes my heart break all over again, so I decided not to be there for now. Plus, Evie's been hugging me more, telling me things like "he's not worth it, honey," and "even innocent, he's still guilty." Everyone has an opinion on who (they think) Bash is and what (they think) should happen to him. But none of them really know.

Not even me.

While Mom and Dad are at the hospital, I rustle through my closet to find something dark, something bleak. Something that screams I'm-sorry-your-Mom-died-and-I-wasn't-there-but-you-got-arrested-for-being-involved-in-the-hit-and-run-of-my-brother-and-you-lied-to-me-and-I've-tried-to-hate-you-but-I-don't. A dress is hanging from each hand when Sarge interrupts. He doesn't say anything, but instead, holds a square of bubble wrap into the air like a siren.

Pop pop pop.

I look up, and he smiles. "Got a minute?

"Sure." I toss the dresses to my bed for further consideration (neither is really an option because they don't convey the right message of being sorry but not *too* sorry). "What's up?" I ask sitting down on the bare spot they leave on my bed.

He moves slowly and sits along the edge of my bed next to me. I feel the warmth of him even though there's ample space between us. "How are you?" he asks.

I hesitate. "Fine."

"How are you *really*?"

My hands fold together between my legs, and I shrug. When we discovered Bash's actual part in the accident, there seemed to be an unspoken understanding between Mom and me. That the heart wants what it wants, despite not always knowing if it's for the best. We've yet to decide if my heart is right or wrong, but I'm banking on the former.

"I realized no one has asked how you're doing lately. Since your friend was arrested. I know how Mom and Brooks and Brynn are. I'm pretty sure I know how Chomperz feels. So I want to know. How are *you*, Birdie?" He points a thick finger at my heart.

"Fine." I feel the tears mounting, so I look away.

"I know you feel a great sense of responsibility for a lot of things beyond your control, things you can't calculate or reason. But you don't have to always be strong or pretend you aren't hurting. If you feel guilty—about Benny, about that boy, about any of it—it's all right. But know this: if you need to fall apart, to release all the pain you've been holding on to all these weeks, I'll be right there to put you back together." He clears his throat, then hesitates. "For a while there, before Benny woke up, you were . . . different."

"What do you mean, *different*?" My voice is small and quiet.

He chuckles. "In a *good* way. Through all the darkness, you found some sort of light. And now that everything's out in the open, I know why."

My heart flutters. "I don't know what you're talking about."

As he pats my leg, his smile grows. "Birds, it's okay. Tragedy rips people apart. It devours every last bit of the soul, and in some, erases all hope or faith or belief anything could ever be good again. But you found a reason to smile, to forget, to *live*. And God damn it, I'm so glad you did. Nan would be, too."

His eyes let me right inside without limit, and in this very moment, I miss Nan so much, I could die. I know, realistically, "broken heart syndrome" is actually a temporary muscle weakness that's been caused by a surge of intense stress, but I wonder if the damage in my own "broken" heart is irreversible and I will, in fact, eventually die from it.

"I know you. You're overthinking, listing all the reasons you shouldn't laugh, or all the ways things could've been different, and are probably weighing your parents' opinions more than your own here. But I'm telling you, as someone with a helluva lot more objective insight, and I think Nan would agree with me if she were here—you're wrong."

My lips tremble as I blink the tears free from my lashes. "*Wrong?* About what?"

"Love."

I gasp, putter through a string of unintelligible words.

His smile widens, revealing the lines of a life well lived around his eyes. "If Nan had given up on me for making mistakes, for being *human,* we wouldn't have had fifty years together. You want my advice? Forgive him. Don't let his mistake keep you from the things you deserve to feel. This doesn't mean you'll forget, no. It just means to decide if it's worth holding on to the anger, or if in doing that, you'll always wonder what could've been."

My body shifts, suddenly uncomfortable inside its own skin.

"Birdie . . . I know it's confusing to care about someone who's hurt you, your family, but . . . he lit you up inside a very dark world. Don't *ever* be ashamed for feeling that light."

I open my mouth to argue, but all words become one jumbled image. Of Bash. With a long, dramatic sigh, Sarge stands and leaves me in this spot. As he rounds the corner, he finishes our heart-to-heart with the only thing that makes sense in this world so full of uncertainty.

Pop pop pop.

* * *

A while later, I'm sitting with my legs kicked up in the hospital chair next to the dream catcher Violet brought by to siphon off Benny's night tremors, while Mom reads a magazine next to his bed. With Benny's progress all over the news, everyone is treating me differently, but this time, in a good way. They're not walking around with their heads hung low, saying "I'm so sorry" or hugging me too much (except for Vi, still). They're smiling at me, saying "good for you," like I'm the one who made it happen, which I don't mind them thinking. And because I never told most people—including Vi—about my complex relationship with Bash, I also never had to explain all the bad things that followed.

I've had Camilla's obituary next to the crinkled mess of Bash's arrest and release articles, stuffed in the corner of my camera case for days where they're safe, even though at first, once the shock wore off, I wanted to pretend I'd never met him, pretend he wasn't part of the biggest earthquake to have ever happened in the Paxton realm. But I can't. He's, like, in my bones, where it's built up, hardened, disrupting the normal process, the usual flow.

Sebastian Alvarez is calcification defined.

I glance at the clock to keep track of time, 8:37 A.M., and tap my pencil on my shiny black leggings. As I'm finishing up the extra-credit work I don't need in an educational kind of way, but more like a keep-my-mind-off-things kind of way, I try, with everything in me, *not* to think of the calcium buildup that didn't just disrupt organ function, but broke the valves of my heart altogether.

Dad drove me over to trailer seventeen a few days ago to get my car and be my shield against any confrontation. With the 7 dangling against the rusted siding, there was no sign of Bash, like he's been gone all along. And thinking back, I guess that's kind of true. Dad must've seen the hurt on my face—the longing to see the mysterious, heartbreaking

Sebastian Alvarez just *one* more time—because he looked up at me with these watered eyes and tight lips, and said, "Sometimes, love and loss are kind of the same," and I remember choking a little, not because he was so wrong, but because he was so right.

The day Kyle Taylor was officially arrested for the hit-and-run, a huge anvil was plucked from my shoulders. Though everyone tried to tell me otherwise, I knew all along, somewhere deep inside my soul, Bash was (mostly) innocent. I didn't use assumptions or guesses, but facts. It is a fact he is not capable of such a thing. I will attest to that one under oath.

And these same thoughts, these truths and facts, haunt me every second of every day.

Suddenly, his face enters my mind.

It's all I see, feel.

I lift my phone. No messages or calls.

I hold my stare long, hope wishing for it will make it so, but every passing second leaves my inbox, and me, emptier than ever. Back to work, I sink into the chair a little farther.

> For the following reaction, predict whether the rate is likely to be fast or slow, based on the physical state of the reactants:
>
> $$H_2(g) + Cl_2(g) \rightarrow 2\ HCl(g)$$

Scribbling the answer—*crazy fast*—I feel Mom's eyes shift in my direction.

"And pretty soon, Benny Boo," she says to him, "you'll be out of this place, and we'll be a whole family again."

I look up from my work to see her eyes. "You're not wearing your glasses," she comments.

"Haven't in days."

She walks toward me, moves to sit in the chair my feet

are propped up on. I swing them down to give her room. "Your eyes . . . they're so . . . pretty," she says, brushing my hair off my cheek.

With a long sigh, she holds my stare. "I know about the scholarship."

My stomach knots. This exact conversation is the very thing that set this horrible trail of things in motion, why I'm even sitting in a hospital at all. My instinct now is to run from it. So as not to cause more pain. I try to stand, but she plants me back down into the chair.

"Birdie, I'm not mad. If anything, I feel sad for you. I know how hard you worked for that scholarship, how hard you work, period. And by the way, even though Brynn takes great pride in burning you at the stake, I'd *never* punish you for sneaking out to a party! You're such a good girl, you deserve to do fun things. Just ask us next time. I trust your judgment. You're almost eighteen. You'll be out of the house soon, and I've got to start learning to let you go."

I bite my tongue, afraid of what she'll say next, afraid I might start crying and never stop.

She tucks a few strands behind my ear; her hand is cold from the hospital air, but I don't mind. "I don't want you to worry about the money part. Dad and I will do whatever we have to so yours, Brynn's, and Benny's needs are met. No matter what. Okay?"

"But how did you know?" I ask.

"Ms. Schilling called. She was worried about you after Benny's accident, and because I know how hard you take news like that, I was afraid to say anything. I didn't really know how to tell you everything would be okay when, at the time, I wasn't sure myself. Now I know it will be. But . . . I've been wondering."

"What?"

"Why lie? It's not like you to keep things from me."

My chest tightens, the air too thick to inhale. "I was afraid you'd be disappointed. I started to tell you in the garage. That's when, well, Benny . . . and it was all my fault—"

"Oh, Birdie," she says, hugging me tight. Her voice expands to a full-on cry. "What a horrible guilt you must've been carrying around." She pulls back from me and cups my face in her palms. "That was an *accident*. It's *not* your fault. *I. Love. You.* And I'm sorry if I ever made you feel otherwise."

She's sobbing now. I press my forehead against hers and close my eyes like we used to do when I was little. A smile breaks across my face, a kind I haven't had since before the accident. She inhales the side of my head and breathes out like it's the best scent she's ever smelled, and I look up at her, and still see, feel, Bash. There is no amount of Wite-Out or erasing that can undo the drawing he's etched on my heart.

She pulls back again to wipe her tears, as she looks deep into the quiet sorrow I'm still clinging to. Her eyes possess more pressing questions but she smiles slightly and pats my arm. "I've never seen you so upset over a boy before. You *love* him."

I fall back to the layers of her, avoiding the statement. If I avoid it, we don't have to talk about it again. If we don't talk about it, maybe it isn't true.

The soft cords of her sweater smother me, but I like it. With a glimmer of compassion in her eyes, she kisses my forehead. "I'm so sorry, Birdie."

She holds me closer, tighter. I don't ever want to let go.

Letting go means it really is love.

But worse than that, it really is over.

LESSON OF THE DAY: If you want to speed up the overall reaction, you should focus on that rate-limiting step, which is THE slowest part. This, for me, is, has been, and probably always will be, saying good-bye.

BASH

The goddamned tiger lilies are in her final wishes.

I can't help but think it's like her last laugh, that as she sits on a white, fluffy cloud next to Elvis and Lucille Ball and Prince, she's pointing her finger at me like she's won. I bring a single calla lily to rest beside her in the wooden coffin, to silently point my finger at her, though. *Who's winning now, Ma?*

The funeral director, Ed Riley, says Nurse Kim and the nursing home staff took care of everything I was supposed to. I should be proper and call him Mr. Riley, but my brain keeps telling me it's Mr. Ed and then I think of the horse from that old television show Ma loved and we just stare at one another oddly while I picture him with a horse's head.

I come dressed in the finest clothes I now own. One old, navy-blue suit with a plaid tie, purchased from Goodwill. It's 9:45 A.M., and no one's here. It makes me worry no one will show up, that no one cares about her like I did. A riptide of pain slices through me. If the pews are empty, I will hurt for her. *It's their loss,* I think.

I'm sitting in the front row, across from Ma. She's surrounded by endless flowers and is wearing the finest dress she owned, a long, maroon sheath of pure silk—something, she said, that made her feel like royalty. Her head is draped in a head scarf that matches perfectly. My face is still buried in my hands as the first person walks up to me, resting a gloved hand on my shoulder.

"Hey," Nurse Kim says. "How ya holding up?"

I shrug. A slew of all the nurses and doctors who cared for Ma crowd in around me. Nurse Kim pulls me up, and I bury my face in her wool coat between the layers of fuzz. Five other hands pat my back, rub the coat of my new suit. It's warm in here, safe. She pulls back, tears in her eyes, and I want to tell her thank you, for everything, but I can't find a single word that's good enough. She smiles, nods, like she already knows what I'm trying to say, and hugs me again.

When I lift my head, a long line of people have formed behind her, stringing around the back corner. Pews are filling. Faces I recognize, and those I don't, have saturated the room with love and tears alike. I move up in front of the golden oak casket, to the place where Mr. Ed directs me, and though it's awkward, I hug every person who passes, feeling more alone with each one, not less. It's a strange feeling, comforting other people when I don't feel comforted. Nurse Kim stands beside me, the other biggest part of Ma's life for the last few months. She pats my back when I must look too sad to carry on another moment.

"Bash." A voice startles me as I'm staring at Ma.

It's Kyle, not dressed in his usual expensive getup. The only thing I really notice is the look in his eyes, which is some degree of sorrow. I can't tell if he's actually sad for me or for himself. His ankle bracelet catches a gleam from the overhead lighting as Mr. Taylor stands behind him. He urges Kyle to shake my hand, hug me, anything, but Kyle resists. His cheeks are tomato red and plump with shame. He reluctantly holds out one shaky hand. I linger in his eyes, look for sincerity, but I realize, no matter how empty his gaze, this is all he's got, all he's ever had, maybe.

If only I'd noticed sooner.

I pull him in for a hug, and he leans into my ear. He's

resisting the weight of me, trying to break free. "Before you embark on a course of revenge, first dig two graves," he whispers. Only Kyle could both begin and end a friendship with words of wisdom he can't understand. And now I know we are finished. Pseudobrotherhood no more, and I couldn't feel better about it. Can't say I didn't try.

He steps back, this time to speak loud enough for Mr. Taylor to hear. "Sorry, bro," he says with total insincerity. "For everything."

I shouldn't be shocked, shouldn't expect more than this, but after all these years of me going to bat for the kid, I am. "I didn't turn you in," I tell him. "I wouldn't do it, you know that."

He manages a slight grin from the side of his mouth, winks at me with that smugness I'm used to. "Yeah, whatever."

I say nothing, don't give him the satisfaction, and take comfort in the fact that he's the one currently on house arrest, not me. *Who needs the luck now, sucka?* Mr. Taylor grabs my hand for a firm shake, wrapping his long arms around me for an embrace. He buries me in his pinstripe suit that probably costs more than everything I own (which, admittedly, still isn't much). When he steps back, his tears have dampened my suit, and his. Our eyes meet, and with a slight smile, he looks to Ma. "Still beautiful, after all these years." He pats my back, but just before he and Kyle move to the last row of pews, Kyle's angry attention never abandoning me, Mr. Taylor leans in close once more. "Oh, and Bash?"

"Yeah?"

"I heard the Paxton boy had an angel donor. Big check."

"I don't know what you're talking about."

He smiles, looks at Ma again. "Of course you don't."

I watch the back of him melt into all the other sad faces, my muscles twitching in weird places. A few more tissues and tears pass through before Vinny pats my shoulder. He and Evie are clutching wads of tissues between their hands.

"I didn't know it was so bad," he tells me. "I'm so sorry. You should've said something." He holds his hand out for a shake, but when I reach for it, he too pulls me in for a hug instead. Evie fights him to hug me next. She unravels Vinny from my new threads, jet-black mascara running down her cheeks. The color bleeds into her blush, creating a master-piece right there on her face.

"Oh, Bash," she cries. "I hate everything that's happened. If you need *anything,* we're here." Dave, Skip, and Janie are behind him. Some of the other rink regulars, too. Teachers, Mr. Lawson—everyone I've ever known is here to say good-bye amidst all these other people I've never seen before.

My heart is swollen as I stand here, knowing this is the last time I'll ever see this shining light again. It's after 10 A.M., time for the service to begin, so Mr. Ed directs me to my seat. He stands at the podium, the people hush, and the only sounds are muffled crying and a song—Johnny Cash's version of "You Are My Sunshine," something Ma used to sing to me when I was little. The sounds of crying get louder, but from no one more than me. There's no bottle of whiskey strong enough to make me not feel this cut. I'm here, in this chair, bleeding all over the funeral home because now I know she's gone—she's really gone. What's worse is, I almost put Birdie through this—I almost caused this for someone else. The feeling will haunt me until I take *my* last breath.

When the song ends, Mr. Ed talks about Ma like he's known her forever—things she'd prepared for him to say so he wouldn't—and he quotes—"screw it up." I laugh because it's typical Ma. He talks about her life in Brazil, how her parents struggled to make ends meet before her dad split, things even I didn't know about her. A few others step up and say the nicest things about her. The room is so warm with love, it could heat Alaska.

My stomach stirs as Mr. Ed calls me up. The room is quiet now, and my limbs are shaking beneath me, threatening to take me down. Everyone knows my face, my story in regard to the Paxtons now, and I hope it doesn't take away from Ma's legacy. Resting my hands on the wooden podium to steady my balance, I can't look up at all the faces who are waiting for my words. From my pocket, I unfold a note I've written to help me.

Though right now, I'd rather disappear.

"I'm not good with words, so bear with me." The paper crinkles between my fingers, my sweat bleeding into each letter. "For those of you who knew my mother, and all the things she loved, you'll understand what I'm about to do." I pull a stick of vine charcoal from my pocket and hold it in the air. "No one believed in me the way she did." I lay the charcoal to the paper and make quick strokes, outlining a mother holding her infant son, similar to the ornament Birdie left. "The last year of her life was spent hooked up to machines, tubes, needles, you name it. She woke up, every single day, with that same ruby-lipped smile and the will to fight. There wasn't a single second she thought about giving up. Not once."

I set the vine charcoal aside and dig into my pocket for a piece of compressed charcoal to gently shade where the light hits. "There were days *I* wanted to, but she'd look at me and say, *You'll never get to tell them 'I told you so' if you quit.* It was that will, that strength, that ferocity that made me the man I am today." I smooth the harsh charcoal lines with the edge of my palm. "She was born in the Morro da Babilônia favela in Rio de Janeiro, which is a neighborhood once controlled by a powerful drug-trafficking cartel—and something my father had become a part of. Being pregnant Ma feared for my safety, so she and my uncle, Ray—who also passed recently—risked everything, and fled before I was born. They came to America to give me the life she said I deserved."

From my other pocket, I lift a chamois, which is like a fancy eraser, to help define the image. "They came with nothing but the clothes on their backs. This woman behind me is the definition of courage. She was fearless the way a mother bear should be, and even when she lost jobs, fell in love with the wrong people, had a delinquent son, and was diagnosed with this death sentence, there was one thing she never, ever wavered on: me."

Careful not to overwork the drawing, I drop the chamois next to the charcoals on the podium. The image nearly knocks the wind out of me. I've never drawn a person before, never tried. It's too boring and never manages to fully capture the emotions I'm looking for. But as I step back, paper in hand, I see something more powerful than any bear or fox I've ever drawn. "To know her is to love her, and to be part of her is an honor I'm not worthy of."

I hold up the drawing, *A Mother's Embrace,* and feel Ma right here next to me as the people gasp in awe at this interpretation of my love. I swallow back my tears, not wanting to smear the charcoal. The final word still rests on my tongue. I spin around and nestle the drawing beside Ma in the casket. My eyes are hard-pressed to her, this unforgettable woman. No life inside, just a body. I lean down, kiss her forehead, and tell her *good-bye*—something I could never prepare for, no matter how much practice I had.

When I turn around towards the rows of the grieving, I see *her* between the doorway and the back pews just as she's leaving. Her thick white glasses are absent, and there's an even bigger hole where her heart should be.

Couch Girl.

birdie

As the service concludes, I round the corner for a tissue, or five, when someone tugs at my black peacoat.

"I just want to tell you . . . I'm sorry," the voice says. It's Kyle, and his greasy fingers are holding on tight. I jerk my arm back, anger coating my throat with such rage, I can't contain it. I shove my finger in his face—this kid who called himself Bash's friend—and let him have it. "Do you even know what you put Bash through—what you put MY FAMILY through? Do you even care? I don't want to look at you. Don't talk to me. Ever. Again."

He's backing away, hushing me with the tip of his stupid finger. A tall man, the same man I've seen talking to Benny's nurses, watches us, but he doesn't intervene. Is this all Kyle Taylor deserves? No. What he deserves is so much more than all the cells in my brain can formulate. I grab the fabric of his silken shirt, lower my voice the way I do to Brynn when she's on my last, frayed nerve. "If it were up to me, I'd run you over and leave you to die."

Kyle is silent, backed into a proverbial, metaphorical, and actual corner. "He's . . . better, though, right? Your brother?"

My lips pinch. "What do you care?"

His eyes dip, and suddenly he seems not as confident as he was at the rink. "It was an accident. If I could take it back, I would."

I release him from my grip. "That means literally nothing to me."

My foot out the door, he stops me. "Haven't you ever made a mistake you wish you could undo?" I hear the pain in his voice, but I don't turn around.

Because, *yes.*

The people are moving from their seats as another sorrowful song ends. When the next song begins, my feet grind to a sudden halt. *Shinedown.* I can't help but smile in the very place no one ever should.

I've lost track of Bash in the sea of black. It looks as if he dipped his charcoal in water and soaked the entire room in the dark drippings. I rewrap the tie on my coat and wait for the back rows to empty before I try to push through. I want to blend in, not stand out. Once the back doors swing open, the air is a thick sheet of ice that hurts my skin. I'm almost to my car when another hand grabs at me. My first reaction is to swing, thinking it might be Kyle for round two. I resist the urge, seeing as it might not be proper or ladylike to brawl in a funeral home parking lot.

"I need to talk to you," Vinny says. He leans in to cup a gloved hand behind my ear as he lowers his voice to a whisper.

My eyes narrow. "What's up?"

Evie is caught behind him in a group hug between the nurses. They're passing tissues back and forth like gold, and Evie's at the epicenter.

"It's about Bash," he says.

My heart momentarily stops.

He pulls me to my car door, away from the people flooding the line that will travel to the cemetery burial. Those cars have flags to say they care; they will support Bash at the cemetery. My car has no flag and I'm not sure if it should or not.

"He wanted me to give you something, but I wasn't sure

when the right time would be." Vinny's sort of twitchy, like we're sharing a secret.

I feel my eyes water instantly. "You *talked* to Bash? I thought he was dead to you."

Evie strolls over just as I say this. She frowns and whops him in the arm. "Vincent Angioli—you did NOT say that!"

He hangs his head. "I didn't mean it, Ev. He knows that. I think."

"I can't believe you," she scoffs. "He's just a kid."

Vinny looks around and discreetly pulls something from his suit pocket to place in my cupped palm. It's the ornament I gave Camilla. I look closer. No, it's not. The figures are different. This one has the same faceless woman, her hair all gray, but she's holding the hand of a small child. On the back, the words *Love that transcends the years*. I'm breathless. Bash knew I was the one who'd given Camilla her special ornament for her tree and in return, he's giving me one for Nan's tree, somehow an exact replica of the one I lost in the move.

"Just told me to tell you"—he hesitates like he's trying to remember—"she isn't gone—she's alive in you. I assume you know what he's talking about." There's a silence, an agreement that I understand. My eyes tear up faster than I can stop them. I blame it on the sun's rays. The surface burns a scorching ten million degrees, and they're all shooting down on me.

He lays his hand on my arm and squeezes. I wonder how this boy I didn't know a couple months ago somehow crawled inside my head and found all the lost pieces of my puzzle.

"See you later," Vinny tells me. He pats my arm.

Evie's fur surrounds me. "Bye, sweetie. Don't be a stranger."

"I won't."

I see Bash beneath the door's frame, and everything inside of me freezes. Through the swarms of black dresses and whimsical flowers, I see him—the *real* him, and every hard swallow he takes. Judging by the way he's enveloped in his own invisible cage of sadness, keeping every grieving hug just slightly at bay, I now realize I'm the last thing he needs. So, I decide to follow Vi's advice via today's horoscope. Before I slip inside my car, I grab my camera and snap one last picture of Bash to resemble something dead, *us*.

And go.

Good-bye, sweet bear.

LESSON OF THE DAY: A body buried in a coffin can take longer than twelve years to decompose to a skeleton, depending on the type of wood the coffin is made out of. Even from the back of the funeral home, I could see Camilla's coffin was solid oak, which means it could take approximately forever for Bash to ever recover from losing her.

And twice as long for me to recover from losing him.

BASH

A week after burial, it's Christmas.

This holiday to me is the celebration of a fat man slinging an iPhone—or in my case, shitty knockoff IPhane—down the chimney (through the flimsy door) while I sleep, glistening snow over dead grass, holiday music known to put an annoying spring in Ma's step, and peppermint *everything* (peppermint meat loaf, anyone?). Ma used to say Santa couldn't give us much, because we already had too much love; wasn't fair to the other kids. I believed her—the lying, old broad.

God, I miss her.

I'm sitting in my new place watching this *totally* overrated movie about a sinking ship and I'm *not* crying about the fact that Jack and Rose won't end up together because that would be *so* incredibly lame. I was going to change the channel, but well, I haven't. So, whatever.

(Still not crying.)

This is the same house Kyle and I used to secretly frequent on those miserable Sunday nights. It's mine until summer, so long as I help finish the thing for whoever bids on it in the fall. That's my rent. It has a working toilet, blinds instead of sheets hanging from the large windows, and electricity—bonus—plus, the walls are thick enough I don't feel wind on my face while I sleep.

The accident on Highway 22 hasn't stopped Mr. Taylor

from keeping his promise to "rebrand" Clifton. In fact, I think it has inspired him to work harder to make this neighborhood safe. And now I'm a little part of that. Ma would be proud.

That old trailer is still sitting there, like a memory stuck in time. I left most of my things (what things?), shut the door hard (because it literally wouldn't fucking shut), and didn't look back. It's easier that way. I still have that little patch of fabric. I keep it in my wallet as a constant reminder—to never stop trying to be better. Not just for Ma, but for me.

I drive by Birdie's house every damn day, and a lump forms every damn time. Probably will until I leave for NYC this summer, but I'm not going for the thing I always dreamed of. Birdie changed something in me. Made me want to be better, smarter. I realized I kind of like chemistry, and I'm sure Ma is laughing her ass off right now, because she knew when she saw Birdie, that was it for me.

Once school and probation are done, and my community service reading to sick kids at Grove City PICU and Trauma Center is served, I hope to be the newest intern at the American Cancer Society—but *not* thanks to Mr. Taylor or his money or any other goddamned person in Clifton. I will do this on my own. I had a sort of epiphany. Not that it's a big deal or anything; I'll still draw, because that's part of me, but for once, I feel like I have something more to give, and I sure as hell have more to prove. I didn't see those things in my *before*.

Birdie did.

Though we still haven't spoken since before the arrest, I guess you can call her my muse. Without meeting her at that party and everything that happened after, I wouldn't be where I am now. Sounds kind of like fate, but as Ma said, fate is a man, so inevitably, he will fuck my shit up again at some point.

But for now, all is good.

Mr. Taylor checks in on the Paxton family almost daily, keeps me informed. Says the little guy opened his eyes and is thriving, but there's a long way to go. The point is, after over a month of hell, he's alive. I can only imagine how happy Birdie is. I'm sure she hates me, if she's even capable of that kind of feeling, and though I'll deny it, it kills. Sure that check Mr. Taylor gave me could've changed *my* life, but Ma raised me better than that; I've never taken a handout before, and I ain't gonna start now.

A jagged piece of charcoal is pinched between my fingers, and I'm sketching my best bear yet. As the snow falls in delicate flakes from the sky, the irony sets in. I have a second chance and can't help but think Ma set it up this way. That's how she could go when she did. She knew I'd be okay before I did.

This doesn't feel like my life. It sort of feels like Kyle's with one MAJOR difference: All this shit that's happening? All me. The good *and* bad.

And I'm okay with that.

He's not speaking to me, not that I (a) want him to or (b) see him in school anymore now that he's on house arrest with a revoked passport (flight risk). It's kind of funny. After all that's happened, Kyle hasn't just lost something, but *everything.* And me? Let's just say knowing I have a plan for the future, however much work I need to do to get there, is enough.

I finish the sketch and grab my bag full of things. *Here goes nothing.*

On the twenty-six-mile drive to the children's hospital, I have one thing on my mind. I throw on a baseball cap, sneak through the front door, and with the drawing in my hand, slide by every set of eyes that might find me. Mr. Taylor says they've moved the kid to another room, so now I have two nurses' desks to avoid. Head low, drawing pinched between my fingers, I graze through the jolly, music-filled hallway, noticing all the open doors where families have gathered to be with their sick children on this fine holiday.

When I get to the room, a thunderous burst of singing begins. I poke my head around the corner carefully, so as not to be seen. A dozen carolers, including nurses, doctors, and the family, are surrounding the kid's bed. Birdie is near the wall, holding a tower of wrapped gifts. She's smiling, glowing, in this big, frumpy Christmas sweater, like the kind Vinny would wear. My heart thumps a little louder just looking at her, and I get lost in the sounds of "Silent Night." When the song ends, the carolers prepare to move rooms. I'm nearly surrounded, so I move fast to idle nearby.

"Merry Christmas," a nurse says with a smile.

I tip my hat. When she's gone, conversation and laughter continue. I try not to listen to what they're saying, because it's not my place. I stretch my eyes to see something so beautiful—*not* pretty—it drowns out all noise anyway: Birdie is still smiling. It's clear to me now, no matter how she feels about me or what I've done, she is better.

Without me.

I've written this apology to her family about a thousand times but can never manage to send the thing. And anyway, I'm not good with words. So, at the foot of the door, I leave the drawing, my magnum opus.

"Merry Christmas," I whisper to the air. "I'm sorry."

And one last time, I lift my arm.

To wave good-bye.

birdie

When Dad gets down on one knee, it makes a loud *CRACK*.

Brynn makes a joke about how geriatric he is, while I'm more focused on the ketchup stain that's splotched all over his left pant leg. With his back arched and a strained look on his face like it hurts to be so low, he holds a velvet box propped open in one palm. A plastic quarter-machine ring sits in the center. Mom is crying with her hands over her mouth, but I can see the smile lines around her eyes that web out when she's really happy—something I haven't seen in a long time.

"A *plastic* ring?" Brynn asks, unimpressed.

"You don't know the story, then," Dad says. "When I first proposed, I was broke, kind of like now, but I was younger and better-looking. But I couldn't wait to spend the rest of my life with your mother, so I dug into my pocket and got one of those twenty-five-cent rings at the drugstore and proposed to her right then and there. Best decision I've ever made."

Mom can't get a word out, she's crying so hard now. The nurses are saying, "Aww," while resting their hands over their hearts. But Brynn is sticking her finger down her throat with her eyes rolling into the back of her hollow head. A lot of things have changed—she's not one of them.

"Bess," Dad says, "we've been through hell."

Mom nods. She's clutching an armful of the gifts the

doctors and nurses brought us since we're spending our Christmas in here instead of at home.

"And God knows, I've made *a lot* of mistakes, and—"

"Who hasn't?" Mom interrupts.

"I don't deserve to share my life with you, but . . ." Dad is crying now, too. Brynn and I smile at each other. "Would you please do me the honor of marrying me—again?"

Sarge clears his throat. We all stop to look at him. "Guess you don't need *my* blessing the second time around. Or the *first,* for that matter," he grumps, scratching his jaw.

"Sarge," Dad says.

"Oh, forget it, ya ninny. Finish what you were saying." He waves Dad off, and we all chuckle.

Mom pauses, bites the tip of her nail, and with a somber face, asks, "Will there be cake?"

Dad grins. "Unlike the first wedding at the justice of the peace, yes—we *will* have cake! We'll have ten cakes, if you'll just say yes."

"Of course I will." She pulls him up from the floor and buries her happy tears in his sunshine-colored polo. Sarge is smiling big now, his head angled away from us all like he doesn't want us to see, just as Dr. Stein walks in.

"Didn't mean to eavesdrop, but congratulations," he says, holding his hand out to Dad for a shake, "again."

The good doctor walks over to Benny, who, though he isn't the same Benny from before, is wide awake. Parts of him have come back, his limbs move more freely, his eyes know us, he fights the nurses when they take his temperature, but there's an obvious speech delay. However, Dr. Stein is hopeful—a word I don't fear anymore—so I am, too. He sticks his light in Benny's ears, then his eyes. Benny lifts one small hand and pushes it away. We all gasp in excitement and gather around him. He's our Christmas tree this year, lighting the whole city. It almost makes us forget it's been a year since Nan passed now. And anyway, Dad and Sarge trashed the baby cypress when Chomperz started using the base as a litter box.

Dr. Stein steps back, his arms crossed. He tells us about all the therapies Benny will be starting soon—that it will be a *very* long road—but the most important part, the most important truth for us to hold on to, is that he is alive. With his eyes wide open.

"Anyway, just wanted to wish you all a Merry Christmas," Dr. Stein says, grabbing Benny's chart. He thumbs through and signs off. "Doctors Morrow and Schwartz will keep an eye until after the holidays. If there's an emergency, call my cell. Anytime. I mean that."

Mom and Dad rush toward him to say good-bye. Because this man did more than save my brother. He saved a family on the verge of collapse.

"Did anyone feed Chomperz today?" Brynn interrupts. Their voices muddle into a pool of fuzz because, out of the corner of my eye, I see a piece of paper resting at the foot of the door. I excuse myself, my heart beating faster and faster with every step, because from here, I see it—a bear—and I know *he* was here.

I hold the drawing close to me to see the detail in the charcoal bear's bleeding heart. The way the pain seems to drain into the sky where it forms, clings, and separates in the clouds. Kind of like me and Bash. I feel the warmth of him in the words written below the bear:

$(Bi)Pax + (Ba)Alv = x$

SOMETIMES GOOD-BYE IS LIKE A SECOND CHANCE
(OR WHATEVER)

On the back, there's a little pink Post-it that reads

MY BIRTHDAY WISH WAS FOR BENNY TO OPEN HIS
EYES. SOME WISHES DO COME TRUE, I GUESS.

My heart is thumping a beat I've never felt before. It's a wash of fear and joy and pain and something else— something I liken to *hope*. The charcoal is so fresh, it clings to my fingertips. I push through Mom and Dad's embrace to look out the window where I see the back of his leather jacket weaving through cars parked on a blanket of snow. I press my hand to the glass and mutter beneath my breath, "Don't go."

"What are you doing?" Brynn asks. She shoves her forehead onto the pane and gasps. "It's that Bash dude! MOMMM!!! DAAADDD!!! LOOK!"

I ignore her. My eyes sting and water as I pound my fist against the pane. Dad and Sarge gather behind us to see the snowy footsteps that lead to this boy who changed it all. He hears me—he must, because he stops abruptly. His feet send an electric pulse into the ground; it travels through the lot, up the building, and directly into my palms. I suddenly lose my breath, and I'm gasping now.

Sarge idles close for a better view. If ever there was a time for him to say something profound, it would be now. Never one to let me down, he pulls my attention away with a firm grip on my shoulder. "Your light is back."

"Ugh—why is *he* here?" Brynn asks with a curl of disgust. "Shouldn't he be in jail or at the skating rink punching my friends?"

"That's enough, Brynn," Mom says. Her hand glides against my arm, too, so I turn to her, my eyes pleading. She looks to Dad. They both smile with a silent acceptance of what I'm about to do.

"Go to him," Mom urges.

I hesitate.

"Stop thinking. Go."

"Thank you," I say pushing past. My feet sprint through the hall, down the emergency stairwell, and out the main door, where the air smacks me in the face. I don't stop to put on a coat or catch my breath or think about anything other than this moment I've thought about so many times since the night of his arrest.

I weave through the rows of vibrantly colored cars, my footsteps barely keeping up with my will to be in front of him. When I reach him, he turns to me with downcast eyes and a slouched, forlorn posture. His breath puffs a thick cloud between us. Mine does, too. I imagine the two masses of vapor combining to form a heart, but even in this thought, there's a big, gaping hole in the center, a pang I can't ignore. With the drawing still clutched in my hand, I search for the words that are shouting, tangled in my brain, where all the files, once stacked, are now in a big old mess.

"Shut up," he says with a slight grin.

My eyebrows scrunch together. "I didn't say anything."

"You don't have to. I hear your brain, Couch Girl."

I dive headfirst into his eyes, but still can't find the words to understand if this is hello or good-bye. Before I can think another complicated thought, he removes his hat, grabs my waist, and pulls me into him. Our bodies smash into one another where all the heat radiates, and right now, I'm not thinking about anything else. His lips press against mine. They're wet, but not too wet, with just the right amount of pressure. Our heads tilt like puzzle pieces to fit into one another just so, and as I squint my eyes open slightly to be sure I'm not dreaming, I see him fall into me, too. He's soft and safe, all the things that I've missed in the days of his absence. When he pulls back, my cheeks are wet with tears. They're not happy tears, and they're not sad.

They're somewhere in between.

Like me; like *us*.

We linger in the cold, connecting breaths between us. There's a lull where he brushes away my tears with his thumb. We both begin to speak: "I'm—" then nervously giggle and shove our hands into our respective pockets. He fidgets, shuffling his boots deeper into the snow, almost as if to hide them. I do the same.

"Birdie—" he starts.

"What are you doing here, Bash?" I blurt out.

He kicks his feet around, and I sense a slight regret in his hesitation. "I just wondered," he asks, pointing to the drawing, "if you could help me . . . balance an equation that's been bothering me."

I step closer, though, as the reality of seeing him again settles, I keep a slight distance now. And cross my arms over my chest to shield my heart and, maybe subconsciously, protect it. My eyes sink into the drawn formula he holds between us.

"You see," he continues. His hands are trembling as he moves the two steps closer that I'd taken back. "We can probably assume x is negligible compared to one reactant's smart, compassionate, *beautiful*—not pretty—concentrations, right?"

My tears cease, and I nod, slowly. The corners of my mouth begin to turn up. "Only if x never meant to be so reckless with the reactant's feelings, I mean, concentrations."

He lifts the drawing from my fingers and holds it so I can see. His eyes water now, the remorse evident. "But"—his voice is breathless, almost a whisper—"the thing is, when some reactants collide, only a lucky few gain enough traction to go the distance. So they can't form new bonds and shit. I think it's the moment of impact that determines this. Like when two reactants meet at a party, or a wretched skating rink, and though they maybe *shouldn't* combine, can't explain why they *need* to. They just know it's where they belong. Feels like home . . . or whatever."

My eyes take in every subtle movement of his lips—the way they twitch before he says my name, and the little dimple only evident when he's trying hard to stow it away. "You're forgetting that a catalyst can change the equation. If one reactant keeps something from the other, like coefficients or car accidents, the equation won't balance. No matter how much you want them, I mean *it,* to."

With the paper clutched in his fist, he takes a stub of charcoal from his back pocket, and looks so deeply into my eyes, I swear he can see every last drop of my being.

"So," he says, "what you're saying is, a successful collision with these reactants in particular is shit out of luck?"

My veins are pulsing, pumping blood in through and out of my heart so fast my body shakes, and I am beaming that light Sarge spoke of. I shrug. "Depends."

"I have it on good authority the reactant in question will do whatever it takes to balance this equation. So the earth can move freely beneath my feet, I mean the formula's feet, again."

"I'm not sure I know the answer to that yet."

He grabs my hand. "Listen, I don't want you to forget a single thing I've done to hurt you, or pretend it didn't tip the world on its axis. There will never be enough apologies in the English—or Portuguese—language to say how sorry I am. For everything."

There is a pause. A moment where my files reorganize, forcing the top one into full view—Bash.

"I know you are. But where do we go from here? So much has happened."

"You remind me of Rose," he says.

"Who?"

"Beautiful girl who lets a poor boy draw her before his icy demise in the North Atlantic."

My grin expands. "I think you missed the point of that movie."

"So then it's fair to assume the answer to 'Where do we go from here?' *shouldn't* be 'I'll never let go?'" His eyes never abandon me. They're intense and electric and all the things I remember feeling the second I saw him at the party.

I chuckle and playfully punch his arm. It's strong and un-flinching, even still. The muscle catches my fist like a net. "Maybe we're the *Titanic*. Destined to sink."

"Nah. Icebergs don't exist anymore. Global warming. Be-sides, you don't believe in destiny. You're a facts kind of girl."

"Touché."

"So . . . before we freeze our asses off out here, how about we go back to the one thing that needs our immediate at-tention. Can we solve for *x,* or is it too late?"

I take the charcoal from him and smile. "I thought you'd never ask."

LESSON OF A LIFETIME: I'm learning love isn't tan-gible, something I can hold in my hand. We are round and flexible, traveling a full 360 degrees to stay in motion—not square, where one of us is left behind, trapped between the angles. When I look at him, think of him, it's a feeling. Like with hope or faith (Sarge), I've got to open my eyes (Benny), feel every single layer whether it hurts or not (Mom and Dad), learn to forgive (Brynn), and mostly, ignore the theo-ries and rationale (me), because when it comes to love, logic doesn't exist.

And now that I've met Bash, I'm okay with that.

(Bi)Pax + (Ba)Alv = x
SOMETIMES GOOD-BYE IS LIKE A SECOND CHANCE
(OR WHATEVER)
X = <u>L(OVE)</u>

I hear and I forget.
I see and I remember.
I do and I understand.

—Chinese Proverb

Acknowledgments

This book was a true labor of love, and I mean that in every sense of the word. For many, many years, I felt a nagging pang to rewrite an ending to a tragedy my family endured in the late 70s, but nothing ever felt quite right. I had to be sure whatever story I told came from a place of love and hope. Thus, I would first and foremost like to thank the McCann family for living the epitome of courage, even in the aftermath of loss. You are perseverance at its best, and I admire and love you more than any words could express, in this book, or otherwise.

Along those same lines, I wouldn't be the woman I am today without the unwavering adoration and support of my beloved Gram, Elsie Carvin. I started this book's journey as she fought death in various nursing homes, and sold it after she passed. She will live on in Sarge and Nan, respectively. Gram—I'll miss you until time no longer exists. Thank you for showing me all the things I never knew I could be. You are absolutely my infinite beacon. Now, please come back. Pat pat pat.

To my mom, Kathy, for pushing me out of your body and feeding me and stuff. Thank you for always being there, no matter how big my hair or how sarcastic my jokes. I'm grateful for our friendship and the material you've given me over the years (like the time you thought someone broke into our house and called police when it was really just a dream). Thank you to my dad, Jay, for continually singing my praises through the years. Your support, however far away, truly means the world to me. And to my brother, Jacob, for constantly reminding me I'll never be cool no matter what I do. Humbling.

Bethany Buck, my B2, I cannot thank you enough for believing in this story, and in me. Your resolve to find a home for *Birdie & Bash* remains to be one of the best things that's ever happened to me. Thank you for your wisdom and for being a gallant cheerleader when all felt lost.

I'd be remiss not to give a Herculean-sized THANK YOU to my fearless editor and badass rock star (#bar), Vicki-positive-kitten-Lame. I don't know who the eff I was before I knew you, but I know who I've become since. You're brilliant and insightful and I can't believe I'm lucky enough to have the chance to know you, let alone work with you. Thank you for totally getting me and loving cats and wearing twirly dresses and mostly, for buying my books. You gave me the chance to shine, and so shine, I will.

I'd like to also thank Jennifer Enderlin and Anne Marie Tallberg at St. Martin's Griffin for bringing my precious book(s) to life. And to my publicist, Brittani Hilles, as well as Ana, Jonathan, DJ, Kerri, Karen, Jeremy, Lisa, Brant, and the fantastic team at St. Martin's Press, for giving me the wonderfully supportive place my stories can call "home."

Bash's story wouldn't be the same without the stunning work of artist, and friend, Wesley Berg. Thank you for bringing the final vision to life and for letting me whine (for years) about the ebbs and flows of this writing journey. Of course we might not have crossed paths if it weren't for Susie Stein and the whole Up and Running team. Thank you for (lovingly) forcing me out of a job so I could stay home and write. Everyone at UAR taught me a lot about myself that I couldn't have found elsewhere. I heart you all. Now buy my books in mass quantities, please.

A monumental thank you goes to my betas, and friends, Patty Blount, for being a continual source of support, and to Kate Walton for introducing me to the agent who would sell this book, and for never doubting my abilities. You're both my author angels, no doubt employed by Gram somehow.

I'd like to give a special thanks to Dan Lazar at Writer's House for your invaluable insight on an early draft of *Birdie & Bash*. You didn't have to, and you did anyway.

Jeff Rivera, you truly are my fairy godmother. Thank you for going above and beyond in more ways than one. I wouldn't be where I am without the opportunities, encouragement, and bling, you've provided.

An infinite amount of hugs to all the friends I've made blogging, particularly (and forgive me if I miss you): TIMMY (aka Matthew Rush), Robin Lucas, Joshua Cartens, Jennifer Hiller, Jen Daiker, Tawna Fenske, Kelly Polark, Elana Johnson, Sheri Larson, Bryan Russell, Rose Cooper, Lydia Kang, Ricki Shultz, and countless others, who've been there from day one. You know how weird Candyland can be and you love me anyway.

This voyage wouldn't also surge onward without thanks to Dan Mandel, Stefanie Diaz, and the entire Greenburger Associates crew, as well as Joanna Volpe and everyone at New Leaf, and Jackie Lindert, for weathering the storms with me. Additionally, thank you to Brent Taylor at Triada, for being an amazing cheering section thoughout the year.

I'd like to thank my biological father, Matt, who I never had the chance to know, but feel he's part of everything I do, my therapy cat, Feathers, for calming my writing nerves—meow, meow (thank you)—and the staff at Winan's for providing my daily writing fuel. I legit could not function without those Milky Way lattes. #truth

The lyrics, although somewhat altered, are thanks to Brent Smith and Shinedown. You write things most of us feel, and I appreciate you. Also, thank you, Steven Tyler, because I've loved you since my first Aero concert in elementary school and without "Dream On," I'd have no anthem to live by.

Last but definitely not least, I want to thank my amazing, wonderful, phenomenal (insert all the adjectives) husband, Erik, for nourishing my every writing whim and dream. It would've been a desolate, somewhat quieter, road without you! You've breathed life into me more times than I can count and a hundred pages of gratitude wouldn't be nearly enough. Thank you for providing for us while I've pursued my passion, sharing your life with me for the last thirteen years (and counting), and for pushing me when I didn't think I could survive another failure. You are now, and will forever be, my platypus.

Also, to my two beautiful children, Lilliana Hope and Sullivan Matthew—my most successful collisions yet. You are the stimuli from which I pull my greatest inspirations. Thank you for making me feel more important than I probably am, more beautiful than I often feel, and more loved than I ever thought possible. This book, and every one hereafter, is for you, always.

If I've missed you, please accept my deepest thanks, from the bottom of my heart.

May you never lose your light (or whatever).

1. Bash allows his friend to drive while intoxicated. How do you think things would've been different if Kyle allowed Bash to drive instead?

2. Birdie says she doesn't believe in love. How do you think her parents' relationship has shaped her views? Do you think she wants to end up like them or not?

3. How has Birdie's mom, Bess, influenced Birdie's decision to keep her part in Benny's accident a secret? How is Birdie's relationship with her mother different than what she has with her father? What about with Sarge?

4. Why does Bash try to keep his distance from Birdie at the skating rink? Do you think he is doing the right thing? How do you think Birdie and Bash's relationship would have changed if there had been no accident?

5. Kyle claims to be Bash's friend. Do you think he is? How has Bash been a better friend to Kyle?

6. Bash's mother was an emigrant from Brazil, escaping with only the clothes on her back. How do you think her sacrifices affected Bash's decisions regarding Kyle? If Camilla hadn't died, do you think Bash's choices to protect Kyle would've changed?

7. Tragedy can often rip families apart or bring them closer. Which do you think the Paxtons fall into? How do you know?

8. Birdie is consistent in wanting to attend school and work, even through tragedy. Why do you think this is?

9. What's the importance of drawing bears to Bash? What about taking photos of roadkill to Birdie?

St. Martin's
Griffin

10. The author often connects the collision theory — a theory that says for a reaction to occur, the reactants must collide with each other — to Birdie's meeting of Bash. What parallels do you think are drawn, if any, to love and theories of fate?

11. How do you think Nan's death inspires Birdie's ideologies on death and fate?

12. As sisters, Birdie and Brynn have a complicated relationship. How do you think Birdie should've reacted to Brynn all the times she acted out?

13. Was Bash right to keep his involvement a secret from Birdie, knowing it would risk any relationship or friendship they may ever have? Was Birdie right to forgive Bash for keeping this secret from her?

14. Why do you think Sarge's influence alters Birdie's decision to stay away from Bash?

15. Do you think Birdie was right to run after Bash in the hospital parking lot? Why or why not? How would you have ended their story?